Born in Zimbabwe, T.M. Clark completed her primary school years at boarding school in Bulawayo, but on weekends and holidays she explored their family ranch in Nyamandhlovu, normally on the back of her horse. Her teenage years were totally different to her idyllic childhood. After her father died, the family of five women moved to Kokstad, a rural town at the foot of the Drakensberg Mountains in South Africa, and the boarding school hostel became her home.

She began writing fiction in the UK while a stay-at-home mum to her two sons and she hasn't looked back.

Now living on a small island near Brisbane in Queensland, Australia, T.M. Clark combines her passion for storytelling with her love for Africa.

Her first novel, *My Brother-But-One*, was shortlisted for the Queensland Literary Award 2014. She is also the author of novels *Shooting Butterflies* and *Tears of the Cheetah*, as well as a novella, *The Avoidable Orphan*, and a children's picture book, *Slowly! Slowly!*, which are companion books to *Child Of Africa*.

Readers can find T.M. Clark on Facebook (tmclarkauthor), Twitter (@tmclark_author) or visit her website at tmclark.com.au.

Other T.M. Clark books published by Harlequin

My Brother-But-One
Shooting Butterflies
Tears of the Cheetah

CHILD OF AFRICA

T.M. CLARK

mira

First Published 2017
First Australian Paperback Edition 2017
ISBN 978 148924118 4

Published by
Mira
An imprint of Harlequin Enterprises (Australia) Pty Ltd.
Level 13, 201 Elizabeth St
SYDNEY NSW 2000
AUSTRALIA

Cataloguing-in-Publication details are available from the National Library of Australia www.librariesaustralia.nla.gov.au

Printed and bound in Australia by McPherson's Printing Group

As always, to Shaun, my love, my life.

To all service personnel everywhere.
Thank you for your sacrifice.

PROLOGUE

Finders Keepers

Binga Area, Zimbabwe, 1996.

The elephant baby lay on its side, its trunk limp in the dry dirt.

'Do you think it's dead?' Joss asked, approaching slowly.

Bongani put his hand on the elephant's shoulder. 'No, it is breathing, but might be sick, as it is unusual for a baby to be separated from the herd—'

'What can we do to help it?'

Bongani shook his head. 'The kindest thing to do would be to shoot it, put it out of its misery.'

Joss ran his hand over the legs of the baby elephant. 'I can't find any hot spots and there doesn't seem to be anything broken. I think it's just tired, and hungry. We can take it home with us.'

'Your mother will not like this—'

'Mum will adopt any animal, you know that! Perhaps if we give it some water?' Joss said. He took his bottle from the webbing he carried across his shoulder. The regulation army-issue flask was too long for him and sat on his thigh not his hip, but at ten years old, he didn't care. Water was water, and when you were out tracking and hunting all day, you needed to carry your own. He poured some in his hand and then put the tip of the baby elephant's trunk into his palm. The elephant was still for a second, then it moved its trunk as it smelt the water.

'It wants it,' Joss said as he pulled Bongani's hands forward. 'Cup your hands and I'll pour the water into them—'

The elephant curled its trunk to drink from Bongani's hands, and put the water in its mouth.

'At least it is old enough to have control of its trunk,' Bongani said. 'A good sign.'

'How do you know?'

'Many years ago, before I came to work for your family, I was with the Parks Board. It was a long time ago.'

'Why did you leave there?' Joss asked, putting more water into Bongani's cupped hands.

'The bush war came. I met your father during that time, and I came to work for him instead, before you were even born.' Bongani paused. 'We could get into lots of trouble from the Parks Board for having a baby elephant. They will want to know where we got it, and how we came to have it at the lodge.'

'Mum will sort that out. Let's try to get it back on its feet.'

'Do not rush it. Give it some more water first. Slowly, in case it gets a tummy ache. It will get up when it is ready, if it can. It needs some relief from the heat. We must make a shelter for it, and then, when it is cooler, we can encourage it to walk.'

They collected dead wood from the forest floor and broke branches off the trees in the mopani forest. Slowly the lean-to took shape around the young elephant, protecting the animal from the harsh African sun.

They sat with the baby for over an hour as it drank all the water from both their bottles.

'If it is to live, it must get up. It must walk to the road,' Bongani said. 'We cannot bring a vehicle in here; the bush is too thick.'

'It'll walk,' Joss said as he returned with a handful of leaves from an acacia tree.

The baby attempted to eat the leaves, taking them from his hand and putting them into its little mouth, but it didn't seem to like them much. For a while it just lay in the shade. Joss sat next to it, stroking its cheek, waiting for the elephant to feel better as the sun began to lower.

'We need to get it moving soon,' Bongani said. 'Is it a boy or girl?'

'Hang on,' Joss said as he bent over and looked underneath the elephant. 'She's definitely a girl.'

'Good. She should not be as moody as a male to look after, and perhaps when she is older, she will come back with her babies to visit, not come back in musth and break the fences, destroying our crops.'

'Come, Ndhlovy,' Joss said, 'you have to get up, you have to come home with us. If we leave you here, the leopards or the hyenas will get you, because your mum is not here and you are all alone.'

The elephant put her trunk into his hand. The tiny hairs on it prickled but he didn't mind. He continued to talk softly to her: 'Bongani and I need to get home; my mum will shout at us if we don't get back before it's dark. It's her one rule when we go hunting: be home before the sun sets. So you need to stand up and walk to the road, then Bongani will get the tractor and you can ride home on the trailer. But first you must get yourself to the road. It's not far.'

Bongani said, 'You are naming her Ndhlovy?'

'Yes. Then you can't leave her behind; she's my pet, she has a name.'

Bongani shook his head. 'We need to leave now. Perhaps if we walk away she might follow us, like the calves do.'

Joss got up and dusted the dirt off his trousers. 'Come on, Ndhlovy.'

The baby lay still, but her amber eyes followed him.

Joss walked further away. He looked back over his shoulder. Ndhlovy had sat up and was watching them leave. 'Come on, ellie, time to go home,' he said a bit more sternly.

The baby elephant staggered to her feet, her little ears flapping. She wriggled her trunk, thrashing it in an uncertain manner, a little unsteady as she balanced her weight.

Bongani smiled.

'Home is this way,' Joss said. 'Come on ...'

The baby elephant walked after them.

Bongani nodded. 'This is good.'

'Keep coming, Ndhlovy,' encouraged Joss.

The baby elephant walked with purpose until she caught up with Joss, then she placed her trunk in his hand, and settled just behind him. Every now and again she bumped him, as if trying to reassure herself he was there.

'That's it, Ndhlovy,' said Joss, 'you just keep walking.'

'You keep heading homeward with the elephant. I will fetch the tractor and trailer and the men from the village to help us load her. Keep sharp now.'

'Okay,' Joss said just as Ndhlovy bumped him a bit harder and he almost lost his balance.

Bongani smiled. 'You keep moving to the road and then home, understood?'

'Yes. We'll be coming.'

'Watch for leopard; we are in their country and they might think you are easy prey. Swap weapons with me. I know the .303 is heavier than your .22, but you might need to use it.'

Joss nodded and switched rifles.

Bongani watched him adjust to the extra weight. 'The ammo belt will not fit around your hips – put it across your chest.'

'This is heavy. Can't I just take a few rounds and put them in my pocket?'

'No. You need to be fully armed out here. If a leopard comes, or something worse ...'

Joss adjusted the heavy rifle and ammo belt onto his shoulders.

'I'm reminding you again, shoot or be killed,' Bongani instructed.

'I got it, Bongani. It's not like I haven't ever been alone in the bush before—'

'But you have not been alone in the bush as much as I have. You are still young. There is so much still to teach you.'

'I'll watch for leopards and hyenas and anything else that can eat me and Ndhlovy while you're gone. I promise, cross my heart,' Joss said as he crossed his whole chest with his free hand.

Bongani nodded as he increased his stride. 'You are a true African, *inkosana* Joss. In your heart. You want to save the babies of this land, not kill them. I am happy to tell your mother about the baby, and have her get mad at me, because you have chosen to nurture this Ndhlovy. Today you have proved you are a child of Africa. I will see you now-now.' He waved as he walked away.

Joss watched as Bongani adjusted the strap of his .22 rifle, which hung from his shoulder tight on his back, then he started to jog back towards the village. He didn't look back.

*   *   *

The sun hovered low above the tree line, a huge ball of orange. Joss watched as their shadows danced along, already three times longer than he and the elephant were in real life. He headed steadily southeast, towards the lodge and safety, with Ndhlovy close behind, her baby feet imprinting like giant saucers over his tracks as she walked. All the while he kept up a conversation with the elephant, explaining how they needed to walk through the village before they could reach their lodge on the bank of Lake Kariba, and about the noise that the others would make when they arrived to help. A coolness descended as the sun sank lower into the horizon.

He heard the sound of whistling, then a donkey bray, and men singing in harmony, before he saw Bongani. He was driving the cart that belonged to his father's village: three donkeys pulled the converted back of an old *bakkie*. Six men stood in the cart, holding tight to the cabin guard.

Joss smiled. Ndhlovy would be able to save her strength. The cart would not be as fast as the tractor, but it would scare the little elephant a lot less. He moved off the road into the bushes so that there was room for the donkeys to turn. The elephant pulled away from him as the donkeys drew near, but he rubbed her ears and encouraged her to be brave.

'Bring it to the back. The donkeys do not seem spooked by it,' Bongani said.

Joss walked towards the cart. The elephant followed, even though its ears flapped at the unfamiliar animals and the new men. Bongani had unloaded the cattle ramp and Joss started to walk up it, still holding the little ellie's trunk.

But Ndhlovy didn't follow.

'Come on, baby. Up you come,' he said.

The elephant looked around, her ears flapping, the white of her eyes clearly visible.

'Trust me,' Joss pleaded.

The men went to move behind the elephant, as if herding cattle.

The elephant turned towards the threat, ears flapping, her little trunk high in the air.

'Stand back!' Bongani shouted.

The men retreated from the threat of the elephant charging them.

Joss came back down the ramp and stood in front of Ndhlovy.

Bongani said, 'Slowly-slowly. Wait for Joss to get her to start up the ramp. Joss, get her to move around again. We are about to lose all the light. As it is we only have one torch to shine the way for the donkeys.'

'Come on, beautiful, come with me,' Joss said as he took her trunk in his hand once again and patted it. 'Come on, turn around, that's it. Just walk with me, that's it.'

The baby elephant slowly plodded up the slope, sticking close to Joss, as if all the bluster she had shown in her mock charge had sapped her energy.

Joss walked to the front of the trailer. 'Okay. You can close up and climb inside. Ndhlovy's real scared.'

One by one, the men climbed up and into the cart. Holding out their arms, they touched the elephant, and braced themselves against the edge of the trailer to help cushion the ride.

The moon had risen and the bright stars watched from the inky heavens by the time they had driven through the village and down to Yingwe River Lodge. When they arrived, Ndhlovy backed herself off the trailer without incident and walked into the stables behind Joss. She showed no bravado, just stayed close to him, as if he were now her lifeline.

The ridgebacks arrived before Joss's mum. Ringo, Paul and John came into the stable, their hackles up, but George remained close at his mistress's side.

'Enough. Outside,' Joss instructed and pointed. The dogs immediately went outside. His mum made her entrance within moments of her dogs being banished and although they danced at the gate, they stayed out of the stable.

'So what have you brought home this time, Joss Brennan?' she asked.

'An orphan elephant. Bongani thinks her herd left her behind, or they got separated somehow ... she was on the border of Chete. She's weak—'

Leslie Brennan walked further into the stable and knelt in the straw. 'Hello, young one,' she said quietly and reached her hand out to the little elephant, who was now lying in the thick straw that Bongani had had the groom prepare.

The dogs whined.

'Stay outside,' she instructed. They lay down quietly near the door. 'Does she have any injuries?'

'No, Mum. Not that I could find. She's just weak and tired,' Joss said, still holding Ndhlovy's trunk.

'She needs some nourishment and something to drink. Mossman, go warm up some calf formula. Let's see if she will take a bottle. I know nothing about baby ellies but I can call around and find out who does.' She pulled her hair back with her hands and held it there, before letting it go. When it fell forward again, she tucked her long fringe behind her ear. 'Bongani, make sure there's someone guarding this little one all night. Armed, in case the leopards decide she's an easy dinner. Get a few of the horse blankets in here to keep her warm too.' She stroked the elephant's trunk as men ran to do as she'd instructed. 'Have you given her a name yet?'

Joss nodded. 'Ndhlovy.'

'It's a nice name. So, let's get her on her feet and better. Then we will find out what ZimParks want us to do.'

'Thanks, Mum,' Joss said. He knew that his mum would always allow him to keep the strays he brought in. The Egyptian geese babies she'd helped raise until they flew away with the migrating birds were regulars at the small dam they had for water at the safari lodge, nesting and raising their own goslings, bringing them to the house to introduce them, and then returning to their wild life, a tiny part of their hearts always with their human family.

Or the tortoises that were kept in a large brick pen by the house. Each had been brought in with an injury – one was missing a leg completely. His mother had sprayed the wound with gentian violet and it had healed over. Although the tortoise would never win a race, it was alive and happy. Joss had wild birds mixed in with his racing pigeons too, those that could never be returned to the wild because of some injury or another. But not nearly as many as his mother had treated and nursed back to health before setting them free again. From birds to baby duikers, now to an elephant, his mum would raise any animal and claim that it belonged to her child, even though her son was at boarding school most of the year.

His father, on the other hand, was always reminding them that the safari lodge was established as a gateway to Lake Kariba, that it wasn't a zoo, and the animals could only stay until they were well enough, then they had to leave. It was survival of the fittest in the real world, and because he'd once been a head ranger in the Chizarira, Joss knew that he understood all about animals, but he just didn't seem to want to take care of them like Joss and his mum did.

Joss chewed his lip, not sure how his father would react to the elephant baby. He remembered that last year a rogue elephant had come from the park and destroyed the village's vegetable patch and flattened their moringa tree seedlings. It had uprooted trees on its way to their village and had even torn a roof from one of the *ikhayas*. When they had attempted to drive it back into the

Chete Safari Area by beating feed tins and hitting metal plough disks, the jumbo had become aggressive and mauled one of the villagers.

His dad had got permission from ZimParks to shoot it.

Joss had thought that perhaps it was just a hungry animal and if they left it alone, it might have walked back into the safari area, then into the national park itself. He didn't think it was a pest until they frightened it.

Joss didn't want his ellie to land up like that – shot and in someone's cooking pot.

What his father would say when he got home was going to be interesting, but first, they had to make sure the baby lived. He would worry about his dad's reaction later.

Mossman returned with a bottle of warm milk, and Joss watched while his mum teased the baby into taking the teat into her mouth. But Ndhlovy refused to drink from it.

'You try, Joss. She seems to already trust you.' Leslie gave him the bottle.

'Come on, Ndhlovy, you need the milk, you need to drink it.' He dribbled a little like his mother had on the elephant's lips tucked up underneath her trunk, and the little trunk made room for the bottle, arching and resting on Joss's arm as she attempted to suck on the teat with her lips.

'That's it,' Leslie said, 'come on, baby.'

Ndhlovy latched on to the teat and began to drink.

'Perfect. Step one accomplished,' Leslie said. 'If she takes milk, we can get her stronger.'

'How often do you think she will need a bottle?' Joss asked.

'Probably every few hours, although she doesn't seem to be a newborn; she's already well over a metre tall. Let's start at two hours, because she's weak and in need of hydration. Mossman, add extra calf supplement in the next feed, double mix.'

Mossman nodded.

'Right. Let me get on the phone to Rodger, see what tips he has. Don't get your hopes up, Joss. She could still die.'

Joss shook his head. 'We can't let that happen, Mum.'

Leslie put her arms around his shoulders as he fed the baby elephant. 'We'll try everything we can. Perhaps if we can just get her well again, you and Bongani can take her back into the reserve, and find her a herd to live with. I don't know if she will be adopted back smelling of humans, but it's worth a try. I don't know how long an elephant baby stays with its mum, but I know it's a long time. I remember watching a documentary where a herd adopted a calf when its mother died … we can only try.'

Joss said, 'Will you make sure Dad doesn't shoot it when he gets home from Durban?'

'I'll talk to him about it, but you know his view on orphaned animals.'

'I don't understand why he hates animals so much.'

She let go of Joss and straightened up, arching her back to stretch it. 'Oh, Joss, he doesn't hate animals, he just doesn't see them as pets. Remember, he was a ranger, and he is a hunter. At the end of the day, he worries that he needs to put food on everyone's plates. Make a decent living. Lots of people rely on him for their wages too. The boys here at the lodge need to be paid so their families can buy food and attend school. The villagers need their cut from the lodge so that they can eat and survive. It's not just you who needs your dad's income to be educated and healthy.'

'It's just one elephant, Mum,' Joss said. 'One little elephant.'

'That will grow huge. Now, we don't need to make any decisions tonight. Let's just get her better, make sure she survives. Then we'll deal with the rest. How does that sound?'

'Can I stay here with my ellie tonight?'

'Sure. I'll bring you some dinner and a sleeping bag, and I'll leave Ringo behind. He can sleep inside the stable with you. That way if a leopard even puts its nose into the area, he'll wake you and Bongani up.'

'Thanks, Mum,' Joss said as Ndhlovy finished the milk in the bottle.

'I'll see you just now,' she said as she kissed his forehead. Once outside she said, 'Ringo, inside, sit. Stay with Joss.'

The dog leapt to his feet and walked into the stable. Still not sure of the elephant, he approached with caution, but Joss called him to his side.

'Come on, Ringo. Meet Ndhlovy.'

As the dog sniffed the elephant, his tail began to wag. He settled in next to the pachyderm, licking her every now and again in a reassuring way.

Ndhlovy didn't seem to mind the ridgeback next to her, and touched him with her trunk.

'Well, look at that,' Leslie said. 'Anyone would think those two were long-time friends.'

Joss smiled. 'You know what, Mum, when I'm old like you, and I'm a Royal British Marine, I can save as many people and animals as I like, and I won't need anyone to watch over me at night, not Ringo nor Bongani.'

'True, but then you'll be an adult, and you will be looking after everything you save, down to every last detail, like all the phone calls, getting all the right food, having enough money to enable you to do that saving, and dealing with all the authorities and their different points of view – and don't forget the local community; they want their say too. It's never a simple rescue, Joss, there are always more things in the background that need to be sorted out that as a kid you don't need to worry about. Enjoy your time with Ndhlovy while you have her. Hopefully she'll be able to go back into the Chizarira soon and live her own life too. Don't rush this time away, my son, it's not as great as it looks to be on this side of the fence, being that adult responsible for others.'

CHAPTER

1

Dreamers

Kajaki Hydroelectric Scheme, Afghanistan, 2008

The four kilometre–long convoy snaked into the Kajaki Hydro-electric Plant. Joss Brennan watched the turbines arriving at the dam wall through his binoculars and wanted to dance around, even though he was just one of five thousand troops who had played their part in protecting Turbine T2. But celebrations would have to wait.

Seven sections of turbine, each weighing between twenty and thirty tons, had been transported the final one hundred and eighty kilometres from Kandahar air base, through the Helmand Valley and the desert and finally up to Kajaki Lake. Some optimist had painted holy slogans and an Afghan flag on the containers to try to dig deep into the patriotism the locals had for their country – T2 belonged to the people. It seemed to have worked, because the heavy convoy had arrived at its destination. The people of Afghanistan would soon have two working turbines, creating power and bringing them electricity.

Chinook helicopters flew overhead, loud as they passed low, sweeping the area.

Ten days of hell were almost over.

The eighty-ton crane was the next piece of equipment to come to a halt. As important as the segments themselves, it would help the engineers lift the parts off the trucks. Each minute the sections sat around was a minute longer that the troops had to protect them from the Taliban.

Joss adjusted his binoculars and looked further up the hill, following the line carefully, looking for anything out of place in the rugged terrain. The word in the barracks was that almost two hundred insurgents had been cleared on the route through and around the dam. He hoped that was true and they were unable to return, but there were always those who, like snakes, slipped through the cracks to come back to bite their butts another day.

He scanned the compound in a grid pattern, making sure no one would threaten this precious cargo, not after the epic mission they had just accomplished. This was his job, the sniper, the tracker, the spotter in his company. Who knew that watching the animals in Africa all those years ago would be such good practice for hunting the enemy when he became a British Marine Commando? Who would have known that the hours spent with his father and Bongani in the bush, learning the skills of a hunter, would help him be the ultimate marine?

Joss went over the grid a second time. 'Check two o'clock on the ridge. Shadow protruding beyond the wall,' he said into his mic. 'Definitely something moving in the compound.' But in the next moment, the shadow had gone, and all that remained was the edge of the wall.

'Affirmative. Suspect unfriendlies,' Mitch's Australian twang answered.

'Don't jump to conclusions, might be the locals. Eleventh troop mobilise. Sweep compound,' Lieutenant Colonel Johnathan Tait-Markham – Tank to his friends – ordered over the coms.

After a quick glance at the convoy still rolling in, Joss packed his binoculars. Mitch put his hand out to help him up.

'Crack on, we have a compound to clear,' came Tank's voice.

Joss bent and ran with Mitch just a few steps behind. The stones at their feet slid loosely until their boots gripped the baked surface beneath.

They reached the compound and were soon hot-footing it along the mud wall. Joss remembered this village well – they had previously cleared an IED from exactly where he walked now. They'd returned a few times since the initial clearing, but that didn't mean that there were no more IEDs. Insurgents could creep in at any time and rearm a place.

'Affix bayonets. Two break left, two break right,' Tank instructed.

Joss saw Mitch and Tank break left. He rounded the corner of the same hole they had blasted in the mud wall a few weeks back, Cricket, one of his fellow marines, with him. He heard the wasp sounds as bullets flew close to his head. He hit the dirt and rolled for cover.

'Contact. Contact,' Tank shouted into the mic.

Crawling after Cricket, Joss slipped into a room. They swept it quickly.

'Clear,' Cricket said.

'Wait,' Joss said as he saw a carpet hanging on the wall move. He indicated with his head towards it. Outside he could hear the shallow *pop-pop* sound of the insurgents' AKs and the deeper sounds of their own rifles.

'Joss, where are you?' Tank called. 'We need a sniper.'

'Clearing this—'

He got no further as the carpet came to life. Someone was screaming, and the whole thing came down, exposing an insurgent with his gun raised.

Cricket and Joss shot him down in a hail of bullets.

Joss approached the body. He kicked the AK-47 away, and looked at the man.

Correction.

Boy.

Joss knelt down and checked for a pulse, but there was none. He was relieved and sad.

No more than fourteen, the boy had only the wispy beginning of a moustache. His black turban still clung tightly to his head. He looked too young to be carrying a weapon and trying to kill them. He should still be in school.

This was someone's son. Someone's child who might not have wanted to be a soldier.

Or worse, this could have been a child who chose this path, thinking it was his shortcut to glory in the afterlife.

Joss swallowed. It was survival – if they hadn't shot him, they would be the ones lying on the floor. 'Dead,' he told Cricket, and together they moved out of the room, to help the rest of the troop.

*   *   *

The stone chips pitted Joss's face, flicked up by bullets that were unnervingly accurate and close. One whistled past his ear. Joss adjusted his scope. 'Bogie at three o'clock.'

He squeezed the trigger.

The man's head jerked back. Joss slid the bolt of his rifle, ejecting the shell and loading another.

'Three o'clock,' he said as he shot the next man who was keeping his troop pinned down.

Again he reloaded.

Taking a breath, he looked for the third insurgent he'd seen. He had gone to ground.

'Lost visual,' he informed Mitch.

Mitch looked through his binoculars, scanning the small hill on the other side of the village. 'Four o'clock, blue/black turban. Behind a wall – must be a ledge beneath it that he's using.'

Joss adjusted his weapon and took aim at the designated place, even though he could see nothing there. The turban rose as the man wearing it peered over the ledge to check where his enemy had got to. Calmly, Joss fired, and the man dropped out of sight.

'Hit?' Mitch asked.

'Affirmative,' Joss said as he reloaded.

Mitch nodded. 'Bad angle, I couldn't be sure from here.'

The firing had stopped. The silence that followed any fight was always deafening. The wait for the next shot terrifying in case it came right for you.

'Any more?' Mitch asked.

Joss took a deep breath and swept his scope over the side of the hill. A single goat nibbled at non-existent grass. 'Wait … look left of the goat.'

Mitch focused on the goat, then left. 'Bogie,' he affirmed. 'He has a rocket launcher.'

They saw the tip of the man's head, his arms outstretched to launch the deadly missile at them or at the precious convoy of trucks.

Joss took him down. The sound of the single shot was loud in the silence that had descended.

The goat bleated and tried to run away, but it seemed tethered to the insurgent. Panicked, it bleated some more.

'Continue to clear area,' Tank shouted over the coms and the men came out from where they had taken cover to sweep the village.

'If we let that goat go, it'll lead us to where they came from,' Joss said. 'Find their base.'

'Negative,' Tank replied. 'It's getting late; we pass that on to the American troops to follow up. I'm in contact with HQ, and they have a command passing us in ten minutes. Check fire. Friendlies approaching from behind.'

Joss watched as the American marines chatted to Tank on their way through. He pointed to the goat, and their leader nodded. Then they were off, along with the goat, over the small hill and out for their night patrol.

Joss's company gathered and headed towards their temporary barracks, spirits high, adrenaline levels beginning to lower. Joss grinned. This was what he had been born to do – to wear his green beret and serve the greater good, just like his grandfather. To help people who were unable to stand up to tyranny. Fight for freedom and justice when those around couldn't.

Tonight he would pen another letter to Courtney, like he always did when something significant took place, then he would watch it burn, as was regulation. He would rewrite it when he got back to England, after he was out of the desert, a more sanitised version. An emotionless version that would never depict the true horrors they experienced out here, or the simple joys of just waking up, knowing that you had achieved something amazing.

It didn't matter that Courtney didn't write back often; he just wanted her to know he was okay out here in the world beyond Africa. He kept the letters he'd received from her in England, and any that he received while on the front line he would read, commit to memory, then burn so that the enemy would not get their hands on them.

Letters to his best friend, and phone calls to Bongani, his lodge manager, were his only connection to his home in Zimbabwe now that his parents were gone.

CHAPTER

2

Whispers on the Wind

Binga Area, Zimbabwe, 2010

Bongani sat on a stool, wiping his father's brow with a cool cloth. Once the chief's skin had barely shown a wrinkle, but now when Bongani looked at him, he saw a man weathered with age and worry. A face of one who knew his time was close, but still insisted on holding on to life, on to the hope that life was eternal and one could cheat death.

The chief lifted his gnarled hand, the skin whisper-thin, and started to push Bongani's hand away, but then clutched it instead. 'This is not your job to attend to an old man. Since your sisters cannot come to my bedside, you should get the nurse,' he said.

Bongani put his other hand over his father's. 'They have lives of their own. Looking after their own families. I live here. This is my place. It is where I want to be. With you, making sure you are comfortable.'

'That was Sibusisiwe's job,' Chief Tigere said. 'Your mother was supposed to live alongside me, so that when it was this time, she could look after me, and not some strange nurse you pay to do the work.'

'It is sad that Mother left this world before you, but if she were here, she would be the one telling you that although I am a grown man, I should still spend time with my father, and ensure that he is looked after. Talk to him about times gone by and times yet to come.'

'Times to come … I will not see those with you, they are your dreams, but I am honoured that you have shared them with me. To know a man's dreams is to have power over his future, and that is a valuable gift.'

'I know,' Bongani said. 'How will I manage once you are no longer here to guide me?'

'You will be fine. I taught you well.'

Bongani nodded. 'That you did, *Ndende.*'

'You are the son who will become chief; you have never been like your half-brother.' The old man coughed, and the fluid in his chest gurgled, the sound painful to Bongani, who was counting the weeks till sickness took his father from him.

'When I die, he will come for you. He will come to take your land, your title.'

'No, he is too busy with his criminal activities now to worry about a small bit of land in the bush.' Bongani knew that his forehead creased with his lie. The only reason he had been safe all these years was that Tichawana was more afraid of his father than he was of any other person in the world.

'Do not underestimate him,' Chief Tigere said.

'I will try not to, because I also remember well,' Bongani said, patting his father's hand and watching as the medicine he had taken with his thin soup at last made him sleepy.

'So you should. Never forget, or that mangy dog will come here and steal everything you have worked so hard to build. Your lodge, your life. Be careful, my son, be careful …' He drifted into sleep.

Bongani let out a sigh, and put the cloth into the basin of water. He placed the basin on the stainless-steel nightstand. The stand was so foreign in the traditional mud hut his father insisted on still living in, as was the *putt-putt* sound of the generator outside, providing electricity.

He watched his sleeping father, letting his head rest against the back of the chair. Lost in thought, remembering the past as if it were just yesterday.

* * *

'*Woza! Woza!*' his mother shouted.

'Coming,' Bongani replied as he ran towards his mother's *ikhaya*. 'Come, Tito, supper time.'

The tan puppy yipped as it pounced from the ground to his hand. Small ears forward, eagerly listening, its unclipped tail whipped around like a *sjambok*. Excitement pulsed through its little body.

'*Tshama,*' he instructed as he approached the door. '*Metse!*'

The puppy looked at him with bright, trusting, amber eyes and sat on the reed mat that Bongani's mother had made for him.

'Stay.' He patted Tito's head and stroked the dog's soft velvet ears for another moment, then entered the family's *ikhaya*.

'Don't forget to wash,' Sibusisiwe said.

He smiled at his mother as he crossed to the basin in the corner. 'You should see Tito track – already he can flush out a pheasant, and then return. He will be a good hunting dog.' He dried his hands on a small towel.

His father was a big man, almost six foot two, strong in his arms and big across his chest, and his legs bulged with muscles. But his real strength came from the inner power that radiated from him. He was known to rule his people fairly, and with firmness, never tolerating drinking or gambling within the boundaries of his lands. He kept an essential peace between all the displaced BaTonga people who had been settled in the area, ensuring they had a home now, where they could live and rebuild the shrines of their ancestors.

'Progress,' his father said. 'It is important that you teach that dog early who is in charge, make sure that if a bush pig comes at you, that dog will want to put itself between its tusks and you. Save your life. Only then do you know that he is a good hunting dog. Did you finish your homework?'

'Yes, *Ndende*, before I went hunting,' Bongani said as he sat on the floor beside his mother, accepting his bowl of *sadza* and *mfino*. She placed a nice meaty chop on top.

'You can give the bones to your dog when you are finished,' she said.

'Thank you, *Bama*.' He knew his pretty mother had a soft spot for his puppy too. It had been the runt of the litter from Bishu Village. His father had brought it home, a rope around its neck, saying he had taken it because if it remained there, it would be drowned.

'I left a bowl of food near the fire too. Remember to feed him outside your sleeping *ikhaya*. I do not want ants in your blankets.' Although the boys no longer slept in their parents' *ikhaya*, his mother was still very much involved with what went on inside the one he shared with his half-brother.

'Where are Tichawana and Tarisai?' Chief Tigere asked.

Sibusisiwe looked downwards. 'Your second wife is feeling ill again. She is not eating with us tonight.'

'Is the medicine making any difference?' Chief Tigere asked.

'Sometimes she is not in pain. Today she kept me company for much of the day, but then she was tired. She is very sick.'

'I know. I will visit her later.' He reached over and patted Sibusisiwe's hand. 'So, Bongani, what excuse do you think your useless *mukulana* will come up with today for being late?'

'I do not know,' Bongani said as he ate his *sadza*. 'I last saw him at school after lunch.' He shuddered, thinking about the look of hatred sent his way by his half-brother from his father's second wife. Everyone knew that his father had taken a second wife to keep peace between two factions within the BaTonga tribe, but it was evident to all that his love was still for his first wife, whom he had chosen himself and paid a big *lobola* for, years before she finally got pregnant.

One son, a child at last to bless a loving marriage.

The second, the expected offspring from an orchestrated arrangement.

Close in age, but only the oldest could be chief when he grew up. This was the main cause of the fierce rivalry between the two boys.

Tichawana had been sitting on the low stone wall, smoking a cigarette that he had definitely stolen, when Bongani had walked past him on the way home from school. His brother did anything he could that was wrong, constantly pitting himself against their father, and always coming off second best.

A yelp came from outside.

Bongani stilled. Listening.

'Leave that dog alone and get in here, Tichawana,' Chief Tigere yelled. 'You are already late.'

Tichawana dragged himself through the door, his feet shuffling, scratching deeply into the mud and cow dung flooring. He leant heavily on his brother's shoulder as he sat down. At almost sixteen, he was just taller than Bongani, and endlessly testing his strength against him.

Bongani shrugged him off. Although smaller in stature, Bongani was still no lightweight. He was seventeen and just over six foot, and while not as broad across his chest as his father yet, he was still muscular, his body already used to the hard labour required to live on the land.

'Go get cleaned up,' Chief Tigere said. 'What is that blood on your hands?'

Tichawana scowled at his father. 'I chopped down a *mukwa* tree. It is the sap from that.'

'Sibusisiwe has cooked you a meal; the least you can do is get here on time and clean up to eat it when she calls, or you will go without.'

'I will go without,' Tichawana said as he rose.

Chief Tigere got up too, still taller than his lanky second son. 'Take one more step, and it will be your last for a while. Do not show such disrespect to your family.'

The man and his son glared at each other.

Tichawana broke eye contact first. 'I can get my own food. I do not need yours any more. I can go to the training camps in Zambia and I can get money and food and clothes and fight like a man.'

'You will not leave. You are the second son of the chief. You are needed here to help the BaTonga people. We have spoken of this before. My mind has not changed on you going across the border to fight. The answer is still no. You are too young to die in a guerrilla war where nobody will ever be a winner.'

'That is Bongani's *pissy* job, he is the first born,' Tichawana said. 'He inherits your title, and your new place within these white man's borders of this Tribal Trust Land, not me.'

Chief Tigere shook his head. 'You need to be here too, to help your brother, help the people. It is your duty. You are not going to war against your own country. Your own people. This white government is changing – they will sort things out. We cannot become a communist state. Things will change for us as black people under the rule of Ian Smith. It will not be like a British colony any more.'

'I want to be a freedom fighter. To have my own gun, be a free man—'

'This is not a discussion. You live under my rule, and the answer is still no.'

As Bongani listened to his father speak to his brother, he kept an ear out for any sound from outside. He inched towards the door, sliding quietly away from the eating circle.

'Bongani, go check on your puppy; it is too quiet out there,' Chief Tigere said, noticing him.

Bongani got up, not taking his eyes off his unpredictable brother until he was well away from him, then stepped outside.

'No!' he screamed. Running back inside, he knocked Tichawana to the floor. He beat him, smashing his fists into his face over and over, rage driving each blow. A strength he didn't know he possessed welled up inside him as he fought with his bully brother. Blood sprayed from Tichawana's nose.

'You killed him. You killed Tito. I will kill you! I'll kill you!' Bongani screamed.

Chief Tigere dragged Bongani off his brother, barely able to restrain the young man.

'That was no sap on his hands, it was blood. My Tito is dead—'

The chief walked to the door, taking Bongani with him. 'Show me.'

Bongani knelt on the mat where the limp body lay, its throat cut from ear to ear. 'Tito never did anything to him, and yet he killed my dog on his way in to dinner. Why?'

'Stay here,' Chief Tigere said.

Sibusisiwe came out a moment later, her expression one of anguish. 'Your father is trying to sort out his second son,' she said as she wrung her hands in her apron. 'I wish his mother was not so sick, she could talk to him. Get him to listen. But she lives in a different world. Soon she will leave this one, the sleeping sickness will take her to the other side. I do not know what we will do with that boy then.'

For three months, his mother had been saying that Tarisai would die soon, yet she had clung to life. Sibusisiwe bathed, dressed and fed her each day, and ensured that she took the medicines from the doctors and the *N'Goma*'s brew, but nothing helped. Tarisai, his second mother, was still dying.

They could hear quiet talking within the *ikhaya*, and then the sick sound of flesh being beaten. Tichawana came rolling out the door, skidding to a stop on his back. He lifted himself up and dusted down his clothes, then used the back of his hand to wipe the blood from his nose and mouth. 'I hate dogs,' he said. 'Just as well he never gave me one too, because I would have drowned it on the same day.' He stalked away.

For a long time, Bongani sat with his dog, his mother standing proudly next to him. He watched his brother fetch something from their sleeping *ikhaya*, then go into the village. Tichawana walked tall, one who was defiant despite the hiding he had just received from his father.

Bongani knew that another beating would do nothing to stop Tichawana's behaviour. His brother seemed immune to feelings, to emotions, and had no empathy to anything. He was a *domba*. It seemed to Bongani that anything he had, Tichawana would attempt to destroy. Tito was not the first pet Tichawana had killed. Yet their father failed to see the danger.

Bongani hated to be beaten, and would do anything to avoid it. The last time, he had been about twelve. The humiliation had nearly killed his pride. To have a switch lashed across his legs, where people would see the welts made by the thin wood, and have to walk around bearing those marks, had made him do everything he could do to avoid punishment ever again. He now did everything he could to please his father, to not attract his disapproval. But Tichawana would provoke their father into beating him, as if it was the only way he could gain his attention. Tichawana didn't care when he was beaten, he wore his stripes and bruises with pride, bragging to the younger kids about how much he could 'take'. Collecting the number of lashes as a sick kind of trophy.

Their father failed to see the pattern he had created with his second son, and he refused to adapt his punishments.

Bongani sat on the mat, stroking his puppy's soft ears. Its blood dried and cracked on his hand, and a fly buzzed around him.

His brother had once again taken what was his.

The only consolation was that the severity of the beating his brother had taken meant perhaps his father was at last beginning to see what a sadistic bastard Tichawana was.

* * *

The sound of people shouting at the top of their voices woke Bongani from his troubled sleep. The flashes from the torches and the smell of burnt paraffin from the lanterns was strong as he got out of his blankets and looked through the crack in the door.

His father was outside his *ikhaya*, his chest glistening in the orange light. Although he had no shirt on, he had pulled on some shorts. His mother stood next to him in a long white nightdress, holding a paraffin lantern.

At their feet lay Tichawana, held in place with his arm twisted behind his back. As he attempted to rise, his father forced him down again, pressing his weight into his arm, pushing him face first into the dirt.

Bongani's blood ran cold. Never before had he seen the villagers so angry and riled up, so vocal against his father. He could smell the fear from the sweat that glistened on their bodies as he listened to the adults shouting.

'My son is damaged. Muzi will never talk properly again. His jaw is broken, and he has ribs sticking out of his chest from your son beating him. There is much blood lost from the cutting,' one of the villagers said.

'Good, hope he dies, the thieving cunt,' Tichawana shouted, and received another kick from his father.

'Shut up. Let the man speak,' the chief said.

'The boys were gambling, and Tichawana lost to Muzi. He attacked him for his good fortune. Now he is probably a cripple for life. My son will not be able to work in the field and grow food, help his father to provide for our family. He will be a burden. This is the last time one of our children suffer because of your son. What are you going to do?'

Chief Tigere looked at his son in stony silence.

'It is not right. If my son dies, I will tell the Native Commissioner that you cannot control your own child, that you are not ruling in the interest of the people. That you are only looking after your own family.'

'That is not true, you know that. Use my *bakkie* to take him to St Patrick's Mission Hospital in Hwange. They have a doctor there.'

'Your son is always hurting people in this village. We cannot wait until he kills someone before we see you take action,' the father of the injured boy said.

'I will deal with my son tonight. He will no longer be a burden on this village,' Chief Tigere said.

The father nodded, then turned away as Sibusisiwe handed him the keys to the *bakkie*. Chief Tigere dragged his second son into his *ikhaya* as the crowd dispersed into the night.

Bongani crept closer to listen, but the voices were muffled. He knew that his father was beyond angry then; when the shouting stopped and the quietness began, you knew to run away, fast as you can. That was the scary father. The one who would calculate how many seconds to wait between strikes with a cane so your skin stopped stinging, and when the next lash would land on the already burning flesh.

Sibusisiwe came out of the *ikhaya*. She held a lantern in front of her to light the path.

'*Bama*, what is happening?' Bongani asked.

She wiped her face with her nightdress. 'Your *ndende* is a good man. He is a fair chief. But this time Tichawana has gone too far. There is nothing I can say to your father to save your brother tonight. First the dog, and now a person. Your brother's cruelty has to be stopped, and if your father cannot beat it out of him, then he needs to get Tichawana out of the village before he murders someone.'

The door of the *ikhaya* opened. 'Get out!' Chief Tigere said loudly so that everyone could hear. 'Leave this village and leave my land. You are no son of mine. You are banished. You are touched by the *tokoloshe*.'

Tichawana laughed and wiped his nose on the back of his hand. 'This is what you want, *Ndende*? You always said I was to stay and be Bongani's pet. But see how I have made you do this? Made you throw your own son out? I could have left if you would have let me, but instead you needed to control me. You will never control me. Never. For so long I have been the second best to your precious Bongani. Now you show just how easily you are manipulated by your people. You are no leader, not like King Mzilikazi or King Lobengula. They would have killed me rather than let me leave this place. You are weak. You let the white man dictate how you rule.'

'My laws are this country's laws, the same laws that govern you too. And the fact that you know that your behaviour has left me no choice sickens me to my stomach. Your attitude towards the pain you have inflicted on others is disgusting. You are sick in the head and the heart. Do not darken my door ever again. Because if you do come home, even in a few years' time, you are not welcome. If that boy dies because of you … Do you understand the cost of a life?'

'Cheap. A few cattle and some goats. He deserved every cut and every broken bone I gave him,' Tichawana said. Then he lifted himself up to his full height. 'Have it your way. I will leave, and I will cross the border and train to kill people like you. Perhaps I will see you when this country is brought to its knees and is begging for mercy.'

'Do not hold your breath,' Chief Tigere said. 'Never return, because I will call on the old customs and kill you myself if you do.'

Tichawana faltered, then turned away, but as he did so, he saw Bongani standing with Sibusisiwe.

'Just wait, my *mukulana*, just wait. One day he will turn on you too, and toss you from your home, just because he is the chief. Your turn is coming.'

'Go. Now,' Chief Tigere said.

Tichawana crunched his fists together and slowly snapped each knuckle one by one. 'I am leaving. But one day I am coming back to take what belongs to me,' he said as he spat on the ground. 'I am coming back and when I do, there will be nothing that you can do about it.'

'How can you do this to us?' Sibusisiwe sobbed. 'How can you do this to your sick mother? This is going to kill her for sure. Drive her to the other side. How can you kill mercilessly, and disfigure that boy? Even if he lives, every day he will remember what you did to him, when he looks at the scars … This is not the way of the BaTonga people. It is our way to show kindness. This is not how your mother and I brought you up. You are not the child I held to my breast, you have become a *domba*—'

Tichawana shook his head. 'All you ever showed me was pity that I was born second, the son who might inherit it all if something happened to Father then Bongani, your own son. I do not want to stay here waiting for something to happen. I already told you I want freedom – from this government, from these people, from living in this *ikhaya* like a child. I want a big house, on a farm with workers. I want everything that every white man has, and lots of money too. To be better than Father ever was. When I come back a rich, famous freedom fighter, you will beg me to stay. To be your son again, and I will laugh at you. When you die, I will dance on your grave, because you did not protect me from my father. From that man who just threw me out of the house. Out of the village. You failed at your only duty as a chief's wife, of bringing up children to serve. I am leaving. Bongani will never be strong enough to rule as a chief, he is pathetic.'

'No,' Sibusisiwe said. 'The chief is right. You have shown great disrespect for your father, your brother, for your own mother, for me, and also for the people in this village. You must go. I will come with you to make sure you say goodbye to your sick mother. I cannot chance that you might try to kill her too. But know this: I agree with the chief. Leave. Never come back.' She turned and walked to the hut where Tarisai lay.

Tichawana shook his head. He went to his *ikhaya* and emerged with a bulging sack thrown over his shoulder. He didn't even look to his mother's *ikhaya* to say goodbye. He just walked away, blending into the night, which swallowed him in the inky darkness.

Sibusisiwe came out of Tarisai's *ikhaya*, looking for Tichawana, but Bongani shook his head and pointed in the direction his brother had gone. She came and stood next to him. 'Do not ever turn your back on that one; he is touched by the *tokoloshe*, and all the unsettled ancestors. He will slit your throat in the night if he can. The only thing standing between you and him is his fear of your father. Watch out for him. Perhaps you had best sleep with us for a few days, and make sure you have a hunting knife close.'

Bongani stood for a long time watching the place that his brother had disappeared. This time his father had seen through to Tichawana's rotten character, to the evil that lurked beneath the surface, and he prayed to the gods and his ancestors that the evil never showed up in himself, because they had the same blood running through their veins.

*   *   *

Bongani's head nodded forward and woke him from his troubled memories.

That same bad blood still ran between the brothers, despite his promise to his mother on her deathbed to try to look after Ticha-wana should he ever return. He had seen him only once since then, and that was enough to make Bongani's blood turn sour in his veins: running along the edge of his father's lands, a small pack and his AK-47 strung across his back, a signature red beret on his head. He was with the dreaded 5th Brigade men, and thankfully didn't notice his brother hiding in the bushes.

He knew that one day he would have to face his half-brother again. Gone was the boy who left and in his place was a *cheelo*, as unstable as the child once was, but now with the power of an organised crime syndicate and a corrupt government behind him.

When his father died, Bongani would face one of the biggest fights of his life.

CHAPTER

3

Homecoming

Beit Bridge Border Area, Zimbabwe, 2010

The deluge came in waves.

Peta de Longe pushed on the lever for the wipers again, but they couldn't go any faster.

'Oh for the mother of God, why now!' she cursed. She braked for the person walking across the bridge and wiped the condensation off the inside of the windscreen. 'Get out of the way, you moron!'

The person walked slowly on.

She hit the hooter, but all that sounded was a pathetic blurp.

'Come on, Nguni, just get us home.' She patted the *bakkie*'s dashboard. 'Just get me over this godforsaken Beit Bridge, through Zim customs and then we are on the home stretch. I promise I'll have Tsessebe look at you when we get home to the reserve ...'

She laughed aloud that she was once again talking to her sister's *bakkie*. Courtney would have reminded her that she was stark-raving mad, and would have asked what she'd do if the car ever spoke back. Technically speaking, the vehicle belonged to Joss Brennan, but he hadn't claimed it, and eighteen months had passed, so she had gone and fetched it from Cape Town. Joss might have given up everything to do with her sister, but Peta hadn't. She never would.

Tears filled her eyes. Eighteen months and still the anger bubbled like a pot of boiling *sadza* deep inside her.

She missed her sister. Despite their eight-year age difference, they had been the best of friends. Not even men or distance could sever the closeness. Only death had managed that.

'Dammit, Court.' Peta wiped her nose with the back of her hand and dug in her bag for a tissue. She glanced back to the road just in time to swerve and avoid the person, who now had his suitcase on his head serving as an umbrella. If she slowed any more she might stall, and then she'd be in trouble. She wound down the window.

'*Suka pangisa!*' she shouted, and hit the side of her door as if herding cattle. *Move your arse.*

The figure turned around. '*Zama uku xolisa,*' a white face, partially concealed under the case, threw back at her. His Ndebele as good as hers. *Try saying please.*

She called out in English, 'You want a lift?'

'I'd rather walk. It's a beautiful storm,' he called.

Something about him was familiar.

A huge bolt of lightning struck close by and the street lights on the bridge went off.

'Oh dandy, now to get through customs in the dark. This is going to be interesting,' she muttered to herself, then raised her voice again. 'If you won't accept a lift, the least you can do is use the footpath. I need to pass.'

The man stopped and put his case down by his feet.

'Lady, you—' He didn't get further. He lifted his suitcase onto his head again and continued to walk slowly across the bridge. It was as if he had self-edited his reaction and chosen to just say nothing.

Peta coasted behind him, lighting his way with her headlights, unable to pass him. There was no one behind her – it was almost eleven o'clock and no sane person crossed the border at this time, except people like her, in desperation to sleep close to Beit Bridge to enable them to get back to customs quickly in the morning, if needed. The post was open twenty-four hours a day, but it just got too hard late at night, and the bribes you sometimes had to pay became too large. The translocation trucks holding her purchases from the stock auction had been waiting on the South African side since four o'clock that afternoon and she had tried everything to get the border inspectors to pass her animals through the veterinary check, but they had been late getting to the border, and now they were stuck there awaiting first light for their quarantine inspection. Then her babies would come through to Zim and be processed. They had a law that animals were to be given priority to cross through first to minimise the impact of travel, but not everyone was sympathetic, and often the trucks were stuck for hours in the forty-degree sun.

Tonight, it poured. God knew they needed it; the season had been long, hard and dry, and the suicide month of October had arrived with its normal brilliant blue sky and hot sunshine. But tonight the heavens had opened, and had stayed open, the storm beating down its rage mercilessly.

She saw the man in front of her stumble on something, and his case wobbled precariously, before he righted it again. He continued his snail's pace across the bridge. She wound down her window again.

'Just get in the *bakkie*. You and I are the only people at the border. It's not like I'm going to beat you up or anything. And I trust that you will not hurt me either. Just get in.'

He stopped and turned to her, then trudged to the passenger side. She leant over to unlock the door as he tossed his luggage in the back. He opened the door and folded himself into the seat next to her. The cab was filled with the scent of a man. He wiped the water from his face with his already wet sleeve before turning to her.

'Hello, Peta,' he said. 'It's been a while.'

'Oh my God! Joss?' she said as she looked at the bushy beard. His long dark hair hung in rat's tails. She would have recognised him anywhere now that she could actually see him. They had grown up together, swum in the water reservoirs in the game reserves and been part of each other's families when they were children. She had last seen him at Courtney's graduation. She'd seen a boy then, but now a man was taking up the seat next to her.

'Of all the people in the world … What are you doing here? Courtney asked you to come home months ago. She wanted her best friend to hold her hand, but you weren't there. You never came back.'

'I couldn't travel at the time. I spoke to Courtney on the phone. She knew it was impossible. She said she understood—'

'Of course she said that. She was dying. She didn't want you to feel bad.'

'I know. But I'm coming home now,' he said quietly.

'You should have been here for her.'

'I wish I could've. But life doesn't always allow us to do the things we want when we want,' Joss said. 'Peta, what more could you ask of me? I spoke to her even on the day she died, you know that.'

Tears fogged up her sight and she sniffed loudly. She let the clutch out a bit too fast and the car stalled. 'Shit!' She tried the ignition, but Nguni just chugged and refused to catch. 'Shit! Shit! Shit!' She beat her hands on the steering wheel.

'Pop the bonnet,' Joss said as he climbed out.

'What? So you're a mechanic now?' She waited while he poked around underneath the hood.

He knocked on her window. She opened it a smidgen to hear him. 'Try now.'

She turned the key and the old girl kicked over.

Joss closed the bonnet then pushed it to make the latch fasten. He walked back to the passenger side and climbed in.

'Thank you,' she said. 'I seriously didn't want to be stuck on this bridge and have to walk back to the South African side for someone to come and fix that.'

'You should have a more reliable vehicle.'

'I do. Nguni belongs to you. Courtney left it to you in her will. I flew down to collect it, as her friend was moving out of their share-house and couldn't store it any longer. I scheduled my visit to coincide with trucks coming through Beit Bridge with some new animals, only they're stuck—' She stopped herself. Her life was none of his business. She concentrated on negotiating the end of the bridge and manoeuvring into the waiting bay on the Zimbabwe side.

'She never told me she left me Nguni. Man, she loved this old *bakkie*.'

'That she did,' Peta said as she climbed out of the *bakkie*, slammed her door and waited for him. '*Eish*, anyone would think you became a sloth not a commando when you left.'

'Something like that,' he mumbled.

She locked the vehicle and strode into the single-storey building, leaving him to walk slowly in the rain. During the day, the area was a hive of activity, with boys running here and there and car guards asking for payment to watch that your vehicle didn't get stolen or broken into while you waited. People would hustle to get to the front of the long queues that stretched around the outside like a colourful python. But at night, the queue-mongers went back to their shacks and homes to sleep, and the lines eventually abated, and only those stupid enough to hit the border late stood looking at the empty counters inside.

Peta went to the nearest window and rang the little bell. '*Woza. Woza!*' she called loudly.

'Coming,' said a voice from the back, and a fat man ambled through. He took his time sitting and adjusting his chair. Finally, he put his hand through the heavy bars, probably once designed for security but required more now to keep irate customers on their own side of the counter, and said, 'Passport and registration papers.'

Peta handed her documents to him.

'Thank you,' he said, already studying them under the yellow lights that fluctuated from dim to dimmer as the old diesel generator throbbed loudly outside. 'You travelling together?' the man asked, nodding at Joss, who was standing by the door shaking the water out of his clothes and hair.

'No. Just happened to get to the bridge at the same time,' Peta said, choosing her words carefully. Despite her surprise at seeing

Joss, she wouldn't give a border authority any power over her by delaying her nightmare trip more because of him.

'Sorry for your loss,' he said as he read through the papers that had the *bakkie* in Courtney's name, her birth and death certificates, lawyer's letter and police clearance stating that Peta could take the car into Zimbabwe. The man stamped her passport with an exaggerated thump, and wrote out an import certificate for her vehicle. 'You waiting on anything else?'

'Three trucks coming through from South Africa in the morning. Buffalo, rhino and one Karoo stallion,' she said as she passed him copies of more papers.

'I cannot pass clearance until the trucks come into Zimbabwe, but my nephew Eric, he will take care of this in the morning for you. I will tell him to watch for them when they come across. We will see you again next time.'

'Thank you,' she said, just as Joss came up behind her.

'Passport and registration.'

'Passport. My *bakkie* and trailer are stuck on the South African side.'

'What is in it?' the customs official asked, now looking at Joss with a curious expression.

'Nothing interesting. They just can't find how to export my custom vehicle,' Joss said. 'They needed to get someone else to come and have a look at it in the morning.'

'Typical you,' Peta said quietly. 'Finally come home and you bring a shiny customised vehicle to Zimbabwe.'

Joss smiled, but said nothing.

She watched the man behind the bars look at the passport. Its blue British cover was very different from Peta's green one, another reminder to her that the life Joss had chosen hadn't necessarily aligned neatly with Courtney's at all, especially since he wasn't even carrying the passport of his birth country.

The man looked at Joss. 'You have been to many-many places. A man well travelled. You planning on taking a room at the motel? It's going to be overflowing tonight with all this rain.'

'Guess so. I don't know how long they will take to clear my vehicle,' Joss said.

'I hope it is not going to be a long-long wait,' the man said.

'It's just time,' Joss said.

'Where is home?' the official asked.

'Yingwe River Lodge, near Binga.'

'Good fishing in Kariba.'

'I hear so. I haven't been there for a few years.'

'*Eish*, a few years,' Peta muttered next to him. 'That's an understatement.'

The man shook his head. 'Too many young people leaving their home, their country. I wish you much luck, and I hope you can find a way to live in Zimbabwe again.'

Peta smiled. The old man was probably thinking Joss was trying to return to a commercial farm that had been taken by the resettlement program, where land was given away because of a political agenda, to move the votes around. Once Zimbabwe could feed her people, but not any more. Now, because of the controversial land redistribution program undertaken by the Mugabe government, there were very few knowledgeable farmers left on the land, very few to organise and grow Zimbabwe's food. Instead, aid flooded in to feed her country's starving people. There were a few farms the war vets had now abandoned, and settlers had moved onto the land. Most were not actively farming but squatting, perhaps subsistence farming. In other places, they were beginning to crop farm in earnest. Some found gold or other minerals, and created microbusinesses despite the dreadful economic crisis that still faced the country. Each person trying to survive and move forward. It was an interesting time to return home.

'*Ngi ya bonga. Kuhle uke bu se inkyaha*,' Joss said.

The old man passed him the passport and touched his hand to his forehead in an unexpected salute. 'Go well, *Inkosi* Joss Brennan.'

'I guess our next stop is the motel. Just hope there are rooms available,' Peta said as she climbed into the *bakkie*. 'I could do with a seriously hot shower and a huge plate of chips.'

Joss nodded. 'Thank you for the lift, Peta. I do appreciate it.'

Peta started Nguni. 'Hey, at least if I have car trouble in the morning I know where to find you.'

He smiled.

She shook her head. It was wrong that someone like him seemed so nice, and yet his friendship with her sister had taken such a bad turn. She couldn't remember exactly what had changed between them, only that, at the end, when Courtney was ill, he didn't come home. But there was no way she could remain bitter towards Joss, it just wasn't in her nature. She'd said her two cents on the subject, and now it was time to let it go. There were only about four thousand white people left in Zimbabwe and their paths were sure to cross over and over again, especially as his safari lodge in Binga was so close to the national parks she watched over.

She waved to the guards hunkered down in their rain gear as they lifted the boom, and continued slowly down the road, the rain so heavy she could barely see. Eventually they came to the only motel that was worth trying to get a bed at. She would rather sleep in the back of her *bakkie* than get bed bugs from the others.

The Beit Bridge Hotel wasn't grand, but it looked inviting and obviously had a generator as it had power, while the buildings around it didn't. The lights beckoned. Peta parked and they walked inside.

'Ah, Miss Peta, nice to see you again,' the night porter behind the counter said. He was a slight man, dressed impeccably in ironed white shirt and black pants.

'Thank you, Phineas,' she said, reading his name tag. 'Can we have two rooms, please?'

'*Uxolo*. There is only one room left, but it's a big room, with two big beds,' Phineas said.

Joss looked at her. 'I'll sleep in the *bakkie*—'

'Don't be stupid. I'm just tired, cranky and hungry. At least we'll both get sleep tonight. It's going to be an interesting day tomorrow, and we both need our strength.' She turned back to the night porter. 'That will be fine. We can share the room.'

Joss put his money on the counter. 'I'll pay for this one, my treat,' he said.

'We can go halves. No way it's getting out that you paid for a room for me.' She placed her money on the counter.

'Peta, other than tonight, if I ever pay for a room for you, believe me, it will be in a nicer hotel than this—'

Phineas took the money from him.

Peta put her half into Joss's hand. 'Just take my share and shut up.'

Joss took the notes and stuffed them in his pocket.

'Second floor on the left,' Phineas said as he gave them each a key. 'I will bring your bags.'

'I can manage mine,' Peta said as she lifted her small bag and slung her briefcase strap onto her shoulder. She looked over at Joss's full suitcase.

'You are going to need to carry that one,' Joss said as he passed Phineas a huge tip. 'The wheels broke first on the bridge, then the handle.'

Phineas nodded, took the case by the middle as if damaged luggage came into the motel every day, and led the way up the stairs.

'You okay?' Peta asked as Joss entered the room. He had taken his time getting there and she was already unpacking. 'You seem kind of slow when you walk.'

'Just tired,' he said as he sank onto the bed.

'Phineas said the kitchen closes at twelve – we only have ten minutes to get our order in.' She threw the inhouse menu his way. It landed on the floor, missing the bed completely. 'Sorry, my aim isn't so great. I'm having those fat, hand-cut chips with mayo, and I'm adding a bacon burger to it.'

'I'll have the same, and a chocolate milkshake.'

She walked over to the phone on the small desk in the corner and placed the order.

'Since you're here, you can answer the door, and I'll go have a shower.'

'Sure,' Joss said.

She took her clothes into the en-suite and locked the door behind her.

* * *

Joss lay on the bed for a long while. If he just didn't move, then he wouldn't hurt.

Damn, it had been a long day.

Knowing it wasn't over just yet, he got up, grabbed his case and tossed it onto his bed. He removed tracksuit pants, a T-shirt and his toiletries and then closed it again. He reached for the fan control and turned the speed to three. Despite the rain, it was still hot. He checked the window. It was an old sash style, the wood painted white. It was stuck and not going to open for anyone. The lock worked, although it seemed an unnecessary addition now that the window was painted shut. He was content that there would be no intruders coming through it. He dragged the chair from the table.

There was a knock on the door as he put the chair near it. 'Food's here,' he said to the closed bathroom door while he tipped the waiter. Although the shower had stopped, Peta hadn't emerged yet.

Once the waiter left, he jammed the chair under the old-fashioned latch to stop anyone with a key entering.

Peta emerged from the bathroom and the steam from the shower emptied into the room, along with a heavenly scent of vanilla. 'That feels better,' she said as she sat cross-legged on her bed with her meal.

Joss watched as she attacked the burger and the chips, and soon her meal was history. Courtney used to eat the same way. He'd teased her often about it.

A heaviness settled deep inside.

'Right. Teeth, then I'm hitting the sack,' Peta said as she went back into the bathroom.

He finished his milkshake with a satisfying slurp.

'That's disgusting,' Peta said from the bathroom, her mouth full of toothpaste, brush still in her mouth.

'Yeah, so is talking while you brush your teeth,' he said automatically.

'*Eish*.'

He took the trays and put them in the passage outside the room before he replaced the chair under the handle.

'I do that too,' Peta said quietly behind him.

'Good to hear. You can't have uninvited guests in the middle of the night.'

'Thanks for clearing those,' Peta said. 'I'm going to sleep and I'm not setting an alarm, just in case the trucks are held up again. I might get a chance to sleep in. They will call me when they're through. What are your plans?'

'A sleep-in sounds great. The South Africa side said they'd let me know when they've processed my *bakkie*.'

'You realise you're going to have to cross the bridge again tomorrow, don't you?'

'Coming over the bridge by foot was probably not the smartest thing, but to be so close to Zimbabwe and not sleep here? I wanted to sleep in my own country.'

'I can understand that.'

'Anyway I'd have had to go back to Musina for accommodation.'

'Makes sense. See you in the morning. I hope you don't snore.'

'Not that I know of,' Joss said, as he lifted his toiletries and went into the bathroom thinking, *Thank God she didn't ask about nightmares ...*

Joss walked out of the bathroom almost forty-five minutes later. He smiled. So much for not snoring – Peta was sleeping on her back, and her soft snore was clear over the sound of the fan that continued to beat out a steady rhythm as it circulated the hot air around the room. She had switched the main light off, but left his bedside lamp on. He ached all over, and his bed called loudly. Putting his toiletries bag on his suitcase, he switched the light off and lay on top of the bed. He was not going to sleep; he couldn't risk it with Peta in the room. He adjusted his weight and began reciting song lyrics, anything to keep from looking at Peta or sleeping.

* * *

Peta woke to the sound of someone thrashing and crying out. It took a moment to remember where she was and that Joss was the man on the bed next to her. She switched on her bedside lamp, but he continued to wrestle with an imaginary demon. He'd curled up into a foetal ball and she could see sweat beading on his forehead. Whimpering. She went to him.

'Joss. Wake up, Joss!' she called and touched his arm.

He moved faster than a cobra. He had her by the neck, choking her.

'Joss! Joss, it's Peta! It's Peta!' she called as she dug her nails into his hand. She could feel them draw blood and she didn't care. He was going to kill her if she didn't get him to wake up. 'Joss!' Peta screamed, yet it came out so quiet.

She was going to die.

She tried to slap his face. Although he still sat on the bed, his legs were now over the side, and she kicked at them, connecting not with flesh, but something hard. Unnatural. She didn't have time to process the oddness as she tried to take her next breath. His hand was tightening.

'Joss, it's Peta, Courtney's sister. Please let me go,' she begged, and she brought her hands back to attempt to break his choke-hold on her neck, trying to wiggle her fingers beneath his.

His free hand pushed on her front, connecting with her chest. For a moment it seemed to grab her breast and squeeze. Then he let go of both her throat and her breast.

She dropped to the floor, clutching at her throat.

He shook his head as if waking up. 'Oh my God, Peta. Are you okay?' He reached out his hand.

'Don't touch me,' she croaked.

'I'm so sorry. The nightmares … oh my God, Peta, I could have killed you …'

'Yes, you could have.'

'I'm sorry. It's not who I am. I don't hurt women. You shouldn't have touched me!'

'A bit late now. One day you're going to kill someone in your sleep.'

'I'm so sorry. They're nightmares from the war zone—'

'I get that. Twenty years on and my father still cries out some nights. But some warning would have been nice!' She still rubbed her neck.

Joss was silent for a while. Then he said, 'I didn't warn you because I didn't want you to know.'

'You didn't want me to know you have nightmares?'

'I told you I would sleep in your *bakkie*, I tried to not share a room—'

'But you didn't say why!'

'Would it've made a difference?'

'No. Everyone has nightmares at some stage in their lives. No wonder you look so tired. Even a marine needs a good sleep.'

'I can sleep tomorrow, when you're gone and not in harm's way. I shouldn't have relaxed in your company.'

Peta shook her head. 'If that's relaxed, I don't want to know you when you're pumped for war.'

'I'm sorry. I've had them ever since I was in the Middle East. They leave me weak, feeling vulnerable, but I've never hurt anyone before. In Headley Court, everyone knows how to wake someone quickly and step aside, get out of the way of a marine's hands.'

'What's Headley Court?'

'Just somewhere Royal Marines go. I'm sorry, I should have warned you, I shouldn't have slept. I'll move to the *bakkie*—'

'No, don't go. It's okay, you're awake now anyway and it's still raining.'

'But—'

'No buts,' she said. 'I'll be fine. You just gave me a fright.' She tried to sound as if he hadn't hurt her but her throat was sore and it came out husky.

'I'm sorry,' he said again. He reached over and put the bedside lamp on. 'Come on, let me at least help you up,' he said, holding out a hand.

Peta was crouched on the carpet, and she saw that Joss still had his shoes on. Without thinking, she reached out and pulled his tracksuit pants up on one leg. There was black plastic and silver bars instead of soft skin.

'Don't—'

She did the same on the next one.

'Oh my God, Joss, your legs are gone!'

'No, I have half a leg still,' he said.

'What the hell happened to you?' she asked as she climbed onto her bed, her throat forgotten.

'How're you feeling?' Joss asked.

Ignoring the question, she said, 'How long have you been travelling to get here? How long can a mighty marine go without sleep?'

His eyes were downcast and his shoulders sagged, as if all the fight had gone out of him.

'I should apologise to you. I sort of insisted, and I didn't give you any chance to talk, to tell me anything.' She wrapped her arms around herself. 'I just bulldozed as normal, just did my own thing, never gave you the chance. Courtney used to tell me I was the bossiest sister around when she was younger.'

'You gave me plenty of chances to say something, Peta; I chose not to.'

'Even I wouldn't mow down a person on purpose. It might just dent Nguni,' she said.

'Come here,' Joss said, opening his arms to comfort her. 'The least I can do is help the shaking stop. I can see you're shivering from here.'

Her knees didn't want to support her weight as Joss took her in his surprisingly strong arms.

'It's okay, Peta, it's shock. The shakes will stop, the anger will come back, and then your body will return to normal,' he said.

'I'm cold,' Peta said as she burrowed into the warmth of him.

'Try to relax.' He held her close. He ran his hands up and down her back as she sat on the bed next to him, his legs still hanging over the side.

Eventually she stopped shaking, and she hiccupped. 'I've snotted on your shirt.'

'I've had a lot worse than snot on my shirt.'

'I'm such an idiot. All the signs were there and I–I didn't see them. You were slow, your custom *bakkie* – it's not custom as in flashy, it's custom as in modified. I'm an idiot. You're an idiot. What type of cripple walks across Beit Bridge?'

'I'm not a cripple, just managing my life in a new way.'

'I bet if we hadn't shared this room, I wouldn't have ever known, would I? Don't answer, it's rhetorical … I know you wouldn't have told me. You never told Courtney. She never knew, did she? Oh no, Courtney – when? When did this happen?' she asked. 'When did you become, you know …'

'May fourteenth, 2009.'

Peta stilled. 'One more question then I promise no more.'

'Don't promise things, Peta. Promises are too easily broken.'

'Did you know about Courtney when this happened? Did you know she had cancer and was asking you to come and hold her hand?'

'No. Not when it happened, but afterwards. And no, she didn't know. I spun her a story about being indispensable to the marines. I was still flat on my back and had only just had my legs taken. Until a few months back when I transferred from recovery into assisted living, I was in no state to travel anywhere, no matter how much I wanted to. Peta, I came as soon as I could, even though I know I was already eighteen months too late. I came home.'

CHAPTER

4

Getting Reacquainted

The sound of 'Walking on Sunshine' by Katrina and the Waves came from her phone.

'Are you going to get up and answer it?' Joss said.

The phone stopped ringing.

She lifted her arm from where it lay across him and sat up.

'Morning,' he said.

The phone started ringing again. Peta slipped off Joss's bed and walked around hers. 'Hello … Fantastic. Give me five minutes to shower and I'll catch up. Any problems … Perfect. See you in a little while. Bye.' She hung up. 'The trucks are through and it's—' She looked at the screen on her phone. 'Oh my God, it's almost one in the afternoon. How did I sleep the whole day away? Why did you let me sleep so long?'

'You obviously needed it.'

She looked at him, still lying on the bed, and at his plastic feet. She dragged her eyes back to his face.

'You've got some game trucks to catch up with. It's time you get going.'

'Right, I need to shower. No news on your *bakkie* yet?'

'Not yet.'

She nodded then closed the bathroom door and turned on the shower. 'Are you going to be okay waiting here?' she called.

'Yeah,' Joss replied. Then he mumbled, 'And I might even get to take my legs off and get some proper sleep.'

He smiled and shook his head. As a Royal Marine, he was used to going without sleep, had even trained to withstand torture, but lying next to Peta and listening to her in the shower was an altogether new kind of anguish for him. He knew once he might have played having a beautiful girl in his shower to his advantage, but that man was long gone. The Joss who greeted him in the mirror nowadays didn't do that type of thing. He had to remember to be responsible, to plan ahead, to avoid cases like last night, where he got into an 'unhealthy situation'.

He should have refused the offer of the lift. He knew he shouldn't have walked across the bridge in the first place, but he'd wanted to wake up knowing he was home in Zimbabwe, knowing he was almost at the end of his long journey.

Peta finished in the bathroom, and came back into the bedroom with the towel twirled around her hair turban style.

He swallowed hard, his eyes drawn to her neck. He had left his mark on her, dark bruises in the shape of a necklace, his fingerprints clearly visible.

'Did you look in the mirror?' he asked quietly.

'No.' She brought her fingers up to her throat as if she had forgotten about the incident, then went into the bathroom again. She didn't utter a sound but came out and dug in her small bag until she found a grey cosmetics case then returned to the bathroom.

She remained behind the closed door for a long time and just as Joss was about to call out, she emerged.

'Ta-dah!' she said. 'Did I get them all?'

She had applied make-up to her face and her whole neck area, and yet she didn't look like a painted geisha. Peta was girl-next-door pretty, but with make-up on, she was magazine-pin-up beautiful, with smoky eyes and sparkling pink lips. His eyes travelled down her neck and there was no sign that underneath the paint and powder was evidence that, for the first time in his life, he'd hurt a woman.

'You're amazing,' he said.

'Thanks. It's too darn hot to wear a polo neck. Anyway, I don't have one handy.'

Half an hour ago he'd held her while she'd slept, her long eyelashes dark against her fair skin, freckles clearly visible across her nose and cheeks, testament to many hours spent under the African sun. But that person was gone and in her place was a businesswoman. She wore khaki shorts and shirt with an Africa Wildlife In Crisis logo embroidered over her left breast. She was all professional.

He knew that their time together was over. He remembered when she had joined her father in Africa Wildlife In Crisis (AWIC), the international wildlife monitoring charity that worked alongside the World Bank and governments to try to manage the wildlife of Africa with transfrontier conservation areas. That was the year his folks had been killed.

'Thanks for being so good about this. It's more than I could expect, or ask, of anyone.' But he wondered how she knew how to cover that type of bruising.

'It was an accident – I don't know anything that's happened in your life since you joined the Royal British Marines, but I do know the Joss I knew as a kid, the one who was Courtney's best friend, would never intentionally hurt me,' she said. 'You're the one who saved orphaned elephant babies, and every other animal.' She paused. 'You're getting help with it, aren't you? The nightmares? Seeing a counsellor ...' Her voice was quieter, as if uncertain she should talk about the subject.

Joss nodded. 'I am. It's better than it used to be. Some nights I don't have them at all.'

'How are you going to continue your sessions in Zim?'

'I've got teleconference sessions set up with my counsellor. Believe me, the other vets in my sharehouse wouldn't have let me come otherwise. I'm surprised they didn't all try to come with me, that they've let me do this alone.'

'You're kidding me?'

'Dead serious. You'll get to meet them someday. I give it a few weeks and they'll rock up here to check out my progress, see if I'm sliding back into a shit pile.'

'Shit pile?'

'There were complications with the procedure and I had to have multiple operations. My progress was slower than others who were injured at the same time. I called it the bandage-stage shit pile, and it stuck. The time when I couldn't walk, even on stubbies, waiting for my legs to recover. And after I started to heal, I just wanted to get back to a real life.'

'So, no anger?'

'Of course there was anger, but then I realised that while I'm not indestructible, I'm still a marine. Once you start on the road to recovery, you soon itch to get back into society. Some even go straight back to the front line, others get rehabilitated, reintegrated into civilian life ...'

'And you?' Peta asked.

'Leave of absence. I've got some time owed to me. I'm in no hurry to make any decisions either way. So the goal at the moment is to get fitter and compete in a triathlon or two. Consider my options.'

'Are you serious? Triathlons?' Peta shook her head as she closed her case. 'At least it's not back to war.'

Joss laughed. 'Not right now. Triathlons, yeah, they're hard work, but I can be just as strong as I once was. It's just going to take some time and lots of energy.'

'If anyone can bounce back, Joss, it's you. Listen, I have to run or those trucks will have a head start on me and I'll never catch up. When your wheels are through customs and you've settled, give me a call,' she said, digging in her purse for a business card and handing it to him. 'You'll need to come and collect Nguni – but you can't drive it, and – oh, dammit, you know what I mean ...'

Joss smiled. 'I do. I'll call you.'

'You do that,' she said as she hung her briefcase from her shoulder, grabbed her small travel case and pulled the chair from under the door handle. 'I'll let them know you're staying another night so you don't have to climb those steps again.'

'I'll be climbing them again anyhow if your *bakkie* needs help starting—'

'Ah crap … Watch from the window. Hopefully Nguni will behave!'

* * *

Joss watched as Peta drove away. He turned back to their room, his room now, and frowned. Somehow he had never imagined his first night home in Zimbabwe would be in a motel room with Courtney's older sister. She had always been there when they were growing up, more reserved but doing everything they did, usually with a caution not to do it first. His heart ached, knowing that his childhood friend had died, that he had missed that whole part of her life. Eighteen months ago he'd been so doped up on morphine and other drugs he wouldn't have known if she'd called him daily or not. He barely remembered having conversations with her, and if it hadn't been for Tank, he wouldn't have even remembered that she'd died.

He was on the way home to her now, to visit her resting place, explain what had happened to him, and to say his final goodbye. He should have called her father's home in the Matusadona National Park, where she had said she was going to recover, and told Uncle Rodger he was coming. Deep down he had not wanted to face the truth, that his coming home was never about Courtney dying, but more about his near death. A slow burn began in his stomach as the memory of so many other good friends he had lost started to come back. Until now he had been able to separate his worlds: his Zimbabwe circle and his military circle. The African circle stood for all things pure, simple, unblemished; the military circle represented war, hatred, and the loss of so much: his innocence, his friends and a land torn apart by heretics.

Courtney was dead, having been beaten by ovarian cancer, and he himself had narrowly escaped the Grim Reaper. His circles had merged into a mess.

He took a deep breath, not sure he was as ready to face the world outside Headley as he'd thought he was. He flexed his hands.

'Courage.' He flicked off the switch that let the anger and resentment surface, and brought himself under control again.

He thought of Peta. She was everything Courtney wasn't. While Courtney used to bubble with energy, laughter and life, Peta had always been the cautious one, the one who stopped Courtney and Joss doing crazy things. Together they had all but run the district; from the time they were about five to the time they were in their teens, if there was trouble, everyone would blame them. It was normally Courtney's idea that Joss took further, so he guessed that it was his fault, but because Courtney was around, she also got blamed. That was when Peta wasn't there to caution her, keep them from being in trouble. She'd always been the older, wiser sister, and had taken her job seriously. Ndhlovy coming into his life when he was ten had united them even more. The girls had shared the feeding with him, slept in the stable, and they had all celebrated when the matriarch had come with her small herd and had taken Ndhlovy back into the wild after her mother One-Tusk had eaten enough moringa trees and had ample milk for her baby again.

Courtney hadn't wanted him to be a Royal British Marine Commando, she had fought with him every step of the way, trying to discourage him from going and getting his arse shot at. Peta had been the one who had told him to follow his dream, be who he wanted to be. And his dream had always been the commandos. From the moment he could remember his grandfather talking about them, showing him his badges and medals from World War Two, he'd known that was what he wanted to do with his life.

Save people.

Help people.

Be a hero.

It was in his blood. His grandfather saved people. His father saved the wildlife. Now it was his turn.

He had left Zimbabwe for England to follow his dream of a green beret, waved off proudly by his parents. But too soon they had died in a car accident on the Victoria Falls Road when the driver of a truck transporting copper travelling from Zambia had fallen asleep and driven over their 4x4. At least he knew they hadn't suffered, that they had died instantly and together. He had almost given up the marines then and come home, but he couldn't. He was committed, and he was determined to complete his tour. Then the next deployment came, and he signed on again, knowing that Bongani was looking after the lodge, running it as well as he could, waiting for Joss to come home.

And it was while he lay in bed, unable to walk, unable to do much but watch the endless drip in his IV line, that he had received his final letter from Courtney: she had cancer and was going home to Zimbabwe to die with dignity and peace. Please would he come home and hold her hand?

So much for being a hero. He hadn't been there for her.

Joss punched the pillow and flipped over onto his stomach. The fan continued to circulate the hot air around the room. He was home. He was in Zimbabwe.

Already it wasn't what he'd imagined, what he had worked so hard for. With his tunnel vision of just getting well enough to get home to his safari lodge, to continue building up his strength and pay his respects, he hadn't focused on how different he was now, or how he would manage with his broken body in a land where so much had changed.

He had been so determined to go and fight against the injustice of the world with the commandos that he hadn't noticed how messed up his own country had become.

*   *   *

Matusadona National Park

In the predawn light where shadows and darkness merge, when lions rest with full bellies after their hunt and the birds begin to serenade the approaching dawn, Peta watched her precious game trucks draw into position after the fifteen-hour slow drive across Zimbabwe. The off-loading area of Tashinga Headquarters of the Matusadona National Park was already a hive of activity. She smiled, watching the men and women she worked with ready the *boma*s for the incoming cargo.

Wayne got out of the front truck and stretched his back. 'That was a long haul!'

Peta grinned. 'Yes, but worth it for my research and this project. So worth it.' She rubbed her hands together, then caught herself, and quickly put them loosely by her side.

'Welcome home, Peta,' Tsessebe said. 'I was worried that Nguni might not make it.' He bumped knuckles then shook her hand, and lightly touched her shoulder.

'Had one or two problems, but mostly she still runs well. How was Dad?'

'He was no trouble.'

'Good one, Tsessebe. What antics did he get up to this time?'

'None, I promise. If he started straying, I guided him back.'

'I'm in your debt, as always.' Lately her dad was getting to be a handful and a half. As head of the rhino project, Rodger had always been the driving force behind the success of the breeding in the parks, keeping the two jewels as natural as possible, ensuring that the wild game was the priority, but after his attack, things in Chizarira had begun to slip. As the onsite large game vet, Peta had unofficially taken on many of his duties as well. They had talked with Africa Wildlife In Crisis about him retiring at length, and letting another take his place, but they had all felt that he lived for his job, and would die if it was taken away; so as long as Peta picked up the slack, they were happy to have him continue. Besides, if he retired, it would send a message to the poaching fraternity that the park was easy pickings without its *ikanka yabo* – 'their jackal' – left to protect it and its rhino.

She remembered the fateful day when her father had been visiting his brother in Nyamandhlovu and the war vets had seized the farm. Her uncle had been killed, and Rodger had been shot multiple times and beaten almost to death. When the neighbours got there to help, they found him still breathing. After months of treatment, when Peta had thought that everything was going to be alright, they had realised that Alzheimer's had set in with the shock. Her father was there some days, but others he was like a child stuck in history and unable to get out.

Since the attack, Rodger was shakier than he had ever been, and he was now blind in his left eye and had limited sight in his right. The only reason he could still drive was because she had changed his *bakkie* to an automatic transmission, and Tsessebe guided him verbally. His fingers were gnarled and bent from being broken and fixed as arthritis set into the joints, and he dragged his left leg when he walked. It was so damaged by the bullet that had shattered his femur that despite pins and plates, he still didn't have full control over it. But none of this stopped him. He could still do most of his work as long as Tsessebe was by his side.

'Where is he?' she asked.

'Still asleep. We had a big day yesterday.'

Alerted to trouble, Peta looked at Tsessebe. 'What happened?'

'The rangers found another poachers' camp, so we raided it. They found nets, rifles and a motorbike, but no poachers. We tracked them to where they had left in a boat, and when they come back there will be a surprise waiting for them. Teach them to poach our wildlife.'

'Tell me he didn't rig another claymore in the park.'

'Just a little one so we will hear the noise and can rush to catch them.'

'Ah man, Tsessebe, he can't do that! Now I have to go and defuse it before some poor animal gets hurt, or a tourist. This isn't the seventies any more, we're not in the middle of a war.' Peta rubbed her forehead. When she had become her father's bomb squad she couldn't quite remember, but she silently thanked his younger self for ensuring she had a sound knowledge of explosives.

'This was not a place any tourist would go, but I will take you there,' Tsessebe said. 'Maybe it is time we started treating it more like a war again. Those poachers keep coming, and we cannot just treat it as anti-poaching forever. It is time we armed ourselves, like a private army, and went to war with them. Like they did back in the day. We should do it now, before there is no wildlife left in our park to protect.'

'I know, and you know the answer. I have asked for more weapons to arm the rangers, but AWIC said that we are here for conservation, not war. I think we need to get a private sponsor on board, someone who can go all Schwarzenegger on the poachers for us, and leave us to our job of looking after the animals.' She shook her head, and looked back at the game trucks. 'Come see what I found at auction. New blood and some unexpected additions.'

They walked to the first truck, where Wayne and Jamison, the owners of South African based Wild Translocation trucking company, were already getting the gangplank ready and the hessian and metal sides in place. The truck was backed up to a *boma*, designed for holding game in quarantine. The holding pens at Tashinga had seen many beauties pass through, and the buffalo bull was no exception; new blood for the Matusadona gene pool. The best thing was that, other than bartering a week's holiday on her family houseboat as transport fees, he was free. Peta watched every dollar of their meagre budget like a leopard watched its prey. She looked through an airhole into the crate on the back of the truck. She turned away from the acrid smell, and grinned as Tsessebe glued his eye to the hole.

'A *duggaboy*? He is beautiful. How do you think he will go with the tsetse flies?'

'I don't know … I'm hoping that he might have seen a few before in his life – who knows? But I do know that he's cantankerous and strong. He's a fighter, this one, and he deserves to keep living wild, not become a trophy on some wall.'

'Used to lions?'

'He comes from the Limpopo area, from a game farm there that had predators, but he's not so fond of people. He's been known to chase a tourist or two. I'm hoping he disappears into the bush here, as he's a menace animal. Let's hope I don't have to be the one to call in a hunting concession on him. I know there's enough room here for him and for us, and since we don't have that many tourists, maybe he'll find a place to live a decent undisturbed life too.'

Tsessebe nodded. 'Did you get the black rhino?'

Peta nodded. 'For even less than I thought I'd have to bid, too. It was a good auction for the buyers.'

'Stand clear,' Jamison called, and they stepped away from the cage. Anything could go wrong with the release of a wild animal into a *boma*, and they moved nearer the giant wooden structure just in case. The buffalo snorted once before putting its head down and slowly backing out of the container, then turned around with surprising speed, and jumped the rest of the way off the ramp and into the enclosure. He snorted, put his head down and charged the trailer. Dust flew up around him as he skidded to a halt and snorted again. He shook his head, his huge curled horns with their thick base ready to rip apart anyone who came too near.

Wayne stood next to her. 'He's magnificent. I can see why you insisted on finding another avenue for him other than trophy hunters.'

'That he is. Now let's hope he likes the wide open spaces of Matusadona and leaves the tourists alone,' Peta said. 'Thanks again for the transport.'

Wayne smiled. 'What's not to love about Tashinga, other than the roads coming in? I thought that they might be the undoing of my trucks, and wondered at Jamison's insisting that we bargain with you, but now that I see this place, I can understand why he was so persistent. Tara and Ebony are going to be so jealous.'

Jamison laughed. 'True, both our wives will be green with envy, and do not mind Wayne, he is always worried about our trucks. If we break down here, the spare parts are sparse and expensive.'

'It was good to see you come all the way through without any problems, both for your and my animals' sakes. Let's get that *chipembele* out after his long journey; my rhino will want to stretch his legs and have a rub on something.'

They turned to where the trailer of the second truck had been unhitched. Moeketsi, the older black man who shared driving with the younger man, Hawk, chuckled as they approached.

Peta frowned. 'What's so funny?'

'Look at your rhino bull – already he is sniffing the air. He knows there are others here; already he is interested,' Moeketsi said.

'We have three juveniles in the *boma*s at the moment. He can probably smell them. Poor guy. We'll settle him down and get him used to his guards before he's let out. He'll never be alone again. Two teams of men will watch him twenty-four hours a day; it's the only way I can keep them alive. The slaughter of the seventies and eighties must not be allowed to happen again. My breeding program here is too important; we can't lose this species,' Peta said.

'Jamison said you were passionate about your wildlife, and you grew up in this reserve, with your dad as head ranger,' Wayne said. 'This park must have been something back then.'

'It was, but times changed,' Peta said, and made a conscious effort to smooth over the frown she knew showed on her forehead. 'For one, we didn't have those white skulls decorating the entrance as you come in; those rhino and elephant were alive then ...'

'Peta! Why are there trucks here so early in the morning?' yelled her father, and Peta groaned.

'Speak of the devil,' she said. 'Over here, Dad.'

Rodger walked towards her. He dragged his leg as if it were a useless appendage, but walked at speed, hopping forward like a buzzard. He wore a black patch over the eye that had been taken out when he was shot in the head, and looked a little like the Hunchback of Notre Dame, grotesque and disfigured despite the plastic surgery. Some days his mind was okay, but there were moments like this when he became startled and she would have to assure him that all was still right in the world. Then there were the bad days. She preferred not to dwell on those.

'Dad, it's fine. Remember I told you I was going to the auction in South Africa to bring back a new black rhino as part of the program?'

'Damn thing will just die of sleeping sickness; not sure why you bother,' Rodger said. 'Then you will need to pay compensation to whoever lent him to you.'

'AWIC bought this one for my research. You know I have to keep trying or the animals could become interbred. We don't want that, do we?'

'Who are you?' he asked, turning to the Wild Transportation team.

'Wayne.' He stepped forward. 'And this is my business partner, Jamison, and the other team are Moeketsi and Hawk—'

'Well at least there's one white face there,' Rodger interrupted.

'Please excuse my father; sometimes he forgets that it's not 1965 and we are not a colonial country any more,' Peta said.

'It is okay,' Jamison said. 'No offence taken. Mr de Jonge, do you remember me? We met before. You had me visit here at Matusadona for two weeks. I used to work for Rose Crosby of Malabar Farm in Karoi. We spoke about creating Amarose Lodge.'

'I remember; you were the *totsi* who came with a letter instructing me to teach you everything I'd learnt in my life in just two weeks. That madam of yours called too, bossy woman. How's she these days?'

'She moved to South Africa in 1992, and I am very sad to say, but she crossed over. She was very old.'

'Sorry to hear that. She was a tough old broad,' Rodger said.

Peta turned to her father and threaded her arm through his. 'Dad, we're about to unload the rhino. Come stand at the *boma* fence with me.' She moved him away from the others, and Tsessebe was soon standing next to them. 'Can you stay here together? I need to check on something.'

'Yes,' Tsessebe said as he began talking to Rodger quietly in Ndebele.

The old man launched into an animated conversation, hands waving in front of him, but Peta knew that, once again, Tsessebe would keep her father safe. Somehow Tsessebe had developed the ability to transform each time the old man's mood changed. When she had moved Tsessebe into their house to look after Rodger, it had been one of the best decisions she'd ever made, as the two of them seemed to have a better relationship than many married couples did.

The rhino backed out without incident, and the moment it was in the *boma*, it pooped, its tail swishing from side to side, then it spread the faeces around with its giant feet, marking its territory.

'He's going to settle right in,' Peta said.

Wayne nodded. 'He's lucky you bought him; I thought for sure that farmer from the Eastern Cape would bid more.'

'I thought so too, but I think he was meant to be ours,' she said as she watched the rhino explore around the boundary fence, all the time smelling the air, its lips curled up.

'Right, just the horse left. Where do you want your stallion?' Wayne asked.

'I'll take him out where that truck is parked.'

'He's a strange companion for the other two animals,' Jamison said.

'Zeus is for me. Dad and I started an anti-poaching unit on horseback. He's from the Karoo, so I'm hoping he'll be tough enough to cope with the tsetse flies. He was trained by an ex-Greys Scout, so he's already battle ready, no bagging even, a match made in heaven.'

Wayne asked, 'Do they still tie them to a tree and throw a sack at them until they learn that the bag won't hurt them?'

Peta nodded but frowned. 'Unfortunately, we need to here. I can't have someone fall off and shoot themselves or their horse because a pheasant flew up next to them.'

'Even with the new "whisper training" that's all the rage now?'

'Most of my guys are not good riders, so I need horses that don't spook. I love the philosophy of building trust with a horse through spending time with it, but we often have different riders on different horses, and believe me, the guards are not generally horse lovers. Most are not naturally riders.'

'You go out on patrol with your anti-poaching guards?' Jamison asked.

'Not as often as I'd like to.'

They came to the smallest of the translocation trucks. When they opened the back, the horse whinnied. Peta walked up the ramp, all the time talking to Zeus as she put her hand on his rump, and then walked into the crate.

'Come on, Zeus,' she said. 'You're home.'

CHAPTER
5

King Gogo wa de Patswa

Tichawana Ndou stood outside the old school building; its white-wash was chipped and peeling, and there was no glass in most of the windows, but the bricks still stood strong. An institution worthy of remaining on Zimbabwe soil, despite its colonial start. He had taken the abandoned building and made it functional again, along with the boarding school next door, which now housed two hundred students.

He stared at the new green and yellow sign on the wall. GWANDA TRAINING COLLEGE, FOR STUDENTS 12–25 YEARS OLD.

When he had asked Hillary, the secretary of his construction business, to ensure that the college ran smoothly, she had been her efficient self and organised everything from the sign to the black uniforms every boy and girl wore. But she would never see inside the school. That part he had to keep her in the dark about. Already she knew too much of his business dealings, and he had nothing on her to keep her silent – she was as spotless as a dry-cleaned suit wrapped in plastic.

He shook his head and walked proudly through the front door. He ran his finger along the old wall inside. It was recently repainted and the smell was strong. He continued through the entrance, then up some stairs, trailing his fingers on the wooden balustrade. Finally, he removed them and looked at the tips.

Clean.

He didn't bother to show an emotion. This college was not built to make the people there happy.

He walked into the first classroom. Once it had held desks and chairs, inkwells and snot-nosed white colonial brats who learnt to write cursive in the Queen's English. It'd probably had coloured posters on the walls of the ABCs and, hanging from the ceiling, the planets revolving around a yellow sun. Now it had waist-high wooden benches arranged in rows. Functional, not fancy.

He passed the lines of teenagers at the benches, all blindfolded. The instructor had waited for him. He nodded an acknowledgement.

'Ready. Go,' the instructor said.

The teenagers each had an AK-47 in front of them, which they dismantled and reassembled, the noise of metal clicking into place familiar to his ears. It brought back fond memories of training in Zambia and in North Korea; of silky-haired girls who never complained but did what they could 'for the good of the people'. If that meant serving some black boys from Africa, sucking them off, taking a beating, then they did that too, and like all good girls, they never complained.

He felt himself stir. Later he would visit his club.

He re-engaged with the group, his eyes flicking around, finding a boy who was slower than the rest. He walked to where the boy stood fumbling at the desk, his weapon still in pieces.

'Time's up,' the instructor said, just as most of the trainees slammed down their reassembled weapons.

The boy had not finished. Tichawana watched as a bead of sweat formed on his forehead and ran into the blindfold tightly bound around his eyes. The youth's breathing was laboured, taking in too much oxygen in his fear. He had much to learn still.

The instructor began walking along the benches, checking the results. 'This one is always slow with his weapon,' he said when he reached Tichawana and the boy, 'but he is good with a knife. Better than most of the other students.'

Tichawana continued to look at the boy. He didn't show any outward signs of being different from the other kids. A regular youngster, the perfect recruit.

'He can also speak fluent Chinese, French and German as well as English and Ndebele, and he is good at teaching the other students languages. He is getting faster with his weapons training. He will be a good asset to have, this one, as he is able to use a computer. Very quick with a computer.'

Tichawana nodded. 'A genius is only an asset if he does not get shot, or cause his comrades to get shot because of his incompetence in the field. Give him extra training, make him prove he is the best with his weapon. If he does not learn before my visit next month, we can let his comrades have him for torture practice. We cannot afford to keep dead weights in training.'

The instructor nodded, then moved down the bench.

Tichawana saw the boy shudder and knew that he wasn't quite immune to his surroundings yet; he still had to be broken further so that he could be built up. Moulded into what was needed for the cause.

The time was almost ripe to strike at Bongani. Their father was seventy-seven and a sick old man. From what his spies said, he now had pneumonia. He would soon become one with the earth, and Bongani would inherit his kingdom.

And it would be ripe for the taking.

Once the chief died, all the *N'Goma* magic in the world would not protect Bongani and his people. His brother would learn the hard way what it was like to lose everything. To have it taken away.

All these years, Tichawana had circled his father's territory, ensuring that when the day came, he could take what belonged to him: the inheritance that should have been his.

If only his mother had been the first wife, and not the second. If only he had been born before his half-brother.

His father was the last obstacle. There would be no one to stop him now.

'I will see you at the same time in a month.' Tichawana walked out of the room and down the stairs of the old school building.

The driver opened the door of his Mercedes-Benz and he climbed in. 'To the office,' he said, then he put his head back on the plush white leather upholstery and closed his eyes, the air-conditioning washing over him. He could almost see his brother's face.

He wouldn't see the takeover happening.

Soon Bongani would be dead, and Tichawana would inherit everything.

* * *

'I need you to take a letter for me,' Tichawana instructed.

'Yes, sir,' Hillary said.

He looked at his secretary sitting in the visitor's chair in front of him and wondered how someone like her was still unmarried and in the workforce. Not that he was complaining – he couldn't function without her.

'Start the letter with "Dear Mr Kamupambe".' He watched her as her pen flew across her page. '"If you believe that the elephant capture is significant,"' he said. Once again, he was instructing the ZimParks board to move a hunting concession to an area that already had a full quota, just below the Mana Pools area, because of the lack of big tuskers in the first area where the original concession was. If they didn't, he would remove the financial support that Crew-Build, his construction company, gave as conservation donations to their organisation.

This was power.

Not that every professional hunter he employed actually closed out every concession on those elephants, but he needed elephants of the right size to match some of the ivory shipments coming in from Zambia and Northern Africa, in order to bring those shipments into the legal market. The authorities, like the police, customs and the Convention on International Trade in Endangered Species, did not tend to look too closely when a hunter said that he had 'moved' the concessions for the animals, and then had the tusks as a by-product of the legal hunt to prove it.

'Make sure that you use strong language, so that they know it is not a request,' he instructed her.

Hillary nodded.

He smirked. She often reworded his letters into a more professional manner. That's what secretaries and subordinates were for, to correct his small imperfections and allow the world to only see him as a professional businessman. Nevertheless, a thick, gold-framed certificate hung on his wall, stating that he had obtained a Bachelor of Commerce at the University of Zimbabwe. No one paid attention to the date on the bottom, which read 1975, when the university was still called the University of Rhodesia.

'Anything else, sir?'

'No, I'm going to the club now. Tell my driver to bring the Mercedes around from the garage.'

She walked to the door.

'Hillary, did you forget something?' he asked.

She turned and curtseyed to him before exiting.

He stood up and walked to his coat rack for his jacket. He looked in the mirror. He did not recognise the man in the suit and tie that stared back at him. Once he'd had an athletic build, but these days he was more fat than well built. He turned sideways. His stomach was widening; he needed to stop his frequent beers at the club. The once strong body of a fighter was now flabby with lack of physical use.

He made a note to begin getting back into shape, and what better way than to spend a few days with his youth army? Take a week or two and retrain himself. He smiled. The government called the camps 'educational facilities where the young would learn "life skills"'. He owned seven. The system worked in his favour. His training camps were slowly amassing him a youth army to rival the president's. To serve him. To fight and die for him.

One day soon, he would call on all the youths he trained in his educational camps and they would rise up, take up arms for him against his brother. Soon there would be bloodshed unlike anything that had been seen in their country for almost two hundred years, since the days of King Mzilikazi and his son, Lobengula, when they killed millions of Shona people, before the white people settled there. There would be a massacre in Northern Matabeleland to rival his days in the 5th Brigade and the slaughter in the name of the *Gukurahundi*. The Shona had such a lovely way of putting things into poetry: 'The early rain which washes away the chaff before the spring rains' instead of an attempted genocidal decimation of a tribe.

The time of the man the business world called Tichawana Ndou, but who the criminals of the country called King Gogo wa de Patswa, the King of Thieves, was near.

* * *

Hillary sat in her small room in Makokoba. She sub-rented her space in the house along with six other people, who had use of a single room each. They were lucky, they had two bathrooms to share; many of the others who crammed into the houses like this one had to make do with one. The housing crisis just never seemed to ease. But it was better than being in a shanty town where the government could come at any moment and bulldoze your home and your belongings. Besides, she needed to be near the city; it was where her job was. But one day, she dreamt of returning to her parents' land, where her father's *kraal* once stood. To build a proper house there, where she could tend to their grave, and acknowledge where they lay in the dark earth, their lost spirits waiting for a proper burial, trapped between the worlds. She longed to enable them to pass over, to journey to the other side and join their ancestors.

Shaking her head, she opened the A4 file she kept hidden in the big pot in her small corner kitchen. Everything she knew about her boss, Tichawana Ndou, was recorded in it. She still had the first book she had been given when she was handed over to the orphanage after the police had found her. She had only drawn pictures then. Sketching his face again and again, so she would never forget. She remembered each face as if she saw them in photographs. They never faded from her memory. When she had learnt to read and write, she began to record details too.

When the men first came into the *kraal*, Hillary and her mother had been crushing maize into *mielie-meal*. When her mother heard the soldiers, she had run with Hillary to the toilet to hide. Through the crack in the door, they had watched the men being made to dig their own shallow graves. Her mother had covered Hillary's mouth so that she could not make a sound. Her brother was shot when he tried to run away, and then her father was killed. They were the last of the men to die.

She did not make a sound, but one of the men came to check in the outhouse. Her mother had lowered her into the long-drop toilet, into the maggot-filled cesspit below. Then the man had opened the door and dragged her mother out.

Hillary had listened to the screaming outside, and to more shots. She had tried to jump up and to get out, but she had been too small. She'd needed something solid to stand on. But when she had felt the shack burning above her, she had been grateful that she was in the pit. When a piece of still burning wood fell into the drop area, she had been able to smother the flame with the poo, the maggots and the moisture. Once the fire had gone out, she leant the plank carefully against the side like a ramp and had only needed a little step to reach up and drag herself out of the hole.

Hillary remembered walking around the burnt-out structures that were once her home, smelling the stench of burnt flesh. The hyenas and the vultures had got there before she had been brave enough to climb out of her hiding place, and she had to chase them away from the corpses that remained in the *ikhayas*.

She found her mother there. She always wore a gold cross around her neck; it was from the days when she had been a nurse at the hospital in Bulawayo. It was blackened, so Hillary took it and shone it on her dress, then put it around her own neck. Finally she had pulled away all the bushes that had been piled onto the mass grave, and reopened it. She buried what was left of her mother, her neighbours and the women in her small village, never understanding why the attackers had buried most of the women with the men, but left some in the ashes.

Knowing that there was nothing for her at her *kraal*, Hillary had carefully washed in the river, taking time to make sure that her dress was dry before she began the long walk to the city to try to find her mother's sister. She knew the road; it was long and many cars and buses would pass her once she was on the main part of her journey. But eventually she had succumbed to the heat and exhaustion and someone had picked her up from where she had fallen on the side of the road and taken her to a hospital. The police had taken her to the orphanage when they couldn't find her aunty.

She had been too scared to tell anyone what had happened, terrified that the men in the red hats would find her and kill her too.

When she was sixteen, Hillary began working as a secretary in the office of the orphanage, where she learnt to type and file paperwork. With her first pay cheque she bought an A4 file and paper to write on. She'd begun recording everything she could remember about that night.

Later she got a job as a checkout girl in the local Spar. She progressed up the ladder slowly, and was a secretary in the office the week before she turned twenty. She worked hard, and in her spare time, she looked for her family's killers. Searching in the streets and the papers and on the TV when she got a chance to watch.

Her diligence paid off when she saw one of the men in the newspaper, standing next to the president, smiling at a birthday celebration. He was older, but she could never have forgotten his face. Once she had his name, she could find out more about him, and in 2007, when Crew-Build, his construction company, advertised for a receptionist, she had applied.

Now, three years later, she had the name of the other man responsible too. He used to be called the Black Mamba. His real name was Philip Samkanga, and he was one of the generals in the Zimbabwe Army. She had amassed not one but eight files on her family's killers. Each man had his own collection of notes, but she had concentrated her energy on the one closest to her – Tichawana Ndou. In her documents were copies of his accounts, and copies of those he showed the world. She had the names of his spies, and the people who were his muscle within the communities of Zimbabwe. She knew who he had meetings with and when, and what they discussed. She added the letter she had written today.

If anyone saw her collection, they would assume it was just her work, brought home and arranged neatly. But in one hidden box was more damaging information. The box was where she put anything linked to the 5th Brigade and the mass graves, along with Tichawana's other crimes, like the purchase deed of yet another Korean slave for his harem.

6

The Heart Calls Home

The sun rose over the trees, its reflection pink on the surface of the water, enticing the elephant herd on. The young matriarch hesitated. She could hear the call of the guinea fowl as it *re-pe-peed* to the flock in a serenade of good cheer, and the doves cooing as they danced their mating rituals in the sand. She could see the tell-tale ripple of a turtle as it swam towards a submerged log to sun itself in the early morning warmth. She lifted her trunk and smelt the air, her ears flapping forward, the two notches in her ear distinguishing her from her herd, as well as the bump above her head where the radio collar, fitted years before, remained securely in place.

She turned her head, cautious of the human smell on the wind. After all these years it was a scent she knew well. Tainted with the faint smell of something sweet, as well as an oily odour that would never leave her memory. This scent could only mean one thing.

Danger.

Men with guns waited in ambush. They had killed her grandmother and her mother. They had slaughtered her aunt, and left the younger elephants to mourn their premature death. When they had died, she'd had to step up and take over as matriarch despite being a young adolescent. It was the way. It had always been the way.

Her mother's mother was matriarch when she was born and had been separated from her herd. It had been her grandmother who hadn't given up on her, and had come back through the poacher's territory, through the charred huts and bushveld to find her. To track her to where she had been rescued by the humans. It had been her mother who had taken over for a few brief seasons when her grandmother fell to the poacher's bullets, despite heading north for security. It had been her mother, with her one tusk, who had kept their herd together for a short time, until she too had been taken. Now the herd was her responsibility. Despite her lack of years, she followed the trails her matriarchs had shown her. She remembered them all. She'd been taught from an early age to remember. Imprinted the details on her memory.

She'd been born to lead one day, and although younger than many, she knew what she had to do now to keep her family alive.

But they were no longer alone. Youngsters whose grandmothers and mother had known each other had banded together as a larger clan. Sticking together, looking to her for leadership. Other herds whose matriarchs had been friends with her grandmother had been affected by the poachers. Their grand dames of the savannahs killed, their teeth chopped out of their heads, and their carcasses left to rot in the hot sun, vultures and hyenas feasting on their bodies.

At first she'd headed north, away from the gunfire and the slaughter. She'd avoided humans, with a new appreciation that not all were good, and she had followed the other herds across a mighty river and into a new land. There they had found peace for a while.

But that time was over.

Closing her mind to the memories, the smells and the hurt from years gone by, she forced herself to be calm. The whole herd relied on her. She flapped her ears, and backed up.

The baby elephant travelling next to her adjusted to his matriarch's change in path and continued walking. Her younger sister, walking directly behind her baby, turned slightly, moving her bulk out of the way for the matriarch to pass back through the herd, followed by the baby. Slowly, and with purpose, the whole herd of elephants turned about fully and moved silently back into the dark shadow of the bush, plodding on through the veld.

They wouldn't drink at this place today. This waterhole was not safe.

The matriarch placed her trunk over the baby who now walked next to her, and gave him a reassuring caress. Technically she was only a teenager herself, yet this little one's mother had been one of the first to join their clan a few seasons before, and this was her second baby under her matronage. It was time to move to safer grounds again so that this baby would see adulthood.

It had been a long time since they visited the high rocky escarpment in the south, and beyond that, the miracle trees. She didn't know if the grove would still be there, or if the humans who once saved her would be living there in their stone and thatch structures, but she knew that when that particular smell of humans and oil came about, it didn't go away until every elephant was dead.

She'd felt the pull towards the south a few days ago, an invisible string, drawing her home, and had ignored it. Now, with the stress of moving her herd quickly and over a long distance, some of the mothers would need the help to feed their babies from the miracle trees she knew were in the south. She would be happier having her own baby near the trees too.

There was a chance that some of her herd might die on this journey across the great river and down into the lands of the southern rocks. She hoped not.

She pushed onwards.

She recalled the map of her life and where that journey had taken her, and adjusted her route to take the whole clan once again towards safety. Towards her birthplace in the steep hills of the big valley, where the eagles cried in the thermal winds, and the green grass grew next to the lakeside, sweet and juicy. Where a refreshing bath followed by a mud wallow on the shores of the vast water was a daily occurrence, and the hunters' guns were silent.

CHAPTER

7

Yingwe River Lodge, Binga

Nothing could keep the smile off Joss's face as he drove his *bakkie* into Yingwe River Lodge, his family home, ten days after his encounter with Peta. The big vehicle had eaten up the kilometres from Beit Bridge to the Binga district in the Zambezi Escarpment. The money he'd paid for the customisation had been worth every cent. Being able to drive only with his hands was the safer alternative and the Hilux didn't seem to have suffered from the customisation. In fact, it purred over the tarred roads and through the road blocks and was now navigating the extremely corrugated and potholed gravel road as if it loved offroad as much as the tarmac.

He was almost home.

When his parents had been killed in 2003, he didn't think he would ever see his home again. But Bongani had been his lifeline. He'd become manager of the lodge, and taken responsibility for it when Joss couldn't. Getting out of the marines at that stage hadn't been on the cards, and then time passed and his accident happened.

Now, his time to return had come. To heal. Maybe to stay, because his friend Bongani needed him now, and he had a debt to repay.

The cows that walked on the road ahead were thin, and behind them ran a young child with a long whip, his shorts tattered and torn, his T-shirt ripped and dirty. On his feet he wore traditional tyre shoes. Someone old school was obviously still living in the village that lay on the outskirts of the lodge. Joss wondered who. He noted that the cattle were unbranded and he was certain that they were a good Brahman lineage.

He wound down the window and whistled to move the cows along. Slowly he edged through the mass, and at last was out the other side. When he rounded the final corner to his family safari lodge driveway, he found his heart was beating wildly. There used to be dense bush on both sides of a graded road, but now the bush was totally cleared and huge potholes had to be navigated. Barren ground baked in the sun where bush shrub used to be. The villages once contained within the old Tribal Trust Lands were spread all the way up to the five-kilometre buffer zone that surrounded Kariba Lake, the only barrier saving the lake on the Zimbabwe side from encroachment by local settlers. Small hedges of aloes separated one family from another, keeping goats and chicken from straying to the next person's home, which were neat mud *ikhaya*s decorated with brown and black geometric images and thatched roofs that puffed smoke from cooking fires.

A few black children ran in the road with wire cars, their wheels made from tin cans, and old people sat under those trees that had not been cleared. No birds flew past. No wild game dared show its face here for fear of being captured in a snare or shot by the settlers in the expanded village.

His heart sank. He knew that his Zimbabwe had changed. Bongani had warned him about the influx of new settlers into the Binga area, Ndebele and Shona people too; people frightened to stay near the cities where the government's dictatorship was being felt daily. He had been the one to organise the settlers, and collected a small monthly levy from them for staying on his land, using the money to keep the communal lands ploughed for the maize, sorghum and vegetables that helped to support them. As chief-in-waiting, Bongani was doing a damn fine job of managing the lodge and the responsibilities of the people, but with his father on his deathbed, that was all about to change. When Bongani became chief, he'd need a break from being the manager of the lodge for a while, until he was sure that everything under his chieftainship was secured. They both knew that he was in for the fight of his life to keep his position: his half-brother, Tichawana, circled in the shadows like a hyena.

A smiling Bongani stood at the back entrance to the safari lodge.

'Bongani!' Joss said as he opened his door. He got out of his *bakkie*, ensuring both feet were on the ground before pushing away from the seat.

Bongani reached out his hand in friendship, but Joss surprised him by pulling him forward and giving him a hug.

'It is good to see you again, my old friend.' Bongani stepped back and held him by the shoulders. He looked him up and down, and tears ran freely down his dark face. 'So much has changed; the boy has come back to Zimbabwe as a man. This is where you belong even if you lost parts of you in the faraway war. This is your place.'

Joss smiled. 'It's good to be home.'

Bongani dusted his feet off at the door to the kitchen. 'I will introduce you to your houseboy, Lwazi, and his grandfather, Madala White. They are giving you a little time to settle in before coming back. They have already moved into the spare rooms as we discussed so that Lwazi is here to help you.'

'Thanks, Bongani, I appreciate it.'

'It benefits them too. Believe me, if I could have moved in here with you, I would have, but my father is too ill; I cannot move out of my home and leave him.'

'You have enough on your plate without adding me to it. I'm just happy to be home. Besides, I need help modifying this place so that

I can be independent, and someone to wake me up when the nightmares happen, which will be for a good while yet. I couldn't get you up at night and still expect you to continue your chief duties in the day without falling asleep.'

Bongani chuckled. 'You always were better with words than I was, Joss. Lwazi will be fine. He already looks after his grandfather, and does it with kindness.'

'How's your father?'

'He is fading fast. I never thought I would see the day he was bedridden, but I do not believe he will be getting up again. I think you have arrived in time to say goodbye.'

'I'm sorry to hear that. I'll visit him first thing in the morning.'

'He would like that; he is looking forward to seeing you again. He liked your father a lot and he was very unhappy when he died, so I think seeing you are now home will comfort him.'

Joss nodded. 'I guess, for me, having my folks taken suddenly was hard, but easier too. You have had to watch your father deteriorate and become a shadow of himself.'

'This is true. If I get to choose, I want to die quickly. Have a heart attack out in the fields, or get taken by a lion. Do not let me suffer as a broken-down old man.'

'I couldn't agree more,' Joss said, looking around. 'So, we have a working fridge and a gas stove?'

Bongani nodded. 'The fridge is an old paraffin one. I bought it because the electricity to the house is not so good any more. We have lots of power failures. The small house generator was stolen long ago. You must not stock the fridge with lots of food; it is not as cold as an electric fridge and the food will go off. I eat mostly in the lodge kitchen, where the generators were bolted down to a concrete slab very well by your father, making them too hard for the *skabenga*s to steal.'

'I brought another smaller generator in my trailer, so that I can use my gym equipment. Sounds like I'll need to lock it up each day when I'm finished with it. Maybe we should be investing in some solar panels.'

'No improvements. You need to understand how this area has changed, and you need to look through your financials for this lodge properly with me. Those settlers will see you improving the house only and say you are rich and should be sharing it with the villagers.'

'Perhaps a solar farm for the village closest us then – that way we all benefit.'

'Maybe.' Bongani nodded slowly. 'But do not start putting money into anything until we are sure they are not going to kick you off and blame the government. The people are still volatile. There are always outside influences that corrupt them. I feel that as chief, I am losing control of the area because my BaTonga people are no longer the majority – too many settlers. I thought that they would be thankful that I had created a safe place for them, but this is not so.'

'That serious?'

'You will see how they look to one in particular, Mary, even though I am not married to her. She is just a worry-monger and she spreads it to everyone daily. She forgets that soon I will be her chief and the government will give the power of the final word to me. It will be me who decides who can live here and who cannot.'

'I take it you have reminded her of this?'

'It falls on deaf ears. But that is my problem, and we can sort that out another day. Right now, we must get you settled into your home again, and make you comfortable so you can finish healing.'

'We both have our work cut out. I'll need to make sure they see me as part of the community, not a *baas*.'

'Good luck with that one,' said Bongani. 'As long as your skin is white and ours is black, it will always be expected that you want to be the *baas*.'

Joss just shook his head as he walked through the passage that led to the lounge and dining area and the bedrooms. 'Wow, look at that, even the family pictures are still on the walls.'

Bongani smiled. 'This is your home. Why would it have changed?'

'I can't thank you enough for watching over the house; it means so much to me.'

'*Inkosi* Joss, lots has changed here, but the bond that your family and mine share, that will never change,' Bongani said. 'No amount of pressure from our president to kick out the white man will ever truly sever the friendship of the Zimbabwe people towards each other. There are those who would go blindly and follow heretics, but there are also those who wait for a strong man to come into power, to heal the land and bring all people of Zimbabwe together again.'

They walked through to the lounge area. It was as if Joss was in a time warp; nothing much had changed – his grandfather's huge kudu bull head still hanging above the mantelpiece of the fireplace. The crimson couch his mother had bought, a lot more faded and used than when last he saw it, but it was still there. The kudu skin that used to cover the floor was gone, but the floorboards gleamed with a recent polish. The house had been well cared for. He found the heavy silver cutlery still in the drawers of the dining-room sideboard, and the cut-crystal glasses sat with their decanter on the silver tray, polished as if he hadn't spent years away. The huge twelve-place dining table had remained in place, the polished surface still a deep burgundy. He had so many happy memories of dinners spent at that table.

'Thanks, Bongani,' Joss said, tears glistening in his eyes.

They walked into the main bedroom. His folks' bed was where it had always been, a huge four-poster in the middle of the room, its netting grey with age.

'Some of the ladies from the lodge came and helped spring clean with Charmaine, one of our best housekeeping staff, when they heard that you were coming home. I bought this mattress new in Victoria Falls last week so that you would have a good sleep at least,' Bongani said.

'Thanks. I'll sort the money out for you. I'll have to replace this bath, put in some rails so that I can be independent.'

'Do not get too fancy,' Bongani warned.

Joss's stomach made a twanging noise. 'Excuse me. It can do with some lunch. I'm starved.'

'We can eat at the lodge,' Bongani said.

They walked back into the kitchen as the back door opened. A teenage boy jumped up the top step into the kitchen then turned and held the door open for the old man behind him, who walked with a stick.

'Good timing. Lwazi, Madala White, meet Joss,' Bongani said.

Joss stuck his hand out. 'Good to meet you.' He looked at the young man. Tall and thin, the boy was obviously still growing. Joss remembered that awkward stage well.

'Lwazi,' the youth said as he put his hand out, but instead of a conventional handshake, he did a sort of slide shake, and Joss smiled as he quickly did the handshake that as kids they had thought was the best brotherhood shake ever.

'You know that Zimbabwe shake?' Lwazi said.

'I'm Zimbabwean,' Joss said. 'Good to meet you. Bongani has told me a lot about you.'

Lwazi just nodded.

Joss shook hands with the old man. 'Madala. Bongani mentioned that you are one of the tutors in the village school.'

'He teaches us to read and write, and to add, to do maths,' Lwazi answered before his grandad could.

'Sounds like your grandson is very proud of you,' Joss said.

'He does me proud too,' Madala White said, smiling.

Lwazi looked at Joss. 'Bongani told me that you grew up here. Did you go to the village school too?'

Joss shook his head. 'I was at boarding school in Kariba until I went to senior school at Peter House, in Marondera, but I would come home to our lodge for holidays.'

'One day, I'll get to go to a proper school, perhaps in a city.'

Joss nodded. 'How old are you now?'

'Fourteen. How old are you?'

'Twenty-four, but some days I feel like I could be one hundred and four.'

Lwazi nodded. 'Would you like me to bring in all that stuff from your *bakkie*?'

'Thanks, that would be nice. We'll get it done faster if we both do it,' Joss said. 'Then after lunch I can do my exercises, or I'm going to be walking like an old woman tomorrow.'

*   *   *

There was a welcome coolness to the afternoon when the sun began its descent into the west. Joss sat on the steps. He looked south, towards the road that led to the safari lodge, and noticed a crowd was forming, people walking down the road to his house. Many were women and children, a few youngsters, but the men were at least as old as Bongani. They walked with dignity and determination and waited at the lodge gate.

Bongani had warned him this might happen. During Joss's time away, things had begun to change. The arid area was being forced to accommodate more and more people as the government's land appropriation program was undertaken, leaving farm workers homeless. Many of them had asked to settle within Chief Tigere's land. Zimbabweans had been holding out hope for many years for a change to improve the chaos they called home, but as yet, it had not come. Instead they were plagued by instability caused by a one-party state. It was a country where everything had been taken to extremes, and never for the better. Somehow a happy medium needed to be found, but to date it had proven elusive to the people.

Bongani had expressed his dismay at the influx of displaced black workers who'd been tossed out of their homes along with the white farmers when they'd begun to assemble in Binga. Chief Tigere had invited them to build their own *ikhaya*s and *kraal*s, and together they had all started to make a new life and eke out an existence from the hard land.

Soon more homeless people had come looking to make a home. Lately they had been greeted by the chief-in-waiting when they had arrived. The new settlers had been prepared to put in the hours to manage the land. Together they had built the fences to keep their cattle and the wild animals out of the fields that they helped cultivate. The windmills that Joss's father, Stephen, had built so many years before pumped constantly so that the sweet, fresh water from deep in the earth filled the cattle and goats' drinking troughs and the reservoirs. They had lands for food that didn't rely on the unseasonal and unreliable rains. Gradually the area was creating micro-markets and Bongani had told Joss they were seeing a difference in all of their lives. The new settlers had been able to make a home, creating a village.

As chief-in-waiting of the area by birthright, they listened to Bongani, but it was still Chief Tigere's word that was law. As the years passed, the people had come to understand that it was Bongani who was really making the decisions and guiding them, before his rightful time. It was a fragile arrangement, one that he controlled only because of the help that he'd given the newcomers.

Bongani had warned Joss that some of the settlers wanted more say, wanted to rule alongside him, and have his chieftain rights in the area removed now that they lived there. They wanted a more democratic approach and they wanted it to be more like the very thing they had tried to run from.

Bongani appeared in the garden below the steps.

'Might as well get this over with,' Joss said.

It had been a few years since a white man had been a *baas* in this area, and many probably didn't know that Joss still owned most of the lodge.

An old woman stepped forward. He recognised her from his childhood; she'd been married to one of the skippers of the houseboats. Their staff house had been on the far side of the safari lodge, and he'd eaten *sadza* and *nyama* at her fire many times when he was growing up. She'd worked with his mother too, before he went away to be a marine.

'Hello, Mary,' he said, and he nodded his head in respect to her. 'It's been a long time.'

'*Inkosi* Joss. It is good to see you again,' Mary said, and she nodded to him. The sign of respect in his name and her manner didn't go unnoticed.

He looked at the crowd. They were not pushing forward, they were not threatening; they waited quietly, wanting to know what was going on.

Bongani stepped forward to address the small crowd. 'Each and every person here knew that Joss Brennan, Yingwe River Lodge owner, was coming home. It is good that you have come to meet him if you do not already know him. I know that Joss is also looking forward to getting to know each of you too.'

Joss nodded. Many of the people in the crowd were nodding too.

Mary looked around. 'Thank you, Bongani. It is good to see you home, *Inkosi* Joss, but it is my worry that you being here could bring trouble to our settlement, living here as a white man in our community, as an owner, not as a tourist in the safari lodge. For some years now we have been a black-only settlement.'

'I'm a Zimbabwean like you, Mary,' Joss said. 'I was born right here, in Chizarira, and my mother and father built Yingwe River Lodge, with permission from Chief Tigere and the land commission.'

'I remember that day, Joss, when your parents came here, and you were a *umfama*. It was a happy time. But things are different now; we do not need a white *baas*. The white owners are being attacked and thrown out of their lodges, like they did to the farmers. You will bring big trouble. The war vets will come.'

'I'm not your *baas*, Mary, unless you are working inside the safari lodge. But then you would be in the safari lodge staff quarters, not in this village. It's as Bongani said, I've come home to heal.' He pulled the bottom of his tracksuit pants up and showed them his artificial legs. The black plastic gleamed and the silver rivets shone in the sunshine.

A gasp went up. Voices joined together in the expression of shock: '*Mywee ...*'

He lifted his T-shirt and showed them the scars on his stomach and his back where shrapnel had peppered his body as if it were jelly, and the still fading scars where the surgeons had taken the skin to graft onto his legs; once they were dark purple, but now they were simply maroon squares. He turned his arm outwards, showing them the keloid scar tissue from where the emergency orthopaedic doctors on the front line had managed to pin his broken arm and save it.

'I deserve to be able to come home, like every other Zimbabwean. Find peace. I came home to my country to heal.'

'You can go anywhere, settle in any town,' Mary said.

'My parents built and lived in Yingwe River Lodge before they crossed over, God rest their souls. I'm the second generation to live here, near Chief Tigere's land. I won't take my lodge away from here and remove the money flowing into this community, not if I can help it. For many years you have been supported by the lodge's profits. My family's lodge. Just because I wasn't here to run it, didn't mean I had abandoned it. Bongani's a good manager. The overseas clients continue to visit, and this very community benefits from them. Many of your parents and grandparents came to this area when they built the dam. Before that, you were in the Zambezi Valley. Some of you came here from other places across Zimbabwe where you have been removed from your land. But as Zimbabweans, we have much in common, and one of those things is that we now live in this same area.'

'Except that you are white,' Mary said.

'Yes, I am. But I have not come back here to tell you what to do. Perhaps in time I can help you all to make this area provide better, so that you are not standing in a queue for food, but are one of the areas in Zimbabwe that can support itself.' He looked around the group. They were silent, listening to what he was saying.

'Bongani has already told me that the people he allowed to settle here are hard workers. That you are not squatters. That you have formed a community and you work together. I'm no squatter either. This lodge has been paying into this very community, providing for this area for more years than many of you have even been here, even before Mary's family came to work in the lodge. This is my home too.'

There was silence.

'What will you do if King Gogo wa de Patswa comes? What will you do then?' Mary asked.

'The King of Thieves? The man who hides from his own name?'

'All this time, we are the only area not attacked.' Mary shook her head. 'There are no mass graves here because he did not come here before. We have had no reason to attract him since your parents were killed, and there have only been tourists. With you here, who is to say that King Gogo wa de Patswa will keep away?'

'I have no control over what the thief Gogo wa de Patswa does or doesn't do, Mary, but I do know that this is my home. Yingwe Lodge is where I belong, and I plan on staying.'

'Do not say that you have not been warned that your return brings a bad shadow,' Mary said.

'Thank you for the warning, Mary.'

Bongani looked at Mary. 'You are the mother of our people. It is good that you have spoken now, cleared the air, and put your position forward. But have you also considered that perhaps my half-brother, Tichawana, who we all know is Gogo wa de Patswa, is cautious of the curse that the *N'Gomas* and Chief Tigere put on the boundary so that he could never come near us? All this time, it has been them who kept that *cheelo* away. If Tichawana visits here, it will be because somehow he learns how to outwit our *N'Gomas'* *muti* and protection, not because a white man has come home to his lodge. My father's time to join his ancestors grows closer each day. Joss coming home does not affect whether my father lives one more day or one more year. And his coming home won't influence that thief either way.'

Mary looked Bongani in the eye. 'I am still worried.'

'We are all worried about the future. It is never stable, but you have to believe me when I tell you that Joss coming home is not going to influence Gogo wa de Patswa.'

Mary nodded. 'I am glad that Joss is home.'

Bongani smiled, although it was a little forced. 'This is a good settlement, a family settlement, and one that is beginning to prosper because everyone works hard. You are welcome here in your home, Joss.'

Agreement could be heard from most people in the group as they started to dance, shuffling their feet back and forth, and clapping their hands as they encircled him.

Joss noted that Mary stayed quiet, although she did clap.

'Thank you, everyone, for the warm welcome home,' he said.

The crowd began to disperse, touching Joss on the shoulder or shaking his hand as they turned away from the lodge and went to their own homes. Soon only the two of them stood at the gates.

Bongani said, 'Let us get you up into the house, so you can rest. I can talk of the changes that have happened. Some you will need to see to believe.'

'I bet,' Joss said.

8

White Crosses

Peta looked at the view from Tashinga Rest Camp in Chizarira National Park and inhaled deeply. The smell of dry dirt, wild animals and burnt bush filled her lungs. Although Matusadona was her baby, this park held her heart. But it was also breaking it.

The burning of the park was out of hand; the thunderstorms the week before didn't mean that the rains were here. Until the good rains came, the burning would continue, and she didn't know how she was ever going to stop it. She suspected the criminal behind it was a newish local resident in the communal lands – the butchery at the market in the small town of Chizarira was never short of bush meat. She supposed the fire was his workers driving the animals further southwest and into the hunting concessions, where they were being shot. All the park rangers and the consultants knew it was the butcher too. But she couldn't do anything about it without substantial proof, and that was something she didn't have.

Chizarira was a park she loved to spend time in, sitting around the fire at night, while the anti-poaching guards and her veterinary team told stories of days gone by, of traditions long past, with gusto.

Their legends almost made her yearn to have been born a man earlier in the century, so that she could have experienced them first hand – none of their stories ever had a white female adventurer in them.

The park held secrets only a few knew of, and she yearned to learn more. The old men had told her of days when they had seen jumbos with tusks so large their tips would touch the dirt when they walked, as the weight of each caused the elephants to hang their heads and rest in the hot sun. They told of bushmen's paintings hidden in crevices, and underground water found deep in caves, in pools the colour of blue skies, even during drought. There were always the stories of the magnificent fish that swam in the river and the giant crocodiles.

There was also the allure of veins of gold found within the park, which had been kept quiet. The location of where the people of the Zambezi Valley's ancestors had once mined was never revealed, and outsiders had never managed to find them. They were said to be protected by the ancient spirits, so they remained undisturbed.

The history of the land was full of stories of adventurers and explorers who had died in the area. They were buried where they had fallen, many of the graves marked by white crosses scattered throughout the park. If they had ever borne the names and dates of those buried there, they had long since faded in the harsh African weather. She'd asked her team to report the location of the crosses whenever one was found. The wall map in her office at home showed sixteen crosses already, and she knew in her heart there were more. Some would never be found. Unmarked and unremembered graves from years of war, simple stacks of stones piled on top of the bodies to keep the hyenas from eating them.

The ones she was interested in were the older ones from the pioneering days, when wagon wheels cut deep furrows into the wet earth as the rains stopped their journey north, or the sheer splendour of the countryside made a family attempt to settle and build a future. This was a land where only the strong survived.

She fiddled with the ring on her finger. Her last gift from her mother, who had died in Peta's first year of university. She no longer thought that her mother was too weak to survive, because she'd found out from her father that Christmas that her mum was as strong as any Ndebele warrior of old. Her mother's soul had been the strongest; it was her body that had let her down in the end.

So much had changed after her mum had gone. Her father, not knowing what to do with Peta and Courtney, hadn't wanted to move away from their home, where he had known such happiness, so they had stayed in the Matusadona, where all the memories were.

At eighteen, she'd gone to university in Pretoria and graduated seven years later. The same year Courtney had graduated from high school.

Despite her time spent at university in South Africa, she and Courtney had a special friendship. Peta never took their mother's place in Courtney's life, but she did become one of the closest friends Courtney had. They became a dynamic duo, ganging up together to make their dad do what they wanted.

Memories of a younger Joss flooded in, and she smiled, remembering how close Courtney and he once were. How things had changed since they'd all grown up.

Joss had gone off to war and Courtney had left for university in South Africa.

Then Courtney had got sick, and come home.

After Courtney lost her fragile hold on life, Peta had buried her ashes under the trees in the small cemetery in the Matusadona, next to their mother.

Still Joss had stayed away, causing the anger towards him to fester deep inside her. Now that she knew why he hadn't returned she felt guilty for having directed her anger at him for so long. It was better that Courtney would never know how broken Joss had become, that when she died she still held him on a pedestal, outshining all the other men in her life.

Peta tipped her head back. A large column of vultures soared in circles in the sky. 'Shit,' she said as she got back into her 4x4 and reached for the radio. 'Chifumba, come in.'

'Chifumba here, hello, Miss Peta.'

'Any reports of a kill this morning? I'm looking at vultures circling on thermals.' She waited while he spoke to the people in the office.

'*Pepe.*'

'No? You sure? I'll go check it out before I come in to the office.'

'Miss Peta?'

'Yes?'

'Is Amos with you?'

'He is. We're at Tashinga Rest Camp already.'

'Good, just making sure.'

Neither of them wanted to mention that if it was poachers, she would need the extra firepower that Amos would provide.

She'd met Amos the week she'd come back from university to work for her dad, when he'd been a new recruit to the game reserve. As the new kids on the block, they had formed an instant bond, fitting into their junior park ranger and veterinary roles in the black rhino breeding program under Jeff, the same vet who had been there since she was a child.

She'd come to understand Amos's initial motives for sticking close to her. He'd been a worker on a farm in Nyamandhlovu when it had been taken over by the war vets, and his white employers had been killed. Many of the workers that day had also been beaten, some even burnt with petrol, their legs broken to stop them running away from the fires. Amos blamed himself for not protecting them better, for not standing up to the war vets who took the farm by force and later abandoned it. When he had seen her, he had taken it on himself to be her shadow. He was convinced he would not lose another madam, another friend.

The Chizarira Game reserve had its share of poachers, and then some to spare. Especially lately. One of the jobs she had taken on from her father was the monitoring and reporting of the anti-poaching units they employed. She feared that the reserve was worse off than it ever had been.

Peta tossed her radio on the seat and stalked back into the main area where the guards were having morning tea. 'Come on, Amos. We're going to check out some vultures. I haven't seen the lions in this area for a while; it might be a chance to see if they have new cubs. If it's an animal hurt by poachers we still might have time to save it or put it out of its misery.'

The other guards put their cups down and immediately went for their rifles. She knew these men. Sixpence, the oldest of the anti-poaching guards and leader of their team, had been in the Zim-Parks employment since he was a boy. She remembered a time she had camped in the Chizarira with her father and Uncle Stephen when she was only about eight years old. Even then, Sixpence had been there, watching 'his' park, looking after 'his' animals. Back then he had been proud to be a park ranger, welcoming visitors and working in the office; now he was proud to carry a gun to protect 'his' animals from the poachers, and use his phenomenal tracking skills to outsmart them.

Simon was a younger guard, and had come into the team most recently, but his passion for the bush and the wildlife was no less than anyone else's. Zambian by birth, he was related to Sixpence through his mother's side, and was always eager to learn as much as he could from the old man.

Moses, Muzi and Valentine were long-term employees, and all carried ugly scars on their faces. Moses had had a run-in with a barbed-wire fence, and Muzi spoke with a slight lisp having recovered from a broken jaw and other injuries from a malicious beating when he was a teenager. Although she couldn't remember when they had started in Chizarira, she remembered well when Valentine had almost died after being ambushed by a poacher, and had his face half hacked off. The deep scar that ran from his hairline across his nose to his jawline was a constant reminder that they were at war with those who sought to take the wildlife for bush meat trade, ivory and rhino horn syndicates, or even for the live exotic animal trade.

They were a motley team, but if there were poachers around, she wouldn't want to go into battle with anyone else at her side. Perhaps she would have liked Joss with her, but only because of his marine training, not because she was still thinking about him two weeks after she'd left him in the hotel in Beit Bridge. She walked out, leaving the young camp gardener behind.

'So many, so fast. We have only been drinking tea for about ten minutes, and already the sky's colour is changed by those vultures,' Simon said.

'We heard nothing last night, so we can hope it is only a lion kill. Because these poachers, some of them are getting clever now; they use darts like you do when you heal an animal, and we do not always hear anything any more,' Sixpence said.

The men climbed into the *bakkie*, while Amos got into the scout's seat on the front, and tapped the bonnet when he saw everyone was in. Peta eased her foot off the clutch and began the drive towards the vulture column. She drove on the rough dirt track until Amos pointed into the bushes, then she turned, trusting his scouting ability. It was strange how their partnership in the bush worked. He was a farmhand, but had been taught by his father to track for meat as a child. He was one of the best trackers she had ever encountered, other than Sixpence. Even her father called on Amos when Tsessebe was having trouble, and that was a huge compliment.

She remembered a time when they had been driving through the back roads near Jedson's camp in Chizarira, when Amos had told her to stop. To go back. She had argued that she thought there was a way through, but he had shown her tracks on the road, and explained the footprints to her. The tracks were fresh, and belonged to King Gogo wa de Patswa, and while he wasn't usually in the bush, the significance of his footprint, with his left foot larger than his right, was clear: if they continued on, she would be killed or raped – the suspected mastermind behind many of the rhino and elephant attacks was a known killer. Peta had quickly turned her Land Rover around and headed back to Mujima Camp. Although she had radioed in the tracks and the position, she knew that by the time the anti-poaching unit got there, it would be too late; he would have gone.

She hit a bump and was wrenched back to the present. She focused on Amos, following his every signal as he navigated them through the brush and scrub.

Finally, she saw his hand in a stop position, and she applied the brakes. She could see a craggy cliff, the vultures soaring above it. They surfed the hot thermals, and then back down as they gathered. Waiting.

'Whatever it is, it's up there,' Amos said to Peta as she got out of the *bakkie*.

'Time to climb. Anyone know of a path up?' she asked.

Sixpence nodded. 'If we drive around to the end, there is a game path that goes up. It has been many years since I climbed this *koppie*. The top is flat, and used to have a clump of marula trees. Many baboons barked at me the day I climbed with *Baas* Stephen, but now it is silent. There is sadness here today.'

Peta nodded. 'Right, back in the *bakkie* then. We'll take the easiest path, and hope that sadness doesn't touch us.' After years of working with her people, she knew better than to pooh-pooh any of their superstitions.

They drove around the bottom of the rocks until Sixpence called the halt. True to his words, a well-used game path led upwards.

'Sixpence, take the front, since you have travelled this path before. Amos, you next, then me. You three come up the rear. Everyone have your weapons ready, in case there's poachers or a predator up here. Keep your eyes peeled for leopard. I don't want anyone attacked by a cornered cat who thinks the way out is through you.' Peta took her rifle from the rack in the 4x4. She put her veterinary backpack on. She went nowhere without it, especially not into situations like this. This was the part of her job she hated the most. It was never the animals she was scared of, but that one day she would come face to face with poachers – and their behaviour was always unpredictable.

She took a deep breath as she checked her rifle and made sure her safety was on. Last thing she wanted was to shoot Amos in the back in an accidental discharge. Pointing her rifle up and to the side, she followed his sweaty back up the path.

'Step right,' Amos said, warning of a loose rock in the ascent.

She did as instructed as they continued, the sun merciless on her head, the sweat dripping down her neck and into her bra, then once that was saturated, continuing its journey down her back, and pooling at the base of her spine. Ignoring the damp clamminess of wet socks in boots gripping uneasy terrain, she pulled herself up the last giant step and onto the plateau with Amos's help.

'Your legs are too short,' he joked.

Peta smiled. At five-foot-seven no way was she ever called short, except by Amos, who seemed to have Shaka Zulu's blood in his veins, because he stood six-foot-three.

The top of the *koppie* was flat, just as Sixpence had said. There were a few marula trees clustered together and a purple bougainvillea, which wasn't native to the area, rambled up a mopani tree and spilled over onto the flat rock. The vine was old, as if it had been there many years. Weaver birds had nested in it, and their beautiful nests swung gently in the breeze as the bright yellow birds chattered happily. What was unexpected was that the bougainvillea had been trimmed away from a single white cross at the base of the tree. The pile of rocks under the cross made her uneasy – they looked too new, not yet weathered enough to be there like the older graves she had found.

'Sixpence, did you know there was a white cross here?' she asked.

'No, Miss Peta, this was not here before. This is new.' He began to walk over to it, then stopped.

Beyond the circle of trees was the reason for the column of vultures: a buffalo lay on its side. She looked closer. It was trapped in a wire snare that ran from its hind legs back to a tree stump that it had obviously been dragging around for a while before it became stuck. The wire had cut deep into its fetlock, and was buried into the skin. The log had finally wedged into a rock crevice, and although the animal had walked in circles attempting to free itself, it had been unable to. Eventually it had collapsed from exhaustion and lay panting, its eyes white with fear, yet the animal was not defeated. It lifted its head and snorted at them.

If nature was allowed to take its course, the vultures soaring on the thermals above would come down and devour it, and the hyenas in the park would feast on the magnificent beast, and so it would provide food for many predators and scavengers alike. But man, the people who had set that snare originally, wouldn't know that this animal had suffered so much, right to its last breath, and they would get none of its flesh to eat, nor its skin to make into leather.

It snorted at them again.

'You can save it, Miss Peta? Or do you want me to shoot it? Put it out of its misery?' Sixpence said.

'Let's see if we can save it first.'

Sixpence looked at his guards. 'Moses, Valentine, Muzi, perimeter check; make sure there are no other surprises lying in wait before Miss Peta starts working.'

The men dispersed into the scrub.

She smiled at Sixpence's use of 'Miss Peta'. He'd always called her that as a child when she visited with her father, or if he happened to come to Matusadona, but after independence, and even after she'd grown up, the old man continued to use it, as if 'Miss Peta' were her name. Despite her asking him to simply call her Peta, he'd shaken his head and told her that to him, in his heart, she was always his 'little Miss Peta', the special child of the bush, and she'd stopped minding at all. Many of the other guards had picked it up, and while it raised a few eyebrows when people first heard it, they soon learnt that it was a term of endearment.

Peta handed her weapon to Amos, then removed her backpack and laid out her darting kit, measuring out some opioid or, as Amos like to call it, the lights-out medicine.

They waited, listening to the birds chatter in the trees and the loud chorus that was the African bush. Somewhere in the distance a baboon barked. The heat on the top of the hill pressed down on them, and more sweat trickled down Peta's back. Amos adjusted his weapon, looking everywhere, while Simon walked around their smaller perimeter, ensuring there was no immediate danger.

Valentine came back first, followed by Muzi and Moses. Each man shook his head, indicating that the bush was clear.

Sixpence nodded to her. Peta aimed the rifle at the buffalo's rump and watched the dart glide easily into his thick skin.

It snorted, but didn't attempt to get up.

'I've only given it a light sedative; in its condition anything more could kill it,' she said, looking at the watch on her wrist. 'Give it a moment, then, Sixpence, if you would put a rope around its horns and back legs, make sure it doesn't gore me while I'm working, it would be appreciated.' She removed a large pair of wire-cutters from her kit, and some Terramycin wound powder. She also measured a healthy dose of antibiotic from a brown bottle into a new syringe.

She watched as the buffalo's head drooped and then jerked back up as it fought the anaesthetic. It rested its head again. Finally, it flopped over at an angle to one side.

'Now?' Sixpence asked, as he took the rope from the pile in front of her.

'Yes, but go carefully; make sure before you get close.'

Sixpence nodded. He removed his hat and threw it at the buffalo. The wind under the brim made it fly at a strange angle and it landed short of the buffalo's nose.

It didn't move.

He moved closer, took his shirt off, and threw it at the buffalo's head. It hung from the horn on the right side, covering its eyes, and remained there. The buffalo still didn't move.

'It's out,' Peta said.

Sixpence moved quickly. He gently shook the buffalo by its horns, but the *duggaboy* didn't react. 'It is sleeping,' he said as he moved his shirt to fully cover its eyes, then tied the rope around its horns, and passed the end to Simon, who took it and threaded it around his waist. Holding tight to the rope and adjusting his feet securely in a rock crevice near him, he sat down, a human anchor. Sixpence tied a second rope around the buffalo's back legs.

'Muzi and Valentine, stay close to Simon in case he needs you. Moses, keep watch on the perimeter, look sharp,' Sixpence instructed.

Peta put a sheet underneath the injured leg and then looked at the wound. The cut was deep, almost to the bone. Flesh and hair had grown over the wire as it got deeper – the snare had been this buffalo's partner for a long time.

'Dammit,' she swore. 'Even if we get this out, it probably won't live long before a lion gets it.'

'*Eish*, Miss Peta, it is a strong one; it might surprise you yet,' Sixpence said.

The game guards were always so optimistic. They claimed their jobs were a calling in life, and that she could believe, because half the time they didn't get paid by the government, and they would get shot at by poachers and often killed while trying to protect the animals in their reserves.

'I'll give it the option to fight another day. Amos, bring the cutters, and snip here.'

She watched as Amos placed the wire-cutters close, and she guided them where she needed his strength to cut the wire. There was the dull *ting* of the wire releasing and, holding the knot where the wire had been wound back on itself, she tugged. The wire slid through the wound, and it was free.

She injected the antibiotic and cleaned the wound with the bottle of water from her kit. Then she splashed the area liberally with antiseptic wash to help the infection. Drying it with a few paper towels, she sprinkled wound powder on it, and sprayed liberally with gentian violet.

'That's about all we can do for you, my boy,' she said, patting the buffalo's rump as she got up. 'Right, guys, release so I can give the antidote, and then run for the path and the safety of the *bakkie*, because when this bull wakes up we are not going to be its best friend.'

Simon let the rope slacken while Sixpence took it off the horns and swapped his shirt for his hat covering its eyes. He rolled up the rope, slinging it over his shoulder and across his chest, then grabbed his weapon from near Simon, and they made to head down the path.

'Sixpence, look,' Amos said, gesturing to the vultures. They no longer soared but were dropping behind the *koppie.*

Sixpence whistled. 'Something else definitely dead down that way.'

'You go on foot, check it out,' Peta said. 'Take Simon with you for extra protection on the ground. Step carefully. The rest of the men and I will exit on the opposite side, and drive around. We'll join you as soon as we can.'

Sixpence nodded. 'Give your antidote quickly, Miss Peta, and hope that this buffalo is kind to all of us.'

Peta nodded. 'Go now, run, everyone.'

The game guards scattered.

She had her pack on her back, and Amos held her weapon. Muzi was already at the entrance to the path that would lead them downwards. She walked back to the buffalo and injected the antidote. Putting the cap on her needle, she returned to Amos and together they ran to the ledge. Peering over, they waited while the buffalo heaved its bulk up and staggered to its feet. It looked around, searching for a target to take its revenge on, but seeing nothing, it tested its foot. It wasn't ready to bear weight yet, but it managed to put it on the ground. It stood for a while before attempting to move forward, still expecting to be anchored to the spot, but when its body moved freely, it stumbled a few steps, then limped into the shade of the bougainvillea, where it waited. A bit later it walked back to the game path and made its way sedately down the *koppie,* in a different direction, thank goodness, from where her men had gone to check on the vultures. The buffalo was a true survivor.

Peta smiled. This was the part of her job that she loved.

'Hang on, Amos,' she said and climbed back to the top of the *koppie.* 'I want to check out that cross.'

It looked no more than a few years old and was made to withstand the elements of Africa. Whoever had put it here had taken the time to move the stones aside, bury the end of the cross deep in the earth, then return the stones to their place. Burnt deep into the wood was CASPER AUSTIN – 1945.

She wondered who Casper was that someone had returned to this place after so long to take the time to re-mark his grave. She took a photo with her phone and walked back to where her men waited for her.

* * *

In front of her was not the first dead human body Peta had seen. However, it was the first dead body she had seen that looked like it had been a lion's lunch.

The bateleur eagle had got the eyes and the vultures had had a little nibble on it too, so there wasn't that much left of the full-grown man at all. A white man. Probably about her height. From the amount of broken and trodden grass, he had been living in the camp a while. The body was half eaten, and by the tracks in the sand, the lion had begun feasting before the man was completely dead – the depth of his pain showed in his attempt to dig into the ground with his fingernails, trying hard to find something to fight the lion with.

The camp around them was small and well concealed. If it hadn't been for the vultures, they might never have found it. A hunters' tarpaulin was strung between the trees, its camouflage pieces blending perfectly into the environment. Underneath was a very new and flash-looking Land Rover, with Zimbabwe importation papers bearing the name Kenneth Hunt in the cubbyhole, and a spacious two-room tent. The ground was covered by a second tarpaulin to keep the site as sand free as possible. In front of the tent was a small fold-up table and chair.

'This is no amateur,' Sixpence said.

But it was the laptop that drew Peta. The computer was attached to a small solar panel. She pushed the trackpad and the screen came to life. She began to read a spreadsheet with details of a game count.

Rhino. There were no comments in the column near that.

Elephant. In the columns were different estimates of tusk sizes. All categorised, with dates and GPS coordinates of the sightings.

Buffalo, leopard, lions and various other animals followed. She scrolled down. Pangolins were listed, as were Angola pitta, African broadbill and crocodiles, with their estimated weight and length.

'Looks like a professional game spotter,' Amos said.

'It does. My question would be, what made that lion kill someone who was obviously so comfortable in the bush? How did it get to him?'

Amos shook his head. 'I don't know.'

'Sixpence, is there any evidence that this lion is hurt?' She bumped the mouse and it changed spreadsheets. She stared.

'No, Miss Peta. Looking at the tracks, it was a loner. Perhaps he is one that hunts men—' He stopped talking. 'What is it?'

Peta was staring at the screen. She sat in the chair and flicked through the other programs and open documents.

'Maps. Look, here is the *koppie*, and it's marked on his map with a cross.' She continued to slowly pan through the map, looking at the sites marked. 'Many of the sites that he's marked are the sites I've marked in my office. Look, every one's the place of a white cross. I wonder what the others are?'

Sixpence shook his head. 'I do not know, Miss Peta. I am sure you will figure it out, but first we need to concentrate on the lion.'

'What did you find?' Peta asked, giving him her attention again. She stood up, closed the computer and took it with her as she followed Sixpence.

'This man, he never stood a chance. Look.' Sixpence walked back to the tracks. He pointed at the ground. 'The man was caught unprepared, and he did not even get close to his weapons. The lion was between him and his guns. His body was away slightly from camp. Perhaps he went for a pee, like he has done often before, pissing around his tent, keeping some predators away. Scent marking. But this time, he ended up getting more than he bargained for: he walked into where the lion lay watching him. This is what the tracks tell me, but in true life, it could have been different.'

'When have you ever read the tracks in the sand wrong, my old friend?' Peta asked.

'Not often. He is the master of all trackers,' Amos said, joining them.

Peta smiled.

'Miss Peta, you need to get back on your radio. If this lion continues travelling southwest like he is doing, he will cross into the old Tribal Trust Lands, and there are people there who could be in danger. It has been a few years since we had a man-eater in this park.'

CHAPTER
9

The Warning

Joss wrapped the towel around his waist and slowly transferred himself into his wheelchair. Now that he and Bongani had transformed his en-suite bathroom into a wet room, showering had become much easier. He had also installed stainless-steel rails along the walls and by his toilet.

The lights flickered and lit brightly again, a sure sign that they were about to have yet another power failure. Thankfully the big generator, now rewired to also power his house, would kick in. He opened the bathroom door and wheeled himself into his room. Once he'd settled on the bed, he lifted his laptop and logged in.

His friends were all on the other end of the computer or a telephone. His commando buddies who lived in England had made noises about visiting, but were still leaving him to his own devices. He thought of his circle, the men he had fought with. Some had died fighting alongside him, and some were permanently damaged. Like him, they bore their scars, and wore their prosthetics.

At least Peta was here, and hadn't been subjected to the horrors of the Afghanistan war.

He shook his head as if to dislodge the thought of her.

The lights went out at the same moment his cell phone rang, its screen bright blue in the darkness. No caller ID. He answered anyway. The generator clicked on and the room was flooded with light once more.

'Hello?'

'Hey, it's Peta.'

'Hi. What's up?'

'A few things actually—'

'Hang on, I never gave you this number. How—'

'No, you didn't, but the receptionist at your front desk did when I asked for it and told her who I was.'

He smiled, lying back and stuffing his pillow under his head. 'Right. And who did you claim to be?'

'Not some damsel in distress, I promise. I told her I was the AWIC veterinary representative of Matusadona and Chizarira National Parks, and I needed to speak with the lodge owner urgently. And that would be you.'

'Ah, in that case I guess I don't need to fire her for passing on my personal information to a stranger.' He laughed quietly.

'I'm no stranger to you, Joss,' Peta said. 'I saw more of you growing up than I care to remember.'

He could hear her smile and could almost see her nose crinkling as she tried to stop herself from laughing, her hand coming up to her chest in the way it always did when she lost control of her laughter. Because any moment she would snort, and she hated snorting, so it would be even funnier, and she would laugh again. He and Courtney used to almost pee their pants making her laugh.

'So, what's so important that you had to call me at this late hour? Not that I mind,' he added quickly. 'It's great to hear from you.'

In those first few days home, he'd so often reached for her card to call her, wanting to talk to her, find out if she was okay, but then become too embarrassed about what had happened in Beit Bridge. He had been a coward, not wanting to own up to the fact that he'd broken one of his own rules: never hurt a woman; always treat her with respect.

He swallowed his pride and opened his mouth to ask, but no sound came out.

'I wanted to know how you are?' she said. 'If you settled in okay. If Bongani had looked after your lodge nicely for you?' She was stalling, her sentences running on too quickly. He had heard people talk like this many times when interrogated, or when in a war zone and scared.

He sat up. 'No, you didn't. If you wanted to know that you would have called before now. What's wrong?'

'I have some bad news. There's a man-eating lion coming your way. We found remains in Chizarira, and then another body yesterday, just inside the Chete Safari Area. The tracks turned south. He appears to be meandering down through the Sijarira Forest Area – towards you guys. My men are on his trail, and I wanted to give you the heads-up. Warn your people, Joss. The last thing you need is a man-eater near your tourists. You will get an official ZimParks notice, if it ever gets done, but I wanted you to know so you could prepare the *kraals* in your area.'

'Bongani will get word to those areas and we'll take extra care with the tourists.' Joss waited for Peta to say something else, but she was silent. 'So, you're sure you have two confirmed kills?' Lions could travel immense distances, so if it decided it was coming to a new hunting ground, the people in his area were in trouble.

'Two that we know of. The first we stumbled on by total fluke, but then some of the anti-poaching guards began tracking the lion, and they came across the next victim. Poor guy riding a bicycle down the road. Two men within a week.'

'How much time do you think we have?' Joss was preparing for a shopping trip to Bulawayo for more timber for ramps through the lodge and, despite Bongani's objections to his improvements, he had a meeting with a pool construction company for the lap pool he needed for his rehabilitation. He couldn't go if there was danger. Bongani would need help to organise his people.

'Another week at most before he's in your area. But he's probably already in range of the outer villages.'

'You sure it's a he?'

'No. I keep calling it a "he" because I would hate to think of it being a pregnant lioness that has to be destroyed.'

'Poor bastard.'

'I'm worried. The area didn't used to be so densely populated and there're many people who don't realise the danger of a rogue lion. This lion's feet are huge, bigger than average, and he seems to have developed a taste for men. It doesn't seem to be that he's old and can't catch anything else. It's as if he's targeted these men specifically, which is madness in itself. There was a woman who was sitting behind the man on his bicycle; she said the lion didn't try to chase her at all. He attacked her husband as if he wasn't interested in her.'

'That's different.'

'I know, weird. I'm worried. You're not as agile as you once were—'

'You're bringing my legs into this?'

'Oh no, just that you walk slower now ... that you ...'

He covered his eyes with his hand, trying to block out the pity he heard in her voice. The pity he'd hoped to never hear from Courtney now rang clearly from Peta. 'Lions can't eat plastic and steel legs. I'll be fine, Peta,' he said.

'Oh, you are a – forget it. Forget that I said anything about it, okay?'

'How did your game settle in?' He switched to small talk to try to keep her on the line.

'My stallion is amazing, although I don't get to spend enough time on him. The *duggaboy* ran into the bushes the moment we opened the *boma*, and I hope he stays far away from the camp. I don't ever want to see him again. The rhino settled in like he's always belonged here. He's already courting a female or two through the *boma* fence. Give him another week or so and we can let him free too. How have you found settling back into the old place?'

'We've had to make a few changes to the house, but mostly it looks like it came out of a time warp. Exactly the same.'

'That must feel a little strange?'

'I needed the familiarity at first. Now, not so much. We're planning on going into Bulawayo soon for more materials. I need to have ramp access the whole way through, and we're running out of usable timber. I'd forgotten how many stairs there are in this place.'

'Joss, you know that there are people in safari lodges who have been kicked out by war vets, had their buildings taken?'

'I know, but these changes are needed for me to be able to get around on days that I need to use the chair rather than my prosthetics. If it will put your mind at ease a little, I went through a list of those lodges with Bongani. All the attacks have been politically motivated, and some didn't have the support of the locals in the first place. Hopefully war vets won't touch me because I'm so far from anything, not even on the edge of a game reserve, in the buffer zone of Kariba and the BaTonga people. Besides, I border Chief Tigere's land, so we should be okay.'

'Be careful with what you invest, is all I'm saying.'

'I will, Peta. I meant to call—'

'No, you didn't. You avoided me because of what happened. I want you to know that I'm okay. No hard feelings, no permanent marks. All forgiven and forgotten on my side. So, if that's the reason, I'm not okay with you avoiding me. You were my sister's best friend. Hell, at one time, we were friends, even if I was older than you. I used to envy you and Court, so carefree together. Full of life and vitality. I could do with you in my life, since she can't be with me.'

Joss blew his breath out. 'Peta—'

'No, hear me out.' Her voice went up a notch. He remembered that tone only too well from yesteryear, and he wasn't about to interrupt. When Peta raised her voice, you listened.

'I'm fine, seriously. Those bruises faded within a week. But I keep thinking of you, wondering how you are. Wondering how you're managing in your home, now that you're so changed. I find myself thinking that you were nothing but truthful with me, and how lucky Courtney was to have you as a friend all these years. The lion was my push to call you. I wanted to talk with you, hear your voice.'

He let out the breath he'd been holding, and knew things were going to be okay between them. The years had passed, and many changes had happened, but underneath all that, their friendship from so many years ago had endured. She'd been brutally honest with him, and now it was his turn.

'Peta, I'm glad to hear from you, honestly. I wasn't sure you wanted me in your life again. You said it yourself, I'm a ticking time bomb.'

'That you are. But friends are thin on the ground these days. I spend too many hours in the bush. Work colleagues come and go. All these years we've known each other, Courtney was always there, but there was a friendship between us too, and friends accept that people change – and they accommodate those changes.'

He chuckled, trying hard to get out of the intense conversation.

'I wanted to say hello. See how you are. Find out if you're okay,' Peta said.

His shoulders relaxed, and he stretched out his stumps. It was going to be alright, the angst was gone from her voice. 'Have you let any of the other safari operators know yet?'

'Only you. The office can do those calls in the morning.'

Joss smiled. 'I'm happy you rang. Sorry about the victims the lion took to get you to call me, but I'm glad to hear from you.'

There was quiet at the other end of the line, then she said, 'How are your therapy sessions going?'

'Difficult, with the constant electricity cuts, and the internet isn't so flash either. I rewired the big generator so I have power in the house when the ZESA goes off. Luckily, the one at the lodge was big enough to share power with the house. I've ordered a new diesel one too. The one my dad put in is getting old.'

'You going to throw it out?'

'Hell, no. I'm planning to relocate it to the village and sink another borehole there for water.'

'You putting in power to Bongani's village?'

'Yes, it's time he came into the twenty-first century.'

'So much for critical repairs and renovations only. What are you planning, Joss? I can hear your brain ticking from here.'

'Nothing major. I want Bongani to have the same comforts he's had in the lodge staff house now that he's moved back to his village to be near his dad. We're going to be doing a bit of renovating, some indoor plumbing, underground electrical work, that sort of stuff. Old Chief Tigere's time is coming, so Bongani needs to be with his people. There's no need for him to live in the past because of the move.'

'Oh, is that all? I know how much that stuff costs. Did you knock off a bank or something while you were in Afghanistan?'

'No, but Bongani was a good manager.' He smiled again, and shook his head, thinking that smiling was becoming infectious when he spoke with Peta. Thank God that the payouts from his parents' life insurance policies had been sitting in an English bank. 'Are you up at Matusadona or closer? You can come on over if you want? Or we can meet you on the road somewhere to share a meal? Picnic like we used to with the folks. I probably shouldn't go out of the area now with the news of that lion, but I could still see you—'

'Little Joss Brennan, are you asking me on a date?' Peta said.

'I guess I am.'

'I'm at Matusadona. How about you come here, and pay your respects to Courtney like you wanted to?'

'I will, but not now. I'm not ready to finally let her go yet.'

Peta paused, then said, 'Believe me, I understand that feeling. Perhaps I can come spend a weekend some time at your lodge? The road isn't in bad condition at the moment, so I can drive down in a few hours.'

Joss felt his heart race in anticipation. 'Been a few years since we were here together; you'll see a lot of changes in the lodge. You sure you're okay with the drive down?'

'I'd love to come. Amos will drive down with me. That won't be a problem, will it?'

'Amos?' His heart stopped beating for a nanosecond. 'Who's Amos?'

'My assistant. I don't fancy driving through your side of the communal lands without him. Besides, if we make our way down, we can check on my guys following that lion, see how far they've got. They might need rations restocked. Do you still have a catamaran or skimmer we can use? Been years since we did any tiger fishing.'

He had forgotten how much Peta loved to fish. She didn't like to eat them, but she loved catching them and throwing them back into the water so they could be free again.

'Fishing, that's all you can come up with?' he said, and couldn't keep the amusement out of his voice, as once again he shimmied down the bed and lay on his back.

'I'm looking forward to seeing my old friend too, I'll be in touch as to when.'

He heard the phone click in his ear and knew she had hung up on him, but he couldn't stop grinning.

Not exactly a commitment to a date to visit, but it was better than nothing. The next week was going to be extremely challenging, but damn if he wasn't looking forward to getting it over and done with, knowing that soon he would see Peta. But first he had a district to get ready for a rogue lion.

No: Bongani would need to get everyone ready. This would be yet another test of his strength as chief-in-waiting, and Joss had to ensure that no one attempted to look to him for help; they needed to continue to look to Bongani.

It wasn't going to be easy, but with any luck, Bongani could contact all his people and they could start being more vigilant. The villagers would have to bring their goats and cattle in and make *bomas* to keep them safe for a while. Most of those on the northern tip of the area did that each night anyway, as they were used to predators. It was only those closer to the lodge who were unprepared.

Joss's job would be to ensure that his guests in the lodge understood the significance of the lion in the area too.

Joss called Bongani's cell phone, punching the speaker button while he dressed in boxers and a T-shirt.

'What is the matter?'

'I'm good, but can you pop over here before going back to your village tonight? I just got off the phone with Peta. She says there's a man-eating lion on its way into the area. You need to warn your people.'

'I'll be right over.'

Five minutes later, Bongani was letting himself through the kitchen to meet Joss in the dining room. He carried a big map of the area and a slim binder. 'I have a plan drawn up for when something like this happens.'

Lwazi came into the dining room. 'Is everything okay?'

'Everything's fine, thanks, Lwazi,' Joss said.

'You sure?'

Joss nodded. 'It's okay, go back to bed; you have school tomorrow.'

'Night, then.' Lwazi waved and walked down the passage. They heard his door close softly.

'Things working okay?' Bongani asked.

'He's amazing. Thank you for suggesting him,' Joss said as he looked at the well-used map and the binder that had seen better days. He knew he shouldn't be surprised; after all, Bongani had proven over and over what an organised person he was. He obviously had systems in place for managing both the Yingwe River Lodge and his father's people in times of trouble. 'You use it often?'

'More than I would like. Although we normally get the call during office hours from ZimParks, so getting it from Peta is a good thing – it will give us more time.' Bongani went through his folder with Joss, familiarising him with the procedure he already had in place. 'This is not the first man-eater we have had in the area. Rogue elephant crop raiders, lions, violent people moving through the reserve – we have seen them all before. Sometimes the rangers or police will catch them and kill them before they get to my people. I will call all the leaders of the villages in the morning and let them know that help is coming. They all have working cell phones now. After those calls, I will tell my village. It is customary that Madala White, Timberman, Julian Seziba and I get everything ready around the village, and we will get the emergency kits for the other villages prepared. You keep to your plan of starting to fix the road. On Thursday, I will take Julian Seziba and Mary's grandson Ephraim with me and we will go to the northern border near the Sijarira Forest Area and start helping prepare the people in the Amaluandi and the Sigara villages. It has been a while since we last had a threat like this, so having me or one of my villagers representing me will help them to be more vigilant, and ensure that everyone is ready.

'Lwazi can accompany his grandfather and Timberman towards Bishu Village, then to the Teti village in the south and do the same, helping anyone who needs to get their *ikhayas* sturdy enough. Some of the elders don't have anyone to help them. Lwazi is good with old folks and he is a very able young man. Do you want to go with them?'

'Of course,' Joss said. 'The priority is to protect the people and their livestock.'

Bongani nodded. He rolled up the map. 'You know, I have to admit that tonight it has been very convenient for me to be living near you again. I have missed you, my friend. I like the man you have become; you are no longer the boy who went to war.'

'You going somewhere I should know about?'

'No, but when my father passes, I will be expected to spend most of my time in my village. And I must marry soon.' Bongani frowned. 'I will need to make a son. I am an old man and I have no heirs, so if I die, that disgusting brother of mine will inherit the chieftainship, and I cannot have that happen. Even now, I have probably left it too late. I am fifty-four years old. And I am not sure I want a wife pestering me, and babies pooping and screaming all day. I avoided it this long with good reason.'

'Then don't, not yet. We can consult with a lawyer and see if the law can be changed. Maybe you can nominate your successor. But this is a conversation for another time; it's already after midnight and we have an early start tomorrow.'

Bongani smiled. 'A lawyer and changing the rules … such a white man's solution. I'm not sure the *N'Gomas* will see it your way at all, to go away from tradition. But I like your thinking. Anything to keep Tichawana out of my area and away from my people.'

'So what are you going to do about him? The people here know who he is, why don't others?'

'That question is with me every second I am awake. I do not know what to do about it. My priority has to be my father. Once he goes, and we have completed the ceremony with the *N'Gomas*, then I can look at the rest of the problems on the horizon, including dealing with my corrupt half-brother.'

Joss pushed his chair away from the table. 'Let's not borrow problems from the future. Sleep well, my friend.'

'You too. I will see myself out.'

Joss listened to Bongani's steps as they walked away from his house and into the night.

He rolled to his room and looked at the clock as he closed the door behind him. Damn, he'd missed his web session with his psychologist. Again.

This was the second appointment in two weeks he'd missed. He was going to be in deep shit. He shook his head. He didn't think that the British Royal Commandos would care that he was too busy getting ready for a man-eating lion to realise that the time of his appointment had passed.

They had their work cut out for them in the next few days and now Joss had the added task of calming down an irate psychologist sitting in snowy England.

CHAPTER
10

Small Steps

Joss bent and tossed a few big rocks into the hole in the road closest to the gates. Using a spade, he added river sand to fill in the spaces before compacting it with the *cymbe*, a crude tool his father had welded together: a T-bar attached to the end of a steel rod. The lodge's grader was broken and he had undertaken to fix the road manually until they could get someone to come out and repair the grader.

He pummelled the rocks and repeated the process. This time the rocks were slightly higher than the ground around them, so it would be rough to take his wheelchair over, but a few car trips would make the repair level. He moved on to the next hole.

Lwazi approached, hanging back to watch him fill the second hole and then the third, a larger one that took up most of the supplies on the *bakkie*.

'What happened to school today?' Joss asked eventually.

'It got cancelled because of the lion. Are you going to fix the whole road?'

'Yes.'

'Why? The holes will just come back when it rains,' Lwazi said.

'Then I'll do it again and again, until we have a decent road for me to train on. I need to be able to practise for the triathlon, without the risk of falling in a hole, so that I can run in it with the guys in my unit next year. The only way to get road fit is to run.'

'What is a triathlon?'

Joss threw in another rock. 'It's a race. Like a super sport for ultra-fit men and women. They do two or three sports together. Injured marines are encouraged to compete in it, to give us a way to test our strength, make us remember we can do anything despite being disabled, that we are still the best of the best.'

'But you don't have legs any more—'

'That hasn't stopped a marine yet.'

'Can I help?'

'Sure. I'm about to fetch a new load of rocks from the river.'

'Okay,' Lwazi said and went to climb in the back of the *bakkie*.

'Get in the front,' Joss said. 'Besides, you shouldn't be out walking alone.'

'Lions have never come this far before; we don't have to worry about that lion,' Lwazi said as he climbed into the front seat and shut the door.

'This lion already killed two men.'

'One time they warned us of a man-eater and it killed eight people before it was shot. But ZimParks rangers, they always get the lion.'

'You have lots of trust in them,' Joss said.

'No, I trust Julian Seziba, and he says they'll get it before it gets here, but for now we just need to be cautious.'

'And by cautious did he mean walk alone in the bush?'

'Oh no, he told us groups, like always,' Lwazi said. 'Because he used to be a game guard, he doesn't like lions. But he is old now, so perhaps the fear begins when you get older. Besides, I could see that you had a gun and could shoot the lion if it came near us.'

Joss laughed. The teenager was so much like he had been at that age – he thought that he was indestructible. That was before reality had made him realise the truth.

He didn't have the heart to force Lwazi to face reality. Instead he showed the boy the size of the rocks he wanted from the river and left him to it, while he began shovelling river sand.

'Much quicker with two of us,' Joss said when the *bakkie* was full. 'Thanks for helping out.' He grabbed his shotgun from where he'd placed it nearby.

Lwazi smiled and climbed in the *bakkie* again.

They drove with the windows down and listened to the silence in the bush.

'There used to be so many birds here; they would call wherever you went when you were hunting or walking around,' Joss said.

'They are here. Sometimes when you are very quiet you can see them. But they are fewer now. I never even find a rabbit in the snares any more,' Lwazi said.

'There's too much hunting going on, too much reliance on bush meat. At the river there used to be monkey troops that played, dug holes to the water that was underneath the sand, and then other animals would make the holes bigger, and for a while the river would be filled with game.'

'The monkeys and the baboons, they still visit,' Lwazi said. 'But they go back into the forest area, away from the people. There are fish in the Kariba, but you can only eat so much fish.'

'Once the road is done we need to do something about that. Have a communal meeting and talk about this problem.'

'The elders have talked and talked, but people need meat to eat, or we starve. They will not kill the cattle or the goats because they cost too much money, but bush meat, it is free and good to eat.'

Joss nodded as he parked the *bakkie*.

They climbed out and Lwazi reached into the back and grabbed a rock. 'How many do you want in this hole?'

'Put a few big ones, and some smaller, then beat it down, fill it with sand and put more in. This hole is going to take most of our load.'

Lwazi lifted the rocks and threw them into the pothole, then he looked up to the road that led to their houses. 'Hey, Ephraim, *woza*, help fix the road,' he called to another youth sitting on his haunches nearby.

Ephraim got up and walked towards them. 'Why are you fixing the road?'

'Because Joss needs a nice smooth road for his wheelchair, just in case,' Lwazi said.

Ephraim pulled his lip to the side, nibbling on it. 'Are you paying Lwazi?'

'No. He chose to help fix our road – yours, mine, all of ours. We could all do with a smooth road,' Joss said.

Ephraim shook his head. 'Why? People use it as it is.'

'The water pump, it's near the bottom of the safari lodge fence, yes?' Joss said.

Ephraim nodded, then he grinned. He understood, because he had fetched enough water to know that a good road was easier to push a wheelbarrow on. He reached in and took a rock, then threw it into the hole.

'Make sure no one gets hurt when you toss those rocks around,' Joss said.

Lwazi smiled and said, 'Perhaps you should be the one to stand near the hole, because you don't have toes to hurt.'

'Good point.' He swapped his spade for the compactor Lwazi held and began crushing the rocks. The boys threw more rocks and added river sand and soon the hole was filled in, a little higher than the road's surface like the others, ready to have vehicles driven over it.

'Three more down and six million to go,' Joss said. 'We can do a smaller one with what's left in the *bakkie*.'

'*Eish*, at this rate we will never finish the road,' Ephraim said.

'We had a saying that we liked to use in the commandos that was really poetic and beautifully written by some guy, but I could never remember it all. But it was about not giving up until you had succeeded, and that you would never give up, but continue to try. Putting one foot in front of the other one, because eventually, that little bit you gain will get bigger and bigger. And you will win.'

'What does that mean to us? We are not commandos,' Ephraim said.

Joss shook his head. 'It doesn't only apply to commandos. It means, do one step, and then the next. Only once you take the first step and then another, can you complete your journey. Like this road. We'll finish repairing it. Definitely not today or tomorrow, but maybe the week after, or the week after that one. But if we don't start, we'll never get it done.'

'I bet you we'll never finish this road,' Ephraim said.

'In what timeframe?' Joss asked. 'Never bet with an open ending or you land up with a tattoo you don't want.'

Ephraim frowned. 'You didn't want that knife tattoo on your arm?'

Joss looked at his arm, where the British Marine Commando insignia and knife were in black ink. 'I wanted that one, it's the spoon and fork on my butt I didn't want.'

'You have a tattoo of a spoon and a fork on your bottom?' Ephraim said, an amused expression on his face.

'Yeah, and you are not about to see it today or any other day. Now, Ephraim, when won't we finish this road by? And what are you betting?'

'I do not have any money—'

'No, but you have time; you can always trade time.'

'Fine, I bet that we will not finish this road before Christmas, and that the rains wash it all away again anyhow.'

'Christmas?'

'Yes.'

'I'll take your bet and add to it. If we finish this road, without you or any of the other settlers sabotaging it in any way, then the time you wager will be used to help me clear the bush from the old moringa grove, and the old vegetable patch near the lodge.'

Ephraim shook his head. 'We can never clear that. It is a mess. Have you seen how overgrown it is down there?'

'Let's see if we do this road first then, shall we?' Joss said.

'If I win? If you do not finish the road in time?' Ephraim asked.

'I guess I clear that grove on my own.'

'And me, can I bet too?' Lwazi asked.

Joss nodded. 'Of course. What's your bet?'

'I bet we do finish this road before Christmas. And you said you would run again on your new legs on this road – I bet you that when you start running, I will run with you every day, and perhaps one day I too can do this triathlon you speak of.'

'Lwazi, that's two different bets. The road, it's a good bet, but the triathlon is held in England; that's a twenty-five-hour flight away. It's expensive to fly there and to take part.'

Lwazi shrugged. 'But you make things happen, you can find a way to make the money—'

'Money like that would be better put into this safari lodge, and used to send you to a proper school—'

'You told us one step and then another. First we have to fix this road anyway, and there are a lot of potholes. Lots of hot work, and many-many hours of hard work,' Lwazi said.

'You know what? I'll take that bet with you too. It's always nice to have someone to train with. Can you swim?'

'No. You have to swim? You never said that, just a long run—'

'Swim, cycle and run, all of it.'

'Can you teach me to swim?'

Joss nodded. 'Let's finish up. I need some food and to rest for a while. We can carry on later when it's cooler.'

Lwazi nodded, and put the *cymbe* into the *bakkie*, while Ephraim swept the sand away from the tailgate.

'I'll drop you at your home, Ephraim, and collect you when it's cooler, say three o'clock? If you want to join me again?' Joss asked, hating to leave the road, but his stomach growled and he knew he needed to get off his stumps for a while, give them at least two hours, rest or they would blister rather than callus.

'I will come again with you,' Lwazi said.

'I will look for you at three o'clock,' Ephraim said.

*   *   *

Joss sat down on the top step to eat, unhitching his legs and putting them carefully next to him. He massaged his stumps as he ate.

'Do they still hurt you?' Bongani asked as he sat down next to him.

Joss smiled. 'Yes, sometimes, depends what I'm making them do.'

Bongani nodded. 'I saw you had company filling the holes in the road.'

'Yeah. Lwazi's willing to try anything new, but Ephraim's sceptical beyond his years, expecting nothing to work. I'm sure he's been sent by the villagers to keep an eye on me.'

'Ah, that is because Ephraim is Mary's grandson. Did I tell you that Madala White used to work on the farm for *Baas* Tarr near Hwange, before the war vets burnt that farm? Many men and women died that day, not only *Baas* Tarr and his wife, but they killed some of the workers who tried to stand up to them and tell them not to take their livelihood. Madala White, he was badly burnt, and it was only because Lwazi took his grandfather and pulled him in a travois all the way to this place, looking for your mother, that the old man survived. Of course, I am not your mother, and do not have half her skills or talent for healing, but I did what I could for him. He refused to die and leave Lwazi an orphan.'

'He's a tough old man and Lwazi is an amazing kid.'

'Have you noticed that Madala White walks with a limp? It is from where they broke his leg and I could not get it straight because of the burnt skin. But he keeps his house neat, and he somehow comes up with enough money to support himself and his grandson.'

'No hospital?'

'He could not travel, and no ambulance will come into an area so far away from everything. Besides, there is only one hospital in this area, and the doctors there never have any drugs for anaesthetic unless a visiting tourist brings them in. We did the best we could at the time, and when he could travel, he was better and no longer wanted anyone to break his healed bones.'

'I'm not sure everyone here's happy I'm back.'

'Give them time.'

'I wish more people here thought like you, but I fear that I'm living on borrowed time.'

'The war vets might come here when they hear of you returning to the safari lodge, but you will have found your place in the community. The people, they will fight to keep you. The war vets are losing the grip they once had on the people, and slowly the land is healing. The dictator is getting old, and one day he will die. Everyone dies eventually. Then the people will elect a new leader, and things will change again. This time for the better.'

'I know, but it's the waiting that's going to kill me,' Joss said and then laughed. He finished his food and put his plate aside. 'Did you have lunch?'

Bongani nodded. 'At the lodge. But I fear you are going to get fat with all the food you seem to eat. You are no longer a growing boy. You will end up lagging behind when we go hunting—'

'I burn more calories with these prosthetics than I ever did with my own legs. Besides, there's nothing here to hunt.'

Bongani nodded. 'There are too many people around these days.'

'I have a plan. How soon is the next community meeting?'

'A few weeks. It is a full district one, not just the villagers' council for this area.'

'Good, then I will table it as one of the people who live in the area. Am I allowed to put an idea forward that will benefit all the people?'

'Of course. You going to give me any inkling about this idea?'

'We start slowly, beginning with a no bush hunting policy, which would entice the animals to come back this way. We try a bit more for the game-viewing market, and the idea that the villages are living in harmony with the wild animals. Doesn't have to be the big game. But the idea would be to begin a local experience – the tourists could sleep overnight in a traditional village. Traditional furniture in the *ikhaya*, food cooked the traditional way. Perhaps learn a few of your traditions, like how to make an *incelwe* for the women or the *intale* for the men. Use it to your advantage and teach people about your culture. I need to do a bit of research, but I promise it won't do anything to disrupt your chieftainship.'

Bongani grinned. 'Just like the young Joss, planning, plotting, always coming up with good ideas. I trust you, Joss, I know you would never do anything on purpose to harm me, or my people.'

*   *   *

It was early Thursday morning when Bongani stood on the back of his *bakkie*, an old but reliable Toyota Hilux 4x4. He looked out over the sea of faces in his most northern *kraal* of Amaluandi, which had now become a village, swelling to over one hundred and fifty people. He realised there were faces here he didn't recognise.

'My people,' he called. 'There is word from the rangers that there is a man-eating lion coming our way; we must be prepared.'

'What are you going to do to protect us?' a woman asked.

'It is you who must protect yourselves during this time. I can warn you of the dangers, and tell you how to keep safe, but in the end, if you do not do as you are told, the lion could attack you. I cannot be by everyone's side to shoot this lion. You need to take responsibility and protect yourselves.'

A restless murmur went up.

'This area of our settlement, it is always having animal conflict, it is nothing new. You are aware what you must do. Make sure that your children are close by and none wanders away from you. A lion is quick to capture his prey.'

'Who will kill the lion?' another woman asked. He recognised her but not the man standing next to her.

'There are men from ZimParks already tracking it. We are hoping that they get it before it comes to our doorsteps. You need to fortify your doors, make sure that if it is going to try to attack, it cannot get inside your *ikhaya*.' He noted that the man next to the woman had now slunk away, but he kept an eye on him, watching which *ikhaya* he went to.

'Do you know if this one attacks in the day or only at night?'

'They do not know yet. We must get ready, and you must stay vigilant until we know it has gone.'

Again, a murmur went through the crowd.

'If there is anyone who is too old to fortify their *ikhaya* themselves, they must tell us so that the other men in the *kraal* can help you. There is no shame in admitting you need help. The shame will come if the lion can get inside your home and eat you.'

Bongani turned to the man next to him. 'This is Julian Seziba; he is an ex-game ranger and knows a lot about lions, and he sits on the villagers' council. His assistant Ephraim will take down the names of those who need help.'

Julian took his bush hat from his head and Ephraim grinned and waved.

'I have a second settlement to call on this afternoon, so let us get working quickly. If you see anything, you must report it to your elder. He will telephone me so that ZimParks can get the lion before it kills again.'

The crowd's murmur rose to talking as they dispersed, everyone speaking at the top of their voices. The people who needed help began lining up next to the *bakkie*, and Ephraim recorded their names in a notebook Julian gave him.

Bongani walked to the *ikhaya* the suspicious man had gone into. He knocked on the door. 'It is Bongani. I would like to talk.'

The man opened it, his head bowed and his eyes darting from side to side.

'What is your name?'

'Elmon Dudzi.'

The name was so familiar, but Bongani couldn't remember where from, as it didn't match with the face in front of him. The numbers were growing so rapidly and he was losing track – his mind had been so focused on his ailing father in the last few months that he simply wasn't paying enough attention to the settlers. 'Do I know you?'

'We have not met. I know your brother.'

Just what he needed.

The door scraped open further, and Elmon shuffled out. The man looked beaten, as if he knew that he was in the wrong, and had no right to be living where he was.

'When did you come here?' Bongani asked.

'Two, maybe three months now.'

'Who gave you permission to build here?'

'Your brother. He said that he had got your permission for me, and I could live here. But I did not build this *ikhaya*; it was here already, waiting for me.'

'I see. So, if you are such good friends with my brother, have you made an effort for a different life, or are you continuing to be a criminal?'

'I am not a criminal, but—'

'But what?'

'It is very-very hard.' Elmon shook his head. 'Your brother said that you do not interfere in the people's business.'

Bongani laughed. 'Did he now? For once he speaks the truth. I do not normally interfere, each person is responsible for their own, and their family, but I see that perhaps it is time that I make it clear that this area is not a squatters' camp. People here work hard, they apply themselves and help the community.'

'I have helped, I am trying to be part of the community in this village,' Elmon said.

'Doing what?'

'This and that.'

Bongani got the impression Elmon was being deliberately vague, a sure sign he was up to no good. 'What exactly have you been doing?'

Elmon shuffled his feet. 'I get meat for the butcher's store in the market.'

'What type of meat?'

'Bush meat.' Elmon looked downwards again.

'You poach? In the forest area?'

'No, it is on communal lands. I would not poach in the Chizarira. I am not a criminal. The butcher Benson, he said that your father allows him to kill the game for his butcher store so that the people have *nyama* for their stews.'

Bongani shook his head.

'Your brother said you would not do anything to me if you came here, and to tell you that King Gogo wa de Patswa knows that no black partner owns more than fifty per cent of Yingwe River Lodge that you look after for your white friend. He said to tell you that when the war vets hear that there is a white man in charge of that business they will come to take it, and he will have Yingwe River Lodge for himself.' Elmon seemed to take a breath, as if this had been information he had held close to his heart.

This was the thing that Tichawana thought he had over Bongani, and he had allowed a nobody to present him the information. Bongani wondered what Tichawana was holding over the man to trust him with that type of knowledge. It must be valuable to Elmon.

'Is that so?'

'Yes.'

'I see,' Bongani said. 'I want you to pack your bags and come with me. As my father Chief Tigere's representative, I choose where you settle, not my brother. I have need of you in a different village rather than make you leave. We can discuss further what you are going to tell my brother.'

Elmon's eyes were large, and Bongani had his suspicions confirmed, that this man had a greater fear of his brother than of him.

'I do not know what my brother is holding over your head, but I will not harm you here. I do, however, want to talk to you further about the other people who are living in this village. Perhaps it is time that I do a count again—'

'I only know that I was sent here by your brother, to live at this village. To listen to what is happening in the area, and once a month report to him. But now, if you change my *kraal*, he will know that I have failed him, and he will kill my son. My real name is Francis Kanobvurunga. I was a man of standing within my community in Bulawayo, I own a second-hand furniture business. I only ever had one wife. I dedicated each moment to my beautiful Rosemary. But God chose to take her from me too soon, and all I have left is our young son. I made sure that he was educated, that he knew many languages outside of Zimbabwe so that he understood there was a world outside our country. My son Thomas is a very-very bright teen-ager. We were looking at sending him to boarding school in South Africa on a scholarship. They stole him in the night from my house. They grabbed him from his own bed, and I could not protect him.'

'Why did they target your son?' Bongani asked.

'I have a good relationship with the people at the Beit Bridge border. One day this man came into my shop and told me that I had to take his shipments with mine into South Africa. I was not to open anything, and I was to make sure that customs did not open them either. Once I had got through the border post, I was to deliver them to an address in Durban. If I did not do this, there would be consequences.'

'You delivered the boxes?'

'I refused. That was when they took my Thomas. The man came back and said that they were training him to be a soldier for the people now. But I know they are brainwashing him, like the kids up in the Congo. I am an educated man, not an idiot. That was when I put the word out on the street that I would do anything to get my son back. Instead of some mercenary coming to me, saying that they would find the camp and save him for a large amount of money, that very same man who had visited me in my store, he came to my house. He told me that King Gogo wa de Patswa owned me now. After a meeting in his office, your brother sent me to this place.' He took deep breaths, trying to stem his panic, and tears had welled up in his eyes.

'He has my son in one of his training camps. My Thomas. You have to understand, I am not a criminal. All my life I have lived in the city, not in the bush. Living here is hard for me. But if I do not do this for your brother, he will hurt my son. Thomas is a scholar, not athletic like a soldier.'

Bongani nodded. 'Pack as if you are visiting someone. We have much to discuss. You will come to the chief's *kraal* with me and we will help you sort this out. I have someone I know who will want to hear more of what you were sent here to tell me.'

Francis nodded, but he looked like a defeated man.

'Do not try to run away; pack quietly and come with me. Julian will collect you later if you are not standing near my *bakkie* within an hour. He tracks better than any man I know and will hunt you down.'

Bongani turned away. Dammit, his father wasn't even dead yet and his brother was already making inroads into the area. Soon Bongani would be chief, but that title was about to cause more trauma and unrest in the area than they had ever known.

A blood feud.

He always knew that King Gogo wa de Patswa was Tichawana Ndou, but having it confirmed again by a stranger wasn't easy. He had to keep his people safe.

Lost in his own thoughts, he walked back to his vehicle.

There was someone standing next to the old *bakkie*. He took in her traditional clothes, her brightly coloured headscarf and long walking sticks. She had a sports bag at her feet that was held shut with safety pins.

'*N'Goma* Abigale. Nice to see you,' Bongani said and nodded.

'Bongani, my old friend.' She nodded. 'It has been a very long time since I saw you last.'

'My father?'

'Not yet, but his time is close. You and I, we have work to do. I was hoping that you would take me to Chief Tigere's village while you have your *bakkie* here, and save my old legs a lot of days' walk through the bush.'

'We are stopping at Sigara Village before heading home, but you are welcome to come along with us.'

'Perhaps, since you are so close, when we travel we can fetch *N'Goma* Thoko and Lindiwe too. They live nearby that place.'

'Of course,' Bongani said.

'*Twalumba*, it will be more comfortable for me in the front of your *bakkie*,' *N'Goma* Abigale said as she moved to the passenger door and climbed in.

Bongani smiled as he picked up her travel bags and sticks and tossed them in the back.

His day had just got a whole lot better.

CHAPTER

11

The Moringa Grove

Joss wiped the sweat from his brow. The furrow between the moringa trees had been cleared of the brown weeds that had choked it, and clean, rich dirt could be seen. The trees themselves were in good shape, old, with roots that ran deep, and had survived the neglect of the last few years surprisingly well.

'One down!' Lwazi grinned.

Ephraim groaned. 'Only about nine or ten left to clear.'

It was amazing that once Joss had begun working on the road with the boys, the villagers had come out to help, and had been happy to continue into the moringa grove with him. Except for Mary, who still seemed to have misgivings about having him home.

The others in the village had proven eager to get the road fixed. It was like they had been waiting for the prompt to start working, and now they were in full swing. The small community worked together pulling weeds and clearing silt-filled trenches to protect the moringa grove. With the threat of the man-eating lion still looming, they gathered in groups to work, taking turns to keep watch.

'That might be, but it's a good start. Tomorrow is another day.' He trimmed a few branches, then he split them into two bunches. 'Here, Ephraim, take these home with you.' Joss passed him a bunch of leaves, keeping the other aside. He put his hands around his mouth and called out, 'Home time!' then listened to the men and women talking as they packed up their tools and headed to the *bakkie.* Two of the female guests from the lodge, Sara and Mel, had volunteered to help clear the grove when they had been talking to Joss the night before.

'You eat the leaves?' Sara asked.

'This tree's good for you. You cook it like spinach,' Joss said. 'Everything used to eat these leaves. We had to dig these deep trenches around here to try to keep the kudu and impala out, and don't even mention the elephants. When I was ten, and I found a baby elephant, her herd came and stayed for about three weeks, eating these moringa trees. It helped the mother jumbo get enough milk and make her strong, so that they could leave again, go back into the wild.'

'If they were so good, why did they get so overgrown?' Mel asked.

'My mother used to keep this grove in order, and make sure that she shared its goodness with the community. I guess after she died, no one took control. I was overseas in Afghanistan, and Bongani had enough on his plate.'

'I thought these trees only made soap,' Ephraim said. 'My grand-mother talks of a soap your mother and she made from these leaves; she says that she remembers how to make it.'

'Tell your grandmother that if she wants to make that soap again, she should come and speak to me about using the trees and the lodge buying it from her.'

'You would help my grandmother even though she says horrible things about you?'

'She doesn't mean to be spiteful – she's worried about the people in the area, and she doesn't like change. She'll see that we can be successful when Bongani is chief. We will do our best to protect her from harm. Having her own business will help her with money, and keep her occupied. Busy people have different problems to worry about,' Joss said. 'The tourists are keen to learn the traditional ways, and to make soap too. It's a memento from Africa and a skill for them to take back to their own countries. There is money to be made in creating an opportunity for them, which will create wealth to help the village. And you get their labour too. You should discuss this with your grandmother.'

'I will tell her,' Ephraim said, 'but I doubt she will come to you.'

'If she doesn't want to earn the income from it, I can teach someone else. I used to spend hours with my mother making soap, and I still have her recipe books and cutters. But I would like to help Mary, and you, because you are a hard worker, even though she makes you report to her.'

Ephraim looked away.

'Are you still spying on Joss?' Lwazi said. 'After everything, you still tell your grandmother what's happening and what we are doing?'

'If I do not tell her she says she will not feed me.'

'Blah, you and I both know she's not going to let you go hungry. She'll always feed you, Ephraim,' Joss said, but he wasn't smiling. 'You are the only family she has left. Mary'll always look after you, until the day she can't, and then it will be your turn to look after her. Those are just idle threats, because she wants to know what's happening, and doesn't want to get involved.'

'I think you are right, but I do not want to go hungry,' Ephraim admitted. 'I will tell her what you said, and if she says no, I will learn to make soap from you so that I can have money to help her.'

Joss smiled at him. 'You are a good grandchild.'

'Soon I will go back to Matilda at Bishu Village to learn how to keep bees, and then I too will have honey,' Lwazi said. 'I will sell honey and beeswax candles to the tourists, and that will make some more money to help my grandfather. Remember you promised you would speak to Bongani about me learning when we visited to warn them of the lion?'

'I haven't forgotten,' Joss said. 'Bongani is a little occupied at the moment with his father and the lion. If Ephraim makes the soap, you can learn too. He should also learn to help you with the bees, in case you are sick. You are the only two boys your age; you need to stick together.'

*   *   *

After dropping the workers at their homes and the tourists back at the lodge, Joss parked his *bakkie* behind his house. Lwazi climbed out and disappeared into the building. For a long time, Joss sat at the steering wheel.

'What is wrong? Are your legs cramped?' Bongani asked at the window.

'What? No. I was thinking.'

'Must have been some heavy thinking, because you have been staring out to space for at least thirty minutes. Look – it is getting dark already.'

Sure enough, the purple cover of night was descending around them.

'Did you ever notice that no matter what you planned in your life, it ends up differently?'

'Always,' Bongani said.

'When I was Lwazi and Ephraim's age, all I wanted to do was go and be a British commando. Wear a green beret and save the masses. But I never truly understood that to do that, I wouldn't be home, I would be away in the world somewhere else, and while I was there, my home would change. And no matter what I do now, it will never be the same.'

'Everything changes. What is important is what you did with that life you planned. Did you achieve that dream?'

'You know I did, but then I paid the price for it, and now ...'

'Now you want more. You want something badly enough to make it happen?'

'Exactly that. Where once I wanted to rip the world apart to bring justice and tolerance, now all I want is to put this world that has been ripped apart back together, only I don't want what it was, I want it to be better.'

'You can do that, Joss; you have always been able to do anything you put your mind to.'

'Not this time. This time my dream isn't about me, it's about our whole community, and it's not something I can do alone. I think that this community can do so much better than it's doing, and today I think I found a way to help make that happen.'

* * *

Joss looked at the road. He knew that today's run was going to be more of a mental challenge than a physical one. While he could achieve kilometres on the smoothness of the treadmill, it was an unreal environment; it lacked the stones, the corrugations and the everyday hazards that he would need to get used to on a road run. His body needed the adrenaline, and the sublime feeling of knowing that if something came at him, he could escape on his own legs. The plan with his captain at Headley had been for him to get on the road and run when he could. He knew that today was a huge step to building up to that competition. One step. But taking that step was making his breathing shallow.

He had chosen to not wear blades but to use his legs because of the unfamiliar and unpredictable surface of the road. Joss bent down and re-tied his laces. Again. His laces were as good as they were going to be. Plastics didn't care about blisters. He breathed in then blew it out, and took his first step.

His legs felt good; there was no excessive pressure on his stumps. He took another step and another. He ran.

It was slow.

He was almost at the first *ikhaya* on the road when Lwazi appeared at his side.

'I said I would train with you,' he said.

'Five houses, then we turn and come back. I need to ease into this,' Joss said.

It felt great to run, to feel his legs turning over. The beat of his heart as the blood pumped through his body. He wasn't ready for a marathon yet, but he was on the right path to participating in that triathlon with his fellow marines.

A ring-necked dove flew onto the path in front of him and he stopped.

'It's a bird,' Lwazi said. 'Come on, keep running.'

Joss shook his head. 'No, it's more than that. The rains have begun healing the land. There's food for the birds now.' He watched the dove, its white underside merging with a darker grey on the top of its body, its distinctive black collar at the back of its neck, and listened while it cooed and scratched in the dirt a little before flying back up into the tree covered in green leaves, above the line where the goats had stripped all vegetation.

He smiled. He had been so busy fixing the road then clearing the moringa tree grove and the vegetable patch that he hadn't noticed that the land was once again bursting with life after the rain they had received.

Joss put one foot in front of the other and ran the small distance to reach the final house. He put his hand in the air to high five Lwazi, and they turned around.

On the road stood many of the people he was coming to know. They began clapping and dancing. Their smiles of happiness as he ran towards them showed that he was not alone in his journey any more. He slapped Makesh's hand as he passed, then Timberman's and Obias's as he continued on the run past their houses back towards the lodge, through the buffer zone and the stables.

Bongani waited on the steps. 'Your new legs might be plastic, but they run as well as your proper ones used to.'

Joss bent over and put his hands on his artificial knees.

'That is all our training today?' Lwazi asked.

'That's it,' Joss said. 'Tomorrow we do a bit more, and the day after that, more again.'

'That was too easy,' Lwazi said. 'Look, I am barely even sweating. I sweat more when I take the cattle down to the lake to drink.'

'Maybe for you it was easy, but then you were not the one lugging around five and a half kilograms of artificial legs, as well as trying to navigate the smoothest path so you don't fall over.'

'That is your problem, your new legs? At this rate, when will we be ready for the triathlon? Next year? Maybe the one after that?'

Joss shook his head. 'In two months or so we should be able to do a half-marathon, twenty-one kilometres, on this road. The full marathon will probably take about six months of training every day, but we will get there. Now, stretches, so we don't get stiff tomorrow.'

* * *

Joss knew to take the bad days with the good.

Just because he was running again didn't mean that he could neglect some of his other duties. It had never been his intention to run the lodge. His dream had always been the military. But sometimes dreams needed to be changed, and he needed to be practical. His parents had left him an opportunity and now it was time to embrace it.

Joss had never meant to totally step away from Yingwe River Lodge, but time in a war zone cut you off from the realities of the world, and you forgot about the outside when you were there. He had been so busy trying to save someone else's country and people that he'd neglected his own. Dreams of seeing Africa again had kept him alive in the desert, and when he was undergoing his surgeries. Getting better and getting home again was one of the main things that had kept him alive.

Now that he was on the banks of Kariba, he felt that he had neglected his responsibilities.

Joss looked at the accounts again. They could afford to renovate the lodge, and then do some advertising to attract a higher calibre clientele. They could be doing much better than what they had been. If he could attract the normal diehard fishing crowd as well as clients with more disposable money, those who wanted the authentic experience of Bongani's village, that would help even more.

He took a pad of paper and began making a list of things to buy for a quick-fix facelift inside, then went from room to room, photographing everything.

'What are you doing?' Bongani asked when he saw Joss on the deck.

'Deciding where to start with the renovations.'

Bongani nodded. 'First you need to decide if you are going to stay. Or if you are going back to your life in a far-off land?'

'I've taken a while to realise that I'm ready to take this on. I've decided I'm staying.'

'What about your triathlon, when you return for that and you see the other side again? What happened to going back to the military, revisiting Afghanistan?'

'The triathlon will only be a holiday. I've seen the other side and I know that I'll still want to come home. Yingwe River Lodge is home. I need to stop running away from my responsibilities. I'm staying. Fighting to protect people in another country was my dream when I was younger but things've changed – I've different responsibilities now. I'm needed here.'

Bongani smiled. 'You have always been a child of Africa. I am glad to hear that you are home to stay. I think that the people have sensed this too, and many are attached to you already. I have many-many chieftain's duties I have left aside while running this lodge, and if you are here then I can begin to catch up, but we will have to ease the people into this, or they will think you are kicking me out. Very few of my people are aware of the legal ownership of this lodge. It has remained a secret for a long time. They all still believe it is yours alone. Even my brother has not found out the truth. It is better to have it like that, or when I become chief, they will think that my property is their communal property and move in. I know how my people's minds work.'

'It's not anyone's business but yours and mine. You know that I would never kick you out of the ownership or management of the lodge, and my home is yours, if you ever need a roof over your head.'

'We are old friends, you and I, and many of those in this area are new; they did not know what this place was like before. One day the house of my father in the village will be my house. When he passes, you and I will need to sort out how and what I still do, so those settlers see that I am the chief, but this lodge, it will be hard to live away from. I still do not understand how you stayed away all those years when I know it runs in your blood.'

'I think we could start with putting a powerline through to your village. Even if it is to a solar farm nearby. Or we could build you a new brick house so that when you get married, there is a smart home to attract your wife.'

Bongani nodded. 'My father, he ran this area with an iron fist. When he dies, I do not want to be like that. Only now I see I have to put some barriers in place. Take control. Not with the excessive brutality of the ancestors, but I need more discipline and acceptance within my area. Having you here means I can concentrate on that more. I can get your guidance, as sometimes you have a different way of looking at things. Perhaps you can help me solve the problem of my useless half-brother trying to take over the area.'

'Yes, we need to talk about that brother of yours soon.'

'We also need to somehow find out if those alleged youth camps Francis told us about are real.'

'I agree. One step then another,' Joss said. 'But know that even if you didn't ask me, I'd still give you my five cents' worth. It's what friends do.'

Bongani laughed, placed his hand on Joss's shoulder and squeezed. 'Come now, we have many plans to make.'

CHAPTER
12

The Camp

Sweat dripped from his brow and onto his vest. He carried a backpack with four bricks in it as weights. All the recruits did, girls and boys alike. He neared the end of their ten-kilometre run and saw the instructor, Mr Emanuel Zheve, standing with his cane ready. He had threatened any person coming in after him with two stripes from his switch.

Tichawana eyed him as he got closer.

As Tichawana was the boss, he wasn't sure if Mr Zheve would beat him yet again, but if he did not, then the children would question his authority. He was out of time. Mr Zheve switched the child in front of Tichawana, and as he ran past, the instructor quickly gave him two whacks across the back of his legs.

The skin on Tichawana's leg burnt as the salty sweat ran over the cut from the thin green switch, but he kept running. During the past week and a half at the camps, he had collected twenty-one stripes. He swore that on the following morning, he would beat the instructor. Tomorrow he would cross the line first. He was already fitter now, the acid that built in his muscles the first few days had at last been reabsorbed into his system and he was running well again. Tomorrow he would not be collecting his twenty-second stripe.

There was a child who came in some distance after him. Mr Zheve administered his punishment then walked to the tap to get some water.

'Last again, Thomas,' one child taunted the student.

Thomas looked at him, waiting his turn for the water.

'Loser,' the kid said and threw sand over his head.

Tichawana smiled. Thomas was much like his father: stubborn and proud. The camp had not broken him yet, but he knew that it would. Break him down to nothing, then build him into a fighter, a soldier. He just had to listen, do everything the instructors said, and learn to be strong. So did his father.

A girl stood between Thomas and his tormentor. 'Leave him alone, you moron.'

'Is that the best you got, Nesta?' the boy said. 'Wait till tonight; I am going to come into your dormitory and fuck you while the others watch.'

'You will be a dead boy if you come anywhere near me,' Nesta said, her voice dropping low. 'I am no boy's free ride.'

The boy grinned like a juvenile baboon, and hitched his balls at her.

Nesta finished drinking and Thomas took his turn at the tap.

'You run like a girl,' the boy continued to taunt him. 'Even the fat man beat you.'

Tichawana swung his backpack at the boy's head. The bricks connected and he fell on the same ground he had so recently been throwing over Thomas. 'You need to learn respect, you snot-snivelling little pig. No one calls me fat,' he said as he stepped over the corpse. He walked away from the tap. It wasn't the first kid he had killed, and he knew it wouldn't be the last. They had an annoying habit of pissing him off, just like this one had. The school would sort out the story of how he died in a tragic accident, fell and hit his head. The girl and the boy who witnessed it would never talk. They knew what would happen if they did – their own bodies would be thrown in a deep hole, just like this disrespectful little shit's would, and left to rot, their souls forever damned as no one would perform their burial rituals.

* * *

Today Tichawana stood at the front of the bunch of children waiting to start their run. He was not getting any more switch lines.

'Ready, steady, go,' Mr Zheve shouted. The mass launched forward. Tichawana ran hard.

He stayed with the front group of boys for a while, then dropped back a little, but remained with the next group. The kids gave him a wide berth, not surprising after the incident with the insulting pig the day before. He was tired. After his run today he was calling it quits, but not until he beat that instructor.

He pushed faster. His chest burnt. He could feel each breath as he drew air desperately into his lungs and blew it back out.

He came around the corner and saw the place where Mr Zheve should have been standing, but he wasn't there.

Tichawana let out his breath. Today he was a winner. No punishment.

He crossed over the end line and walked away.

He had done it.

It was time to go hunting instead of this running around like a youngster. Time to face the world of responsibilities again, and get back to his business.

It had been interesting training with the recruits first in his camp in Nkayi and now outside Gwanda, the latest addition to his portfolio. They were making him good money. The soldiers he produced were being used in the conflicts in the Ivory Coast and the Sudan. He was being paid well for their training. He'd got a commission for every soldier he trained and sent north to fight. Those he kept were his disposable army, ready to bear arms for him against his half-brother, and the time was coming closer to call them up.

It reminded him of when he was put on an aeroplane the first time and taken to Korea to be trained there, only this was much simpler; everyone spoke the same language. In his camps, he got to control the training, and he got to keep the trainees' services if he wanted to. The excess were unloaded and sent north. Unemployment was at an all-time high in his country, and he was creating an avenue for jobs that many would not normally consider. He was helping them.

He cleared his room of his bag and called his tracker, who had been waiting in the kitchen all week for him.

It was time to go hunting.

*   *   *

Tichawana clenched his stomach; it was flatter than it had been in a long time from the sit-ups and crunches he had recently done. He was not quite as fit as he had been as a young man, and not as fit as when he had got out of prison on amnesty, but much better than he had been of late. He doubted that his brother would be in such good shape. His reports on Bongani said that he was too busy running the Yingwe River Lodge and looking after his father's affairs to bother getting any exercise.

He swished a fly from his face, grateful that today he had worn long pants for the hunt, keeping the flies off his shredded legs.

The buffalo bull stood under a tree, hiding from the heat. It chewed its cud, secure in the knowledge that it was the king of the bush in this area. Lions were few and leopards wouldn't bother a fully grown male.

Tichawana took a deep breath and swallowed the excitement that bubbled up from his chest. He held it. He placed the crosshairs of his rifle firmly on the target, directly behind the ear. He squeezed the trigger.

The shot exploded from his Ruger.

The buffalo's legs collapsed underneath it as it fell in slow motion. Half a ton of mammal hit the ground.

Tichawana let out his breath.

*   *   *

Tichawana drove slowly back through the bush to the training college and parked under a tree where a block and tackle were set up, the ground stained dark from previous butcherings.

'Meat for the students,' he said, 'protein after all their running this week.'

The tracker smiled as he cut the skin of the buffalo's back fetlocks and pushed the hooks of the Y-frame through. Then, using the block and tackle, he began to lift the carcass. Slowly the beast rose into the tree and Tichawana moved the *bakkie*. The buffalo swung on the chains, its head about twenty centimetres off the ground.

The tracker pulled an old tarpaulin under the carcass. Tichawana stepped up and, using his own curved skinning knife, neatly sliced through the skin and sinew of the giant ball sack to join the cut he'd made earlier. He moved the skin aside, then cut deeper, severing the flesh and muscles. The intestines and stomach tumbled onto the mat as he separated them from the body, careful not to pierce them. He removed the other internal organs and dropped them onto the tarpaulin too, except for the kidneys. Those he took and put in a yellow enamel bowl in the back of the *bakkie*.

Once the offal was on the tarp, the tracker and one of the kitchen staff dragged them to the side and Tichawana began to skin the buffalo. He carefully separated the hide from the meat, almost like a doctor performing a skin graft. He sliced with precision, ensuring that there were no puncture holes in the leather. Cutting up to the knee point on the back legs, and then the front, he worked the whole skin off, until it spilled like a pink and white blanket around the buffalo's head. Finally, he completed the cut behind the neck that his tracker had started, and the skin came free.

Only then did his shoulders relax. He smiled as he watched the tracker and two other men carry the skin to the *bakkie* and lay it, hair side down, in the tray. They threw handfuls of salt onto it before carefully folding it into a bundle.

Tichawana stopped then, cleaned his knives and washed his hands at the outside tap. He sat on his bonnet and watched the cook bring out his own knives and sharpen them before he began to dissect the carcass.

'See you next month,' Tichawana said as he left the carcass in the capable hands of the cook and climbed into his *bakkie*.

'There is another hunter in that area. A large leopard, *Baas*,' the tracker said.

'Bigger than the one in my lounge area?'

'Yes. Feet almost the size of a trophy lion. He is proud, he walks with purpose, as if he is at the top of the food chain.'

'Do you think he will attack anyone in the training school?'

'You never know with a leopard. He obviously accepts the training school as part of his territory, but if someone comes out of that school, he might keep their silence better than a man.'

'That is good. Perhaps next time someone thinks they can use the bush to hide away from their destiny they will learn an important lesson instead.'

He dropped the tracker at his hut in the outskirts of Esigodini and watched in his side mirror as the man rolled the skin from the *bakkie* to land on the ground. The tracker held his bowl of kidneys to him as if it was a precious gift and lifted one hand as Tichawana drove away.

* * *

The Shanghai Club was situated in the premises of the golf course in Killarney, once a prestigious suburb of Bulawayo. The club was no longer used by golfers; it was now owned by a Hong Kong Chinese businessman who catered to his elite clientele's every wish, as long as they paid huge fees for annual memberships, and fees for any event they attended, as well as fees for the time they spent inside the premises. What happened inside the walls of the club was guaranteed to stay there, especially now that the clubhouse had been expanded to include accommodation.

'Ah, my favourite customer,' Mr Ling greeted Tichawana warmly.

'You say that to all your customers.'

'With you I mean it,' Mr Ling said with a smile. 'Your normal suite?'

Tichawana nodded.

'I'll send your girls once you have had time to clean up.'

'Give me at least half an hour, and get someone to clean my *bakkie*, and lock my guns in a safe.'

'Of course,' Mr Ling said and he smiled again, passing Tichawana an access card and taking the vehicle's keys.

Tichawana walked out of the clubhouse and passed rooms screened off with thick thatch. When he saw a small mongoose carving sitting on top of a rock he stepped onto the path that meandered around a huge old jacaranda tree and through some bamboo growing on both sides, effectively creating a corridor. Finally he walked into the suite.

He opened the door and inhaled. The faint scent of sex always remained in the room, but it was masked expertly with cedar wood and furniture polish. Walking directly to the bathroom, he dropped his clothes on the floor and stepped into the hot shower.

Lathering his hands with the soap from the dispenser, he scrubbed himself from head to toe using his nails, cleaning every crevice and line. He rubbed the deep scar across his left cheek. It had almost killed him, almost put him in a shallow grave of his own. So many memories flooded into his head, but that day was a turning point in his life, the day he learnt to never trust a man – even when he believed he was defeated, broken, something would always fight for life.

The scene played like a movie in his head.

* * *

The darkness of the night contrasted to the brightness of the burning huts behind the men standing at the edge of the large pit they had dug for themselves. They knew it was their grave, and yet they stood like the proud and stupid Matabele they were. They knew that when the men with the red berets visited, there would be no one left alive, but still they had hope. Defiantly standing tall, knowing that death was around the corner, they believed that by dying they would protect their women and children from the carnage.

They were so wrong. Steeped in tradition and influenced by the colonials who once ruled them, they had no idea the ethnic cleansing was happening for a good reason: so that the president could control the people. To ensure that those who still opposed him after the long bush war were stamped out and he could run the country any way he liked.

Tichawana sneered. His father was like these men, living in a bygone era. One day Tichawana would get back to his own village and not only make his father and his brother watch the other pathetic males die, but he would keep them alive to watch as he and his comrades shared the women. Only when he knew they were broken would he run his knife slowly across their throats so that they would suffer. No quick death for Bongani or Tigere.

He only had to manipulate his lieutenant, Black Mamba, into taking them into his homeland area. He was sure that the bloodlust that his lieutenant seemed to revel in would rule his head. A few more kilometres to the west and they would cross over into the land that he'd own once he had killed the reigning chief. Then he could settle there and be home once more.

'Tich,' Black Mamba said, interrupting his thoughts.

He looked over to him.

Black Mamba gave a grunt and scratched his balls. He took the toothpick from his teeth and spat on the ground. 'Shoot them, then line up the women.'

Tichawana jumped to do his lieutenant's bidding, opening fire with his rifle, watching the men fall in a heap, some clutching their stomachs, others dead right away.

'One body, one bullet,' the lieutenant shouted. 'We will run short of ammo and I do not want to go back to base again this month.'

Tichawana stopped spraying the bullets across the falling line. 'One body, one bullet?'

The Black Mamba approached him and punched him in the face. 'You questioning my authority?'

Tichawana bent slightly, showing his respect for his lieutenant. 'No, no, you have it wrong. I am not sure that I can shoot as well as you expect, that is all. I would never question you.'

'You would not? No, because you are an idiot and you do not learn. You do not listen. You want to kill and kill. You need to learn. You take this knife and you finish those men, cut their throats like the cattle they are, and push them in that grave. We have the troublemakers. There are women over there who will keep me warm for the night. You get this over with before you join in the fun.'

He turned his back to Tichawana, and walked towards the burning huts. The chief's wife stood taller than the other women. Like her husband, she carried excessive pride. Tichawana smiled. He knew where that pride would be by morning – broken in a heap and in the same grave as her husband.

He turned back to the men, who, seeing the lieutenant and four other men walking towards their women, began to struggle against their bonds. He looked at the line and knew that he would leave the chief and his teenage son till last – they could watch, and they would always know that they had not done their duty, hadn't protected their people.

Grabbing the first man's hair, he pushed his head forward, and his combat knife slid into the neck like it was butter. The artery sliced, and his warm blood seeped over Tichawana's hand. He pulled the head backwards, and the blood splashed out. He thought it was what painting a picture would be like, if he knew how to paint. He pushed the man, still twitching, into the grave, and moved on to the next. The teenage boy's eyes showed white with fear. His body glistened with sweat.

Tichawana laughed. 'This one is because you are too much like my half-brother,' he said, but instead of killing him and pushing him into the pit right away, he pushed him into his father instead. 'Here is your precious first born, your heir to your everything. Say goodbye, because he will be dead. So will your wife; you can hear her screams already as my lieutenant shows her what a real man can do.'

The chief defied his years and jumped his feet through his bound arms and then swung his fists at Tichawana's head. The blow to his ear made his whole head ring and he found himself knocked to the ground. He remained stationary, but saw the chief come at him again, dropping to his knees next to him. Tichawana had lost his knife, so he scavenged by his side. He found his AK-47 and let off a short burst of bullets into the chief's gut.

The man folded, the top of his head hitting the dirt first.

'Run,' the father shouted at the boy, who now attempted to hop away, but was still bound to his father and all the other bodies. He toppled over.

Too late, Tichawana realised the father had his knife and was cutting his son free.

'Run!' he screamed, as he lunged again at Tichawana.

Tichawana's cheek erupted in fire as the knife slashed his face. The chief knocked him back again, only this time Tichawana didn't fall. He brought his gun to his hip and emptied the magazine into the chief. 'Die, you stupid fuck!' he screamed.

A second burst of gunfire was heard nearby, and Tichawana saw the boy fall on his face, unmoving.

'One job, Tich. I gave you one job and you screwed it up,' Black Mamba was shouting at him, his pants still around his ankles, AK-47 at his hip.

'I am sorry,' Tichawana said. 'I did not expect that old chief to be so strong.'

'I hope you learnt. Put those two into the grave. I left a few women strong enough to start covering the bodies, then they can follow. Finish up and then see to that cut on your face, or the maggots will eat you alive.'

Tichawana nodded, bringing his hand to his cheek. The tips of his fingers traced the cut. His cheekbone and teeth could be felt from the outside. His stomach heaved.

'On second thoughts, face first,' Black Mamba said. 'Keep your dirty paws out of that. Come to the fires, and get your belt and bite hard, you are going to need it.'

'He was so strong,' Tichawana said again, still shaking his head.

'The most desperate ones always are,' Black Mamba said. 'Earlier you mentioned that there is another village only a day's walk from this one? Bend down, put your head here.' He pointed to a small mat on the ground near a fire.

'West. Amaluandi Village, it is within spitting distance,' Tichawana said as he put his head on the mat. He watched Black Mamba thread some cotton through the eye of a needle, then pass the pointed end through the flames a few times.

'And you think it is a good place for us?'

Tichawana went to nod, but found he couldn't as Black Mamba had put his knee on his ear and was holding his head in a vice-like grip. 'Second best. I hear that Yingwe Village, further south, is better, but it will do.'

'Then there is even more reason to get your cheek healed, so that you can enjoy these spoils with us,' Black Mamba said, as he took the heated needle and plunged it into Tichawana's cheek.

Two days later, he was finally almost home. Almost over the boundary line from the Chizarira and into the old Tribal Trust Lands.

His father's kingdom.

Amaluandi Village was on the edge of the forest. After they had slaughtered those villagers, they would head south, towards Yingwe Village, where his father had moved his main *kraal* to. Tichawana was so close to victory he could taste it.

He lifted his fingers to his cheek and winced. The cheek was still sore even now it was stitched, but the burning had almost gone. Getting his unit here had been easy, but making sure that he would be the one to kill his father and his brother, that was going to be a little trickier, and he had not quite figured it out.

Black Mamba stopped, looking up at the tree in front of him. 'We can go no further. Look, there is bad *muti*. We shouldn't cross into this area. There are powerful *N'Gomas* that protect this place.'

Three of Tichawana's comrades talked in quiet tones.

'Tich, *woza*,' Black Mamba called him forward.

Tichawana ran to his commander.

The lieutenant pointed to the bags that hung on the tree. They were not subtle at all, not like the other *muti* he had seen previously. There were five of them, looking like giant drops of dried leaves and twigs, all tied together with bark. 'You told us of this place, but you did not tell us of this *muti*.'

'I did not know of it. But the *N'Goma* here, she is weak. I remember her, she was very young,' Tichawana said.

'You know this place?' Black Mamba asked.

'I grew up here,' Tichawana said, 'before I came to be with my comrades in Zambia. The chief banished me. Threw me out of my own home.'

'A revenge killing.' Black Mamba shook his head. 'Have I taught you nothing in the whole time you have been with us? You cannot go into an area you know; they will recognise you and they will tell the bush drums to watch for you. They will get their *N'Gomas* to make *muti* to keep you out permanently.'

'I do not care.'

'You should. The *N'Goma* has power over you if they know your name, and if they have anything that belongs to you, it is even stronger. If this was your home, the *N'Goma* will have your things, and the *muti* will be very strong.'

'I do not believe in *N'Gomas* or their *muti*. If you do not believe, it cannot affect you.'

'You are mistaken. The *muti* from the *N'Goma*, it works on all men, white, black, yellow, everyone. This *muti* here, it is made to keep someone out of the border of this land, and if you are from this area, it is probably you.'

'We can enter further south, away from this tree and its *muti*,' Tichawana said.

'I have seen this type of *muti* only once before, in Zambia, years ago. We tried to pass through an area, we never saw *muti* when we entered the area, but when we began walking, strange things happened.'

Tichawana raised his eyebrows. 'Strange?'

'A lion attacked us. He killed a man, and even though we shot it, it did not die. It was as if this lion was possessed, as if it was one of the Shona people's *Nehanda,* and the spirit was commanding the lion's body. We ran away, and the lion chased us, but it stopped at the tree where we had not seen the *muti,* and it would not pass further. It was as if it was inside the barrier and the *muti* hanging in that tree was the border.'

Tichawana said, 'But that would take a great *N'Goma* to perform such *muti,* and I know that the girl in this area was young when her teacher passed over to the other side, and she was left alone to learn her witchcraft.'

The Black Mamba shook his head. 'This is powerful *muti.* You can go over there and see if anything comes out of the bushes for you and die alone. Or you can come back with us, and we avoid this area. I am not ready to die today for revenge on your family. I will not cross this boundary to test the *muti*'s strength. You must have done some bad shit for them to put such strong *muti* here to keep you out. We will skirt this border and head southeast, towards Hwange instead.'

Tichawana didn't want to believe in the power of the *muti.* He shook his head and ran to the other side of the tree, and then took a few steps further into his father's lands.

There was no lion to greet him.

He turned to his comrades, laughing. 'Look, it does not work on me, it is not here for me. There is no lion here.' But as he said the words, he began to feel as if a million bees were stinging inside his stomach. He bent over and vomited. There was a red splash where he had spewed. Blood. His head was pounding as if someone was inside hitting a hammer on his brain, and his eyes streamed water.

Black Mamba swore. 'You are a fool.' He picked Tichawana up and ran back to the other side of the tree, out of the protected territory. 'Can you not understand that the *muti* works differently for different *N'Gomas?* So what if there is no lion in this one? Look at you. She made you sick. Very sick.'

Tichawana threw up again, only this time there was bile, no blood. The bees were no longer stinging his stomach and the *tokoloshe* in his head had gone.

He wiped his mouth.

'It is as I said, you cannot go into this area. Some very powerful people live here, and until they die, you will never get into this place. You can kiss your revenge goodbye.'

* * *

Tichawana's mind switched off the past as he stood under the spray of the shower, the scalding water on his back reminding him of his position today, and how far he had come since 1988, the day the *N'Goma* stood with his father when he had tried to return home, tried to enter his father's area, and had suffered his only defeat while taking part in the *Gukurahundi*, the cleansing of the Matabele people by their Shona president.

He had been repelled by the ancestors and his father.

Soon that would change. The old chief was dying, and then he would once again test the strength of the *N'Goma's muti*. His time to strike was fast approaching, and this time there would be no stopping him.

He switched off the shower and wrapped a white towel around himself. Walking into the bedroom, he saw three Korean women already sitting on the bed, naked except for the leather straps around their necks, each one padlocked to the heavy chains that tied them together. They had been expertly trained, and today he was looking forward to their services.

He wanted to forget about ivory shipments and rhino horns, and how much money he was making or not making in shipping these commodities at all. Today he wanted to lose himself in the softness of the women willing to service his every wish, no matter how perverted. He wanted to feel the blood run through his fingers, and know that they would remember forever that he had marked them as his.

And know that they would never be able to turn him away.

He owned them.

CHAPTER

13

Surprise Package

The sun had not yet risen when Joss walked into the kitchen. He'd heard Lwazi moving around so he knew he was awake. Joss grabbed his water bottle from the fridge before heading out to begin his warm-up, but as he stepped through the door, he almost fell over something in the way.

The basket was woven in a beautiful manner, and was obviously locally made from Zambezi green reeds. There was a lid covering the contents. In another land, Joss wouldn't have touched it. He couldn't have trusted that it wouldn't blow up.

Bongani came around the corner, carrying a coffee cup in one hand and a plastic carrier bag in the other.

'You know anything about this?' Joss asked, pointing.

Bongani shook his head. 'Give it a prod to make sure there is no snake in it.'

Joss nudged the basket with his foot. It moved a few centimetres, rocked, then toppled down the ramp and, without turning over, landed with a thud.

The basket began to scream. The shrill sound of a child woken from sleep, and now extremely unhappy.

'Oh my God,' Joss said.

'*Eish*,' Bongani said at the same time.

Before Joss could yank the lid off, a tiny black fist lifted it slightly. The screaming got louder.

'What the fuck?' Joss bent down to remove the top completely, and looked inside. He reached in and tried to pick up the child, but it squirmed away against the wicker, its eyes wide in terror, the crying increasing. 'It's okay, I'm not going to hurt you.'

He tried again. The child screamed even more and tried to hide itself under a *kaross* that was inside the basket with it.

He stepped back a little. 'You get it; it seems scared of me.'

Bongani stepped up to the basket. '*Thula thula, umntwana.*'

The child looked out from behind the skin, as if recognising the language.

'Ha, so you speak Ndebele.' Bongani reached in and picked up the white dummy he saw lying in the basket, shoving it into the child's mouth. The toddler began suckling while staring at Bongani with huge brown eyes.

'A few days ago you were lamenting that you didn't have any children. Guess the stork heard you.'

'Very funny,' Bongani said.

The child began to cry again. Bongani reached into the basket and grabbed the dummy once more, putting it into the child's mouth like a stopper. Carefully he put his hands under its arms and lifted it from the basket. He held it at arm's length. It was dressed in a little pink jersey top and long tracksuit pants.

'Hello there,' Joss said in Ndebele. 'Guess it's a girl.'

The baby looked at him. She sucked on her dummy as if her life depended on it.

'*Woza, umntwana,*' Joss said as he took the child gently from Bongani and held her against his shoulder. He bounced her a little, making soothing noises. The smell of the child reminded him of Afghanistan, of carrying children to safety away from IEDs, of wishing he could continue to carry them out of Helmand Province and away from the fighting altogether. The child stilled, hiccupped and moved slightly, then settled her head into his shoulder, as if lulled by his heartbeat.

'At least she is no longer screaming,' Bongani said. He took the basket and walked inside with it.

Joss followed.

In the dining room, Bongani took everything out of the basket – there were four cloth nappies neatly folded at the bottom, together with a second set of clothes, a bottle with a teat and a small tin of S26 formula. He turned the basket upside down and shook it as if there might have been a hidden compartment with more goodies in it.

'No note? Nothing to say who she is?' Joss asked.

Bongani shook his head.

'She has to belong to someone. Surely somebody will know something about her?'

Bongani humphed. 'In the meantime, what are we supposed to do with a child?'

'I don't know, and less of the "we" – she's certainly not mine.'

The child moved back from his shoulder, looking at him. Then she screwed up her face and began crying again. Joss rocked her, tried to give her the dummy, and patted her back.

She continued to scream.

'Maybe she's hungry?' Bongani suggested.

'Let's read those instructions and get some formula into her,' Joss said.

'You keep holding her; I will do the milk,' Bongani said, taking the tin and holding it at arm's length. 'Did they have to make the writing so small?'

Joss chuckled. 'You need glasses, old man. You take her for a minute and I'll make it.'

Bongani reluctantly took the baby. The crying stopped as she studied him.

Joss made the formula as per the instructions then when it was ready, he squirted it on his wrist.

'That is a small tin. Why are you wasting it?' Bongani asked.

'I saw the nurses in Afghanistan test the heat of the milk before they fed the orphans. I've had a little to do with babies during my military days – it's not all about shooting terrorists; it's also about humanitarian care.'

'Good. Then you can feed. You do know how to do a nappy when the milk comes out the other end?'

'Yeah, but I prefer disposables.'

'*Eish*. This is a woman's job. Charmaine would be good; she has a baby on her back most of the time, so she knows about these things.'

Joss took the child and put the teat in her mouth. Her small hands immediately wrapped around the bottle. He turned her and she settled into the crook of his arm.

'What is that noise?' Lwazi asked from the doorway. He stared at Joss. 'Where did the *umntwana* come from?'

'She was on the doorstep. Do you recognise her?'

'No, it does not look like Charmaine's. Her baby is fat, with big cheeks and rolls on his arms. That child is bigger than hers. Is it sick?'

'I don't know,' Joss said.

Lwazi frowned. 'You going to keep it?'

'She's a human; you can't pass her around like a parcel. We have to find her family,' Joss said.

'Why would someone give you guys a baby?' Lwazi asked.

'That is something we are going to have to find out. As soon as she finishes this bottle, we can go see if Charmaine minds if her duties here are changed a little. Actually, Lwazi, if you can go and fetch her from her house and ask her to come here,' Bongani said.

Lwazi nodded and left.

'At least she is quiet with that bottle,' Bongani said.

'For now,' Joss said, as the baby drained the last of the formula. 'But it won't last long. We'll need to take her into town to the Binga clinic; they'll know what to do with her.'

'You going to give her to someone else if you cannot find her parents?' Bongani asked.

Joss frowned. 'What else are we supposed to do with her? She isn't mine and she isn't yours. Besides, there must be some legal implications – we can't take someone's child. A doctor needs to look her over, make sure she's okay. Like Lwazi said, she's thin; she doesn't look like a healthy child.'

'She looks like any other child to me,' Bongani said, but he didn't touch her.

Joss smiled. 'Are you sure you want marriage and to have a son, Bongani, because you seem scared of this kid?'

'Scared is the wrong word for it, Joss. I would rather face a raging buffalo than hold that little girl again.'

Joss laughed. He looked down at the toddler, her bottle now empty. He put her back to his shoulder. Humanitarian training in the commandos hadn't all been in vain, he thought, as she rewarded him with a loud burp. He continued to give her reassuring pats on her back.

'Move my stool so I can sit on it. I don't want her to scream again if I move her.'

Bongani moved the furniture and Joss carefully manoeuvred himself onto the stool. The child didn't make a sound. He felt the wind through her padded bottom as she passed it, but nothing could have prepared him for the smell that followed.

He gagged. 'Oh my God,' he said, holding her away from him. 'How can something so small smell so bad?'

Bongani took a step backwards. 'I have no idea.'

Charmaine and Lwazi came through the door.

'Thank goodness,' Bongani said. 'We have a situation. The child, she has made a poo.'

'I can smell that, Bongani,' Charmaine said. He looked at her and she giggled. Despite her own baby strapped to her back, she put her arms out for the little girl. 'Whose baby is this?'

'We don't know. She was in a basket on the stoop,' Joss said.

'Someone gave you a child?'

'Not me,' Joss and Bongani said at the same time.

Charmaine shook her head. 'You are a couple of sissies. Come, little one,' she said and made cooing noises. 'Let us get you cleaned up and show these men that we girls, we stick together.' She took a nappy from the table. 'Where can I change her?'

'Bathroom. She smells like she needs a full bath,' Joss said.

Charmaine shook her head and muttered something about useless African men as she headed to the bathroom, followed by Joss, Bongani and Lwazi.

'I need a towel put on that counter,' she said, and Joss grabbed one out of the cupboard and spread it flat.

'No, put it in half, or even a quarter, as it is a nice big towel. She needs something soft to lie on.'

Joss did as she asked.

'I also need a toilet roll and a clean facecloth.'

Joss gave her both.

'Now please run the water and make the cloth warm, and I need a bucket.'

'A bucket?' Joss asked.

'To put the dirty nappy inside so that it can soak and then get washed.'

'I will get that,' Lwazi said as he fled the bathroom.

Charmaine put the baby on the folded towel. Then she pulled the tracksuit pants down so she could change the nappy.

'Oh Jesus,' she said, and made the sign of the cross.

Joss and Bongani looked at the baby.

'I guess now we know that this baby was given to me,' Joss said, staring at her badly deformed legs.

'Poor little girl,' Charmaine said, gathering her composure. 'It does not change things; she still needs a fresh nappy.' She undid the big safety pins holding the cloth together.

Joss gagged again.

Bongani turned his back and left.

Joss turned on the tap to get the water warm.

Tears dripped from Charmaine's eyes as she cleaned the toddler, and she sniffed. 'This is why this little one is so thin. The mother, she would have hidden this child away. It is an old custom that the Ndebele people do not show weakness. This little girl is not strong.

The mother was ashamed of her. If she did not give her to you, this child, she would probably have died. She would never be accepted into their society. She would be better to be dead.'

'But she's a child,' Joss said.

'Now, but when she grows she will be another mouth to feed who cannot help. She will be useless.'

Joss frowned. 'Even today, with medicine and everything?'

'Even more so today, because everyone is broke. A child who can help you plough and reap the harvest, they are welcome. One who cannot, they are shunned.'

Joss shook his head. 'How can they still be so cruel?'

'It is the way things are,' Charmaine said.

Joss sighed. 'I assumed no one would actually practise such a ritual any more.'

'That is life here. Perhaps when she is older, she will be used by the men and pay her way, but even then, someone would probably need to help her everywhere, and that would not happen. I can understand her mother giving her to you. She has seen your new legs when you have been here. She knows that you can give this child everything that she cannot, and this is her gift to her daughter: to give her to you, so that she can have a happier life than she could give her.'

'How can I look after a baby girl?' Joss asked.

'It is not my place to tell you what you must do, but as a mother, I know that she did not give her to you to abandon her. She has trusted you with her child, that you will stand by her when she cannot or could not any more. You need to take some time to have a good think about the future of this baby with you and without you.'

'But there are laws. Even in Zimbabwe there must be child welfare—'

'No one will care about a crippled child. If you give this little girl to the orphanages, she will die early, or when she is old enough, she will be on the street. No one will save her. No one except someone who understands what it is like to not have legs. Someone who can pay for her to get metal legs like you have.'

Joss stared at the toddler, who lay still on the table.

'You will need to get her some creams; she has a rash,' Charmaine said. 'I will look after her during the day, as her nanny, instead of being a cleaner in the lodge rooms, but please do not ask me to take this child into my home.'

'Would you be able to come into Binga with me to get her some supplies, and make a list of what else I need to get from Bulawayo?'

'Yes,' she said as she put the clean nappy on, and then carefully put the girl's deformed legs back inside the pink fabric and pulled up the pants. The baby sucked her fist.

Charmaine held her out, giving her back to Joss. 'Take her so I can clean up here. You need to name her; you cannot keep calling her "the child".'

Joss nodded.

'You should call her Nosipho; it means "gift",' Lwazi said, smiling from the doorway as he stood next to Bongani with the bucket.

'I'll think about it,' Joss said. 'How long till the next nappy change? It's thirty kilometres into Binga.'

'You can wait a long time at the clinic,' Charmaine said. 'It is better to get her more clothes, some waterproofs, a proper baby blanket before we go to the clinic. Not take her skins in there.'

'Can I come?' Lwazi asked.

Joss nodded. 'Check with your granddad that it's okay.'

Bongani still stood by the door, shaking his head.

'What?' Joss asked.

'Are you sure that you want to be involved with this child? I can take her to the clinic.'

Joss shook his head. 'I'll do it. It's the least I can do.'

His thoughts drifted to Peta, and he wanted nothing more than to share the news of the child needing a home with her. She was coming to visit him tonight, but it felt like years away instead of a couple of hours.

She was not going to believe that he had been given a baby girl.

* * *

'Sophia Leslie Yingwe,' the nurse called, and Joss stood up.

'Come on, Charmaine,' he said, and she leapt up and followed him. Lwazi stayed seated.

The nurse looked at him. 'Hello, Joss, long time no see.'

'Hey, Maggie,' he said. 'You're still here?'

'I am. I heard you'd come home. I'm so sorry to hear about what happened to you.'

'Thanks. I'd forgotten how fast the bush telegraph travels,' Joss said. 'This is Sophia's nanny, Charmaine, and her baby, Samson.'

Maggie nodded. 'I know Charmaine, and little Samson. What brings Sophia in today?'

He explained the situation, all the time holding Sophia on his shoulder. 'Do you happen to know this child, or anything about her mother?'

Maggie shook her head and put her arms out. 'Let's take a look at this little one.'

Sophia went to Maggie without any fussing, but her eyes were huge.

'Hello, Miss Sophia, nice to meet you.' Maggie moved to the changing table that was set up near the scale. She took Sophia out of her clothes and examined her.

'She has feelings in these legs,' Maggie said as she ran her fingers lightly over them, 'but I doubt she'll ever walk on them as they are. I would have said talipes equinovarus, club foot, but this seems to be worse than that – not only are her feet in the incorrect position, but she seems to have defects in the formation of her limbs too. She'll need a full examination, X-rays, an MRI to see what's going on in there before any proper diagnosis can be made. You'll need to take her into Bulawayo, maybe South Africa. See a paediatrician, preferably one who specialises in birth defects and skeletal corrections. This is interesting – she has thick calluses on her knuckles and on her legs. Have you seen her crawl? Move at all?'

'We've been carrying her the whole time.'

Maggie placed Sophia gently on the floor. Her legs folded at their own strange angle, forty-five degrees to her body and side-on to the floor instead of knees upwards, and she rested on her bottom. She sat very upright.

Maggie stepped back about a metre and knelt down. '*Woza, woza,*' she said and smiled, putting her arms out in a welcoming position.

Sophia looked at her uncertainly.

Charmaine took Samson and put him down next to Maggie.

Sophia put her little fists on the floor and used her arms to help steady herself as she hopped like a springhare on her bottom towards Samson and Charmaine.

'She can move,' Joss said.

'Kids are resilient and inventive. She's worked this out herself. Clever girl.' Maggie picked Sophia up and cuddled her, giving her a kiss on the forehead.

Joss nodded.

'I do need to do an HIV test. If she shows a positive indicator, will it make any difference to you?'

Joss frowned. 'I don't know, but I want to make sure she's alright while I decide what to do with her.'

Maggie nodded, and she gave Sophia to Joss to hold while she put on gloves and took a blood sample.

Sophia screamed at the needle.

'It'll take about half an hour.'

'We're not going anywhere.' He soothed Sophia, and wiped her tears away with a tissue. 'Come on, beautiful. It's okay. You're fine now. That one was for a special test. Come on, shh ...'

Sophia looked at him and hiccupped, and he put her dummy back in her mouth as she settled in his arms again.

Maggie put the blood sample in a dish and the needle in her sharps bin before she removed her gloves.

'Is she healthy, other than her legs?' Joss asked.

'If you're asking if she's also mentally handicapped, I don't think so. She seems fine. Alert. Her eyes follow perfectly, she listens and responds. I'm not sure why she doesn't talk, but that might be that she's shy. She needs more tests than I can do here to confirm that.

I think she's okay, a little underweight maybe, but then as I don't know her birth weight it's hard to say; she might have been a small baby. Unless you can find the mother, we'll never know. She looks to be about eighteen months old, looking at her teeth and size, so she will be at that stage when she's about to enter the terrible twos.'

'Great, so the mother gave her up as she starts to be hard work,' Joss said.

Maggie smiled. 'You don't know the circumstances as to why she left the child with you. Don't be so quick to judge.'

'I'm not judging—'

'Since you are undecided, I'm going to fill you in on a few things. Zimbabwe Welfare don't like black babies going to white families. Not without good reason. But in this case, it looks like the mother gave her to you, so if you can prove that you are a good father, there shouldn't be too much of a fuss. You would possibly get custody of her.'

'I understand that. Is there any way you know that we can find her mother?' Joss asked. 'I'd like to look for her first, give her a second chance with her baby.'

'If they bring their kids to the clinic, I see them. I haven't seen this child before, which means either she moved here after the birth, or she's kept Sophia hidden. I'm not going to do any of the vaccinations, in case she did them at another clinic. Until you can take her to Bulawayo and run proper tests, I don't want to stress her little body. Other than some nappy rash, which I see you already have cream on, she appears to be a healthy girl.'

'Perhaps I should look in at an orphanage in Bulawayo, see how they handle children with special needs there?'

Maggie nodded. 'Give yourself time; don't rush into anything.'

'I won't,' Joss said.

'Do you have everything needed for a toddler at home?' Maggie asked.

'Charmaine and I went shopping before we came here. I bought what we could locally, and I'll go into Bulawayo next week to get the rest.'

'Stop by Mrs Jenson's; she has some nursery furniture that she offered me last week and I haven't had a chance to collect. Take it, use it while you need it, then once you have made a decision either way, you can either keep what you want or you can bring it back to the clinic for another person who needs it,' Maggie said.

'Thanks, but—'

'No buts, Joss. You are going to need to accept help from people with this little girl while you have her. You have a lot on your plate. Having a child thrust into your life is not easy. Having a disabled child will mean extra challenges too. Go see Mrs Jenson. She'll love to be able to help you; it will make her feel needed.'

Joss nodded. 'I've only recently relearnt to be independent.'

'Phaaa … being part of a community isn't about being proud and hanging on to your independence, it's about learning when to let other people who need something in their lives help you with something in yours, even if you don't need help. It's not always about you.'

'Suppose you're right.'

'Let's take a look at Samson since he's here.' Maggie took Samson and examined him. 'He's putting on weight nicely; I'm very happy with his progress.' She looked back at Joss with Sophia on his shoulder. 'I take it you are employing Charmaine full time to look after Sophia?'

Joss grinned. 'As full time as she wants, but I do understand that she has her own family.'

Maggie smiled. 'Good to know.'

'You realise she's in the room and you are talking about her like she's not?' Joss said.

'Of course. That's why I'm saying it so that she can hear too. She would never ask you for anything; it's not her way. She might be our age, but her upbringing is old school.'

'I treat all my employees well, Maggie.'

'I've heard that. You know the bush talks, and since you've come home, they're all talking about you. That even with your steel legs you are still very strong.'

'I think the bush exaggerates,' Joss said.

* * *

They put the white wicker crib and rocking chair that Mrs Jenson gave him into his room. When Sophia was accustomed to the house, he could move her into one of the other bedrooms.

Sophia slept in the crib while he tried to make sense of the day. His head was spinning.

Bongani came and sat on the bed next to him. 'Your mother, she would have liked this, having a child in the house.'

Joss nodded. 'Taking on this little girl is not a light decision—'

'No kidding,' Bongani said.

Joss snorted. 'I tell you, the disposable nappies are so much easier than those cloth things, but they're going to bankrupt me. I'd no idea how much baby paraphernalia cost, and we didn't even buy that much of it.'

Bongani humphed. 'Do you remember Ndhlovy, when you were ten? You put all your energy into that elephant and I can see you have that same mindset now with Sophia. You want to do what is good for her. Letting that elephant go almost ruined you: you began to get into all sorts of mischief; you were in trouble all the time.'

'You think that I was in trouble because Ndhlovy left and went to live in the bush where she belonged?'

'You telling me differently?'

'Yes. Most of that trouble was because of Courtney. She was always braver than me, and I followed her lead and did everything with her. It was way more fun that way.'

'Ah, she was a wild cat, that one. I am sorry that she died and you were not here to wish her well on her crossing to the other side,' Bongani said.

'Me too. But I think perhaps this time, with this little girl, I will have a chance to be more like Ndhlovy's matriarch. I'll do what I need to for the good of Sophia.'

Bongani was nodding. 'I hope so, my friend, I hope so.'

14

Dames and Dust

The sign to Yingwe River Lodge could still be made out despite the failing sunlight. She tried her phone and to her surprise, there was a signal. She called Tsessebe's number, which rang once before he picked it up.

'Peta. You okay?'

'We're fine. We've just got to Joss's.'

'Good to hear.'

'The lion seems to have doubled back. Sixpence and the others are still following it.'

'I will let your father know,' Tsessebe said. 'Be sure to tell Bongani; he knows that park better than any other person, except maybe old Sixpence.'

'I will. Bye for now,' she said, ending the call.

Amos shifted in his seat.

'What?' she asked.

'This Joss, he is a good friend of yours, and you have talked of him often since he came back. He is a British Royal Marine Commando. A trained soldier.'

'When I was growing up, he was almost like a baby brother. Joss was my sister's best friend – his parents and mine, they had lots of history. To be honest, I can't believe that I've taken so many years to come back here after his parents died.'

The headlights shone through the gate. She slowly drove up to Joss's house and parked next to his *bakkie*. Joss came out the back door as she jumped down from her Hilux.

'Welcome to my humble abode.' He put his arms out and she stepped into them awkwardly. He wrapped his arms around her and held on tightly. 'Hello, Peta,' he said, close to her ear.

She could feel the goose bumps forming on the back of her neck. 'Hey, Joss, it's great to be here after so long.' She cleared her throat as she stepped back; her body's weird reaction she would examine alone later. 'This is Amos.'

'Good to meet you at last,' Joss said. 'Come on in. We've had an interesting day, and I think you will be surprised. Amos can meet Bongani …'

'I know Amos,' Bongani said from behind him, and they shook hands.

Peta smiled. 'I'd love to freshen up a bit, get to look a little bit more like a tourist for the weekend and less of a khaki worker. Amos and I jumped in the *bakkie* after breakfast, so we're starved. When's dinner, Joss? You did remember the warthog pie?'

'As if I'd forget. But before I walk you to your room, you need to meet Sophia,' Joss said.

'Sophia?' Peta took her small overnight case and three plain *knopkieries* from Amos. 'Who's Sophia?'

'A baby that I was given this morning.' Joss put his hand out to take her case but she shook her head.

'A baby what?' Peta asked.

'Human. She's more of a toddler.'

Peta frowned. 'You have a baby? Biologically?'

'No! She was put on my doorstep in a basket.'

'You got given a child? Why?'

'She's got crippled legs, so I guess her mum thought she would be better off with me.'

'That's terrible.' Peta put her hand over her heart. 'How are you going to tell her when she's older that her mother abandoned her? How are you going to explain that she was given to you because she was deformed?'

Joss shrugged. 'I don't know.'

'How old is she? Is she pretty? Don't answer that last one, it's a stupid question ...'

'She's beautiful, a little on the thin side, but she's quiet, unless she's hungry, then she's very loud. I'm not sure how something so small can be so noisy.'

'I'm lost for words!' Peta said.

Joss laughed. 'I must warn you, she stinks when it's nappy time. Charmaine said it's because her diet wasn't so great.'

'I'm a vet, Joss, I think I can handle a little kid's poo.'

'I'm betting ten bucks you can't.'

'The bet is on. I want to see a royal marine changing nappies.' She laughed.

'All part of the job description.'

They dumped the bags in the kitchen and moved into the lounge, where Sophia sat safe in a playpen, surrounded by soft toys.

'Do you want to hold her?' Joss asked.

'Me? No. I love the idea of kids, but they don't love me.' She stepped back so that he couldn't do what so many of the women in the camp did when they had babies, pass her their offspring, saying that she would be a natural if she just gave it a chance. 'They always scream when I hold them; it's like they know I'll drop them or something ...'

'They are no different to a young animal, or a sick baby monkey, and I know you've nursed plenty of those.'

'Not quite the same. They don't have possessive parents who would never forgive you if you drop them,' Peta said, shaking her head.

Joss frowned. 'Okay.'

She watched Sophia playing with her toys and eventually reached over the small fence and touched her face. 'Hello there, Sophia. Aren't you so beautiful,' she cooed. 'Oh, Joss, she's so sweet.'

'Wait until she farts. Then see if you still think so.'

Peta laughed and continued stroking the baby's cheek.

'She's due her night-time bottle and bed. Give me a second and I'll be right back,' Joss said. 'Make yourselves at home.'

He returned, shaking a bottle of formula. He picked up Sophia and then sat in the lounge chair and fed her in the crook of his arm, as if he'd been doing it all his life.

Peta sat on the couch. 'It's quite overwhelming that you've been given a child.'

Bongani laughed. 'I think that is how we all feel at the moment, so welcome to the club.'

Sophia finished the bottle and let rip with a loud burp.

Peta looked at her. 'Did that really come out of something so small?'

*   *   *

Sophia was sleeping at last. She had been fussing in Joss's arms, then she curled against him and was asleep. Even moving her into the crib in his room hadn't disturbed her. This toddler slept like the dead.

'Take Peta and Amos to their rooms. I'll stay with her,' Bongani said. 'You should join them for dinner. I'll eat with my dad later.'

'Come on, I'll show you the way,' Joss said, standing up.

They walked through to the kitchen to collect their bags. Peta picked up her three *knopkierie*s.

'Strange luggage, that,' Joss said as he took her case and stepped out the door.

'It's for if we come across the man-eating lion,' she said.

Joss shook his head as he led the way down the path, walking carefully in the low light, even though the lanterns he'd installed were on. 'You have access to all the tranquilliser guns in the world and real guns to defend yourself with, and you chose a stick?'

'Never underestimate what a *knopkierie* can do.'

Joss laughed. 'You are good for the soul, Peta.'

Amos was laughing behind her. 'She is playing you. Tsessebe asked us to get one of your guys here in the village, Julian Seziba, to carve them for Rodger. Apparently, his walking sticks are looking a bit dry and Tsessebe wanted new ones made. Julian is the best woodworker in this region.'

'I didn't know that,' Joss said.

Amos said, 'I will sort this with him tomorrow.'

They walked a little down the path towards the lodge and then stopped.

'This is your room, Amos; Peta is in the next rondavel along. See you in about half an hour – is that enough time?'

Amos nodded.

Joss opened the door of the Shangaan Suite for Peta and she walked in. Each lodge had been decorated differently, either portraying a tribe of Zimbabwe or a bird native to the area. The Shangaan Suite had been one of Leslie's favourites when she decorated it. Unlike the Livingstone Suite that Amos was occupying, which was packed full of antiques and old travelling cases to depict the colonial lifestyle of Livingstone's era, this one was decorated in all the colours and patterns of the Shangaan people: bright oranges and burnt browns, with grass mats and simple wooden furniture with *riempies* strung into the seats. There were big paintings on the walls too, of pots and silhouettes of black women walking on a road, carrying water on their heads. The picture had always called to Joss when he was a kid, made him want to join in the walk.

The small lounge area opened onto a patio area, which held a small plunge pool, and off that was an open-air bathroom, which faced the cliff and the lake; secluded but natural. Even in here his mother had kept the vibrant colours of the Shangaan with big glass double basins and a green bath.

The bedroom was huge, with a king-size bed dominating it. A heavy four-poster, its posts were carved with pictures depicting Shangaan life, and its drapings in faded hues of purple, orange and turquoise. The room had a large grass and leather mat on the floor, which enhanced the effect of being old world and yet belonging to a nation. The bedspread was tie-dyed orange, blue, green and yellow.

Peta heaved her case onto the bed. 'Thanks. Now I'm going to use that outdoor shower, and then I'll meet you in the dining room.'

'Sure,' Joss said, as he turned to walk out. 'Peta, I wanted to say thanks for coming; I'm so glad you're here.'

'Me too,' Peta said.

*   *   *

Early Saturday morning, Peta stood on the deck of *The Ladies' Plan*, looking at the lake. The wind whipped her hair all over the place but she didn't care.

Bongani and Amos had plans to disappear into the village later, looking for Julian to carve the *knopkieries*, and Charmaine was watching over Sophia – Lwazi had insisted on helping her. When Joss had suggested they go out on the lake, Peta had jumped at the chance. Now, skimming over the water as Joss piloted the catamaran with the natural abilities born of growing up around boats, she felt a little like a water nymph.

'I think that bay over there looks good; we can try for some tiger fish,' Joss said as they came around a small island.

'Perfect.' She paused. 'How are the nightmares?'

'They're still there, but not every night. Lwazi wakes me like I showed him. Actually, the first time I had one, he had his grandfather's walking stick, and was poking me harder and harder with it: "Joss, wake up. Wake up, Joss!"' he said, mimicking Lwazi perfectly.

Peta snorted, then stopped herself. 'I shouldn't laugh at that.'

'I know, but it was like something out of a comic book. He was too scared to shake me and then step away like I'd shown him to do. I think I had bruises from him having to poke so hard. He's got a bit braver now, shakes me quickly and steps away, which is a lot less painful. I'm lucky he's a light sleeper.'

'Lucky for all of you.'

They lapsed into silence for a while. Then Joss said, 'Bongani thinks I should get a dog. He's convinced that something like a Labrador or a German shepherd, or even a ridgeback like my mum used to have, would be good company while I'm around the lodge and when I go running, for days when Lwazi can't be with me. He seems to think it would wake me up when I need it too, quicker than Lwazi can get to my room, so the nightmares wouldn't get as bad.'

'There's a place in South Africa that could help you with a dog like that. They're pre-screened for good temperament, obedience, socialising skills and their ability to interact with people with different types of problems. Some are really good with physical disabilities, like one I heard of that was paired up with a disabled child. When the dog met him, he licked his toes in greeting, then sat next to him, forcing his hand to touch his coat. He would lick the little hand every now and again, and continued sitting there. Then the small boy turned his hand and gripped the dog's fur. This was the first time the child had ever shown any emotional response, as well as a conscious control of his muscles, and he did this every time the dog sat near him. I have also heard of dogs for older people that can be trained to pick up remote controls that fall on the floor, open the fridge, even wake people from PTSD night-mares. Bongani's right. It's a great idea. You'll be given a slightly older puppy, but they'll help you train it. I can put you in touch if you want?'

A cormorant flew past them and settled on the top of the mast. It surveyed the surrounds, looking for its next meal. 'I'll think about it,' Joss said. 'Especially now that I have Sophia.'

'You do that. In the meantime, I'm fishing.' Peta disappeared into the hatch, returning with two rods.

Joss grinned. 'Guess it's time to drop the anchor.' He attended to the setting of the catamaran so she wouldn't drift onto the rocks, then lifted the small bucket and tackle box next to him. 'Bring those rods.'

They moved to the bow, where the soft lattice ropes made a comfortable cradle to lie on. He took the meat from the bucket and baited her hook for her.

'Here you go. Your *gillie* has done well, madam?' Joss mocked.

She laughed and took the rod from him. 'And a great looking *gillie* you are too. You could be a bit friendlier with the guest, but you are forgiven for that. What would I do without you here? I still hate that part, and am forever grateful for anyone who baits the hook and guts the fish and does anything related to fishing. I'm glad that all I get to do is bring it in. Thanks.' She cast off the starboard side and he did the same off the port. For a time they sat on the lattice, holding their rods, listening to the sounds from the water, the silence between them comfortable.

The cormorant flapped its wings and put them out to dry, squawking.

Peta let out a sigh. 'Ah, how did I let so much time pass before coming and enjoying this again?'

'Life tends to get in the way of these little pleasures.'

'Your dad used to say that all the time. I remember when you found Ndhlovy. I was dreading Christmas because it was the first without my mum, then Aunty Leslie called my dad for help, and we came over. You had that tiny elephant, and were so determined to save it.'

'I remember.'

'That little elephant made me major in large animals in my degree.'

'Really?'

'Absolutely. She was the best thing that happened at that time. I was so lost.' She spun her ring around her finger. 'Then we saved her. And the matriarch and One-Tusk, the baby's mother, came, and needed help. It got me thinking about the social interaction necessary for a herd, how they never got close to us, but accepted our help anyhow.'

'She brought them back. When I was fourteen. One morning, they plodded into the lodge. It was as if One-Tusk needed the extra nourishment from the moringa trees to feed her new baby again. Ndhlovy was bigger, naughty. She still interacted with me more than the others, but the matriarch kept calling her away when I tried to play with her.'

'Dad told me they'd returned. I was deep in exams then. I wish I could've visited to see her again.'

'My dad said she came again the year I left for the marines. He said she'd walked around the lodge looking for me, and kept going to the back door, waiting. Something she'd never done before.'

'That's so sad.'

'At the time I didn't think anything of it. But when I was in Afghanistan, I would use the memory of her visits as a reason to keep going. Knowing that if I didn't make it, she would forever be visiting and looking for me. I couldn't let that happen. I had to come home to her and, the next time she visited, show her that I was okay and that I was alive.'

Peta reached out and touched his arm. 'If she's what helped you stay alive, I'm glad you knew she looked for you.'

'Me too. My dad used to always tell me that they couldn't stay; it was time for them to continue their journey – just because they chose to visit us didn't mean Ndhlovy belonged to me. It meant that as a free animal, she chose to be my friend. He never understood that it was never about possession of her, more that I liked knowing she was doing okay as she grew older, that I'd helped her. That's all I wanted to do in the marines. Make a difference. In the end, I'm not so sure we made any difference at all.'

'I'm sure you did, even if you couldn't measure it.'

'Perhaps.'

'You know, I did a paper on her when I was in uni, and the lecturer questioned everything about it, wanting to know how I knew they had a structure with such a small herd, and that they were intelligent enough to get help. It was a heated discussion, because

I could back it from experience, and he hadn't seen anything like that.'

'I can imagine you giving stick to your lecturer. You were so good at telling Courtney and I what to do.'

'I wasn't! I just didn't want you guys in constant trouble,' Peta protested.

'You were no fun. Good to see you've improved over the years,' he joked.

'Oh, I improved heaps, Joss Brennan! So did you.'

Joss looked over the water. 'What happened with your paper?'

'The lecturer came around. Actually, he's taken to visiting me every July semester break, coming up to work at Matusadona as a volunteer.'

'He's probably got khaki fever around you,' Joss said jokingly.

'It's not like that at all. He brings his wife, and they help with game counts and at the rhino research centre. He and I have talked about Ndhlovy and if I would recognise her, and if she would ever interact with humans again, now that she is grown. He says I should try to find her, do another paper ...'

'I often wonder where she is now. If she made it into adulthood,' Joss said.

'I'm convinced that she would recognise us. I often look at the elephants in the national park and call out her name, seeing if any of them react. I'm almost certain that if she came back, she would know us. You especially. But I like to think me too.'

'We can only hope. When I was in the desert getting my arse shot at, I used to close my eyes and see her, free in the Chizarira, perhaps with a baby herself. I would know that she was still waiting for me to come home.'

'It must have been terrible out there. Not what you thought you were going to be doing at all.'

'It wasn't how I'd dreamt of it, but it wasn't terrible. If I had the chance, I would do it all again. I would go back and fight without hesitation.'

Peta's rod jumped in her hand and the spinner ran.

'You hooked one,' Joss said, as Peta moved to the fibreglass part of the deck and stood up. He wound in his line so that her fish wouldn't get tangled in it. Soon she had landed a fat tiger fish, and Joss reached for it with the net, bringing it up onto the deck of the catamaran.

'Careful of its teeth,' Joss warned as he held its slippery body and took it out of the net, angling it slightly away from her.

'Hell, I don't remember them having such big ones,' Peta said.

'It's a good size. Take it to eat or toss it back?'

'Toss it back,' Peta said.

The beautiful striped fish bit the line, and Joss let the wriggling creature go. The fish flip-flopped on the deck, then fell over the edge and into the water, its jaws still trying to bite anything it could get at.

Peta and Joss stared over the side after it was lost in the ripples its splash had created.

'I'm getting a drink; you want one?' Peta asked.

'Sure, grab me whatever you're having,' he said. 'I'll rig up the shade cover or do you want to suntan?'

'Shade is good. It's going to be a hot one,' Peta called as she disappeared into the galley.

Joss unfurled the tarp and soon had it secured in place. Peta returned and handed him a bottle.

'Cheers,' he said, clinking his bottle against hers.

'Here's to a new chapter for us all,' Peta said. 'Yours. Mine. Little Sophia's. Whatever they might hold.'

'I'll drink to that.'

'You know, I'm still in shock, but Sophia's beautiful and if anyone can handle a little girl, it's you, Joss.'

'I'm not so sure. I'm thinking of paying the Australian-run orphanage in Bulawayo a visit, seeing what it's like.'

'You going to give her to an orphanage?'

Joss frowned. 'I need to see what it's like there. Make sure that I'm doing the right thing by her.'

'When you go to the orphanage, I can come with you if you like?'

'I'd like that.'

'The orphanages are full of children whose parents have died. Many of the children are HIV positive now too. It's a sad situation.'

'Sophia's initial test said she was clear. And having lots of parentless kids is nothing new.'

Peta took a deep breath, then blew it out. 'If you don't want Sophia, would you consider me taking her? I would rather see her have a home with one of us than go into an institution, and I feel like I've missed the boat in the kids department. I'm thirty-two years old, and there are no prospects on the horizon. No one is going to accept me and my dad as a package deal, and I'm not prepared to get a turkey-baster baby from a stranger somewhere.'

Joss looked at Peta. 'Your father would freak if you brought home a black child. He's the biggest racist out, or at least he used to be.'

'Worse since the war vets tried to kill him. Even so, I don't know how long I'll have him with me. Between the damage from that bullet and his Alzheimer's, I lose a little more of the man he was every day.'

'I'm so sorry about that, Peta.' Joss laid a hand on her arm.

She smiled at him and didn't pull away. 'It's hard sometimes, but what if he reacts positively to having a kid around the place, and it awakens something inside him? It could be a good change.'

'It could. But she'll be with us until at least the first few weeks into the New Year, so why not bring your dad and Tsessebe and join us for Christmas? Then we can see his reaction to her.'

Peta moved her arm until the back of her hand touched Joss's. 'Why do you think that you're incapable of looking after Sophia?'

'I'm a disabled single male,' Joss said. 'I live in a safari lodge in the middle of nowhere. She should have better than me as a father. She needs a family group.'

'You're coping with your disability; she will too. The only difference is she has you to help her along. You have Charmaine, and all the other workers in your lodge. How's an orphanage going to be more homely than what you can give her?'

'She'll need to know about her customs, her roots,' Joss said, turning her hand over in his and threading his fingers through hers.

'You live in the ideal place for Sophia to learn all about those. It's not as if you're planning on taking her overseas, where she won't have anyone to tell her. She'll have plenty of people to help her with customs.'

Joss looked out at the water. 'I don't know anything about bringing up a child except what I read.'

Peta laughed and squeezed his hand. 'Neither does any other parent.'

'I guess one of my main worries is that welfare will take her from me because I'm white. So rather than have them come and take her and put her where they want, I want the chance to choose a place that I could visit, where I can keep an eye on her, one that is up to my standards. I want to have that choice before they take her away from me totally.'

'Oh, Joss. Everything you have said pales in comparison to that. Welfare would be stupid to take her from you when you're the one who can afford to have her. I'm sure that the chances of them interfering in her life if you choose to keep her are very slim. You already support so many in the area.'

Joss pulled his hand out of Peta's and looked out at the water.

'You okay?'

'No, not really,' he said quietly. 'When Ndhlovy walked away from me into the bush to live her life, I thought that my heart would break. I thought I was losing her forever. It was like someone had a spoon and was trying to take my heart out of my chest with it. Now I know I didn't understand what real loss felt like. I hurt so much when my parents were killed in that car crash. I was lost, empty. Directionless. Real loss shattered my heart. But I was employed by the military, so I had a purpose set out for me. I buried that pain deep down inside, and I continued with my job, knowing that accidents happen.'

'Oh, Joss ...' Peta put her arm over his shoulders and pulled him close to her. Slowly his arms came around her too. She shifted her weight and looked up into his face. 'It's okay, Joss. What are you thinking? You know you can tell me anything ...'

'I loved your sister, she was my best friend, and she was taken from me. After that happened, I swore that no woman would ever cause that type of pain in my heart again. When Courtney died, I was spaced out on drugs, but later, when the realisation that she was gone hit, I hurt. I hurt so bad that at one stage I didn't want to get better, I wanted to be left to die. It's not that I'm scared of death – I've seen enough of it to know that you can never escape it in the long run. Everyone dies. It's living that's so hard.

'It's the pain that comes with caring that I'm shit scared of. Of letting someone else into my life who will be taken away from me, because everyone I love seems to die. My parents. Courtney. I loved them and they were taken away.

'What if I keep Sophia and love her like she deserves, and something happens to her too? I don't know if I could survive that. I'm already in too deep emotionally with her to give her away. I knew on the very first day that she was wriggling into my heart, and I was beginning to care for her. I can't leave her at an orphanage, no matter how nice it is. I already knew that I wanted to keep her when she arrived on my doorstep, but I have to make sure that's what's best for her, not what's best for me.'

Peta smiled. 'You can't control life. You can't control what happens to other people, but as a father, you can control what happens to Sophia. And you know what? You're a survivor, Joss. If, God forbid, something happened to her, you would survive. It would be your life spent with her that would help you accept that hurt and make it part of you, and carry on. Because in remembering your folks and my sister, they live on. In your heart and in mine, and in the memories of anyone who knew them too. You have to live life and continue to experience it fully. You can't stop loving people in case it hurts you. That's an unhealthy attitude to have.'

Joss shook his head. 'I know.'

'This is about giving Sophia a loving home. Being her dad. Of course there'll always be a risk, but if she was your biological child, those risks would still be there.'

'Like I said, irrational. But who's to say that I'm what's best for her? She doesn't get to choose.'

'Biological fathers don't get to make the choice for their child. Their children don't get that luxury either. You're lucky. Sophia needs you in her life, Joss, but only you can decide if you need her.'

He was quiet before he looked at her and smiled. 'My choice is already made. We're already family, Sophia and I, but I still need to follow up with that orphanage, as a back-up plan. I have to make sure I'm doing what is right for her, putting her needs above mine.'

Peta put her forehead against his. 'You'll be an amazing dad.'

'If something happens to me, would you consider being Sophia's legal guardian?'

'In a heartbeat,' Peta whispered. She hugged him to her. Of all the scenarios she had dreamt about as a kid, never had they included being in Joss's arms on *The Ladies' Plan*, talking about Sophia and families. The thought sent shivers across her chest and into the bottom of her stomach.

'You do know that thirty-two isn't old for a woman. You're not an old maid yet.'

Peta pulled away. 'I know, but can you imagine trying to fit an ordinary man into my life? I live in the bush and travel whenever there's a hurt animal. No matter what plans I make, they always get disrupted because some elephant or rhino needs me. He'd feel second place in my life. Besides, I can't ever move from my home, or leave my dad. He might live for another twenty or even forty years, and every day I'll be reminding him who I am. If I bring a new man into the fold, he would get even more confused. It's never going to happen.'

Joss stared out across the water. 'You could still meet someone with the same interests as you.'

'And move to their farm? Be tossed off by war vets? I don't think so.' She shook her head.

'There are other countries. You do get visitors passing through the park – plenty of opportunity to let them fall in love with the khaki chick.'

Peta shook her head. 'I'm happy that you came home. At least now I have a friend close by again.'

'I'm grateful for that too.'

'I want to show you something.'

'Cloak and dagger stuff?' Joss said.

'A little. It was on the computer that I took from the camp where the lion killed that man, Kenneth Hunt.'

'You stole evidence?'

Peta shook her head. 'I told Gideon Mthemba, Amos's cousin who's the member in charge at Binga, that I needed that computer after the police had taken Kenneth Hunt's body and everything out of the park, because I didn't want the animal information sold to anyone. He was happy for me to hold on to it for a while. They had another body to collect in the lands east of the park that day and were worried about it being stolen.'

She disappeared downstairs and came up with the backpack she'd brought on board. She took out a folder and unfolded an A3 page. 'This map was one of the files that were open on his computer.' She passed the map to Joss and pointed. 'This is the place near where we found Kenneth's body. I think that Kenneth has something to do with my white crosses.'

'What white crosses?' Joss asked.

'There are crosses scattered across both the Matusadona and Chizarira. Some have names on them, others are too old and I can't read them. Most are white, or were once white, but some are too old to tell. I always thought that they were pioneer graves, so I started making a list of them, plotting them out to see where they all were and if they were connected.'

Joss lifted his eyebrows. 'That's a tad weird.'

'It's our heritage. If I had the names and information down, then if one got damaged at least there would be a record of what it said.'

'What is so significant about them?' Joss asked.

She pointed to the map. 'This grave on this *koppie* is old and I have no name recorded against it in my office. Only now, it has a new cross on it, with a name and date to match that on the map. I think that Kenneth replaced the old cross with a new one.'

'Why would he do that?'

'I don't know. But it doesn't excuse that he was spotting in our park. I know that some of the spreadsheets were counting our game and tracking them through the area. But this map doesn't fit into that category at all; it's all about graves, not game distribution. If Kenneth could find this old grave on a map like this, he probably knew the bush well.'

She passed him a second map, more detailed than the first, with latitudes and longitudes marked on it clearly. 'This was also on his computer, and this map highlights a more serious problem for me and the parks. With the use of a GPS system, anyone could follow a map like this, enter our parks and find any place on his spreadsheets. They don't even need to know the bush well. Nothing will be safe inside our fences.'

'And both these maps were on his computer?'

Peta nodded. 'I worry about who will come to take his place in the bush now Kenneth Hunt is dead. I put everyone on high alert because, from this, I think that we can probably expect a poaching attack soon in the area he was surveying.'

'Have you asked around about him?'

'No. I didn't want to draw attention to the park or to me.'

'That's probably a good decision. You said you had his computer still?'

'I do. I could access a lot of spotter files, which I printed off to study, but there are a few folders on it that appear to be password protected, which is strange, because there was no password to get onto his computer when I started it up.'

Joss downed the last of his drink. 'You think he's hiding something?'

'I don't know. I hope not, because it's not like we can ask him. There are twenty-five crosses marked on this map. Not all of them are in the park; they're all over the country.'

Joss smiled. 'You know, I have friends who could spend some time on getting into those protected files. We could give it a try before you have to give it over to the police. Do some digging in his computer, see if there is anything else to explain those crosses. Have you had time to do an internet search on this Kenneth Hunt?'

'I tried. I couldn't find anything.'

'We aren't known for being front runners in technology here in Zimbabwe, are we? I forget that sometimes,' Joss said.

'So you don't think I'm nuts, following this through? Finding out more about this dead spotter and why he was upgrading the crosses?'

'No. This man was trespassing in your park. Your home. You have every right to ensure that you, your staff and your animals are safe.'

CHAPTER
15

Friends

Chaos reigned supreme at Victoria Falls airport as people exited the plane. Joss had to laugh, because despite Zimbabwe Airlines being late, the ground staff were on a go-slow over Chinese migrant workers being brought in to construct the new international terminal.

Joss watched as Marine Mitchell 'Mitch' Laski bounced down the steps, always the clown, despite being a bit older than the others in their unit when they had been thrown together in commando training at Lympstone in the UK. Joss knew that Mitch would take a little time to get his luggage and have his visa issued. He also knew that they would take more time clearing his sports rifles.

Now that Joss was living at Yingwe River Lodge full time again, and Sophia needed to be watched over, at least for a while, the chances of him going back to England had gone from maybe to zero. He hadn't been surprised when Mitch had said he was coming for a visit and followed through this time. His marine friends had said they wanted to visit Africa so many times before, but somehow they had never got around to doing it as a group during their time off. Joss wondered why.

He grunted. He knew the reason.

He was an idiot before. Being young, he'd thought that there was always time enough to visit Zimbabwe another day; they had visited cities like Bangkok, Beijing and Utsjoki in Lapland instead. They were going to get around to visiting Africa – one day. To him, there was time enough to do so many things later, but things were different now that he knew he was not indestructible. And it seemed to be the same for Mitch, as he had got on a plane and was now on Zimbabwean soil.

Finally, people began to spill from customs and immigration into the main area of the airport.

'Mate!' Mitch said, pulling him into a bear hug.

'Welcome to Zimbabwe.'

Mitch stepped back. 'You're looking good.'

'I am,' Joss said as he grabbed one of the bags Mitch had put on the floor. 'Hold your luggage; it'll grow legs if you don't.'

Mitch laughed and took hold of the handle. Despite pushing a trolley, he still had luggage that spilled over.

'You must have paid a mint for extra weight.'

'Gifts from everyone, for you and your kid, and shit for your lodge. Damo sent you a new fucking laptop because he said you need a better one with more power to stay connected out in the sticks. Cricket insisted I bring some cooking thing that does everything, so yeah, I have lots of shit.'

'Tell me the laptop is in your hand luggage or we can kiss it goodbye,' Joss said.

'That it is. One of your customs officers wanted to know why I had two computers, and I told him I was a researcher. He looked at my other equipment and shrugged, asked if it was all on the import list, and I said yes, so he stamped the paper and I was allowed to leave. He was more interested in the computers than in my weapons.'

'Lucky,' Joss said as they walked through the doors.

The heat hit Mitch like a freight train. 'It's as hot as the outback.'

Joss smirked, knowing Mitch's upbringing was in Sydney, filled with sea, surf and beaches. 'And you spent so much time in the outback?'

'I didn't say I'd spent time there. I've watched the weather report, mate, it's hot there. Like this.'

Joss laughed and guided Mitch to his *bakkie*. They loaded his bags, putting the electronic stuff in the front, and drove north towards Binga.

'I saw the falls when we were coming in; they look spectacular.'

'You sure you don't want to spend a few days in the area before you come north?'

'You crazy? I'll have plenty of time to do that. I want to get back to your lodge, crawl into bed and sleep for two days. Too many parties before I left—'

'It's about a four-and-a-half-hour drive, so you're welcome to put your head back and sleep,' Joss said.

'And miss the sights?'

'Bush and more bush,' Joss said. To make a liar of him, they travelled for about fifteen minutes before Joss had to slow down for animals on the road.

'What's that?' Mitch asked.

'Impala. They're everywhere. You'll get used to them real fast.'

'They're kind of like our kangaroos, all over the place?' Mitch said as he put his phone out the window and took a photograph.

A car blasted its horn behind them, and the impala all scattered.

'Idiots,' Joss said as he began driving slowly through where the impala had been as a minibus taxi flew past him, the heavy beat of music blasting through the open windows polluting the tranquil scene.

'This is what driving here is like?' Mitch asked.

'You mean the impala or the fool? We have animals on the road all the time, so you can't speed. Donkeys, mostly, as you get into the more rural areas, but you need to watch out for the wild game.'

Mitch nodded.

'You got anything you want to do while you're here?' Joss asked.

'I'd like to go see some of the game parks. I've heard about this rhino sanctuary in Matu-something-or-other that I want to visit so I can check out their volunteer program.'

Joss laughed. 'Matusadona. It's a game park north of us. My friend Peta is one of the researchers and vets. Ask her if you want to go spend some time there.'

'Cool.'

'When are you due back at headquarters?'

'I've taken a year's leave of absence. After this last tour in Afghanistan, I don't know if I want to go back. We always said, "third time's a charm," then you got taken out, and Cricket and I still went back for another round. I think going again might be like holding an armed grenade. I don't know what else to do, though. I love being a soldier, but I don't want to get killed. A bit of a dilemma there.'

'Teach at the academy?'

'About as exciting as watching paint dry. Death by boredom.'

'You're welcome to stay as long as you want. I have a big house, so you won't be in the way, but I do live in the middle of nowhere. It's not a decision you want to make in a hurry. Sometimes having a bit of space, quietness and nothing to do is what you need to unwind and see the future clearly.'

'Space and quietness. I'm looking forward to the downtime,' Mitch said. 'Maybe I should get a vehicle while I'm here?'

'Use one from the lodge. They're just sitting there now that most of the game has gone from the area. We use them to collect guests from Binga and Vic Falls if they need it, but that's about it.'

'Beaut.'

Joss stopped again.

'Shit!' Mitch exclaimed. 'Look at those elephants. They're huge.'

Two large bulls crossed the road. One turned his head towards the *bakkie*, shook it and flapped his ears.

'Is he going to charge us?' Mitch said.

'He's just curious.'

They sat watching the elephants as they decided to walk down the opposite side of the road rather than cross.

'They certainly are a sight to behold,' Mitch said.

Joss put his elbows on the steering wheel. 'Those're actually some decent-size tusks on the front one. I hope he gets lost in the bush quickly.'

'Is that about the size they hunt them for trophies, then?'

'Unfortunately there's no size limit. They can hunt them with small or large tusks. Larger's obviously better. This old guy would be a prize ...'

'Who would want to kill something so majestic?' Mitch said.

'Hunters pay big money for the privilege. A single elephant will feed a small rural village through a drought season if they dry the meat and keep it well enough. Poachers wouldn't blink twice before taking him down to sell the ivory on the black market. To many of the people here, the wild animals are just another commodity.'

CHAPTER
16

Precious Time

Bongani stood next to his father, holding the cup to his lips. 'Father, you need to drink.'

'I am not thirsty. Just because I am old and weak does not mean I do not know what I need. And that nurse you have watching me, she gave me tea not even ten minutes ago.'

'She told me that you hardly touched it,' Bongani said, putting the glass on the locker and sitting himself next to his father on the bed.

'That is because she gave me a cup not even half an hour before.'

'It is hot; you need fluids.'

'I have drunk enough. If I drink any more I will spend all night going to the toilet. I love the night sky but I prefer watching the sunshine dance on the bush to the night creatures.'

'At least eat your dinner. I brought you some warthog pie. Yedwa made it especially for you when I told him I was visiting today.'

'You visit every day,' Chief Tigere said.

'He cooks something special each time – he misses seeing you walking around. Joss asked if he could come over and visit, bring little Sophia to see you. He seems to be a natural with that child.'

'I am very tired tonight. Joss can bring her tomorrow. You need to write a letter of support to the Welfare Department so that I can sign it before I cross over. If he decides to keep Sophia, they will think he bribed you into it. A letter from me, they will accept.'

'I will do that later tonight and you can sign it in the morning and Joss can visit another time.'

Bongani smiled as he opened the cooler. The plates were covered with silver dishes and wrapped in large dishtowels, keeping the heat in. Putting the plates on the table across his father's sick bed, he lifted the lids and inhaled the aroma.

'That smells like your mother's cooking,' Chief Tigere said.

'I remember when she and Leslie Brennan made this recipe together, both of them in the kitchen, trying to blend the colonial and the native worlds into one dish.'

'They were both special ladies.'

Bongani cut the pie on his father's plate into little pieces.

'I think I will try to feed myself.'

'You sure? It is no bother to help you.'

'I am old, not dead yet. Crank up this bed further so I can eat my own dinner.'

Bongani smiled again. Sometimes his father's determination to live shone through and reminded him why this man was such a beloved chief. He placed a white linen napkin across his father's chest and lap and put a spoon into his hand. He took the cover from his own food, lifted his knife and fork and began to eat. He ignored the tremble in his father's hand. He ignored it when the food fell from the spoon, keeping his eyes downcast so as not to cause unnecessary embarrassment for the older man when he lifted it in his fingers and put it in his mouth.

'And?' Bongani asked.

The old chief smiled as he ate the next mouthful. 'Patience, my son, remember – slowly, slowly, catch a monkey.'

Bongani laughed.

Soon his plate was empty, but not his father's.

'Do you remember when you caught that monkey with your grandfather, Bongani?'

'Like it was yesterday.'

'I remember it too. Your brother, Tichawana, he was there. Even then he was already cruel. Your grandfather saw it before I did; he warned me not to let him near you and that I was not to treat you equally. You were the next chief and he was not. But I did not listen. I was too proud to listen.'

'It is not something to think about now,' Bongani said, looking at the branding on his arm, one of the many scars that his younger brother had given him before he was banished.

'Your grandfather was a great tracker and he knew the Zambezi Valley as if it all belonged to him, not only this little part the government told him he could have. He once tracked elephants for Cecil Rhodes himself. When you asked him to show you how to catch a monkey, I thought he would say no, that it was beneath him, but that day, happiness radiated from his face, as his grandson sought his knowledge.'

'I remember.'

'You were so impatient. And when he began your training, you were like the resurrection plant in the Matopos – you blossomed with a little bit of knowledge, but instead of dying again, going back to a brown and dead state, you carried on blooming like a strong protea.'

Bongani's eyebrows raised. 'Are you calling me a flower?'

The chief laughed, then coughed and took a while to settle again. 'Of course I am calling you a flower. You were tiny at first, timid like a bud. Then you stretched your face towards the sun, and you grew. The more you knew, the more knowledge you soaked up, the brighter you became. Your mind moulded into that of a chief, even at that young age. Everyone could see that you were already the right choice to take my place. It was never in your brother's nature.' The chief reached for another small piece of pie.

The quietness inside the thatched *ikhaya* washed over them, and the night critters began their evening serenade.

Bongani glanced at his father's plate. Only a little had been eaten, but it was more than in the last few days. The nurse ensured he drank protein shakes during the day and took vitamin tablets, but even those were getting harder and harder for his father to swallow. He seemed constantly tired. He was frail now, as one would expect of such an old man. But inside, his soul still danced with life and vitality and it was this part of him that Bongani was not ready to let go of.

'Are you finished?'

'I am still eating, and you are still like you were with that monkey. Impatient.'

Bongani rolled his eyes.

'Slowly, slowly, catch a monkey,' Chief Tigere said again as if he could turn back the clock and witness the boy and the monkey. 'Remember when you caught one, how you tracked it, and set the trap to capture it? How that stupid monkey would not let go of that gourd?'

'I remember. You were so sure I was too short, too young, and that a hyena would get me if I ventured outside the village.'

'I was right. Only I had the wrong kind of savage.'

'It is in the past, it does not matter. Do you remember when I eventually caught that stupid thing? I let it go, back into the wild?'

'Yes, and it probably raided the *mielie* crop and the sorghum plenty after that, but always looked twice to see if you were there. Bongani, promise me something. When you catch your brother, make sure that you deal with him. The biggest mistake in my life was that I let go a juvenile snake and did not kill it. Now a full-grown mamba will come to try to kill you once I am gone. He will be back soon, making no good in our land.'

'*Ndende*—'

'Just do it. Remember that burn on your arm, remember how he taunted you that day, saying you were a coward for letting that monkey free and not killing it. He burnt your arm to remind you always. To cause you pain. But it was he who was the coward, not to learn patience, not to spend time with an old grandfather whose most precious gift was passing on secrets of the bushveld.'

'I always remember.' Bongani rubbed his arm, even though the scar had not hurt for many years. 'He is making mischief – people have settled in our lands without your permission. There is poaching on the northern border. Our people and the park usually help each other, unlike many other safari and forest areas. The Chizarira never had to look to us as poachers, because our people had honour. Now, there are some who hunt where it is forbidden.'

'They must not be allowed to get away with this.'

'I know.'

'Soon you will be chief … it will be easier then.'

'No, Father, it will be harder. Tichawana will bring with him years of hatred and try to take our lands by force. Having you alive is the only thing keeping him out for now. Even after all these years, he is still afraid of you.'

'So he should be,' Chief Tigere said. 'But now it is time for him to be afraid of you. It is almost my time. I know that three of the five *N'Gomas* are already here. The other two must be close, and will arrive for my burial any day. They will need your help as chief to do new boundary *muti*, to stand with you and keep him out. I do not know how long their *muti* will last once I am gone, and before you are named chief. This is the time he will come. Gather the *N'Gomas* close to you. Keep them with you, because if he is not scared of you, at least he has a regard for the angry *tokoloshe* they can call to aid them.'

'Abigale said the same as you.'

'Good. That will give him a surprise if he dares to come here.' Tigere's head nodded to the side, and Bongani lowered the bed halfway.

The nurse came into the room with a small knock, just as Bongani had finished putting the dishes into the cooler.

'He is sleeping?' she asked.

'Just nodded off.'

'Did you get some food into him?'

'A little warthog pie.'

'That is good. He is counting the days to his crossing over.'

'How many do you think?'

'Hard to say. A week at most.'

Bongani nodded.

'Your father is old. You need to prepare for the funeral, for the procession and for his burial.'

'No, I will take care of that once he is gone. For now, I will spend as much time as I can with him. If you get him comfortable for the night, I will sit with him. He might wake up again before morning.'

He sat in the rocking chair he had placed next to the bed and watched his father sleeping. He remembered doing the same thing when his grandfather had died, only then he sat on his father's lap silently as that chief slipped away to chase fireflies in the dark night.

It was too soon to be his father's turn.

Bongani had no son to sit with him. He did not want any of his nephews from his sisters there either, not when their mothers were all 'too busy' to help look after their own father. Joss had been the son Bongani had never had, the one he had mentored in the bush and, despite their colour difference, the one he still loved as if he were his own, but it was not acceptable to his people for Joss to be in the chief's home when he died.

Bongani wondered who would sit with him when it was his turn to cross over.

* * *

The next morning, Bongani held his father's cold hand.

Five *N'Gomas* surrounded Chief Tigere's bed, chanting songs and burning herbs. They sang the traditional sounds of *Kuyabila*, the poems to the god *Chilenga*, who created all, and to the ancestors to help the family left behind, and to grant them wisdom during this difficult time. Abigale raised a drum and began beating it. Lindiwe and Thoko joined the steady beat. Thully shuffled to the doorway to begin a slow walk around the outer perimeter of the *ikhaya*, continuing to beat her drum. Cludu followed, chanting, her song solemn. A sign from the *N'Gomas* that their chief was dead.

Each of the *ikhayas* in the area joined in the chorus. In the distance, other drums could be heard, and then still more as the bush spoke across the vast distances, each signalling to the other that Chief Tigere was dead.

Joss got up from where he sat waiting. He walked into the *ikhaya* and stood behind his friend. He put his hand on Bongani's shoulder. 'I'm sorry.'

'All this time to prepare and yet I still cannot believe he took his last breath and crossed over,' Bongani said.

'At least you got to spend this time with him.'

'That I am grateful for, and that he was at peace.'

'What now?'

'My mother was spared *Kukala Ku Chilyango*. She has passed so she won't be covered in *meilie-meal*, but I will have to do that for a day, while I get everything organised for the feast. With the help of these five *N'Gomas*, I am going to follow every tradition, for my father, and especially as chief, so that when Tichawana attempts to take away my chiefdom, he will get nothing. It will all be sanctioned by these women, and there will be no doubt in the eyes of the people who will be their next chief, by blood and by law.'

*   *   *

Joss lay the now-wilting flowers at the base of Courtney's tombstone. Flame lilies had always been her favourite, and he was lucky that his mother's garden had pots of them flowering profusely at this time of the year. Despite her being gone for years, the plants were hardy and had survived. The red and orange petals were a stark contrast to the white marble with the black writing.

It was time to let her go.

Courtney Jean de Longe
Time is eternal.

It made him smile that Peta had not put dates on her resting place and chosen a saying that Courtney always used instead. But her time walking on African soil had not been eternal, even if her spirit remained.

'Hello, Courtney. It's been a while,' Joss said.

The sounds of the bushvelt answered him back. The unrelenting cries of the cicadas and crickets filled the silence, with the chatter of distant birds as they went about their day, oblivious to him trying to say goodbye to his best friend. Closer to the camp, men sang as they tended to their tasks, their voices deep and harmonised, the rhythm soothing. He could hear the shrill whistle of one of the rhino handlers, herding the babies back into the safety of the camp for the night.

'This is a great place to rest, you know,' he began. 'There are worse patches of dirt. You can hear the sounds of the bush, and still be part of the people around. We all know how much your loved being near people—' He stopped because he felt stupid talking to her as if she was still there. He hadn't even done this at his own parents' grave.

When they died, he knew that they were at peace together. But not Courtney; she was so young – in his head she wasn't the person below his feet, but a free spirit, not like the pictures that Peta had shown him, of how thin she was at the end, with dark shadows under her big eyes. That person was not the Courtney he carried in his heart.

'I wanted you to know that I kept my promise. I didn't let you down. I was late, but I got here. It's really important that you know that. I came home.

'I know that you of all people would understand because it's all changing, Court. What I felt for you was like the love of a sister. I don't believe that we would have ever taken our friendship to a different level. You were always my best friend. But with Peta it's different. I feel differently now about her. I don't want you to hate me for it, but I have changed. I've seen things no person ever should. I've seen such cruelty and madness, and losing my legs. I should be angry, but I'm not. Not any more at least. Now I have to believe that I'm a better person because of the experience. Not such a *windgat*.' He laughed dryly. 'Peta sees me differently too. She hasn't tried to boss me around for at least a few hours. We seem to have a more even footing now.'

The sound of whistling grew closer and he could see the baby rhinos plodding along in front of the game guards.

'At least you get to see the animals each day here, and you are not resting in a city somewhere. No matter what, you will always be looked after here. These are men of the bush, and they will respect your resting place. You would be so proud of your sister; Peta is doing amazing research with those babies who walk by you each day, and the photographs she showed me of their interaction at night are amazing. Who knew that rhinos had such a social life?

'So, while I was off fighting a war in a country that didn't want me there, you and Peta were doing just fine here in Zimbabwe. You were living a safe life, and were where you wanted to be. There's no use me having regrets about not visiting more, it is what it is, and I can only hope that in the end you were not in pain.

'I know that you visited me after you were gone, and you knew why I was breaking the promise to come home. I know that you were there, and you told me I wasn't allowed to give up. That I do remember, despite all the drugs in my system. Making me choose to live because you had chosen to leave this world, but you didn't want me to as well. You wanted me to carry on. To keep my promise and return home. I always knew that you were aware that I had lost my legs, even though I didn't get to tell you myself.

'At least I got to continue living, and for that I'm grateful. I'm not sure that Peta has come to understand exactly how much it's changed me yet, but us getting to know each other better is a dance worth dancing. I know deep down that you would be making jokes about us, about me and older women, and her being a cougar, but you would continue to love us both.

'I do love you, Courtney, I always will. You were everything to me growing up, you made my life exciting, and challenging, and filled every moment with madness and activity. Your relentless enthusiasm for life influenced me so much more than you would believe.

'I wish you were here now.

'I wish I still had my legs.

'But we both know that some wishes are never granted. There's no turning back the clock.' He stood looking at her grave for a long time, remembering better times in the quietness, until he sensed he was no longer alone.

Peta. He knew her step already, the rhythm of her breathing, and the smell of her as it drifted in on the breeze. She walked up to him, and stood looking at the tombstone for a moment before she slipped her hand into his and gave it a squeeze.

'I'm not sure why I took so long to come and say goodbye,' Joss said.

'I'm sure that you had your reasons.'

'Now that I have done it, they don't seem that important. I should have come earlier.'

'It doesn't matter. You okay?'

'Far from it, to be honest. But I will be.'

'Yeah, I know that feeling. Tomorrow will be a better day – isn't that what every Zimbabwean always believes deep in their souls?'

He felt her move away, but instead he pulled her towards him, and he took her in his arms, holding her closer to him. His arms wrapped around her and pinned her body to his. He felt the moment when she relaxed and leant into him. He let out a sigh of relief.

It was supposed to be a sombre moment, but he felt a glimmer of hope inside, as if saying goodbye had let part of him that had been burdened and held back go free.

He hoped the same was true for Peta.

He knew that Courtney would be smiling at them both.

17

Across the Mighty Zambezi

The matriarch moved with purpose and patience, waiting for her herd to cross the river. The last time she had traversed it at this place, the water had been higher on her body. She had been younger then. Not as young as many of her herd, but young nonetheless. Now the water was below her belly. The river was low for this time of year because the rains had not arrived in earnest.

Hippos gathered together in the deeper pools to her right, grunting loudly. The dominant male bared his huge yellow teeth in a show of strength, but she ignored him. He was not about to move from the sanctuary of his deep river pool and attack the herd today; he was more worried about the rival male in the next pond as they competed for females and breeding grounds in the vanishing water. A lazy crocodile lay sunning itself on the opposite bank. Its teeth gleamed, but it made no move to approach the herd either.

She stopped and drank some of the refreshing water. She knew that the others were behind her, and they too would satisfy their thirst before crossing. She threw the water over her body and continued her journey. Finally, she lifted herself up the small ledge on the other side. The mud was packed hard from many feet treading the same path, but the step was high. The youngsters would need help here.

Once out of the water, she flicked the warm river sand over herself, and turned to help the mothers in the herd get the infants up the small ledge. She watched the crocodile as he remained on the bank, aware of their movements, but not a danger.

A fish eagle called. She looked up and saw it circling above her, its black body and white head so distinctive. It owned these skies and wasn't afraid to tell the world about it. When she was younger, she had been so used to the serenity of their calls, taken both them and the vastness of water in the lake for granted as part of her life in the bushveld. But that was before she had travelled north. Before she had the responsibility of her herd.

She was closer to home now, the place of her birth, but she knew she wasn't out of danger yet. Hunters were still around and she had to lead her herd up and over a huge escarpment before they would be safe.

One baby was in trouble; it was attempting to get up the step, but its legs were too small and it repeatedly slipped back into the water. The calls between it and its mother were frantic.

The crocodile slithered into the dirty water and disappeared.

The matriarch stepped down from the small shelf, her feet in the water. She turned her bulk around until she was behind the baby. Slowly she angled it between her tusks and lifted it, while the mother soothed it with her trunk.

The baby's feet trod air before it was up, and then it was running beside its mother.

The matriarch looked around for the crocodile. He was closer now, but seeing her in the water, he moved slightly away as if acknowledging she was a formidable foe, the protector of her family, and he wouldn't get an easy meal from her herd.

She helped another baby up and over, and then she stepped up once more. The herd took time to cover themselves in sand, creating a barrier from the hot sun and biting insects, and once everyone was ready, she slowly made her way to the front of the column again.

The matriarch pressed her herd. They passed near the town with the large power lines, and the strange sensation under their feet that tingled and yet threatened at the same time, warning of impending danger. Vibrations from thundering water and man-made machinery.

They left the town with the thundering water behind them, seeking the cover of the bush. South towards security.

CHAPTER

18

Brewing Storms

Joss watched the sky as it threatened a summer storm. The clouds towered above them, darkening, foretelling the mother of an electrical storm about to break.

'I think it is going to rain,' Lwazi said.

'You think? Anyone can see it's going to rain. I'm just hoping we get into the lodge before it pours down on us.'

'How much further?' Mitch asked.

'About an hour, but there's a river between us and the lodge and if that cloud bursts, we might have an interesting crossing.'

'What about all the shopping in the back; can it get wet?' Lwazi asked.

'Yes, and believe me, we'll put those bicycles through worse than this storm,' Joss said as the wind battered the side of his *bakkie* and he gripped the steering wheel tighter.

A fork of lightning lit the sky in front of them. It hit a tree and the trunk split in half, then shattered, the shards scattering around the bush. Smoke didn't even get a chance to accumulate before blowing away in the wind, but they could see that the tree would never recover, as the half that hadn't shattered fell, its magnificent green canopy plunging to the ground.

'Lucky that didn't start a veld fire,' Joss said.

The sky darkened even more, and huge drops started to splash against the windscreen. It reminded Joss of the last time he'd seen rain this hard, the night that Peta had picked him up off the bridge. He thought of her smile, and how much he'd messed up around her, and yet she had still asked him to call her. Now they spent most weekends together, and saying goodbye on Monday mornings when she was ready to drive back to the Matusadona was becoming harder and harder.

He braked for a thick branch across the road.

'Shit,' Joss said, as he saw a boy of about twelve run from the tree. He came towards the front of the *bakkie*, waving his arms. 'Mitch, stay sharp, something isn't right here.'

Joss kept the engine running and wound down his window. The boy ran to the driver's side, banging on the body of the *bakkie* as he got closer.

'*Baas! Baas!* Help us, he is stuck under the tree on the road.'

'Who is stuck?' Joss asked.

'My brother! He is underneath the tree!'

'Is he still alive?'

'I do not know. I was running away when it fell on him.'

Joss looked at the tree that had fallen into the road. It didn't look cut – it had a jagged end – but it was too dark to see for sure. The boy seemed to be genuinely distressed. Joss switched off the engine, pocketed his keys and climbed out of the *bakkie*. 'Lwazi, stay here for now. Mitch?'

'Hijack. Unfriendly in the ditch!' Mitch called as he left the *bakkie*, but his warning came too late.

The youngster had pulled a *panga* from the back of his pants and was threatening Joss with it. 'Give me your keys,' the youth demanded, his voice wavering slightly.

Joss looked at him. In his peripheral vision, he saw the man in the ditch stand up. He was armed with an AK-47. The man pointed it at Mitch's stomach. Slowly Joss raised his hands and walked to where Mitch stood. The youth with the *panga* followed him, still far away enough from him that he wasn't a real threat.

'Give me your keys,' the man said.

'Do you know who I am?' Joss asked.

'It does not matter. I am taking your *bakkie* and all your stuff,' the man said.

'No, you're not. I'm Joss, I own Yingwe River Lodge in Binga, and have Chief Bongani's permission to travel through his lands. This land is in his territory. You're attempting a hijack on the chief's land. Do you think there'll be no retribution from him?'

'I am not scared of him. King Gogo wa de Patswa told me to take your *bakkie*, so I will take it,' the man said.

'He did? You sure he said my *bakkie*? Joss Brennan's *bakkie*?'

'He said anyone who comes this way this afternoon, past this point in the road, we must take their *bakkie*.'

'I see,' Joss said. 'That is unfortunate. Did he give you any other instructions?'

'No.'

'Why? You are not a killer, and your son, he hasn't done this before either. See, he's shaking – he's afraid to hurt another person. He's a good child.'

The man's eyes darted to the boy, and when he was distracted, Joss struck. Lunging forward, he grabbed the barrel of the gun, bringing it and the unsuspecting man towards him. He twisted the weapon from his grip and punched him hard enough in the stomach that he fell to the ground. Joss sat on the man's back, his arms held up so that he couldn't move.

Joss turned his head to the son as Mitch advanced on him. 'Drop the knife and no harm will come to you, and I won't break your father's arm.'

The boy dropped the *panga*. Joss could see the urine running down the inside of his leg.

'Step backwards. Five steps away from us.'

The boy counted aloud to five, then turned and fled into the bush.

The lightning flashed, and almost immediately a deep roll of thunder was heard. The storm was closing in.

'Mitch, get the *panga*.'

Mitch grabbed the huge knife and returned to where Joss was sitting on the man.

Keeping his metal knee right in the middle of the man's back, Joss reached for the AK-47. He unloaded the rifle, removing the curved magazine and the round in the chamber and pocketing them, then handed the disabled weapon to Mitch. 'Put the *panga* and the gun in the front seat.'

Lwazi took the butt of the gun and the *panga* as Mitch handed them to him.

'If I let you up, are you going to try to fight me?' Joss asked the man.

'No. Please do not hurt me.'

'You and your boy can now drag that tree away from the road, and I'll drive through. You can tell your Gogo wa de Patswa that he has no control in this area. He won't even attempt to hijack anyone within Chief Bongani's territory again or there will be hell to pay.'

'Yes, *Baas*,' the man said as Joss slowly released his weight, allowing the man to stand. He stooped and clutched his back, clearly in pain.

'I had to do this. King Gogo wa de Patswa, he will take my son if I don't give him something of value.'

Joss looked at him. 'What is your name and what did you do to get into debt with him?'

The man looked down. 'My name is Chipinduka Joseph Nandoro.'

'And what did you do to him, Chipinduka?' Joss asked, using his Shona name.

The older man said, 'I gambled with him. I always win at cards, but I never knew that he cheated. I did not know it was him who was playing cards that day.'

'And you gambled with the life of your boy to ambush a *bakkie*. You're not a very good father, putting your own son at risk like that.'

'I had to do this, or he will hurt my family. He told me that today, a new *bakkie* would be coming, filled with goods from Bulawayo.'

'He did, did he? Where can I find this man? This king of thieves?' Joss asked.

'He cannot be found. He finds those he wants. But his lieutenant, Danisa Mlilo, he drinks in the shebeen every Friday night at Binga.'

'Where were you to take my *bakkie*?'

'To my house. He will send Danisa Mlilo to fetch it.'

'Tonight?'

'Tomorrow, early in the morning.'

'Perhaps tomorrow I need to be there with you, to have words with your King Gogo wa de Patswa's lieutenant.'

The man shook his head. 'I will not be there in the morning. He will take my son to one of his camps and probably kill me now. I must leave, run away. Flee into Botswana or South Africa, where he cannot harm me or my son.'

'Chief Bongani and I will speak with Mlilo in the morning when he comes for the *bakkie*. Where is your house?'

The man explained his home in detail, and then he said, '*Baas*, if I had known it was you in that *bakkie*, I would not have stopped it. Everyone in this area knows that only you can drive that vehicle with its special gears. I feel only shame that a man with no legs could still beat me to the ground.'

Joss smiled. 'There is no shame to being taken down by a Royal British Marine Commando, even if he doesn't have his own legs any more.'

* * *

Joss, Bongani and Mitch waited for the sun to rise.

There was no smoke coming from beneath the thatched roof of Chipinduka's home, and all around there was an uneasy silence. Chipinduka had left his *ikhaya*, disappeared into the night, taking his cattle and his son; proof that his fear of King Gogo wa de

Patswa went deeper than his belief that his new chief could protect him.

'It looks like Danisa Mlilo is a no-show,' Bongani said.

Joss ran his hand over his neck. 'I'm thinking I've been played.'

'Perhaps,' Bongani said.

'You need to find out who that man was, because I have a feeling that last night I met with one of your brother King Gogo wa de Patswa's lieutenants themselves. Something else bothers me: the boy with him was terrified. I thought it was of me, but he might have feared someone else.'

'Perhaps the boy was terrified of the man in the ditch?' Mitch said.

'Perhaps. The man said something about the boy being taken to a youth camp. That's a worry.'

'A few years ago, the government ran youth training camps to train our youth, give them skills for trade, but they were in fact camps, used by the government to indoctrinate a youth army. Everyone referred to the kids trained in those camps as "green bombers". But those facilities were shut down when they ran out of money,' Bongani said, looking out over the *kraal*. 'Francis, a man I found settled in Amaluandi Village, mentioned that his boy Thomas had been taken to a camp. I do not know him well enough to know if it was a lie or not, but Francis is still there, spying on me and passing misinformation back to Tichawana.'

'Too much of a coincidence that two different men mention youth camps,' Mitch said.

Joss frowned. 'Sounds like someone resurrected them. We should see what we can find out.'

Bongani nodded, and took one last look around. 'My homeland is much changed. I have tried to ensure that no one looks at our area too closely, walked a tight rope for so long between what is right for my people and what is right morally, that perhaps I have given too much to people who did not deserve to live here. My people have suffered enough – I am hoping that they do not suffer more because of my allowing others to come here to try to rebuild their lives with us.'

'That might be so, but you've always ruled them with your heart and done what's right, which is more than a lot of other corrupt chiefs in Zimbabwe have done. Your brother's pushed at your boundaries significantly. We're going to need to strike back,' Joss said.

'I need to find out as much as I can about him after he left here if we are going to do this within the law,' Bongani said. 'When he goes down this time, he needs to stay down. It must not look like foul play from my side.'

Joss smiled. It was time his friend Bongani began exerting the authority of his chieftainship, and the first step was to gain control of all the people living on his land. Bongani had officially been named chief by the *N'Gomas* and all the thousands of people who were at the chief's funeral and his burial feast had witnessed that.

Tichawana was in for a surprise when Bongani exerted that authority.

* * *

Christmas morning had dawned bright, with the copper sun in the bright blue sky. The heat was already becoming oppressive as it beat down mercilessly on the people gathered around the table on the lodge deck.

Joss looked around, and smiled at the gathering of people he would never have expected to see sitting together.

'Can I give Sophia some more duck? She seems to like it,' Lwazi asked, seated on the other side of Sophia's high chair.

Joss nodded. Madala White had put on an old suit for the occasion and sat next to his grandson, wearing a paper crown on his head that absorbed the sweat.

'Who hides in the bakery at Christmas?' Mitch asked, reading out yet another of the jokes from the crackers.

'A cat,' answered Mary.

'No, a mouse,' Ephraim said.

Mitch shook his head. 'A mince spy.'

Scraps were all that remained of a Christmas dinner fit for any Michelin star restaurant, but better for having been contributed to by everyone gathered at the table. With the only two safari guests over Christmas included in the main festivities, the German visitors had wanted to add their tradition into the meal. Yedwa had allowed Hansie and Cyndine Hoffman into his kitchen to cook, and even had Peta in there too.

The roast duck with sauerkraut had sat perfectly next to the roast lamb and ham already on the menu. Joss knew that the German butter cookies that were to be served with the dessert of flaming brandy over Christmas pudding would be a hit – he'd stolen one from the kitchen already.

Bongani laughed. It was good to hear, especially after losing his father so close to Christmas.

Rodger was having one of his good days and was in the Christmas spirit, sitting next to Peta and joining in the conversation. Tsessebe had been constantly by his side, ensuring that he didn't get lost or disorientated.

Sophia smacked her food-covered hand into Joss's face, smearing fat across his cheek, and his attention was snapped back to his daughter sitting on his lap.

'Miss Sophia, that's just rude. Don't you know that this Christmas celebration has all been because of you? You are a guest of honour and this is how you repay me? With fat make-up?'

Sophia giggled. Joss took his serviette and wiped her hand. Then his face. Peta laughed.

'It's only funny because it's not your face getting coated,' he said.

'You do realise she won't remember today? This big celebration might have been because of her, but for everyone around this table it had been worth it. Look at them; they all look so happy. Even my dad.'

'Your dad? I hear my name. What about me?' Rodger asked.

'Nothing, Dad, I was just saying what a nice lunch this has been.'

'Here's to many more,' Rodger raised his beer.

Mitch raised his glass too, and everyone joined in the toast. Sophia leant over and tried to grab at Peta's glass, and the contents spilled all over Peta.

'That's cold,' she said, shaking the ice blocks off her lap. Joss stood up and thrust Sophia into Rodger's lap. 'Here, hold her. I need to help Peta.'

'I'm good. I'm cooled down. Did Sophia get any on her?'

'She's fine – she was just trying to get a drink from you. She—' Joss turned to where he'd dumped Sophia, and realised where she was sitting.

He stopped talking.

Sophia was facing Rodger. Her small hands tracing the scars on his face. And he seemed completely at ease with it.

'Dad? You okay?' Peta asked.

'She's so happy. Despite the fact that she probably won't walk, she still looks at everything in awe. Just like you did when you were a baby. I remember you at this age, and Courtney.'

Sophia tugged at his grey hair, scrunching her fingers into it.

Rodger didn't attempt to move her hand, and let her continue exploring.

'She's a beautiful child. A beautiful soul,' Rodger said.

Sophia giggled again as she put her forehead against his, then wrapped her hands around his neck and hugged him, laying her little head on his shoulder.

Tsessebe was staring at Rodger, tears running down his face.

Peta was shaking her head slowly from side to side.

Joss watched the interaction between the two. His instinct was to get his child back, to correct his mistake in giving her to Rodger, but now he hesitated. The moment was too precious to break up.

Joss heard Peta's intake of breath. He reached for her hand and gave it a squeeze.

'Dad, you want me to take Sophia?'

'No, she's fine just where she is,' Rodger said.

Mitch started on another joke. 'Why are Christmas trees so bad at knitting?'

'No clue,' said Lwazi.

'Because they do not have hands to hold the knitting needles?' Ephraim called out.

'Close. Because they always drop their needles.'

'*Eish*, that one is even worse than the last one,' Lwazi said.

Bongani was laughing again. Hansie and Cyndine were laughing too.

Joss smiled. In losing his legs he'd lost much, but in coming home, he had gained a whole lot more. He'd renewed old friendships, made new ones and expanded his family.

This was a good Christmas.

CHAPTER
19

Grape Vines

Tichawana could hear his secretary talking through the wall. Not that he would ever tell her.

'Hello, Miss Hillary, is he in?' a voice he recognised as Denisa Mlilo's asked, the bell on the outside door still ringing.

'He is, but it is Tuesday. He has a booking at the club for lunch,' she explained. 'I can make you an appointment, Mr Mlilo. Perhaps tomorrow?'

'It will only take a minute—'

Hillary said, 'One moment. I will ask him if he can see you.' He heard her stand and walk towards the office, knocking lightly on his door before she entered. 'Mr Mlilo is here to see you, but he doesn't have an appointment.'

Tichawana purposely didn't look up from where he was studying a topographical map. 'Send him in.'

He heard her return and say in her ever efficient tone, 'Mr Nhou will see you now.'

Tichawana folded the map and put it in his drawer as she led his visitor into the office.

After they had shaken hands, Hillary showed Mlilo into the visitor's chair and asked, 'Can I bring refreshments?'

'Tea would be nice, Miss Hillary,' Tichawana said before turning his attention to Mlilo. Denisa Mlilo was a tall man, thin but extremely muscular, his body honed from many years of bush work and fighting. He was also one of the better spies Tichawana paid to keep him abreast of what was happening outside of Bulawayo.

Hillary walked back into his office and set the tray on his desk. She took her time in pouring the tea, and he noticed that Mr Mlilo sat on the edge of his seat, bouncing his legs. Tichawana smiled at the man's obvious signs of agitation and anxiety.

'Thank you, Miss Hillary,' Tichawana dismissed his secretary, who curtseyed to him as he liked, then exited the room, leaving him and Mlilo in peace at last.

'I had the unfortunate pleasure of meeting your brother's friend, the white man Joss Brennan. He is trouble for the Sijinete area and the whole Chete area too. We had planned an elephant hunt there – there were many large tuskers we could have taken. Now we will have to move further north, perhaps nearer the Matusadona. He will cause us difficulties.'

'How can one crippled man be so much trouble?'

'He is a commando. He is fit. And fast. I still have a bruise on my back from him,' Mlilo's voice rose slightly. 'He knows my face now, and he would have told the new chief.'

'You have not found my half-brother's weakness then?'

'No. Not yet. But we are going to need to watch his friend the commando carefully, closer than your brother, perhaps.'

'So does Brennan have a weakness you could see?'

'Other than being a cripple? No. He has another white man visiting; he talks with an Australian accent. The visitor is staying in his house, not in the lodge.'

'Did you try to turn Madala White to work for us?'

Mlilo shook his head. 'It would be a waste of time. He is loyal to your brother. But he is old.'

'What else does Brennan do?'

'He spends a lot of time with your brother, and with his white friend, who is not a cripple.'

'Always my brother, he finds a way to have security around him.'

'Your brother and this man, they are acquainted a long time. He knew this man when he was a boy, and that is how he became the manager. Remember after the accident that Stephen Brennan and his wife met when they discovered your boat on Kariba? Your brother suspected nothing then, and he was Stephen's right-hand man. We have one who is close to him: Mary. Remember her? Some rats sometimes escape the traps and they take a while to come back again.'

'That piece of shit. Yes, I remember her. Is she still alive? I thought by now she would have died from the thinning's disease.'

Mlilo laughed. 'She still lives in your brother's area. Rumour has it she is the one behind the butcher in Amaluandi, and has built up a small gang of men who work for her business, mostly obtaining bush meat right under Chief Bongani's nose. It would not be too hard to convince her to watch over the white soldier too.'

'This is a good idea. Get the rat to earn her keep. I want to know about everything they do.'

'I will organise it.'

'Now, what of my spotter team? Any news?'

'We have lost Kenneth Hunt; a lion ate him in Chizarira. Zim-Parks took a few days to warn everyone about the man-eater, but my contact in the game reserve says that when they found him, the lady vet, Peta de Longe from Matusadona, recognised what was on his computer, and she was very interested. She spoke with the old tracker and her sidekick, Amos, about the files. They are never far apart. Our man, he was not on site when they found Hunt, he had been left behind, but they were all talking about it in front of him when they got back to camp. Apparently they are tracking the lion now. He killed a black man who was cycling through the reserve too.'

'How can that be? Hunt was expensive, but he was a man of the bush. How did the lion get the jump on him?'

'It seems like he was not paying enough attention. He got too comfortable in the bush and forgot to sleep with one eye open.'

'This is unfortunate news,' Tichawana said. 'So where is his computer, and my reports?'

'I thought it would be in his personal possessions at the police station at Binga, but when I organised for it to "get lost" in transit to Bulawayo, it was already missing. Someone else got to it first.'

'You think one of the policemen we are not controlling has sticky fingers?'

'I think someone else wanted that computer, and took it,' Mlilo said.

'We need that computer back. It has our information on it.'

'Yes, sir.'

'Come, it is lunchtime. Join me at the club for a beer. I am sure it has been many months since you last found a waitress there to cater to your exotic taste.'

'They have a new Korean waitress?'

'Petite and with these perky little tits, perfect for a handful, and long nipples.'

Mlilo smiled. 'You already sampled her?'

'Would I offer you anything I have not tasted before? What happens if it is poisoned?'

Both men laughed.

'She will fuck anything – she could do us both with energy to go around. Come,' Tichawana said as he pushed his chair back and got his jacket from the rack in the corner of his office. 'I will be out the rest of the day, Miss Hillary,' he said to Hillary as they passed her desk. 'I will see you in the morning. If there are any urgent calls, please put them through to my cell, but only if you cannot convince them that tomorrow will be another bright new day in our beautiful Zimbabwe.'

'Have a good lunch,' Hillary said and nodded.

As they walked out, Mlilo asked, 'So, have you sampled your secretary yet?'

'That one is not for anyone to touch. I need her for my businesses, and anyone who even tries to date her and causes her to lose focus will have to answer to me. No fucking my secretary; she is off limits to everyone. Is that clear?'

'Yes, sir,' Mlilo said.

The Journey Home

The grey morning yielded larger drips of moisture from the acacia trees as they filtered the light raindrops that floated downwards but it wasn't sufficient for the herd. The matriarch ignored the trees that they sheltered under, and instead dug the heel of her foot into the base of the small rise. If her memory served her, the rise was a lifeline in the scrublands – there was sweet water running beneath the surface. Scrapes in the ground where other elephants had done exactly as she was doing showed on the side of the knoll. Tree roots and layers of sediment were testament to the forest hiding its jewel from those who would not know of the water site.

She reached with her trunk and pulled on a deeper root that blocked her access. It came up long, almost vine like, and white as the outer layer of protection was stripped off. A small baby appeared next to her and got gently onto her knees to stick her head into the hole, exploring. The matriarch left her to find the outer part of the root, wrap her trunk around it, then pull with all her might, breaking it and stumbling backwards with the force of the break. She watched as the baby played with the prize, then came back to the hole, still inquisitive to see what she dug so diligently for. The matriarch remembered a time she had done the same thing, first with her grandmother, then with her mother.

Once again, she widened the area with her foot, carefully moving the sand away with her trunk. The baby mimicked her, and although her small trunk could hardly clear away any dirt, she had the general idea. Together they carefully dug the hole.

Water began to seep upwards. The sand turned darker and became mud and easier to move away. The baby squealed as the tip of her trunk felt the first kiss of cool water.

She waited while the baby drank her fill, knowing that this young cow was imprinting the day onto her memory, in order that she could return again when she needed to, and to pass the knowledge on to the next generations.

The mud moved slowly as the water bubbled up from the spring released by the hole she had dug. She drank deeply, quenching her thirst with the sweet taste. Then she moved aside to let others in the herd drink.

The herd took turns in an orderly fashion, as if sensing it was not going to be a mud-bath time to clean off insects and parasites, or to keep the sun off their bodies; this was just a drinking stop. Another time, later today, they would bathe in the sand.

The matriarch browsed the trees nearby, picking delicate leaves away from white thorns. It was almost time to press on. There were bones on the small path that led south from this place that she wanted to pay her respects to.

Slowly, she moved away.

The herd, finished in the waterhole, began to follow as a noisy troop of baboons noticed the new watering place. Chattering loudly among themselves, they moved forward. The matriarch stopped, looking back as the baboons stretched their bodies down the hole and drank deeply. The biggest male bared his teeth at a younger troop member who came to drink. She turned her back on the squabble that ensued. The water would stay bubbling to the surface for a while, but she knew that the mud would refill the area and as the surface water dried, the earth would crack once again in the harsh sunshine. This was only a temporary relief for the baboons who wouldn't have the sense to dig the hole as nature covered up its secret again, and they would once more be forced to travel longer distances to the river or another hidden spring for their water.

Plodding down the path, the matriarch turned off near a huge baobab tree and stopped. In front of the tree was an area once cleared of vegetation, but now green grass reached up to her knees. Above that she could still see the bleached white bones of her grandmother. They had long been picked clean by the vultures and hyenas. Her skull still stood as testament that once a gentle giant had walked here. Fallen here. Down onto the hard earth when a human had killed her to strip away only her tusks and her tail.

To the hunter, her grandmother had been a commodity. To the matriarch and her herd, she'd been the leader of their family, in the finest sense; right to the end, when she challenged the hunter and gave her life for the herd so that they could run away. Her grandmother was the one who had returned to find the younger elephant, despite the threat of the hunters, when she was a baby. She'd overcome her fear and retrieved her granddaughter from the small humans who had fed her and kept her alive during that dark time.

With her trunk, the matriarch caressed the skeleton that was beginning to deteriorate and return to the earth, where the ants and worms burrowed into the thick bone. She was content knowing that her grandmother would once more contribute to life, even in her endless sleep. A quiet moment spent with her now after many moons had parted them. The seasons passed so fast.

The other elephants paid their respects too. Some who travelled in her small herd remembered the great matriarch, but many had never known her and now met her, sombre in the knowledge that this fallen ancestor was held in high regard by their matriarch. Even the baby who had so recently learnt to dig for water touched her trunk to the bones, committing the place to her memory.

In her mind, she still saw this older matriarch, whose tusks and trunk had rescued her from fast-flowing rivers, who had defended her from a hungry lion, boldly chasing the lionesses away so that she was safe. She remembered other times, how her grandmother had led the herd north, away from this place, to a quieter grazing ground, until danger had encroached there too.

She was too young to take on her grandmother's position in the herd; she hadn't even had her own offspring yet. Soon that would change – her time was approaching. She'd been training to lead her family all her life. When her mother was taken too, she had stepped into her place.

Moments like this, comparing the size of her grandmother's skull with her own, were a reality check. She still had so much growing to do, so much life to experience, and this wonderful elephant now resting under the African sky would never see her do it.

She said goodbye to her matriarch, and hoped that one day she would be as much of a leader as this old elephant had been. That she would keep her herd safe, and ensure that the younger ones learnt her knowledge, the migration paths and the areas to avoid. She turned south again, following the deep calling within her. Something that had been missing for many years called to her in the bottom of her heart.

She followed that instinct.

The land was much changed. Many of the trees that had once stood proudly over the land were gone. Instead, open grasslands and human settlements dotted the landscape. Men were always changing the land, putting up large metal fences and wires that the herd had to walk over, the silver barbs menacing and dangerous to the whole herd. She had to constantly make sure that the babies were not separated from their mothers by these fences.

She would keep her herd inside the thicker forest for as long as she could before walking through the newly landscaped world. Her destination was a place near the water's edge where sweet green trees grew.

A land she hadn't seen in many years, yet it called her home.

21

Unlocking Secrets

Peta hit another bump. Hard. She knew she was travelling too fast for the road. Joss would still be there when she got to him. If she didn't break her Hilux before then with stupidity.

'Sorry, Amos,' she said as she noticed him rearrange himself on the seat. 'Right. That's the last causeway.'

'Good. I swear my kidneys are never going to be the same. That road needs fixing.'

'Think of it this way: if the poachers can't get away fast on the road, then they'll go somewhere where it's easier to poach, and leave our animals alone,' Peta said.

'I wish that were true.'

As they drove up the river bank on the other side, Amos looked out his window. 'There are some fresh tracks here, but not our lion. The team said he was still in the Sijinete area. But plenty others.'

The road flattened out for a while, but the bush on the sides closed in tightly. She heard the scratches it left in the *bakkie*'s paint.

'I am glad I am inside,' Amos said.

'Me too. Can you imagine how many thorns we would be picking out of our skin if we were walking in this?'

'You sure this still counts as a road?'

'I think so.'

Suddenly the bushes gave way to a T-junction. On one side was a pile of stones, but no direction markers.

'Told you. To the right, Binga, to the left and forward, more of the same,' she said, turning right.

'How long since you were last here?'

'A few years. My father and Joss's dad were best friends, and they walked every inch of both parks. Dad reminded me about it when I explained where we were going to drop off supplies for the guards tracking that darn lion.'

'What are you going to do when he gets worse, when his mind is gone? So much knowledge will be trapped, and you will not get to it.'

'I don't know. At the moment it looks like the medicine the doctor gave him is working. It's keeping things in check, at least. The disease definitely isn't progressing as fast as it was.'

'But one day soon.'

'I know. But it's not Dad I worry about, it's Tsessebe. They have been together for longer than most marriages. Tsessebe will be lost without Dad.'

Amos shook his head. 'I think that Tsessebe will not be lost. I think that he will be sad, but then he will join us on our adventures, and he will keep working, keep protecting his park. Tsessebe is family to you.'

Peta nodded. He had proven it over and over too. It was Tsessebe who had driven her to university in January when she was in her third year before she bought a little car. At year end, she had called her father and told him that she wasn't going home that Christmas, and Tsessebe had borrowed her father's *bakkie* and come to fetch her. When he had found her battered and blue, he had asked her what had happened. She hadn't known how to tell her father that she had been beaten by her boyfriend. Tsessebe had left her in her dorm and, armed with a photograph of the man, his name and his parents' address, he had disappeared for three days.

Tsessebe hadn't cared about the charges he could have faced, even in the new South Africa. He had done what he did best: he'd tracked her *windgat* boyfriend to a place that was good for an ambush, and delivered his retribution. He had beaten the man to within an inch of his life, and told him that if he ever laid a hand on Peta again, next time it would be three black men who would beat him up, and they would take his testicles for *muti*.

When Tsessebe returned, he had helped Peta to pack her things and driven behind her all the way home. He had been in her father's *bakkie* when they drove back for her fourth year of university, and he had stayed in the shadows for two months, watching out for her, without her even knowing he was there. When he found out that the ex-boyfriend had dropped out of university, he had come out of those shadows to tell her he was going home, now that he knew she was safe.

She let out a breath.

'What?' Amos asked.

'I'm thinking of Tsessebe. My dad gets to make a new friend every day, but Tsessebe has to watch his best friend drift away.'

'They are lucky. Tsessebe has been with your dad so long that if your dad regresses into the past, Tsessebe can also talk about those times.'

'I know, but it's so sad.'

A kudu jumped across the road in front of them and disappeared into the bushes. Peta stopped in case there was another one with it, and sure enough, three big bulls jumped out of the bush and across the road. She eased forward slowly.

Amos looked out his window again. 'Stop.'

As she brought the vehicle to a halt, Amos got out and examined the tracks in the road.

'Look, someone has laid down an arrow on the bank.' He pointed to the sand that had been graded off the road and was now compacted next to it. 'See these sticks? They make a marker.'

'Pointing to the road we were on.'

'Yes, but no car tracks there since the last rains, only ours. I looked all the time when we were crawling through that area.'

'So maybe whoever put them here does not know our park well enough to trust their tracker.'

He nodded. 'Hang on, I want to look at the sand on the other road.' He crossed in front of her and walked a little way down the road. Soon he bent down. 'A double arrow here,' he called. 'Sticks arranged carefully on the sand.'

She got out of the *bakkie* and joined him. 'This road leads from Chizarira and eventually into Sijarira forest. The road in front leads through the park, towards the hunting camp in the Gokwe North hunting concession. The road to the left takes you up towards Tashinga, but gives you access to a few more tracks. Hunting tracks mostly, not easy to pass. How old do you think those sticks are?'

'The sticks and the logs used are old, and they have been here for a while – look at the colony of army ants that has built a nest here in this dead log.' He pushed the log and the ants boiled out.

'The stones we passed are the marker that says there is a road here. The rangers before Stephen and Dad already had the system in place. Binga markers are always on the right if you see them. Tashinga never has a marker. We must speak to the guards about these, have a look for more.'

'Yes, but right now, we need to keep moving. Joss will be waiting for us at his lodge.'

Peta shook her head. 'He'll understand if we're a little late. I'll radio him while we drive.'

They returned to the *bakkie* and she climbed in. Amos got into his tracking seat on the bonnet. She started the powerful engine and swung around, heading towards Gokwe North.

* * *

Forty-five minutes later, Amos tapped the bonnet. She stopped and got out. He hopped off and she followed him to where he stood looking at another marker. This one still pointed east, like the one they had passed. On their left was a break in the gravel, as if it had been cleared away and there should be a road there.

Amos pulled at the bottom of the dead bush, having found a cut branch, and a huge area of the covering came away. 'You know this road heading north here?'

Peta shook her head.

'I think we need to get the office on the radio,' Amos said.

'You're right. Who hides a road except a poacher? Or someone looking for something they shouldn't be,' she said, turning to her *bakkie*. 'Tashinga Headquarters, come in,' she said into her radio.

No one answered.

'Tashinga Headquarters, come in,' she called again. 'Dead spot,' she said, checking her cell phone too.

'I think we should go have a look. There are no recent tracks. Perhaps it is old and no longer used.'

Amos cleared more of the trees from the road, dragging them to the side. Once the dead bushes were moved it was clear that they had found a two-track road heading north. The middle *man-netjie* was grass and not too high, so the road hadn't been used for a while. He took his weapon out of the carriage in the front of the *bakkie* and loaded it, putting a bullet in the chamber. Peta took her 0.9mm from the cubbyhole where she kept it and checked it too. Only when she nodded to Amos did he walk to his seat on the front and climb in, his rifle on his knee, the strap wrapped around his large hand.

Peta dropped the clutch and they moved forward. She could hear her heartbeat even above the roar of her diesel engine as the blood rushed through her ears. She watched her tracker on the front and kept herself alert as they checked for danger.

Slowly they bumped over the rough road, the sweat running down her back and pooling at the waistband of her shorts. She fanned the front of her T-shirt, trying to get a bit of airflow. Despite her open window, the heat inside the cab was stifling.

Amos tapped on the bonnet. She felt the vibration through every nerve in her body.

They were at the end of the road, in front of a low *koppie*. Amos dismounted while she remained in the *bakkie*, the engine running. He started walking in circles around the vehicle, before moving towards the *koppie* itself. When he gestured for her to follow him, she shut the vehicle off, took the keys out of the ignition, and started in his direction, keeping her 0.9mm in her hand.

Amos was pulling dead bushes away from the side of the *koppie*. When he pulled the last bush away, she stared.

'Oh my God. This is almost the same layout as Kenneth Hunt's camp, except there is no body and no *bakkie*.'

'Another spotter's camp?'

'Looks like it to me,' she said. The canvases on the floor were covered with leaves that had blown in while it had stood abandoned. The net above her was still in good condition. She took pictures with her phone.

'I was expecting a poacher's camp or remnants of one at least, not another spotter's camp,' she said. 'Bloody cheeky swine! Right under our noses!'

'What are we going to do about it?'

'I think we should cover it all back up once we've had a good look around, and cover our tracks out too. Make it look like we turned around near their road. It'll take us a while, but if they don't know we were here, we can come back again, check if they are here or not, and they won't know we are onto them.'

Amos looked to the sky. 'I do not think we will need to worry about our tracks. We cover this back up and close the hole in the road, but Mother Nature is going to take care of the rest with a storm tonight.'

'Let's not take that chance. I want to poke through his stuff a bit, look in those boxes at the back against the rock, see if there's anything that can lead us back to who this camp belongs to.'

She ran her finger along the wood, looking for a way to open the box. The crate was about one-point-five metres by eighty centimetres, and crudely constructed of pine, nails hammered into the soft wood at an angle. The lid was fitted into the structure of the box. She went to her *bakkie* and brought out her tool box.

They decided the screwdriver might work. She looked over the lid until she found where it had been previously damaged, and she put the screwdriver in the seam, wiggled it down a little, then levered it.

The lid popped up and Amos ran his fingers underneath it, to lift it more. Inside was packing material, and it had a horrible smell.

'I have seen this before,' Peta said. 'Smugglers and poachers pack tusks in it. The smell of the fibres is supposed to discourage the dogs from sniffing too close and finding the ivory.'

'So why is it out here, in the middle of nowhere?'

'Mmm,' Peta said, then went and got a stick, which she used to remove the matted fibres.

'You are making a mess,' Amos protested. 'Remember we need to cover that we were ever here.'

'We can tidy once we make sure there are no tusks in here,' she said, but she was relieved when all the packing was out and the crate was empty. She took a photograph of it and of all the packaging on the lid. Now knowing that there was no ivory in the straw, they threw it back in, and carefully picked up all that had spilled. They put the lid back on, and moved to the next box.

Peta looked inside. She brought her hand up to her mouth. 'Oh my God.'

Pre-made white crosses were packed into the box, and it was only half full. She took one out and turned it over. There was no marking on the cross, no name.

'Why?' Amos asked. 'What did the spotter want with the white crosses?'

'This is another of Kenneth Hunt's camps. Remember when we found his last one, Sixpence said that the cross on the top of the *koppie* was new? It hadn't been there before. And then you and I checked those others in the park on his maps to names we already had, but none of those had been replaced. Joss and I have a theory that perhaps Hunt was replacing the old crosses with new ones. Perhaps this is the proof we were looking for.'

Peta flipped the other crosses in the box to check if any of them had names. All were blank. She placed the white cross back in the box with the others, and took a couple more photos.

Together they put the lid back on.

'This is interesting, and weird,' she said. 'Let's cover up our presence here.' She walked a little away from camp and broke a branch off a tree. She began dragging it over where she'd made footprints in the ash and onto the canvas.

'Why not go to the top of the *koppie* and call Tsessebe so he can relay to your dad?' Amos said. 'I will finish covering all the tracks here so if that storm misses this area, no one will know we visited. I will cut some more bushes to cover the tracks of the *bakkie* as we drive out.'

She nodded and began the trek up to the top of the *koppie*, all the time checking for a signal as she went. As she neared the top, she got two bars.

'Thank you, Econet,' she said as she dialled Tsessebe.

The phone rang twice before he answered. 'Hello?'

'Tsessebe, it's me.'

'Are you at Joss's already?'

'Not yet. Remember that road Dad used to use that cuts through the bushes across the river, and out to the east? There's a road towards Gokwe North hunting camp as you cross the Tashinga gravel road?'

'I know it.'

'Amos and I found another spotter's camp in the park off that road. The layout is the same as Kenneth Hunt's camp, so it might have been one of his, or it's someone else like him, who knows him or trained with him. It's so similar it's spooky.'

'Okay, understood.'

'Keep Dad out of this area; there is danger here.'

'More dangerous than your father and his homemade explosives?'

'Yes.'

'This is an interesting find.'

'There's a dead spot here. No radio or cell coverage. I'm halfway up a *koppie*,' she said. 'Please mark that on the map in my office.'

'I will do that. You sure you are alright?'

She looked out across the bush. There was no tell-tale dust sign of another car anywhere that she could see with her naked eye. 'This camp hasn't been active for a while. We're fine.'

'I would still be on your toes, in case,' he said. 'Call when you are out of the area.'

'Promise. Bye, Tsessebe.'

She hung up and took one last look at the surrounds. She could see elephants moving nearby, and there was movement closer to the road, where some birds flew up as if disturbed by feeding impala, but no dust, and she felt herself relax.

She'd never been a big adrenaline junkie, and she wondered what had made her believe that being a large animal veterinarian in Zimbabwe was ever going to be an easy profession.

* * *

At last the gates of Yingwe River Lodge came into view.

'We're so late,' she said.

'Your Joss, he will not mind that you are late, only that you got here,' Amos said.

She smiled at that. *Her Joss*. She didn't remember when she had started thinking of him as hers, perhaps when he'd finally come to Matusadona and laid a bunch of flame lilies on Courtney's grave. She had watched as he conversed with her sister, allowing him the space to grieve alone, until finally she couldn't take it any more, and went and stood with him. She had slipped her arm into his, and he hugged her tightly as they stood together saying farewell to someone they both loved deeply.

After that, they had spoken each night, about their days, their dreams and their hopes. Lots about Sophia. About the renovations Joss was planning or what was happening in the community in his area. Her parks, and what was happening there, and the people in both of their lives who were connecting them.

Somewhere between phone calls and visits, their friendship was blossoming into something more. It scared her, because if she crossed over that invisible line and changed the footing to something else, there would be no going back to friends if it didn't work. And she didn't want to lose her friend. This was a mature friendship unlike anything she had experienced before, and she hated to admit it, but she was fast becoming used to having him to talk to. To laugh and scheme with. With Rodger's mind ailing, and Tsessebe so focused on her father and his needs, it had been a while since she had someone like Joss to talk to.

She forgot that he was years younger than herself when she was in his company, and no longer saw him as little Joss Brennan. Instead she noticed idiosyncrasies like how he absentmindedly stroked the smooth plastic of his left leg, and never did it to his right one. He would reach forward and tuck a stray hair behind her ear when it got out of her hairband, or straighten her hat when it wasn't on right. How he never attempted to move out of the way when she had to reach across him, appearing to welcome the contact with a small smile, a laugh or by helping her where she was going by lifting her over himself, as if she weighed nothing, just because he could.

Her stomach clenched as she drove the familiar track up to his house. She was already climbing out when Joss appeared at the kitchen door. He hugged her, and she hugged him back. Once their hugs were stilted, awkward. Now they were full body contact, and she was sure that he held her against his chest just a little longer than normal as his hands ran up and down her back, keeping her in the embrace.

'Glad you made it without more delays. I was worried about that river crossing.'

'It's high, but not over the causeway yet; we were good.'

'You want to freshen up before dinner?'

'Actually, we want to talk to you and Bongani first.'

'Intriguing. We'll do it at my place. Come on in and I'll call everyone together. Sophia is almost ready to go down for the night. Lwazi and Ephraim have gone to Bishu Village to learn about bees and chilli plants and how to use them to keep the elephants out of the crops.'

'Lead the way. At least I get to say goodnight to Sophia.'

*   *   *

Peta got her phone out and called Tsessebe.

'Hey, is Dad with you?' she said, putting him on speaker. 'Can you hear me?'

'Loud and clear,' Tsessebe said.

'Mostly,' Rodger's voice came over the line.

'Joss, Bongani and Mitch are on the line with us.'

'What mischief did you get into this time?' Rodger asked.

'Amos and I were travelling on the Gokwe North road, and he noticed these large log arrows on the curb.'

'Arrows? Did you say arrows? What type of arrows?' Rodger asked.

'Yes, arrows, like pointing in a direction. We followed them and they led us to another spotter's camp.'

'You shitting me?'

'No, Dad. I've got photos, and there was more. I found a huge crate of white crosses. The crate wasn't full either, as if some had been used already. I think this is proof that Kenneth Hunt was putting these crosses in our park.'

'You sure it's a spotter's camp?' Rodger asked.

'It was similar to the camp we found Hunt's body in.'

'This is bad news,' Bongani said.

'Remember the map I found at Hunt's first camp? It has references to people who died all across the area, and names and dates. Amos and I have been checking those sites, and a few of the names match his map, but so far we haven't found another cross that had been replaced, other than Casper's. A few of those old crosses are real graves from pioneers passing through the Zambezi Valley – they match names I've already collected – and they cross reference with the map. This new spotter's camp adds more to the mystery as it doesn't tell us much about the man himself.'

'That's okay. I'm sure you won't find all your answers in one day,' Rodger said.

'Mitch, how's the hacking of those other files on his laptop going?' Peta asked.

'I've got a friend working on breaking the codes on those we couldn't open,' Mitch said. 'I'm hoping to hear from him soon.'

'Bongani and I looked through those spotter files you printed for us,' Joss said. 'There're definitely two sets of files with similar data. One file excludes all the big tuskers. It's as if he's either making up that there are big tuskers there, or they're there and he's excluding them from the reports he's passing on. We looked at the police report that Amos got from his cousin for us. There wasn't even a trace of dead animal in his camp, so we don't think Hunt poached in the parks himself. Even looks like he was living on food that he brought into the area.'

'A spotter with a conscience? Now I've heard everything,' Tsessebe said. 'Have you found out anything about him yet? Anything at all?'

Peta looked at Mitch.

'A little. I've done an internet search and also tried to ask questions around, discreetly. His family were Zimbabwean pioneers. Their farm was taken in 2000. He wasn't married, and had no siblings. According to his social media page, he completed his schooling and then studied African history as a major at Wits University; after that he returned to Zimbabwe and started an overland hunting safari business,' Mitch said.

'At least we know a little more about him now,' Peta said.

'All you know is what he wanted the world to see on those stupid computers,' Rodger said.

Peta grinned at Mitch's frown. 'We don't have enough to go to the police with this yet?'

'Not really,' Bongani said.

The others shook their heads as Tsessebe and her dad said, 'No.'

Mitch's phone pinged, and he looked at it. 'We have progress. Damo has cracked the files. Let me go grab my laptop.' Mitch hopped up and disappeared into the guest bedroom. He came back with the machine already open. There was a Word document on the screen. Peeking out behind it was an image.

'How did he do that?'

'I wasn't making progress, so I gave Damo remote access. He ran some fancy program he wrote. Cracking passwords is his hobby.'

'What do the files say?' Tsessebe asked.

'Hang on,' Peta said as they all gathered around the small screen, reading the document. 'There's thirty pages in this file. We'll call you back once we've read it.'

'Speak to you later,' Rodger said as he ended the call.

Mitch scrolled through slowly as they read.

'Can you print us off a few copies?' Peta asked.

'Sure.'

'While we wait for those, does anyone want a drink?' Bongani asked.

'A cold Coke,' Peta replied.

'I'll have a beer,' Joss said and Mitch agreed.

'I will help you.' Amos stood and disappeared into the kitchen with Bongani.

'I've been meaning to ask if I could visit your project at Matusadona?' Mitch said to Peta. 'Your research into the nocturnal behaviour of rhinos sounds interesting. Joss suggested that I ask to come over and help out for a few days.'

'Sure. If you don't mind staying in the volunteer accommodation.'

'Perfect, thanks, mate,' Mitch said.

'Told you she'd be fine,' Joss taunted Mitch playfully, as if they were still teenage boys.

Bongani and Amos came back, and Joss went to his room to collect the pages from the printer. He returned and put four neat piles of paper on the coffee table.

There was silence as they began to read in earnest.

After a while, Peta dug in her bag and unfolded the taped-together duplicate of her map on the table. She took a pencil and transferred the crosses from Kenneth's new computer file onto her topographical map, making notes of the GPS coordinates of the others that were off the map on the back of one of the pages in the pile.

There were only twenty-five crosses over the whole of Zimbabwe on the original map, sixteen situated within her parks and the surrounding areas, including Tjolotjo and Nyamandhlovu, seven in the concession area, and two near Masvingo. Kenneth Hunt's new map had sixty-three crosses in Matusadona, Chizarira and the surrounding areas, including down in the Tjolotjo and Nyamandhlovu areas. In the Masvingo area alone, there were an additional seventeen crosses.

Peta's eyes filled with unshed tears, and she sniffed. 'If Kenneth's maps and notes on these pages are true, then we are in possession of the location of some of the *Gukurahundi* massacre graves.'

'We have to be sure,' Bongani said. 'We have to substantiate what Hunt said in this file, because this could open many old wounds in the community.'

'I agree,' Joss said. 'When they found mass graves in Afghanistan, we had to send personnel to protect them from the villagers digging them up to see if they could find their loved ones to re-bury them with dignity. But the forensic evidence around the graves needed to be preserved, in case the people responsible for killing all those villagers could be prosecuted. I know a few guys who had that detail, and they can probably tell us more about what to do, who to go to.'

Amos cleared his throat. 'There are many people who have stories of these atrocities, and who cannot speak about them publicly because our government has not changed. They are still scared. For these villagers to have told a white man, and allowed him to mark these graves, they must have trusted him. If we go there, we will break the trust of these people, even though the man is dead. The bush drums will talk, and all these crosses will disappear.'

Bongani nodded. 'Amos is correct. We are going to have to move very slowly and carefully on this information. When does the policeman want Hunt's computer back?'

'Gideon told me they would let me know when it was needed,' Peta said.

'That is good, because the fewer people who know this information, the better,' Bongani said.

'I agree,' Peta said. 'What about Dad and Tsessebe?'

Bongani shook his head. 'Not on the phone. Fill them in when you get back. Everyone be careful with this information. We already know that Tichawana is sniffing around. We cannot afford to have him destroy the evidence. Our people, they need justice for these killings.'

A loud clap of thunder rumbled nearby.

'There's not much food in this house, so we had best go grab some dinner in the lodge before that storm hits,' Joss said.

*   *   *

Joss sat on the couch in Peta's rondavel. Decorated in blacks and whites with monochrome pictures of African fish eagles catching fish in front of majestic vistas of drowned trees, her lounge area had an overstuffed couch and two chairs, excessive for a single person. It was the nicest suite that he had available for her and Joss had purposely not let it out for the next ten days. He yearned to offer her a room in his home, to show that to him, she wasn't a simple guest, she was so much more, but with Sophia in the nursery, Mitch in his own old room, and Madala White and Lwazi in their rooms, the five-bedroom house was suddenly feeling rather small.

'Dinner was lovely, thank you,' she said. 'And I loved the new idea of the serviettes being different animal prints and folded to look like each of the animals. It's a nice touch.'

'The waiters were so excited to spend hours practising that folding and this is the first week they're trying them out. I just wish we could have relaxed a bit more. I think that the universe has thrown us quite enough curve balls for now.'

'You think? The lion, then Sophia, these crosses and the potential for them to be mass graves ... At least I can honestly say that since you came home, life hasn't been boring.' She slid open the door to the private patio. The cool wind off the lake flooded into the room, carrying with it the smell of imminent rain. 'I love watching electrical storms.'

'You always have. I remember you'd sit out on the veranda until my mother would drag you inside.'

'The rain at this time of the year is refreshing,' she said. 'It cleanses your soul.'

Joss raised his eyebrows. 'Excuse me if I don't sit out in it tonight.'

'Seriously, you don't want to try?'

'I might rust,' he joked.

'Joss, you are incorrigible!' Peta said as she flopped onto the couch next to him.

'You sure you still want to come to Bulawayo on Monday, with the spotter problem in your park? They might send a replacement for Hunt at any moment.'

'They won't move fast – there's too much trust in a spotter. They need to know the area well, and also how to move through it unde- tected by the locals. Like Hunt was, using the crosses as his excuse to be where he would normally have raised suspicions. Being away from the parks for a few more days isn't going to matter.'

'I'm still planning on visiting the orphanage, and I've appoint- ments with both the paediatrician and my lawyer. I'm going to ask Charmaine to go with us, to look after Sophia.'

'Too many bodies to fit in either of our *bakkies*,' Peta pointed out. 'Besides, I think you, me and Sophia can cope. Spend some time together, just the three of us.'

Joss looked at her. 'You sure?'

'Yes.'

He stared into her eyes for a long time, searching them, but all he could see was honesty. She wanted to give the three of them a chance. No maid around for Sophia, no Lwazi around to wake him up.

'What if I have another nightmare?' he said.

'Then I shake you and step away, just like Lwazi does. I think we can cope, Joss, and it's only for a few days. See how we go. I adore Sophia, you know that already, and it will give me time with her too, without anyone else hovering to take her away. I won't feel like I'm always being watched with her.'

'You feel watched?'

'A little, but Charmaine is just being herself. She is an extremely nurturing person, even towards Sophia. There is a protectiveness to her that Sophia is lucky to have. I'm not sure I'm built like that.'

Joss tilted her head with his finger and stroked her cheek. 'It's there, deep inside; you just have never been given the opportunity to show it. Remember when Ndhlovy was here with us? You were pretty protective of her, and really nurturing then. But it's not Sophia I have doubts about.'

'You? You think we can't share a room as adults?'

'We already spent one night together, but there is so much more to us now. I don't want to blow our friendship. It's become too important to me.'

'I don't think that a few nights away together will damage us. I'm hoping that the time away could help us decide if we want to take it further.'

Joss smiled and squeezed her hand. 'I agree. I need to make sure that just because I said goodbye to Courtney, you're not simply substituting for what I lost ... we both need so much more than that—'

'Gee, thanks, you know how to make me feel so special,' Peta said, pulling away.

'You know I don't mean it like that. I need time too, to make sure that this shift is what I hope it is. Thank you for your honesty and, as always, your frankness.'

The lightning crackled outside and a clap of thunder shook the ground. Fat drops of rain began falling on the veranda and soon became a sheet of driving rain. A fine mist drifted in on the wind.

'I should close those,' Peta said, standing up and walking to the doors. She slid them together, cocooning them in an artificial quietness. She returned to the couch and took Joss's hand in hers. 'I'm scared. If we become more, and it goes wrong, what if I want to come back to this time and place, and go, this is where I liked you. This is where we were firm friends. Where we shared more than just Courtney between us.'

'I don't have the answer for you, and I'm not sure we can come back; it would always hang between us. But I'm happy to give it a try, like you said, and just go slow. A few days with me, seeing my scars, having to help me in and out of the bath or the shower, being faced with seeing only Mr Half-a-leg.'

'We have time to look forward to the week away together. Doing a few fun things too, like dinner and a little dancing, and having Sophia with us. Just us.'

He smiled again and brought her hand up to his lips. 'Okay, no pressure; that I can handle.'

They sat there, Peta leaning on Joss's shoulder, watching the storm rage outside. He wallowed in the scent of her next to him, the heat radiating from her body as they watched the storm. He watched her eyes grow heavy and close.

Still he sat there.

CHAPTER
22
Bulawayo

Hillary was shopping in the market when she saw him, the white man with the iron legs. It had to be him. Mr Joss Brennan. There couldn't be too many white men in the country with black and silver artificial legs sticking out from the bottom of their shorts. She got her phone out of her bag and typed in his registration number, vehicle type and colour.

She watched as Brennan finished loading the goods from the baby store into his *bakkie*, and that was when she noticed there was a woman with him who carried a child in her arms. She smiled, watching the family, seeing how he laughed when the woman talked, and smoothed her hair aside, tucking it behind her ear. Then he lifted the child and gave it a little wiggle and a kiss before putting it into the front of the *bakkie*.

Even from where she stood, she could see that the baby was not theirs, not biologically. Hillary found it hard to equate this family man to the story of the ruthless commando who unarmed Mr Mlilo within seconds and bruised his back. Brennan was causing her boss to move his 'importation' shipments of ivory and rhino horn to a different boat crossing point away from Binga, and a planned targeted poaching exercise to a different area too, something he had never done before.

Brennan made Mlilo uneasy, and her boss was dismissing him as nothing more than an inconvenience. Watching him, Hillary knew that Tichawana had made a huge error of judgement. Joss Brennan was not a man to be underestimated. Despite his iron legs, he moved with the grace of an athlete, held himself proudly, and he had shown kindness to the woman and child.

The woman and the child. Mlilo had not yet reported either of those, so his intel was not as complete as he thought it was. She wondered what else had been left out of the report, or had been overlooked and not passed on to her boss.

She continued watching as Brennan closed the door of the *bakkie* for the woman. He touched her arm through the window before he moved to his side of the vehicle and climbed in. She watched them drive further down the road, stop and get out again at the Private Medical Centre. They walked into the building and she couldn't see them any more.

Realising that she was standing in the middle of the pavement, staring at nothing, she forced herself to continue walking to the taxi rank. Now that she had seen him, her mind reeled with possibilities. It was getting close to the time that she would have to admit to herself that she could no longer just hold on to her files. Tichawana Ndou was planning something against his half-brother, but she did not know what. She didn't yet know how the many threads she had collected knitted together. She knew that if she took her information to Brennan, he would know what to do with it.

He would help her to bring down her family's murderers.

*   *   *

The paediatrician's office was already running four hours late.

Peta sighed and looked at the clock on the wall, willing it to stop or the appointment would run into the one they had with the lawyer at five-thirty. First the orphanage had cut their shopping trip short, now the doctors were on the same track. Everything ran on Africa time. She noticed the other mothers in the room openly admiring Joss as he returned from fetching her a scarf from the bakkie to put around her shoulders. The way he moved, his physical appearance, but, as they ran their eyes down his body and legs, their looks changed to pity as they noticed the gleaming metal and black plastic, and they averted their eyes.

He sat down next to her, peeking at Sophia, who slept soundly on a mat on the floor. 'She still out?'

'I think she could sense your turmoil this morning at the orphanage, and it drained her,' Peta said. 'I'm glad we went and had a look, but I'm more glad it's over.'

He put his hand on Peta's neck and massaged it gently. 'Thanks for coming. It confirmed that I've made the right decision in keeping her. Jarryd and his orphanage are definitely only Plan B if welfare give me trouble.'

Peta moved slightly so that he could massage her shoulders. 'I could get used to this.'

'Me too,' Joss said.

'Brennan family, you can go in now,' called the receptionist.

Joss picked up Sophia, who had become restless in her sleep, a sure sign she was waking, while Peta collected the rug and the bag.

The doctor was writing something at her desk, and motioned them in with her hand, not looking up. After a few moments, she finished and stood up as Joss and Peta reached the desk. 'I'm Kim Swart, nice to meet you. Sorry, I was just finishing up a report.'

'I'm Joss, this is Peta, and this sleepy girl is Sophia.'

'Hello, beautiful,' Kim said. She reached over her desk, and patted Sophia's back as she lay against Joss's shoulder, before sitting down. She gestured for them to take a seat and glanced at her file. 'So, little Sophia was an abandoned baby, left at your home, Joss?'

'That's right.'

'She has deformities in both legs.'

'Also correct.'

Kim's head snapped up. 'You're willing to keep this child, even though she might never walk?'

'Yes. What difference would that make?'

'About five hundred thousand US dollars and counting.'

'I didn't pay for her—'

'No, you misunderstand. That's going to be the cost of having a disabled child, above and beyond what you would normally expect to spend raising a child in Zimbabwe in the private education system. You don't have to keep this child; she can go into an orphanage and be cared for by the state. Deformed black children are often shunned by their Ndebele playmates; the old traditions still run strong. Being a cripple will cause you more trouble as she grows up—'

'Dr Swart,' Joss interrupted her. 'There's something you should know, before you say another word. I recently became a double amputee. Sophia was given to me because I know what it's like to be a "cripple". Who better to be her dad than someone who has no legs and understands her needs?'

Kim nodded slowly. 'I guess I owe you an apology. This will make explaining the whole process easier.'

'Also, she has already been living with me for a while. We visited the Baobab Tree Orphanage to see if she would be better off there than with me, and the answer is no – she'll be better off with me. I'm keeping Sophia, and our next stop after here is the lawyer's office to begin the adoption process. What I wanted to know is how bad her deformity is and if it can be fixed. Is she healthy in every other way? Because if she isn't, then I need to organise other treatments for her, besides her legs.'

'It's wonderful to see your passion for her. You three, you'll be fine.'

'Three?' Peta said. 'Oh no, there is no three. Just two. Joss and Sophia live a few hours from me.'

Kim looked at Joss. 'You're a single white man trying to adopt a black child? Did your lawyer explain how hard this is going to be for you?'

'He did. Hard, but not impossible.'

'Okay. Let's get looking at your precious bundle. Pop her on the bed and get everything off except her nappy.'

Joss put Sophia on the examination bed and removed her clothes. He blew a raspberry on her stomach and she laughed.

Kim began with Sophia's mouth and worked her way downwards.

'Can she get around on her own at all?'

'Yes,' Joss said, and explained her hopping style of moving.

Kim was making Sophia giggle as she tickled her and rubbed her feet. 'Other than her legs, Sophia appears to be a healthy child.' She lifted her up into a sitting position, and Sophia adjusted herself to balance on the bed. 'She's got good balance. I'd like to do an X-ray of her legs. See what those bones look like inside.'

'Sure,' Joss said.

Kim lay Sophia back down. 'I'll take some blood, then she's free to go get those scans.'

'Do I need to hold her?' Joss asked but Kim had already put a needle into Sophia's arm. Sophia was trying to bat away a large pendant that swung from Kim's neck.

'All done,' she said, placing the tubes of blood on the table next to her. He watched Kim dress Sophia, then unwrap a lollipop she'd pulled from the jar next to the bed and give it to her before passing her back to her father.

'My receptionist will walk you through to the X-ray department. Once you're done, please come right back. I'll fit you in as soon as I can to review the films,' Kim said.

*   *   *

Kim put the X-rays up on her light box. 'I'm not going to sugar coat this. There are going to be three schools of thought on Sophia's prognosis. One would be to just leave her, wait and see what happens as she grows. Others will suggest breaking her legs and operating on them, putting in pins and plates, then have her learn to walk. But she might have to have multiple operations, and keep having them as she gets older. A third option would be to have these legs surgically removed once she's a little older, and helping her learn to walk with artificial legs.'

'If we take option one for now, and just wait and see how her legs go as she grows?'

'You'll have a little girl who'll have immense upper body strength, having to drag those useless legs around behind her. But she'll never walk without intervention. We can't perform any major operation on her legs until she is older, so you have time on your side before you make a final decision.'

'Is there any indication when she'll begin to talk?'

'I think she's choosing not to. She has her every need taken care of, so she hasn't needed to. It might be she's only learning English now, so she's working on being bilingual. Give her more time to settle into your home and she'll begin to talk more. If she isn't talking by the time she's about three, then we can look into it. Kids are resilient; they find out what their bodies can and can't do. She'll develop at her own rate, but by twenty-one she'll be exactly like any other 21-year-old, except she'll have fought a huge battle with her legs, and we can only speculate on that outcome. Just remember to toddler proof your house. Things that you think are out of her reach, she will get to.'

Joss smiled. 'We've already found that out.'

'She's totally normal. Living with you, she'll never think herself as anything but. She is lucky to have you. I guess that mother knew what she was doing when she gave her up. Just be careful – you are going to have to ensure that the area you live in knows that you are not a private orphanage, that this is a one-time thing with little Sophia, or you will end up with more children than you can imagine.'

Joss nodded.

'I'll see you as soon as her blood work comes through so we can do her inoculations and get her up to date, and here are some papers to get an MRI. You might need to take her down south for that, as the machine here is broken again. Once those are done, we can discuss the prognosis of her legs and what other specialists we need to involve in getting her walking.'

Joss knew that their journey was only just beginning, but he also understood it better than anyone else. He was going to be with Sophia every step of the way.

*   *   *

Peta was kneeling on the floor of the nursery, sorting through the stuff they had brought home, packing clothes and blankets and sheets into the new cupboards. Joss took a step towards her, then stopped himself. She'd looked so happy when they were buying the stuff for the nursery but she'd been pretty adamant in Dr Swart's office that they were only friends.

She turned as if sensing his presence. 'Is she down at last?'

'Yeah, she was exhausted from the trip, I think. Overtired. She played with that new doll almost the whole way home, instead of sleeping like I thought she would,' he said, slipping down to sit next to her.

'You're going to regret getting down so far,' she said.

'No regrets,' he said, smiling.

'I bet when you were sixteen and leaving to go to the commandos, you wouldn't have even considered taking on a crippled orphan child.'

Joss nodded. 'I guess I've grown up a little since then.' He ran his fingers up her arm.

'We're all forced to,' she said. 'It's called maturing.'

They sat looking at each other. He searched her face for some sign, for something to say what she wanted now that their time away was over, and if she had made a different decision on them and their friendship.

Then she leant forward and kissed him softly on the lips.

'I'm sorry—' She broke the kiss but didn't move away.

'There's nothing to be sorry for,' he said and dipped his head for another kiss.

He felt her arms wrap around his shoulders, her fingers in his hair. The sound of Sophia crying on the baby monitor interrupted them.

'This isn't finished,' Joss said as he clambered up and went to settle Sophia, his mind filled with images of where he and Peta could have ended up if they hadn't been interrupted.

* * *

Joss knocked on Peta's rondavel door. He heard her check who was there before she unlocked the latch, and opened it.

'Hey, you,' she said. 'Come on in.'

'Hi. I asked Lwazi to watch over Sophia for a few hours. He's so excited with some of her toys we brought home, I feel that I should be showering him with the gifts I bought for him too, not waiting till he's ready for them. He's going to love those sports sunglasses we picked up.'

Peta laughed. 'He's still a big kid at heart. I know you think of him as grown up and mature, but remember what you were like at fourteen? I remember you were just as energetic as him, and it was as if you couldn't sit still ever. I remember when you tested your boundaries with your folks, a lot. You and Courtney got tossed out of a nightclub in Harare, if I remember rightly, and she was suspended from school for two weeks for some prank you guys did together.' She sat on the couch.

Joss laughed and ran his hand through his hair before sitting next to her. 'Bubble bath. They were rationing the girls' bathwater, but they had the fountain bubbling up and looking great. It was Courtney's idea, to protest that they couldn't have bubble baths. I just helped. I never understood why I didn't also get suspended.'

'You didn't go to her school. And you were a golden sports star at yours. They never would have punished you for anything, as long as you kept winning their rugby matches for them in the winter, and their swimming carnivals in summer.'

'I just didn't get caught and she never ratted me out. Besides, it wasn't my fault I was good at sport. Lwazi doesn't test boundaries, he doesn't have the same restrictions put on him that we did. He's fourteen and already earning his own money, and Madala has him learning to save and budget already.'

'Well, I'm glad he's watching out for Sophia for the next couple of hours at least,' Peta said, grinning. 'I wish that I had let my hair down more like you and Courtney did when I was in my teens.'

'Me too,' Joss said, taking her hand in his. 'But I'm not sure that at twenty-two you would have got away with half the pranks we did. You might already have been too old even then.'

'Gee, thanks for reminding me that I am so much older than you,' she said, attempting to pull her hand out of his.

He held on to it. 'Not happening. We are staying connected for this conversation.'

'What conversation?' Peta asked.

'The one that is happening now. About that kiss …'

Peta let her hand go slack, then turned her fingers to thread them through his. 'What about it?'

'I wanted to know if it means what I hope it does. That the look of my mutilated body didn't repel you this week, nor did the fact that you need to be as strong as you are to actually help me sometimes.'

'You are an idiot, Joss Brennan. If you think I'm going to look at you differently because you are missing one and a half legs and have a few scars …'

'I think we already established that I'm definitely an idiot. But I was asking if you would take me as your idiot?'

Peta grinned. She leant towards him and he matched her stance on the couch, putting his forehead to hers.

'I think that we both know that what's happening with us isn't just a transfer of friendship from Courtney to me. We both know that I'm going to be called a "cougar" by many people, and I don't care one ounce for their opinions. I would like to believe that you knew my answer was always going to be that you were already my idiot. From the moment you walked in the stupid road at Beit Bridge. I should have run over you and done away with a lot of the heartache I know will come from us being together.'

Joss tilted her head and kissed her. He said against her lips, 'I don't know how I got so lucky to have found you again in my life, but I thank the universe that you can see past everything, and still see me. The real me. I want you, Peta. I can't say it was that first night together, but I can honestly say this was inevitable for me. I can't imagine life here without you. I love you. I want you in my life, always. And even though I know that we'll still have obstacles in our way, I want to believe that together we can achieve anything we want to.'

'Rewind to the part where you said, "I love you", and I'll be happy.'

'I love you,' he repeated for her, between kisses and holding her close.

'I love you too, Joss.'

CHAPTER

23

An Elder's Secrets

Amos moved from his hiding place on top of the *koppie*, throwing a small stone down the side, hoping that it would reach Julian Seziba waiting at the bottom. Julian quietly moved away from the face of the *koppie* where they had set up camp and signalled that he was ready for the next instruction. Amos pointed down the road. A column of dust rose into the air where a *bakkie* was moving at high speed. If the traveller was legitimate, they would carry on past the hidden turn-off to the hunting camp on the outskirts of Chizarira.

They didn't.

Instead the dust seemed to hang, before changing direction and heading towards the *koppie*, to where the spotter's camp was. Amos took his binoculars out at the same moment that Julian began climbing for a better vantage point.

At first Amos hadn't understood why Bongani had insisted that he take Julian with him, but now he had set out to learn all he could from the old man because, although he moved more slowly than the younger rangers, his mind was sharper than an *assegai* honed for a fight. Julian had proven that he was a mine of information.

'Two men. One white, one black,' Amos said.

Julian looked through the binoculars Bongani had given him. 'That man who drives does not respect machines. Look at the speed he drives at. It means he has more money than sense, and he does not care about destroying things. Machinery. Lives. He has potential to be a killer.'

'That is three-quarters of the white men in Africa,' Amos said. 'The black man, he looks ahead; he has not turned his head to the side. Not once. He is used to travelling like this. They are used to each other.'

'I see him. He looks like an Ndebele.'

'Can you see in the back?'

Julian raised his binoculars again. He shook his head and made a gesture to indicate that the back was covered. They had waited a whole week for someone to arrive and now they watched to see what the men would do.

'Can you read the plates?' Amos asked.

Julian read the 4x4's number plate through the binoculars and Amos texted it to Bongani.

When Peta had found Hunt's body and been so insistent that she get to keep the laptop, Amos had not fully comprehended why she was worried. She had understood the significance of those numbers and images on the computer. When they had stumbled on this place, and then got the confirmation from the files, the pieces had begun to fall into place for him: Peta was walking into trouble if she carried on looking at these graves. Someone was using the information that Hunt had been collecting, and no one leaves a dead man's possessions in the bush for long. Not any more, not with the communication available nowadays. Whoever his partners were, they might have left his body to be claimed by the police, but the equipment and his belongings, they would want to collect those.

He took the cover off the camera that Mitch had given them to use, with its lens that was so big it had meant he had had to leave a whole extra week's worth of rations behind, and began taking photos.

The men parked their vehicle under the hunter's net before they retrieved deck chairs, lit a fire and settled in for the night. The fire glowed red, but if they had been at ground level, it would have been difficult to see. Once the smoke had begun to disperse on the breeze it would have been difficult to even tell where the fire was. It would take time to track down a fire like that.

The white man had climbed to the top of the smaller *koppie* right next to the campsite, stretched his back, urinated, and then sat on a boulder to watch the sun set.

Amos said, 'Guess not even a small fire for us tonight and cold food.'

'*Yebo*, but I cannot remember when packet stew last tasted so exciting. The camp food that Mitch loaded us up with is better than any rations I ever got working in these parks.'

'Exciting? Are you sure you are using the right word? We might have to run for our lives if they discover us.'

Julian nodded. 'If we simply do our jobs right, we will not be found, young man. Bongani, he told me to show you some of the older tracker skills while we are watching them. This is the first one: I am sleeping first; wake me at three am.'

Amos chuckled quietly. 'Why did they let you go? You still have so much to pass on to others who need to learn.'

'Because the men who took over are stupid; they are there for power, not passion for the bush and the animals they are supposed to protect. They see an old man, one who cannot read a paper or write his name, and they believe he is the past. They think we are useless. They do not realise that the old ones, it is where much of the real wealth, the knowledge, still lies.' He pointed to his head. 'They are *penga*. They do not understand. They put all our animals in danger, because they allow mistakes that have happened before to reoccur, because they do not ask the old people; they get rid of us. Chief Bongani, he is a clever one. This is his area, and he knows what is happening in it, and no one is going to hurt this park while he can help it.'

Amos sat quietly for a while. 'Has this happened before? Has someone set up these spotter camps in the game park while you have been alive?'

'Always. White, black, private or government. The Chizarira, it is a sanctuary for beasts, birds and *skabenga*s. It is always the job of the rangers to remove the *skabenga*s.'

*   *   *

The sun rose bright red in an indigo sky, caressing the African bush with the hope of a new day. If the men in the camp had been more observant, they would have noticed that the *koppie* had grown a few new plants overnight: Julian and Amos had fortified their position, fearing the reflection from their binoculars and the camera now that people were in the spotter's camp.

The silence was disturbed by a string of profanities as one of the men washed in cold water in an outdoor shower.

Julian lay on his stomach next to Amos. 'See? I told you they would take the water from their *bakkie* to wash in the morning. They do not know this land as we do. These men were told of this place on a map; they know nothing about the spring that lies just around the corner.'

The white man came out of the shower area quickly, his hair wet.

The black man was laughing at him. He opened a beer and passed it to the white man before he crossed over to their camp kitchen area and cooked them breakfast on the small fire.

'What are they waiting for?' Amos asked.

'I do not know,' Julian said.

They watched the men begin to dismantle the spotter's camp. The large crates were brought out, the straw emptied and piled against the rocks, then the crosses came out and were thrown where the fire had been. They packed both crates in the *bakkie* and filled them with all the items that had been in the camp.

Julian stretched a little then resettled under the tarp. 'These men, they are not listening to the earth with their poaching, so she will send in someone to bite them, and they will feel her vengeance.'

'Hopefully that is so. Perhaps in time we will get a chance to confront them, but today is not the day.'

'Those two men are marked for destroying this ancient land, for destroying the animals of the BaTonga people.'

Amos looked at the sun, and then at the two men. The black man was burning the crosses. Black smoke swelled into the sky, a by-product of the paint covering the wood, but the man threw on a bush, turning the smoke white as you would expect from a bush-fire, and the breeze gently blew it away.

'The white man is still very colonial. He just sits in his deck chair while the black man does all the hot work.'

'No, look, the white man is sick; he is sucking on an asthma pump.'

Julian clicked his tongue. 'You sure? Perhaps that is just his manner. Like *Ikanka yabo.*'

'I work around *Baas* Rodger all the time,' Amos said. 'It is not his manners that are faulty, just his brain.'

'He always said he had no love for a *kaffir* boy. I have seen him string up a poacher by the ankles, and start to gut him like a buck before he got information from him. Another time, I saw him pull the pin from a grenade and tape it in a poacher's hands, then tape them up. He would cut the tape so that if the poacher wanted to he could break it, but in breaking it, the grenade would go off. He marched that man through the bush until he got to his camp, where he arrested the other men.'

'I knew that *ikanka yabo* earned his Ndebele name, but I never knew you worked with him.'

'For many-many years we worked together. When he first came to the Matusadona. With him and Stephen, Joss's father. I was always thankful that I was on their side, and not a poacher. But even with the news of how the poachers were treated within the reserve getting out to the people around Chizarira and Matusadona, the poaching continued. Then the armies came and shot so many animals, and I saw both those men weep over elephant herds that were killed for no reason other than their ivory, because someone far away wanted a pretty ornament.'

'Rodger cried?'

Julian nodded. 'When independence came, Stephen built his lodge. Rodger stayed for a few more years, and I was let go.'

'Any others rangers who knew of these ancient sacred places we will visit?'

'There was a young white ranger; his name was Hunt. Albert Hunt. And his tracker, Elmon Dudzi.'

'That is interesting,' Amos said. 'Did he have a son, or a brother that you knew of?'

Julian's mind raced back in time. 'I cannot be sure. He did not stay very long in the Chizarira before he went away to war.'

They lapsed into silence.

Half an hour passed before there was more movement at the spotter's camp. 'Look. The white man is getting into the passenger side of *bakkie* – perhaps they are almost done.'

The black man closed the chairs and put them in the back. Finally, he walked to the *koppie*, slashed a few bushes and dragged them to cover where the camp had stood. He went to the driver's side and climbed in. Slowly, with a lot more respect for his companion than he had been shown as a passenger, he drove away from the site.

Amos continued taking photographs until they couldn't see the small dust cloud in the distance.

* * *

Peta sat on the edge of her chair at the dining table in Joss's house listening to Amos recount his adventure with Julian in the parks. Joss put his hand on her thigh to steady her leg as she bounced it up and down. But then his finger started drawing circles and she had to put her hand on top of his to stop it creeping upwards. She was still trying hard to digest the change in their relationship, but one thing was for sure – being together was now a reality. Everything else they could work out.

'What else did you find, Amos?' Bongani asked.

'Julian said that there were two more people we had to check who knew about the old prospectors' camps: Elmon Dudzi and Albert Hunt,' Amos said.

'I knew Francis was not Elmon. Francis came clean with me in the hope that I would help him. He is still in Amalunandi Village, feeding my useless brother the information we ask him to. We should get him back here and ask him more questions because we still do not know what has happened to the real Elmon,' Bongani said.

'Your brother has two spies that you know of watching you,' Joss said. 'And he's doing something suspicious with children—'

'I'd hazard a guess there's more than that,' Mitch said.

'The white man, Albert Hunt?' Amos asked. 'Do you remember what happened to him?'

Bongani shook his head. 'I do not even remember him at all. Although the name Hunt is familiar—'

'Albert Hunt was the spotter Kenneth Hunt's father,' Peta said. 'I'm pretty certain that there was something about an Albert Hunt in the file that we got off his computer.' She went and got her copy from her bag, and flicked through until she found the passage she was after. 'Here, Albert died in 1978, in the bush war.'

'The Hunt family again,' Joss said. 'I think they're worth looking into a little more.'

Peta nodded. 'Perhaps it's time that we include Gideon Mthemba. We're going to need the police's help with this. These people are clearly trespassing in the parks.'

'Do you trust Gideon, Amos?' Bongani asked.

Amos nodded. 'He is the type of man who cannot be bought. He has helped us before when Peta wanted to keep the computer.'

'That may not be such a bad idea then,' Bongani said. 'With the spotters' camps and the continual talk of my brother taking children into youth camps, it is probably time to investigate exactly what Tichawana is up to.'

'We need to take this further up the chain in ZimParks,' Peta said.

'No,' said Bongani and Joss at the same time.

'You can keep Tsessebe and Rodger in the loop because they already know of the crosses, but no one else,' Bongani said.

'I will approach Gideon,' Amos said. 'According to Julian, there was a powerful *N'Goma* in the old days who, along with *Nyami Nyami*, protects the ancestral land and the sacred ground within the park. He said that if someone is making a profit at the expense of the people, they will face the *muti*, and their death.'

'You believe in that stuff?' Peta asked.

Amos shook his head. 'No, but I respect that others believe in it.'

Bongani said, 'It was always said that the curse was to ensure that any money made from these lands was used for the good of the BaTonga people, or there would be a blood price to pay.'

'Nice curse your *N'Goma*s came up with,' Peta said. 'But how exactly does it work?'

'They claim that it had always been here, since the days of the Portuguese slave traders. Each *N'Goma*, they add to it when they learn their trade, protecting their people, who they will serve. That is how the legend goes. But the people who it affects have to be on BaTonga land for it to work. The curse doesn't work outside the borders, but no one can be sure.'

Joss cleared his throat. 'I'm not so sure on this magic part, but it seems to me these men who burnt the crosses had no idea what they were for. So we can probably believe what is written about the crosses in Hunt's computer files. His information is too accurate to have been an elaborate hoax or anything like that. His passworded files were precious, even though he was in the middle of the bush. A cautious man, with the information he was in possession of meticulously documented. I think we have three different problems here. We have the crosses, and what they might possibly represent, and then we have the game-spotter problem, and then the youth camps.'

Bongani nodded. 'Four. Add Tichawana in there too, because I bet he had a hand in there somewhere. I think, too, that we need to be wary of speaking in front of Ephraim, who repeats everything to Mary, who still reports to my half-brother. Perhaps the boys need to learn more about those beehives and chilli plants in Bishu, at my cousin Anton's fishing village. Spend another week there, so that they are not around here for a while. We need time to sort this out, without Tichawana knowing what we are planning, just in case he is involved.'

'Lwazi will be pleased; he seemed quite taken with the bee queen, Matilda, from the last visit,' Joss said.

'He won't be so keen after he's been stung a few times,' Peta said. 'Bee stings hurt.'

24

Recognition

Joss, Lwazi and Mitch were getting ready to take their bikes out together. For the first time, they were going to ride to the tar road that went up towards the Sijarira Safari Area, and then towards Binga and back, a big circle.

'Put on your helmet, Lwazi,' Joss instructed.

'I look stupid,' Lwazi said. 'You see the black people riding their bicycles all the time, and no one wears a helmet. And no one wears these tight girl shorts with a big pad between their legs either. If anyone sees me, they will think I am a poofter.'

'There is nothing wrong with being gay,' Joss said.

'No one wants to be seen as being one or they come and take you into the camp for correctional training. There was this kid, I saw him in Binga at the store. He said that I had better behave and not act like a poofter, or the green bombers would come get me. They take kids to the camps and they train them so that they can fight and stuff.'

Mitch frowned. 'Fight? In a youth camp?'

'That's what he said,' Lwazi said, still looking down and tugging at his new cycling pants.

'Ridiculous,' Joss muttered under his breath, but made a mental note to speak with Bongani about it – this was the third time the youth camps had come up. Then, louder, he said, 'You'll be happy for that extra padding in an hour or so. The helmet is still a deal breaker. We already discussed this – wear it or you don't ride with me. If you fall off when riding at our speeds, you'll crack your head open, and Madala White will never forgive me.'

Lwazi nodded, then gave his pants a last tug.

'You can wear normal shorts over them if you want,' Mitch said, 'but that padding will help. Believe me, these are better than shorts and if us marines can wear them, so can you.' Joss smiled and pulled his latest surprise for Lwazi out of his pocket. 'Perhaps if you stopped moaning about your clothing, you might see these, and think they are okay. Looks like they will go with that stupid helmet just fine.'

'These are mine?' Lwazi asked, looking at the polarised sports glasses swinging from Joss's fingers.

'You don't have to wear them if they're going to make you feel like a girl,' Joss teased.

'Awesome. Thank you,' Lwazi said, putting them on.

Joss shook his head.

Mitch laughed. 'You willingly signed up to be a father, and will have to put up with this type of backchat from your daughter one day.'

'No, everyone says girls are easier than boys.'

'When they are *younger*,' Mitch said slowly, as if trying to get the word into Joss's head.

Joss had changed the attachments on the end of his prosthetics for cycling grips, and was now mounting his bike using a small wall for balance.

'Come on, Joss,' called Lwazi, who stood with his bike between his legs.

'Let's go,' Joss said and he pushed off, wobbled for an instant before the momentum of the bike picked up and he glided as best he could across the gravel.

Cycling on the road was never as easy as using the stationary bike in his gym, but Joss used the gears, finding one that worked for him on the small incline. He could see Lwazi hadn't changed gears. Like any teenager, he was hurtling along headfirst, just knowing that he would have enough energy to ensure he'd get through the day – if he had to dig deep, he would. Lwazi had the temperament of a natural competitor. Of a winner.

They were booked into their first biathlon later in the year and although he hadn't told Lwazi yet, Joss knew he would do well. He'd held off booking into the Ironman triathlon because, although it was still a dream to compete in it, it was no longer so important to him. The restlessness he felt when in England had abated in Africa, and he was content. The importance of competing paled in comparison to seeing the joy of Lwazi learning to ride and run and watching the lap pool being constructed, knowing that soon the boy would learn how to swim. Competing in the triathlon would take Joss away from watching Sophia wake each morning and giggle and reach up to him. He knew that she would begin to talk one of these days and if he was away, he might miss her first words. His heart broke that Peta would probably miss them anyhow, even if he got his camera in time to record it, as despite wanting to be together all the time, her work was in Matusadona and Chizarira, and his lodge wasn't part of that. For the moment, she was the one doing all the travelling. Keeping Rodger as settled as possible was high on both of their agendas. While they had told him they were 'dating', they hadn't discussed him possibly moving to the lodge if Peta did. After all, they were a package deal: Peta, Rodger and Tsessebe. He'd known that from the onset. And he wouldn't have Peta any other way.

Just thinking of her had him smiling, wondering what she was up to.

He glanced at his watch. Already an hour had passed; it was almost time to turn back on the road.

'Come on, move it, slow poke,' Mitch called as he passed him, and Joss showed him his middle finger. Only to see Lwazi jam on his brakes, his bike skidding to a halt.

Mitch almost hit him, stopping just in time. He stood there like a buck in the headlights.

Joss turned small circles as close to Lwazi as he could, keeping his bike upright.

Crossing the road in front of them was a herd of elephants. The matriarch was already halfway across. Behind her, a baby followed closely, but it was playing, dragging a stick with it. The matriarch was big, and she wore an old and worn collar behind her ears. She flapped her ears at them, smelling the air as she did. She seemed to hesitate, then the elephant behind her nudged her forward, and she moved about two steps before turning again to Joss. This time she stepped towards them.

'This is not good,' Lwazi said. 'She does not look happy with us.'

The matriarch continued to flap her ears, and had her trunk raised, smelling.

'Hold on to me while I unclip,' Joss said, and he stopped next to Lwazi, who already had his feet firmly on the ground.

Lwazi held tightly to the frame of the bike as Joss got his 'feet' out of his pedals.

The elephant listened to the strange noise, but she didn't back away. Behind her, the herd continued to cross the road, confident that the matriarch would protect them, her rumbles soft and reassuring.

She took another step forward.

'Ndhlovy,' he called. 'Is that you? It's me. It's Joss.'

The elephant flapped her ears again and she took another step towards them.

'Lwazi, go down the road with Mitch. She looks like the elephant I saved, and I'm not sure if she remembers me.'

Lwazi shook his head. 'If I leave you here, and she charges, she will trample you.'

'If she was going to charge, she would have done so already. She's smelling us, she's curious.'

The matriarch took another step. Now her trunk wasn't held high, she had brought it down, and made a loud, long, rumble sound.

'You're crazy, Joss,' Mitch said. 'Been nice knowing you. We thought you were nuts in Afghanistan; now I know you're certified crazy. Have you not noticed the size of that thing?'

'I know, but I think she knows me,' Joss said.

Lwazi made sure that Joss was standing, then slowly backed away.

'I'm not sure why I'm agreeing to this,' Mitch muttered as he backed away too.

'Come on, Ndhlovy. Come on, old friend. Come and say hello.'

The elephant took another hesitant step, then Joss began whistling like he used to when he was a boy, making calls through his hand, trying to imitate birds, like Bongani did, although he had never perfected it. He had spent many hours around the elephant, practising, driving both Courtney and Peta mad.

Ndhlovy took another few steps until she was near enough to him that he could see the black hairs on her grey body. She reached her truck to his outstretched hand, and put the tip into his palm.

'Hello, girl.' He smiled. 'It's good to see you. You've been on my mind a lot lately.'

She shook her head like a dog would and placed her trunk back in his hand, then slowly began smelling him all over, across his face, checking him out, getting to know the man he'd become. He patted her trunk, and she stepped closer to him.

'I know, girl, I know. An older me. A man now. Look at you. A matriarch. Good to see you are still safe.'

Her trunk found the prosthetic blades he wore for cycling. She stepped back, and her ears flapped. A low rumble vibrated through him.

'It's okay, girl, these are my legs now.' He took her trunk in his hands and slowly moved it back to his legs, showing her that they were part of him.

'I lost them, girl, I left them in Afghanistan,' he said. 'Shit happened there, and they were lost. Just like I see you are no longer travelling with your mother and grandmother.'

She smoothed her trunk over his cheek, much as she had when he was ten years old.

'It's good to see you are so big.' He patted her and she brought her head against his, as if trying to comfort him. He scratched her ear. 'Look at this; so much has happened to you too. You're in a tracking program. I wonder if whoever did that even knew that they were tracking my elephant?'

Ndhlovy made a rumbling sound that vibrated up her trunk.

'I know, girl. So many years have passed, but I'm back. I'm home now. And I'm not leaving ever again.' He ran his hand along her tusk.

An elephant from her herd trumpeted, and she moved her head slightly. Another deep rumble came from her.

'Listen to you; you are the matriarch now. The protector. The decision maker. I wonder what happened, how both your grandma and your mum passed over so early, that you are already in this position? They visited me, you know, when I was drifting, after my accident. They made me come back; perhaps they knew that we needed to meet again.'

She stepped away, but she left her trunk on his shoulder.

'I know. You need to go. Look after your family. I'll see you at the grove soon,' he said. 'Be safe, Ndhlovy.' He held his hand out to her.

She put the tip of her trunk into his hand once more, before turning away and walking slowly back into the bushes, where she blended into the environment.

Joss watched her go.

He wanted her to turn around, to look back at him, to come back to him again. But he also wanted her to continue her life now that he knew that she was alive. Relief lifted his heart. He hadn't realised that not knowing about her all these years had been so much a part of his life. He had always hoped, but now he knew.

'If I tell anyone about what I just saw, no one would believe me,' Lwazi said as he came up behind Joss. 'You and that elephant really do know each other; it is as if she was sad about your legs.'

'Holy shit,' Mitch said. 'I took photos of that whole meeting, mate. That's the only way anyone would ever believe me when I tell them about this.'

'I was ten when I rescued Ndhlovy,' Joss said. 'You have no idea how glad I am to see she's still alive, that the poachers and hunters haven't got her. Come on, Lwazi, help me back on my bike.'

'You rescued her when you lived in the lodge? Not in the game park?' Mitch asked.

'Yes.'

'No way,' Lwazi said. 'Ephraim and I thought you were exaggerating when you told me about her – we have never seen an elephant here. Ever.'

'She'll come back. We must warn the villagers that she'll go right past there with her herd soon. They'll come through the gate up past the old stables, then down to the grove. It's an old elephant trail; that's why there were no buildings there – the track was there when my dad and Bongani set down the plan for the lodge. It's sad that she is now probably the only one who remembers this path to the trees that heal.'

CHAPTER

25

Glowing Embers

The rhino bull was huge, probably one of the biggest she had seen in the park. She looked through the binoculars. This old bull had witnessed many years. No ear notching, so he definitely hadn't been caught before, and judging by the size of his horns, she was glad she had got there before the poachers or the trophy hunters.

He smelt the air.

A go-away bird called, announcing their presence, just as Peta released her breath and squeezed her trigger. The shot sounded loud in the early morning. Immediately the rhino turned towards where she was concealed, his big feet planted firmly on the ground, his head up, as if knowing that was the direction the pain had come from. For a split second he seemed to watch her, even though she knew he couldn't see where she hid. They had chosen their spot well, downwind so that he couldn't smell them. While their sense of smell and hearing were keen, the rhino didn't have great sight, and couldn't tell the difference between a tree and a human at fifteen feet.

He began to run, 3600 kilograms of angry animal hurtling towards her.

He veered left and ran past her and the team in the bushes. For about fifty metres he ran, then slowed and began to stagger, the opioid she had administered via the dart taking effect.

'Go,' she shouted. Her team ran to the rhino.

Mitch let out the breath he'd been holding. 'Shit, Peta, I can't believe you do this day in, day out. He ran right at us and you didn't so much as flinch.'

She grinned at him. 'Just make sure you don't put any shots of my fat butt in your photos. And remember to keep out of the way unless I ask you to do something.' She went to join her team. Amos was right next to her, carrying her Husqvarna chainsaw.

The team of men were skilled and well practised in dehorning and they clambered to get a rope around the rhino's snout, a soft blanket around its eyes, and then pushed it over onto its side.

'Slowly, careful,' she said as she always did. At this stage the rhino was pretty much out of it, and special care needed to be taken to ensure it fell onto soft ground, not rocks or tree branches that could cause unnecessary lesions. She moved closer. Amos stepped forward and stuffed some cloth balls into the animal's ears to cut out as much noise as possible and make the treatment easier on it. He put the chainsaw on the ground and knelt next to the rhino's head.

Peta checked the rhino's front leg to ensure it didn't get muscle strain from being at a bad angle, patted him on the shoulder as she knelt and put her stethoscope to its chest, listening to the heartbeat.

'Sounding good,' she said, and looked at Amos.

'Breathing steady,' he said as he glanced at his watch to check the time.

Peta nodded. 'Let's start then. Pass the scalpel,' she said, and took the instrument from Assan, her latest vet student. 'Watch carefully.' She took a scraping of hair and passed the scalpel back to him. 'Now you do it.'

He copied her and soon had the hair samples tucked away in his bag.

'Syringe,' she said. He passed it with the needle pointing away from her. She removed the covering from the needle with her teeth, then inserted the needle directly into a vein at the back of the rhino's ear and drew out a sample of blood.

'Amos,' she said, and he moved close and held a cloth soaked in Betadine on the pinprick. Moving slightly away and taking the cover from her mouth, she sheathed the needle again and passed the sample to Assan.

'Got it,' he said, closing his left hand on the syringe, and holding out what looked like a couple of large pairs of scissors with his other hand. One was a clamp and the other razor-sharp surgical forceps.

Assan held a picture in front of her and she followed the notching that they had chosen as the identification for the rhino bull.

'Good boy, you are not bleeding too much,' she said as she sprinkled Terramycin powder onto the wound, then sprayed it with gentian violet to seal the cuts as well as help them heal.

'There you go; you'll be purple and fashionable for a few days, but it'll help keep infection out,' she said as she passed the sample of the ear to Assan. She measured the horns, marked out where she would cut, making sure she left at least an eight-centimetre stub so as not to damage the rhino's sinuses. She stood up and stretched her back. Amos removed the chainsaw from its case and handed it to her.

'Everyone clear,' Peta said, and once she had checked they were, she flicked the switch and the chainsaw roared into life, the sound totally alien in the African bush. Carefully she cut the biggest horn. 'Water,' she said when she was about halfway through, and Amos splashed water on the horn to keep it cool. She continued to cut.

Once that was cleared, she began on the smaller horn.

She hated the dehorning program and was convinced that a better anti-poaching control would stop the poaching of the rhino, but until someone came up with it, the Matusadona and Chizarira, like every other park in Zimbabwe, was dehorning almost all their rhino to try to stop the rate of decline as the poachers killed them and sold the horns to Vietnam and other Asian countries.

One of the saddest parts of her job was attending rhino who had survived being shot by poachers. She often had to put them down after their faces had been viciously hacked apart, and their horns cut away too deeply for any hope of regrowth at all. At least this way there was less horn for them to poach, so there was less chance of the rhino being a target. That was the theory behind the dehorning program anyhow. She had her doubts and reservations; many of the people on the ground did, especially after one of their rhino had been poached within twenty-four hours of being dehorned.

She cut through the last bit and it came free. She powered down the chainsaw and called to Amos, 'Grab the horn.' She patted the rhino again, and ran her hand along the edge of the stumps to check that there were no sharp bits. 'Sorry, boy, I know they were magnificent, but that's just what the poachers want.'

Amos took the horns and wrote the rhino's number on them with permanent marker, then put them in a bag. He used a cloth to dust the shavings from the blade of the chainsaw, which were put in their own bag, before he put the chainsaw back into its case. He also collected all the shavings from around the rhino, adding them to the bag before he sealed it. Amos placed each bag on the portable scale and weighed it. The larger horn weighed 605 grams and the smaller one 71 grams. The shavings were 47 grams. Amos wrote the weights onto the bags, along with the rhino's number.

Peta turned to Mitch. 'Amos is holding about forty-five thousand dollars' worth of horn. And it doesn't do any of the things the Chinese herbalists claim it does; it's just like my fingernails.'

'Why would they kill this beautiful animal for that, when it regrows anyway? Why don't they just dart and dehorn them? Let them regrow, like a renewable resource?'

'Don't even get me started on that,' Peta said. She looked back at Assan. 'You can administer the booster now.' She watched closely as Assan gave the rhino a vitamin injection. She smiled as he finished and punched the air.

'Don't celebrate just yet; we still need to get him up and moving,' she said. 'Breathing?' She looked at Amos, who checked the animal again.

'Steady,' Amos said.

'Everyone ready?' she asked as Assan passed her the syringe containing the antidote: naltrexone.

Amos removed the cotton from the rhino's ears and took the rope off its head and back legs. The rhino now only had the soft blanket over its eyes.

Amos passed the chainsaw's case to Assan. 'Take this with you, in case I need to run.'

'Assan, take the men to the *bakkie* and get it started,' Peta instructed.

The men disappeared into the bushes, only Amos and Peta remained. They heard the vehicle start and come closer. Only then did Peta administer the antidote. Then she and Amos ran for the *bakkie*. Mitch put his hand out to her, and she took it and climbed on the back. They watched as the mighty rhino flicked his head and the cloth fell to the ground, then he rose up, staggered once, and walked away in the opposite direction.

One of the team laughed. 'Not like the last one, who chased us. This one, he liked you from the moment he didn't run away when we were upwind of him, getting into the right position. He liked your smell.'

'How do you know it's my scent he liked and not yours?' she asked as Assan turned the *bakkie* away from the retreating rhino and made for headquarters.

'Because I know this one. We call him Mumparie, because he is very-very naughty. He is the one who chased old Chifumba last year, when he had to climb a tree, and stamped on his bicycle.'

'Why didn't you tell me that before I got so close?' Peta asked.

'Because you always treat the animals here like they are family. Mumparie is the number one in this area.'

Peta stared at where the rhino had disappeared. She couldn't put men on every rhino like she wanted, but as long as Matusadona was inside the Intensive Protection Zone, they were safer than anywhere else, but it didn't stop the pain in her chest at taking the horns from such a magnificent specimen, leaving him defenceless against attacks from lions and hyenas.

She turned her head, then groaned as she rubbed her neck.

'You need a massage,' Amos said. 'You should make that trip into Kariba you keep threatening, or perhaps you should spend more time at Joss's place and see that new masseuse he hired at the lodge. I tell you, she has magic fingers.'

'She does, does she?' Peta asked, laughing. Then she frowned. 'But you are right, I do and I should – maybe when I see Joss at the weekend.'

'You like him, lots,' Amos teased.

'I do,' she admitted.

'You know, you should just move in there, stay with him,' Mitch said. 'He's mad on you too. I've never seen him so much as look at another woman the way he focuses on you when you visit. And he leaves his lodge to visit you too; it's not easy getting him to leave that place.'

'He suggested that, but we thought we should give it more time. For now, it's easier if we commute to each other. Other couples survive being apart during the week; I'm sure we can too. Besides it's not only my job that requires me to be here in the rhino nursery, it's Dad and Tsessebe too. That's quite a crowd to take on, not just one old lady vet.'

Amos smiled and said, 'Old. *Eish.*'

'Old? What? If you are old then I must be ancient.' Mitch laughed. 'And it's not like he has no baggage either; he comes with a lodge and a heap of needy people he helps Bongani look after.'

Peta smiled. 'Okay point taken, from both of you. Assan, you can stop driving now.'

Assan stopped the *bakkie* and bounced out of the driver's seat. Peta and Amos climbed off the back and into the front. Mitch stayed in the back. Having him here for the rhino dehorning was great timing, and she was even contemplating having him do the shooting of the rhino for her, instead of the photography, after he had proven just how good he was with his hunting rifle on the range.

'Thanks, Assan,' Peta said as she slammed her door. 'Where's the next one?' she asked and Amos looked at the list.

'It is the big male you introduced from South Africa. Ngozi.'

'Bladdy hell,' Peta said. 'I don't know who put a hot poker up head office's butt. We've been telling them for years that we are losing our rhino, and now they give us a quota to dehorn. It's madness.'

'We have lost many guards along with the rhino,' Amos said.

'I know. The graveyard at Matusadona grows bigger all the time.'

'I fear that the poachers will not care that there is only a little horn; they will kill the animal just so they do not have to track it again,' Amos said.

'I worry about that too,' Peta said. 'What direction are we heading in to find Ngozi?'

Amos looked at the paperwork. 'He was last seen on the banks of Kariba, so let's head west.'

Peta slowed, and stopped. 'Drat. That means navigating the steps down. Any other rhino still in this area I can chase instead?'

Amos shook his head. 'No, Mumparie was the last one. The rest are all down in the valley, and their guards' last contact with us was about three days ago.'

'I wish they'd given us a helicopter to do this job; it would have gone much faster,' Peta said. 'I know I'm wishing on an empty well, but it's hot, and those big warm winds are not helping.'

Amos pointed. 'Look.'

There were black plumes of smoke coming from the direction of the main office and camp area.

'Oh God,' Peta said as she got on the radio. 'Tsessebe, Tsessebe, come in. Are you guys alright?'

No answer.

'We have to help,' she said. She ground the gears in her haste to get moving.

Amos reached for the radio. 'Tsessebe, Tsessebe, come in,' he called.

Still no answer.

They raced as fast as they dared towards the smoke while Amos continued to try to hail Rodger and Tsessebe.

They came into range and could hear the other units were all out fighting the blaze that had been started just outside the Matusadona, had quickly spread inwards and was now threatening the main camp, the rhino orphanage and the tourist accommodation.

Peta tried to go faster. 'I hope Dad listened to Tsessebe and left the fighting of the fire to the staff.'

'Surely they won't let him fight the fire in his condition?' Mitch said.

'I hope you're right, Mitch.'

'Mind the pothole on the left,' Amos said.

Peta steered right. 'You are good for me, Amos. You know that?'

He nodded. 'Something is off about this fire.'

'Look,' Peta said. 'It's getting worse. Something is feeding it – look at that black pumping upwards. There's accelerant in that smoke.'

They came up out of the small depression they had been in and the radio was now busy with different guards talking about small fires that were starting to merge into a single front. Jeff was on the radio: 'The original front itself looks like it's still on track to hit the main camp. We have not been able to back burn. We've alerted the tourists and all staff to evacuate.'

'My dad and Tsessebe?'

'They said they were going to take the horses and the rhino babies and get to safety. They left a while ago.'

'Thank God,' Peta said. But she didn't slow as she headed towards the main camp – directly for the fire front.

The smoke on the wind now reached them and pieces of blackened material fell on the windscreen.

'This is a bad one,' Amos said.

She could see that there was not one but two fire fronts, driven by the winds.

'There's still a gap,' Peta said and adjusted to drive between the roaring columns of flames. 'As long as Tsessebe and Dad got out okay, we'll fight this thing and stop it getting further into the reserve.'

But as she spoke she noticed another fire front to her right. The fire danced about the tree tops, swirling in turrets of orange and red as it caught whispy-whirls and touched down once more in front of the burning bush, igniting the tinder, then swirling again.

'Shit. Shit. Shit. Look.' She stopped. The high winds were driving the fire, and the gap had closed.

'We're fucked,' Mitch said. 'We have fire on three sides.'

'Not if I can help it,' she said. She had to think fast and move even quicker. No longer was her objective to try to get to the housing complex to help; now she had to save her men and herself. If she could get to a road where she could go faster, get out in front and around the side, or to a place where she knew the fire would pass over with the wind, where they could stop the small creeping fire that came after the inferno, they would be okay.

She needed to head for the deepest ravine she knew: Picnic Pool, a rivulet not far from where they were. It had been a favourite picnic spot for their family when her mum was alive.

'Hang on, everyone,' she warned as she spun the wheel one hundred and eighty degrees and headed back the way they had come. They bounced along the track, past where they had so recently dehorned the magnificent rhino, and she breathed a sigh of relief that he was nowhere in sight. He'd also run from the fire.

She kept heading west. She gunned her engine, pushing it for everything it could give her, knowing that if she could just get them all down into the depression at Picnic Pool, and if there was water, they could hide as the firestorm blew over, and would be protected from the hottest part of the fire – if there was water there. If not, they would have to hide under the *bakkie* and get out quickly after the fire passed to extinguish any flames it had ignited in the vehicle. The tarps – they could soak them and use them as a giant fire blanket.

She began the steep descent into the ravine, ensuring she took it slowly despite the urgency, because she didn't want to roll her vehicle. When she stopped near the pool, she explained her plan to the team and they all rushed to wet the tarps. All the time they could hear the crackle of the fire as it grew closer.

The pool was not big enough for all of them and a fat hippo that had claimed it this season. But he seemed to recognise the urgency with which the humans were working, and he didn't begrudge them wetting the tarp and filling canisters. Despite showing them his huge yellowed teeth, he didn't attempt to exert his authority over his territory. Peta worried that if they attempted to hide in the water he might attack them.

They threw the wet tarps over the *bakkie* and slid underneath just as the first large sparks began raining down on them.

The roar of the fire as it danced over the ravine, skipping as if the gaping hole in the underbrush didn't exist, sounded like a freight train. They could feel the heat even under the *bakkie* and the tarps. Peta put her arms over her head as she lay on her stomach, sand-wiched between Amos and Mitch.

As it quietened, Mitch peeked out. 'It's jumped us. It's gone right over. Look,' he said as he pushed the tarp up and pulled himself out.

Sure enough, the fire had skipped them, and the fat hippo now showed his teeth to challenge something else: a wave of small animals that had bounded into the ravine in front of the flames.

'Don't relax just yet. The fire is still coming – this time it's at ground height. We need to get up that side and stop it. Tear the tarp and use it as a beater.'

She used a scalpel from her bag to help cut the tarp. The men took a few pieces each. They wet them again before going up the ravine. They only made it about halfway before the flames crept over the edge, and they began fighting the fire in earnest, beating the front line with their pieces of tarp. Peta also cut smaller pieces to put over their mouths to help with the smoke inhalation. She pressed hers to her mouth and ran to help.

They stopped the fire just as it reached the plateau at the bottom, but they could see that the rest of the front had burnt around them, and was now over the edge on the far side and moving away from them. Many of the smaller animals had stopped running, realising they were safe, but were still on the other side of the water, watching the humans with great caution.

'We did it,' Amos said and Peta hugged him, jumping up and down.

'We did it!' Mitch said too, joining in their excited embrace.

'You are one badass vet,' Assan said, putting out his hand to shake hers. 'If anyone asks me what I learnt during my time with you, I will tell them it is that you never give up. I thought that fire had us.'

'Believe me, Assan, today we were lucky; it could have been so much worse. Someone was smiling down on us. Come on, let's see if we can get back to camp and see what damage it did there.'

They drove over blackened ground that crunched beneath the tyres, and stopped whenever they saw a fallen animal to make sure it was dead. For those that weren't, Peta would tell the boys to put them in the *bakkie* with them, and use the pieces of tarp to bind their legs so that she could treat their burns when she got back to camp. Mitch helped her euthanise those that were too badly burnt.

She drove on. Already they had enough small buck, tortoises and other animals, including a small genet cat, on the back for one to be sitting on each of the boys' laps, with more by their feet.

As she neared the outskirts of the entrance to the camp, she saw Nguni, her sister's *bakkie*. It appeared to be stuck against the upright of the gate and it was burnt out, still smoking.

'No ... No ... No ...' she whispered as she drove towards it.

Peta stopped with a jolt. Nguni's windows and headlights were blown out from the intense heat. She ran the short distance to it.

'Dad! Tsessebe!'

Mitch got out as fast as she had and tried to stop her getting too close to the hot metal. 'Wait, vehicles can still be hot up to half an hour after being burnt out.'

'Dad! Tsessebe!' Peta called, but she had stopped, Mitch holding her.

There was no answer.

Peta noticed that the tyres on the side facing the fire front were burnt to only rims, and the once lovingly painted brown and white cow paint job that Courtney and Joss had spent hours doing on their last Christmas holiday before he went away, was black. A layer of thick white ash lay around the vehicle. Peta gasped for air. She could imagine the fire as it engulfed the *bakkie*. She turned away, not wanting to look any more.

Mitch glanced into the burnt-out shell. 'They're not here.'

'Oh, thank God,' Peta said as her legs threatened to buckle under her.

Mitch pulled her closer to him, holding her tightly. 'Your work isn't done yet. If they're not here, we need to go and find them. Amos, check with the others on the radio and phones. You okay?'

She nodded, and Mitch let her go, testing that she was once more strong enough to walk.

'Do you want me to drive?' Mitch asked.

'No, I'm okay,' she said as she climbed into the driver's seat and pulled her phone off the dashboard. No signal. 'Looks like the fire has burnt the cell tower too.' She picked up her two-way radio. 'Rodger. Tsessebe. It's Peta, come in.'

She waited, then repeated her call.

Nothing.

Then a crackling sound and Jeff came on, loud and very clear. 'Peta. Your dad and Tsessebe are safe. Where are you? We need your help.'

'We just found Courtney's burnt-out *bakkie*. I'm at the west gate coming into the camp.'

'Head north towards Kariba Town. You can't miss us.'

Tears streamed down Peta's face as she turned away from the carnage in front of her, the camp still smoking, and headed north.

They passed a point where the fire had not burnt, and a little further along they came to the makeshift camp where all the vehicles had been parked to form a huge circle. It looked like an old-fashioned *laager*, only with modern machinery. She noticed her horse, Zeus, running around inside the circle, and a few of the other horses following him. They had halters on, but were not saddled. The baby rhinos were corralled in the middle, but some were mingled in with them. She frowned and pulled up next to where Tsessebe, Rodger and Jeff waited.

She got out and threw herself at her dad. 'Oh God, Dad, I saw Nguni burnt out and I thought you were dead!'

Rodger held his daughter. 'No, my girl, the Grim Reaper didn't catch me this time either.'

'Tsessebe,' she said and held out her hand to him.

'It is alright, Peta. We managed to back burn and congregated here, where the fire was not so intense,' Tsessebe said and squeezed her hand.

'That stallion of yours is highly strung!' her father complained. 'You said he was well trained. I tried to get on him and I couldn't. He would not let me mount.'

'Did you get all the other horses? The rhino babies?' She was trying to look past her dad into the *laager*.

'All safe,' Tsessebe said. 'No casualties, and no one left behind.'

Jeff was laughing. 'You should've seen your father. When your stallion wouldn't let anyone ride him, Tsessebe put Rodger onto one of the anti-poaching horses, used his belt to strap his dodgy leg onto the saddle so he wouldn't fall off, then he gave your father Zeus's lead rein. We gathered the other horses and the anti-poaching guards had those ones that weren't mounted on leads. Your father tried to lead that stallion, but Zeus was having none of this being led thing, and he took off.

'Tsessebe and the other anti-poaching guards were pushing the baby rhino along with their mounts, and your stallion ran right through them all. Then the fun started. The baby rhino and half the horses all decided they were racehorses too, and galloped after him.'

'The babies were running after Zeus?' Peta asked.

'He led them at full tilt. When he got to the *laager*, it was as if he knew this was where to stop. He's been running circles around them since, keeping them in the middle as if they are in the centre of a show arena. We parked all the cars in formation, thinking he'd stop, but he's just kept going. The guards and the grooms can't go in there to get the horses and tie them up or check on the baby rhino because he keeps chasing them away. Peta, you need to get Zeus to stop running about,' Jeff said. 'He's sure not listening to any of the grooms. If you can't make him stop, we may have to dart him – he's exhausting the babies.'

Peta smiled. She slipped over the bonnet of Jeff's *bakkie* and approached Zeus, who was cantering slowly towards her. He snorted, arched his head and his tail, and slowed. He threw his head, and the lead rope snapped on his flank. Then he took off faster, past her.

'Oh come on, boy, settle,' she said and waited for his next approach.

'Be careful of the other horses,' Mitch called as they thundered past her.

'Did you save some of their food?' she asked Jeff.

'In the far *bakkie*,' he said, and pointed.

Peta helped herself to a few handfuls of pellets and turned back to the running horses again. This time she held one hand full of horse cubes in front of her. Zeus slowed as he approached her, eyes still white with fear.

'Come on, boy. Calm now, come, come, come,' she said.

Zeus nodded his head. The trailing lead rein jiggled, but this time didn't whip him. He pawed the ground, arching his neck, his nostrils flaring.

'Come, come, come. You can smell what I have here. You love these,' she said, dropping the tone of her voice and keeping it as steady as she could. She gave no ground to him, waiting for him to come to her.

The other horses had stopped behind Zeus. One of the older mares could smell what Peta had too, and walked to her. Peta fed her.

Zeus edged closer until he could just touch her fingers. She let him smell the pellets, then brought her hand closer to herself, forcing him to come nearer.

'This is not like you, my beautiful boy,' she said as she looked at the sweat that had lathered all over him.

He stepped closer. She fed him a handful, then slid her hand up his head to his lead rope and grabbed it, showing him that she now held him and he was no longer leading his herd.

A gelding came for food too, and the mare pinned her ears back. 'Don't be nasty; there is food enough for all,' Peta said as she fed the gelding.

One of the older rhino babies, Minjama, was inquisitive and walked past Zeus for a handful of cubes too. It made the most adorable sound as it asked her for food, which made her smile. The baby rhino had a whole range of sounds that she had learnt and mimicked. She repeated their sounds, and made a few more as Minjama rubbed her hand, asking for more food.

Mitch and a few of the grooms had joined her and were shaking buckets of food to lead the animals away from where they gathered around her, feeding them nearer the head ranger's car.

While the others fed, Peta walked Zeus out of the gathering. He breathed heavily, his powerful chest heaving as it laboured to bring his rhythm back to normal after the extended exertion. Slowly she walked him to where she had parked.

'Assan, find out if anyone has a towel I can rub this horse down with, then get the back of Jeff's *bakkie* ready to start treating those animals we brought in with us.'

Tsessebe came to her. 'I will walk him for you.'

'It's going to be a long walk. Will Dad be okay with you away from him?'

'Your dad was helping Assan with the animals even before you called to him. He had already begun sorting them, getting them ready for you and Jeff. That Assan, he has a good heart and is not scared of hard work. Your dad is in good hands.'

'What happened with Nguni?'

Tsessebe looked away. 'We got everyone here and safe, and your father, he realised that we had left Nguni at home. He got one of the other anti-poaching guards to go back with him.'

'He gave you the slip?' Peta said. 'Thought he only managed to do that to me.'

Tsessebe nodded. 'Yes, he got away. The groom came back, but when your father did not show in Nguni, he came and told me what they had done as he was worried. Jeff and I went looking for him. We saw that he had tried to go out the wrong gate, and hit the radiator on the big new upright. Nguni was not going anywhere. Without me there as his eyes, he had got disorientated. He was lucky he did not hit his head or anything. We put him in Jeff's *bakkie* and came back. The fire was close then.'

Peta put her hand on his arm. 'I wish he had just left it like it was, that he hadn't gone back—' Zeus nudged her, reminding her he was still there, looking for food as he smelt her top.

'That would be expecting your father to be something he is not. Nguni is one of the last links he has to Courtney. He loved that old *bakkie* – it represents freedom to him. Sometimes we drive into the park, and it does not matter where. No one asks him where he is going, or how he is feeling when he drives slowly. It is just us and the bush. It is a good feeling for both of us. I can understand him wanting to save Nguni from the fire.'

'Courtney wouldn't have wanted him risking her life for a stupid old *bakkie*. I didn't even realise that Dad was driving around. I can buy him another *bakkie*, Tsessebe, you know that. I can't get another dad.'

Tsessebe nodded. 'I know.'

Amos brought her a large towel. 'Assan told me that Mrs Peterson said you can have that one – she doesn't want it back.'

'Thank you,' Peta said. 'Amos, can you check that the grooms are walking the other horses, and not just drying them off and putting them in with the others? They need to cool down or we might have problems later.'

'Sure,' he said and walked off to sort out the grooms.

'I will walk your stallion,' Tsessebe said, taking the lead rein and towel from Peta. 'You go and save those animals that you picked up. Zeus will be fine.'

Peta hugged him. 'Thank you, my friend. Thank you for everything.'

CHAPTER

26

The Spark

Francis Kanobvurunga's right eye was swollen shut and the cut above it was covered with a plaster, but anyone could see that it had crusted dry and was not stitched, although it needed to be.

Tichawana stroked his own scar, knowing that injuries like that never healed well.

'You were tasked with watching. You left your post unattended,' Denisa Mlilo said.

'I tried to tell you—'

The sound of flesh hitting flesh as Denisa struck Francis again was like music in Tichawana's ears. 'And you decided to come right to my office? To tell me what?'

'I found the weakness at last. I found it,' Francis sobbed.

Denisa went to hit him again, but Tichawana put his hand up. 'Tell me, and it had better be news to me, or there will be further punishment for your useless son.'

'The chief, he does not have a weakness. But the white friend, his weakness is children. He has these two black teenage village boys who do everything with him. Chief Bongani, he sent one to my village, Ephraim, to write for the old game guard, who is illiterate. The other one lives in the cripple Mr Joss Brennan's house; his name is Lwazi. He also has a new black child; he calls her Sophia.'

'Joss Brennan has a black child? How did a white man get his hands on a black child?' Tichawana asked, his voice rising.

'Someone put her on his doorstep, and then ran away.'

'Do you know who?'

Francis shook his head. 'No. It was not a child from Amaluandi Village.'

'You are sure that it is Brennan who has claimed this baby and not Bongani?'

'The baby, she is a cripple. Her legs do not work. Her parents put her there so that he could buy her legs like he has.'

'How can we trust you, Francis?' Denisa said.

'You have to. I was scared for my life, for the life of my son if I did not bring you this information quickly.'

'You should be,' Tichawana said.

'There is an old lady in the village who passed me the information about the chief. She has ambitions to rule when Chief Bongani is gone. She waits in the shallows like a crocodile. Patient, cunning and in camouflage.'

'What is so great about her? She sounds like every other power-hungry African woman in every village.'

'Yes, but she is the grandmother of one of the children, Ephraim, who Mr Brennan has let into his circle of friends. She has her grandson telling her everything that happens every day in that house.'

'Mary?'

Francis nodded.

'She reports to us too, you idiot,' Denisa said.

Tichawana shook his head. 'You think this is good enough news? To get your son back? That you tell us of our own spy?'

'No. There is more. The boys Lwazi and Ephraim have learnt how to keep bees. Now, to pay for their own bees, they must go help Bishu Village to harvest their bee hives.'

'Why do you tell us about bees?' Denisa asked.

'It is not the bees that are important. The boys will be in Bishu Village soon. While it is considered one of Chief Bongani's villages, it is not actually on his lands – it encroaches into the forest area. It used to be inside his boundaries, but the village flooded with big rains every time, so the government agreed that it could be relocated five kilometres north. That is why they now have river access to Kariba when no other village does. But the maps have never changed for the boundary of Chief Bongani's lands. The boys will be unprotected by the white commando and their chief when they are in this village. They will be outside the protection the *N'Goma*s placed on the boundary that you are afraid to try to cross, even though the—'

Denisa hit Francis again. 'King Gogo wa de Patswa is not afraid of anything.'

Tichawana said, 'Enough. You were saying?'

'The five *N'Goma*s now are very strong.'

'No. About the boys,' Tichawana coaxed.

'The boys were given bee hives to look after. To pay for them they must return to Bishu Village and help Matilda the bee queen to harvest her honey.'

'You have done your job well. Your debt is repaid. I will let your son out of the camp and will send him home,' Tichawana said.

'Thank you. Thank you.' The relief could be heard in Francis's voice.

'Get up off that floor and get out of my office. Do not ever come here again, and never let me see you,' Tichawana said.

Francis Kanobvurunga rushed out of the office, barrelling through the door as if a pack of wild dogs were nipping at his heels.

Tichawana buzzed the intercom. 'Miss Hillary, bring tea into my office for myself and Mr Mlilo.'

'Right away, Mr Ndou,' she said.

She put the tray on Tichawana's desk and served tea.

'That will be all,' Tichawana said.

She walked to the door, her back straight, and then she curtseyed. 'I will be at my desk.'

'I still think you should sample that one,' Mr Mlilo said after she had closed the door.

'You touch my secretary and you are dead. I thought I already made that clear. Understand?'

'Yes, sir,' Denisa said quickly.

'So, now that that idiot has left, what other news do you have for me? I need to know what is happening in my kingdom outside this office.'

'The shipment in the west came through without any problems, and should show in the Cayman bank account in a few days. The delay happened because the hunter had an asthma attack on his side errand into the Chizarira to clear out the spotters' camps. He had to go to hospital in Harare.'

'*Eish*, he should be more careful,' Tichawana said. 'Any news on the computer at Binga?'

'Nothing. I need to spend some time with that policeman who attended the site and collected the body. Find out who is not on our side.'

'My side. Never forget you work for me!'

'Yes, Mr Ndou,' Denisa said quickly.

'Deal with it. I need to plan. I have an opportunity to take those boys from the chief and put them in my educational camp at Gwanda. They will soon learn who it is they should be friends with in my country. I will be there when my team snatches those boys, but I only wish I could see my brother's face when he sees that he left the children open for leverage against him.'

CHAPTER

27

Trust

Ndhlovy moved through the villages. It had been years since she had been here, and her memories had faded, but she was sure that she was on the right track. She had seen the boy who had saved her, and now she wanted to visit the miracle trees. But more importantly, she needed to get the large bull to the boy's family. The wound in his side was festering, and she knew that if she could get him to the boy, there would be help.

Slowly they trekked further southwest. The amount of human settlement had increased considerably, but she knew that she was in the right place. As she passed one hut, a small child came out of the doorway, but it backed away, retreating inside. Silent in the predawn morning.

She could feel the road beneath her feet had been strengthened with man tools – it was smooth now, compacted. She looked up, and could see the silhouette of the buildings that were so familiar to her.

The bull limped behind her. The rumbles in her stomach reassured them they were almost there; help was within reach. She lifted her trunk and tested the air. Already someone had lit a morning fire. The light of the day was brightening with a pink splash of colour across the buildings as she walked inside the gates towards the old stable.

Once again she spoke with her herd, telling them to follow her and leave the bull behind. She would show them the trees in the grove and return to him, to ensure that the humans understood that they were here because he needed help. The younger one would remain with him, as she hoped that the human boy would take the wire snare off his trunk too. Already the youngster had lost condition, but she hadn't allowed him to fall behind. Finding the bull along the way had just been lucky for him. The youngster with the damaged trunk had also come from a different herd, which mingled in with hers on the journey. Remnants from another massacre. After she saw the boy again, smelt him, she knew that it was safe to bring the herd here for help.

Her stomach ached. Her time to birth her first baby was coming nearer. She was happy that her child would be born almost in the same place she was. The human was here. He would keep them all safe.

She sniffed the air.

She could smell the boy, now a man. Ndhlovy wondered where his real legs were, and how he had got such an injury. She remembered other elephants in her migrations who had the ground beneath them erupt with a deafening noise, and how most of them had died. Men had put something under the ground to kill. There was one youngster of a herd they had met who had lost half his foot, who lived permanently damaged. His matriarch had not run from the noise; instead she had urged her herd to remain close to him. Protecting him. Not ranging far for a long time, until he had had time to heal. He relearnt to walk, but never put his foot on the ground except when he was resting, to counter balance his weight. Only when he could do that had she moved her herd away from that area, such was the determination of the matriarch not to lose yet another member of her family.

Trumpeting, Ndhlovy told her herd to continue following, but the hurt bull and the youngster remained near the human buildings, pacing nervously. The way to the miracle trees was clear. When her herd was sheltered, hidden within the trees, she left them there and returned to the human settlement, to stand guard over the injured elephants.

She felt the communication from the bull that a human was looking at them, that a man was close by. She hurried along, reassuring him not to be afraid. She told him that the man who had light skin and strange legs would help. He had saved her own life many years before.

She broke through the bush and saw the man. She slowed, and walked towards him.

He wasn't alone. The old man behind him was also familiar. The man had aged, but she knew him. The humans were a family, despite being different colours. The men moved towards her.

She reached out her trunk, wanting them to understand. Her herd needed them. She breathed deeply. She touched her trunk into the light-skinned one's hand, then smelt him again, reacquainting herself with his scent as he was today. Less smelly than their last encounter, and this time he was walking on the shiny legs that stuck out of his clothes. She was happy that he had found a way to still be mobile.

'Hello, Ndhlovy,' he said and his words were as familiar as the sun rising over the hills and spilling over the green trees. He stepped forward and put his forehead to the top of her trunk. Once they had touched foreheads together easily – she had been so much smaller; so had he. He had grown, and now that he stood at his full height, he was tall. But she was still much taller than him. She brought her head down and touched her forehead to his, before lifting it again and wrapping him in her trunk in a warm greeting.

She could feel the muscles of a man, yet she was not afraid. They were bonded. She knew that he would help her once again.

'So, old girl, what have you brought us?' the older dark man asked, as he too put his hand out and touched her trunk.

She raised her trunk and tasted the salty wetness on his cheeks. Then she turned to the bull and the youngster.

The dark man walked in front of the light-skinned one as if protecting him, as he had when he was still a youngster himself. Always the protector, just like she had become. She understood wanting to shelter those in your family.

The bull came forward slowly, urged on by her soft murmurings. He swayed, then touched his trunk to the dark man's hand, just as he'd seen the matriarch do, and turned his flank to the men, to show them why he needed help.

*　*　*

'For fuck's sake,' Joss cursed. He turned his attention back to Ndhlovy. 'We'll help them, but we need to get Peta. You remember her?'

The little calf came forward. Bongani tsked as he saw the wire snare on his trunk. 'Not sure that one will keep its trunk; it looks like it has already cut too deep and he is breathing out of the top of it. It's amazing she got them here at all.'

Ndhlovy trumpeted a warning to the men approaching behind the two humans that they needed to keep their distance.

Joss turned around. 'Hey, Lwazi, Mitch. Walk slowly. Meet an old friend. Look what she brought us. Two elephants in her herd need our help.'

Joss knew that Ndhlovy could feel the tension radiating from Lwazi. His whole life he had been warned of the ferocity and the danger of elephants. He had reason to fear her, but she surprised him when she reached her trunk towards Lwazi first, as if curious who the newcomers were.

'She won't hurt you. Let her get used to your scent,' Joss said.

Lwazi stayed still as she sniffed around him. He didn't pull away. 'She is beautiful.'

Ndhlovy touched her trunk to his chest. He giggled. 'Hey, that tickles.'

She took a step back at the sound, but she came forward again. This time, she put her trunk into his hand. Not to be outdone, the baby elephant attempted to put his trunk into Lwazi's hand too. He wasn't as good with the control of it since the snare had damaged his muscles, and the trunk landed on Ndhlovy's trunk, and then overshot Lwazi's outstretched hand. The baby didn't give up – he attempted again to put the tip of his trunk into Lwazi's palm. He failed once more. This time he simply left his trunk dangling next to Lwazi's arm area, close but not what he was obviously trying to achieve with his damaged trunk.

Lwazi laughed. 'Can I touch him?'

'You can try. Help him to trust us,' Joss said as the youngster flipped his trunk over Joss, and this time it landed with a heavy thunk on Mitch's shoulder.

Mitch was quiet before Ndhlovy gently pushed the youngster away from him so she could make her introductions, get to know Mitch's smell.

Joss pulled his cell from his pocket and dialled Peta's number.

'Hello?' she croaked.

'Peta, sorry to get you up, but you're not going to believe who has come for a visit. Ndhlovy's home and two of her herd need help.'

'Ndhlovy came home? She's at your place?'

Joss could picture her sitting up in bed, wide awake now.

'There's an adult male here with what looks like a bullet or a spear wound in his side, and the most adorable baby with a snare already cutting into its trunk.'

'She brought them there, for you to help?'

'I'm certain of it. She's standing here, keeping guard.' He could hear her moving about already, and he smiled, knowing that she would have the phone between her shoulder and her ear as she attempted to put on some clothes.

'Amazing. After all these years, you see her in the bush, and now she is ... where are you?'

'At the old stable area.'

'Oh my word, Joss. That's incredible; this proves my theory that the elephants will come to humans for help if they know that they'll get it. It proves so much of their intelligence, and their behaviours—'

'How fast can you get here?'

* * *

Torn-Ear, the bull elephant, lay on his side, his ear over his eye, and a few wet towels over his body. Lwazi and Ephraim sat next to his head, petting his trunk, making sure that his airway remained open.

Joss, Bongani and Mitch stood with Ndhlovy, present but not in the way.

Peta took a pot by its handle and put her elbow into the water to check the temperature. She waited while Jeff squeezed antiseptic into the pot then she poured the water into the wound. It ran out clear, with a faint trace of pink, but no yellow pus.

She wiped away the residue.

'Looks okay now. I think we got all that muck out,' she said.

'We have done what we can; it's up to him now to fight the rest,' Jeff said as he dabbed at the wound with a sterile pad, drying it as best he could.

Peta smiled. 'I think Ndhlovy brought him far to get help, and I like to believe that he'll continue to fight and heal.' She patted the elephant's stomach then packed antiseptic powder into the open wound and sprayed it with healing ointment.

'Pass the syringe out of the pink box,' she said to Amos, who was handling her drugs and equipment. 'Time to wake you up, Torn-Ear. We'll stay here, close by.'

'You sure about this?' Jeff asked. 'He's huge and he might not remember where he is when he comes around. He could be raging and ready to defend himself.'

'We'll be nearby, and Ndhlovy will calm him. She has remained here with them the whole time. Look how she helped the little one when he came around. Despite him losing the bottom half of his trunk, she will caution him. He won't hurt us.'

Jeff lifted his eyebrows. 'You think she'll stay here if you continue to feed them so we can do this again in a week?'

'We might need to dart them in the bush next time, but the likelihood of her keeping her herd close is high,' Peta said. 'She's made her own rules since Joss and Bongani found her. Don't underestimate her; she's a force to be reckoned with.'

Jeff laughed. 'As are you.'

'Remove the towels. Remove his ear from his eye so he can see when he wakes and make sure his trunk is clear of anything, so when he moves it he can feel solid ground. Everyone get away.'

They watched as she administered the antidote then joined them in the stable area, behind the wooden fence posts.

The elephant began to come around. He heaved himself up, but as he did that, Ndhlovy was already communicating with him, her rumbles audible above the noise of the bush. He swayed, put his ears forward as if he was going to charge, but didn't, just changed his footing and swayed a bit more. Then he trumpeted to let them know that they had hurt him and he wasn't pleased. He shook his head as if attempting to clear his vision.

The humans remained behind the fencing of the stable – a flimsy barrier between them and the elephants, but Joss and Peta had firmly believed that Ndhlovy would keep him under control. They had been right.

Torn-Ear stumbled once more, then he walked away, out the back towards the moringa grove, as if food was now the most important thing on his mind. Ndhlovy followed him, flanked closely by Half-Trunk.

The humans emerged from the stable as they watched the departing elephants. Bongani, Amos and Mitch walked after them, and soon they too had disappeared.

'Reminds me so much of Ndhlovy when you first found her,' Peta asked. 'Where did the years go, Joss?'

'I don't know, but come nightfall, I suspect those three will come back, just like she used to.'

Peta nodded.

For a moment they stood shoulder to shoulder and watched the silent bush.

'Right,' Joss said, 'let's get this area cleaned up, make it as nice as we can for them. Thank you, everyone, for your help. Lwazi, Ephraim, get those cadacs and the pots back to the kitchen, then come back here and help spread some sand over this area – the less it smells like a hospital, the better. We have a tough week ahead of us to ensure that those wounds don't reinfect.'

'Yes, Joss,' Lwazi and Ephraim said.

'Then we need to get you to Bishu Village; the honey harvest is waiting.'

'Aw, but with the elephants, there is more for us to do here,' Ephraim complained.

'No. You keep your word,' Joss said. 'You said you would help Matilda today, and although you are a little late, you will. Your word is your honour, always remember that.'

Lwazi nodded. 'What time do we need to be ready to go?'

'Let's say everyone who helped gets to eat breakfast in the restaurant, and then we leave?'

'Deal,' Lwazi said and high-fived him on his way to collect the cadacs.

'Neat,' Ephraim said as he did the same.

Joss smiled. 'You know, with the two of you helping Matilda, if you work hard we might get word to collect you in a couple of days, and then you'll be here to help again the next time Peta has to sedate Torn-Ear to check his progress.'

'You bet,' Lwazi said as he went by, loaded down with cadacs and pots, Ephraim close on his heels.

'You spoil those boys,' Jeff said.

'They deserve it most of the time – they actually do work hard. Besides, if we don't teach the next generation to love their wildlife, how are we ever going to expect them to protect it?'

28

Threads of Terror

Francis Kanobvurunga waited in his house, everything packed. Ready to flee when his child was returned. At one-thirty, he still waited, watching the minutes tick by on his watch. They said they would bring him his son.

He was beginning to think that Tichawana Ndou had broken his word. After all, he was a crook, so why would he keep his promise?

He heard a quiet hum outside the door, but dared not open it to see who was driving the vehicle. The less he could tell about them the better. When his son was returned to him, they would flee to South Africa. He would rather face the crocodile-infested waters of the Limpopo than King Gogo wa de Patswa again. He would rather face the lions in the Transfrontier Park as he walked through Mozambique and into Kwa Zulu Natal, where he had family.

He heard a thud and then a car door slam. The vehicle drove off.

He opened the door and ran outside to see if his son was home.

There was a sack at the fence of his property.

He approached with caution. 'Thomas? Is that you? Can you hear me?'

Only silence greeted him.

He reached the sack. It was still. The smell was putrid and even in the dim light of the street he could see that the bag was soaked with something. It was bound together at the top with wire.

'Thomas, talk to me,' Francis said as he felt through the bag, to see if his son was inside the dirty sack, or if they had tricked him and given him a sack with a snake inside.

It felt human, but it was cold, not how his son should feel at all.

He struggled to open the thick wire; it was hard to bend back, but he got it undone. He pulled the top open.

'Thomas!' he screamed into the night air. 'My Thomas is dead!' he yelled in sorrow and pain as his heart broke into two.

His son had been dead for a while. Someone had hacked him into pieces. There were arms and legs and a torso in the sack. Francis clutched the decapitated head to his chest.

His neighbours came out with torches to see what was going on. Soon blue lights flickered over him. He couldn't let go of Thomas's head.

He had done what they asked, yet King Gogo wa de Patswa had still killed his son.

*   *   *

Tichawana Ndou was out of the office, having left instructions for his secretary to hold his calls, when the phone rang.

'This is Detective Sargent Kudzanai Mathobeni. I need to speak with Mr Ndou.'

'Mr Ndou is out of the office right now,' Hillary said. 'Is there something I can help you with, Mr Mathobeni?'

'No, it is imperative that I speak with him right now.'

'He is not here. I am dealing with everything while he is out. What can I help you with?' she said again, trying hard to make her voice sound as commanding as she could.

There was silence on the other end.

Hillary let out a quick breath, hard into the receiver, to make sure that she sounded fed up. 'Fine. When Mr Ndou finds out that you kept something important from him, and you would not allow me to help you on a simple matter—'

'Francis Kanobvurunga,' Detective Sargent Kudzanai Mathobeni said, 'he has created a complicated problem. He has landed up here in the police station, with the body of his son in a sack. I was lucky enough to be on duty, so I took his statement. It has been recommended that he gets admitted to the mental ward in the hospital as I have told everyone that he is *penga* upstairs. He is saying all sorts of things about your boss and what they did to his son.'

'What do you expect me to do, Mr Mathobeni? You want me to come fetch him; is that what you are asking?'

'Yes. I can get him out of the police station, but I need you to take him from here. Get him to Mr Ndou so that he can silence him. He is going to blow everything if he continues to carry on like this; someone might begin to listen to his ravings.'

Hillary took a deep breath. Tichawana Ndou was visiting an old friend to borrow helicopters to raid Bishu Village for its children. This man at the police station was going to die if she did nothing. They had killed his son. More children could die.

She had to stop this madness. Surely with what she had now, she could get Chief Bongani and Joss Brennan to listen to her? If she took Francis with her they would surely listen? They knew him.

Trying to sound calm, she asked, 'What time are you taking him outside for the transfer?'

She took notes on her pad and hung up the phone, sitting quite still in her chair.

She could not believe that she had just decided to take action to save a man's life and potentially save the lives of not only the children who were about to be taken, but perhaps all those Tichawana Ndou kept in his camps.

Joss Brennan had better be a kickass commando or everything she had worked for would be in vain.

She would be found in the bottom of a mine shaft in Inyati.

* * *

Hillary could not stop her hands from shaking as she drove to the police station in the company *bakkie* that the foreman had signed out for her. She already had her bag packed and in the back, and her files were all there too, neatly stacked on the backseat of the double-cab ute. She was transporting her revenge.

Detective Sargent Kudzanai Mathobeni was waiting outside with Francis Kanobvurunga in handcuffs. She pulled up next to him, and he opened the front door and pushed Francis inside.

'Buckle him in,' she instructed.

He did and tossed her the key. 'This problem is all yours now.' Mathobeni turned and walked away.

Hillary looked at Francis. His skin had taken on a pallor. The man was broken. He shook as if he was withdrawing from ice or ecstasy like she had seen the drug addicts in Hillbrow do when she had been on holiday in South Africa.

'Mr Kanobvurunga, you are in shock.'

'They will find me there, they will kill me. I need to be free now. I need to leave. I need to make this right.' He didn't seem to notice that he was even in her *bakkie* as he babbled.

She drove away, hoping that perhaps he would stay like this and not turn violent on her. 'How can you do that? You cannot bring your son back from the dead.'

'No, but I know where the *domba* lives. I can kill him in his sleep.'

Hillary shook her head. These were the words of a man who had suffered a great loss and experienced great trauma. The threat was not real; it was the adrenaline talking, the fear and the pain in his heart, not the brain of the man. They were just empty words.

'I need to warn Joss Brennan; they will take his children too,' Francis said. 'I have to warn him. The king is coming to take his brother's throne and he will kill whoever is in his way. He has grown in strength.'

Hillary stiffened, hearing the very name of the person she was driving towards. 'Why must you warn Joss Brennan? What has he to do with your son?'

'Because he is friends with the king's brother. Because to hurt the brother, the king will take the children. It is my fault. I found the weakness. I tried to use it to get my Thomas back. Now he will exploit it.'

'Who?' Hillary asked.

'King Gogo wa de Patswa. I can tell you everything because he has nothing left to take from me. He will kill me anyway.'

What this man was saying in his grief was very interesting indeed. And it was backing up her view that this was the time to reach out for help. 'Do you believe he will kill you?'

'I will die today. His spies are everywhere, even here in the police force. Someone will cover up yet another murder.' He looked at her. 'How do I know you are not one of them?'

Hillary glanced at the terrified man. 'Because I am a woman of integrity, of honour. A Matabele.'

'He is a BaTonga and he kills Matabeles. He does not care for the law,' Francis warned.

Hillary glanced again at Francis Kanobvurunga. This man was telling the truth. She knew it and the proof was travelling in the backseat with them. He was right: Tichawana's network would kill him. The only place that he would be safe was with her, and the only place they would be safe was inside the boundary of Chief Bongani's land.

She could contact ex-Zimbabwean Reason Sazulu in the International Crimes Court again, and they could finish her father's killer. His reign of terror could be stopped. It was like Reason had said, she would never get Tichawana Ndou on war crimes, but if she was patient, and gathered substantial evidence, they would get him on international criminal charges, and the ICC could and would prosecute him on those instead. He was shipping ivory across borders and they could step in with proof. They just had to give Tichawana Ndou enough rope to hang himself.

'They will get me anywhere I go.'

'Let us hope not, or they will kill me too. Put your head back and rest now; I am taking you somewhere safe.'

'You are going to dump my body—' He began fighting against the seat belt.

'No, Francis. Listen. I give you my word,' she said as she pulled over to the side of the road.

He went quiet as he looked at her, then he began struggling in earnest. 'You. You are his secretary!'

'Stop. Stop struggling. I am not on his side. He killed my family. I have been trying to find evidence to bring him down for almost three years. Before that, when he was 5th Brigade, he killed my father and my brother, and he raped my mother before he closed her in an *ikhaya* and burnt it to the ground. I hate the man. I am not on his side.'

A fire lit in Francis Kanobvurunga's eyes, and he stilled. 'Do you know where his camp is?'

'I know almost everything. I need your help. You need mine. Let me help you because, believe me, if we stay on the side of this road, and he finds out what I have just done, we are both dead.'

He looked at her. 'May God strike down your whole family if you are lying to me.'

'I am not,' she said.

Tears welled in Francis's eyes. 'He killed my son, even though I did everything he wanted me to do. I told him how to take the children. He is going to hurt them too.'

'Shush. You need to have a sleep, so that you are calm when we speak with the people who can help us.'

'And these handcuffs?'

'I have the key, Francis; I just cannot take them off you right now, not in your state. I am scared to remove them, as you are unpredictable. If you show me you are calmer, and once again in control of yourself, we can talk about it. Perhaps in another three or four hours. Depending on if this GPS is right,' she said as she pressed the accelerator to the floor again and sped along the tarmac towards Binga.

CHAPTER

29

Taken

Joss woke to the incessant ringing of the house phone.

'Lwazi!' he shouted, but then he remembered that even though it was the weekend, the boy wasn't home; he was still at Anton's village, gathering honey with Matilda.

He heard Mitch answer the phone and muted tones as he spoke with someone, his Australian twang audible in the still of the night.

Peta turned over next to him and snuggled close.

Through the baby monitor, he heard Sophia start to complain in her sleep, then settle again.

Mitch's footsteps came down the passage and stopped outside his door.

He checked that Peta was covered. 'I'm awake, come in.'

'You need to call this number. It's Matilda at Anton's village. She said it's very urgent but she wouldn't talk to me. She said there's trouble and Bongani is not answering his phone.'

Peta stirred next to him, and he tucked the sheet around her as he dialled the number on his cell, his hand on her shoulder. Joss switched his phone to speaker. 'Hello, Matilda?'

'Thanks be to Jesus. Joss, you need to find Bongani and come here. Quickly. Quickly. We have been attacked. Someone has taken the children,' Matilda said.

'Are you alright?'

Peta sat up, clutching the sheet to her.

'I am unharmed. My grandfather was struck down, but he is going to be okay. There are others who tried to stop their grandchildren being taken, and they were hurt too. But I do not think anyone is dead. They have burnt a few of the boats. They have destroyed our fishing camp. They came in three helicopters. Who comes in helicopters and steals children?'

Mitch sat down on Joss's bed.

'Could you identify anyone? What language were they talking?' Joss asked.

'They spoke Ndebele and English. They were dressed in camouflage clothes. They were asking for Lwazi and Ephraim by name. They took them. They took our children too. Seven boys.'

'What can you tell us about the helicopters?' Mitch asked.

'They looked like army helicopters, but they didn't have numbers on them.'

'Did you get a look at any of their guns?' Joss asked.

'Hang on,' Matilda said, and they heard her put her phone on speaker too. Chief Anton's voice came over the phone; he was shouting as if not understanding that the microphone would pick up his voice.

'Matilda said you wanted to know what guns they had? They all carried hunting rifles, like they were doing an elephant cull. The bullets that went through our boats have made big holes when they went out of the other side.'

'Did they shoot anyone?' Joss asked.

Peta put her hand on Joss's.

'No. They shot a lot on the ground, and into the *ikhayas* and our boats. But they knew your children were here. How did they know that those two boys were here?' Matilda asked.

'How long ago did the attack happen?' Mitch asked.

'About half an hour. I was too scared to come out from my hiding place before that. They said if we did they would shoot us with their long-range scopes.'

Joss's ears strained in the night, trying to listen to not only the phone conversation, but to see if he could hear the helicopters too. Bishu Village was north of them, then it was just the whole of the Chizarira between them and civilisation on the other side. Alternatively, Zambia was a short hop across Kariba Lake. If they had taken the boys there, they would be difficult to follow. 'Anything they said, anything at all that you can remember?'

'The one man, who was tying the boys up, he said something about the king being happy. He could be there to take the boys and now he could come back and take his crown next,' Anton said.

'Are you sure?' Joss asked, sitting straight up.

'Yes. He spoke in English, not in Ndebele,' Matilda said.

'I will find Bongani and we will be there by first light. If you remember anything else, you need to call us right away.'

'The people in this village, they are hurting; we do not know why they have done this to us. Even during the bush war, nobody would take our children. There is something rotten going on here. Children, they took the children.'

'I understand,' Joss said. 'Matilda, believe me, we'll do everything we can to get them back.'

He stayed quiet as he pushed the end-call button.

Mitch looked at him. 'Joss?'

'When I came home, I believed I'd closed the door on fighting. I always wanted to be the hero, save people, and look where it got me.' He gestured to his legs. 'When I left Afghanistan, I believed I would never need to lift a gun against a person again. But these people have taken Lwazi and Ephraim. I have come to think of them as my sons, as older brothers to my little girl. Now I'll hunt these men down and kill everyone who's involved.

'I have always been driven by honour and good intent; now I find myself facing a battle with hatred in my heart. That scares me. I can't ask you to fight with me and Bongani, but I could use someone I trust to have my back. A friend I can walk into battle with again. My only wish is that we'll all have our souls intact when we come out of the other side of this madness, along with the boys they have stolen.'

Mitch nodded. 'I'm in. Having met those boys, I'll gladly fight for them. You do realise we can't all go rushing up to the village? If they have helicopters, what's to stop them raiding Bongani's other villages?'

The baby monitor on Joss's night stand burst to life with Sophia crying.

'I'll go grab her,' Mitch said and went into the nursery, leaving Peta and Joss alone.

There was a light knock on the door. Joss looked at Peta. She nodded.

'Come in, Madala.'

The old man shuffled into the room. 'Is everything alright, Joss? I heard you and Mitch talking loudly and—'

'Come, sit. There is something I need to tell you, and you're not going to like it.'

*   *   *

The heat of the day was making mirages on the water in front of Yingwe River Lodge. Mitch, Peta, Madala White, Amos and Julian sat around the table in the dining room collecting information as Bongani and Joss drove back after their dawn visit to the village.

Mitch was not surprised by how much the bush telegraph knew. Abigale, the head *N'Goma*, along with Lindiwe, had appeared at the lodge just before nine o'clock, asking for Bongani. Thoko had arrived half an hour later, with Cludu and Thully arriving soon after. They were settling in with tea and scones on the veranda.

The phone at the lodge hadn't stopped ringing. It was as if the world knew that Chief Bongani needed help and people were calling to offer their services, vehicles and weapons. Hunters with lodges in the area had even begun arriving with their trackers and anti-poaching personnel. From talking to the other villages in the area, the group had been able to work out which direction the helicopters had come from, and in which direction they had left. Now they were getting ready to follow.

Two guests were shown into the dining area by one of the reception staff. She came to their table. 'Miss Peta, these people, they said that they are looking for Joss and for Chief Bongani.'

'Thank you, Alice,' Peta said. 'What can we do for you?'

'My name is Hillary Shambira, this is Francis Kanobvurunga. We are looking to speak with Joss Brennan or Chief Bongani.'

The name 'Francis' jumped in Peta's head. 'They are both busy elsewhere at the moment,' Peta said. 'They shouldn't be much longer.'

Hillary frowned. 'We will wait, thank you.'

'We are here about the children,' Francis said.

'Look around you – so is everyone else,' Peta said.

'The children have been taken already? Is there some place more private we can talk?' Hillary said.

Peta frowned, Hillary's words clanging like a huge bell in her head. 'We can talk in Joss's office. Amos, please will you keep an eye on what's happening out here? Mitch, I think you should come.' She led the way from the dining room and into the office. 'Sit, please.'

Between the desk and the visitors' chairs, they found a place to sit, except Mitch, who stood next to Peta as if he were her bodyguard.

'This is Francis Kanobvurunga; your Chief Bongani knows him,' Hillary said.

'Peta de Longe and Mitch Laski,' Peta said.

'I saw you that day in Bulawayo with Mr Brennan and the dark child,' Hillary said.

'You saw us?' Peta said. 'You've been watching us?'

'Yes. No. Not like that. It is complicated, and there is a lot of the story that we are still trying to piece together, but we have run out of time,' Hillary said. 'Your children have been taken and we are here to help.'

'I'm listening.'

Francis shook his head. 'No. No more talking. He killed mine and he took yours. You have to stop this man. You have to stop him.'

'Calm down, Francis, we need to explain why we are here,' Hillary said, 'or they are just going to think we are a pair of babbling idiots.'

Francis sat back in his chair, but his legs jumped to an unnatural rhythm, his palms silently tapping his knees.

'Perhaps we need to start at the beginning,' Hillary said, and was just about to fill Peta in on the details of what had happened with Francis and their escape from the Bulawayo police when the door opened and Joss and Bongani walked in.

'Apparently you have visitors in here,' Joss said, going to stand next to Peta. Bongani flanked Mitch.

'You. What are you doing back here?' Bongani asked Francis. 'You skipped out of Amaluandi over a week ago. Why are you back?'

'Go easy on him, he is still in shock – they killed his son,' Hillary said.

'And you are?' Joss asked Hillary as she passed Francis yet another tissue.

'I am – was Tichawana Ndou's secretary. It is not a position I was ever comfortable with, as he murdered my family.' She explained what she had been doing, and how she had files in her car to back her up. 'How did he take the children?'

Bongani told them what they knew of the attack from the accounts of others.

'It is an open declaration of war,' Hillary said quietly.

'Pardon?' Joss said.

'He is trying to get Chief Bongani to come out from where he is safe and fight him, so that he can go behind and steal what he believes belongs to him.'

'Tichawana truly believes he should be chief of this area?' Joss asked.

'Yes,' Hillary said. 'He will stop at nothing to attain what he wants.'

'So why is this man here?' Chief Bongani asked quietly.

Hillary related the situation in detail.

'What exactly did Francis tell him about me?' Joss asked.

'That Chief Bongani had no weakness until you arrived. But you have a weakness: children. If Tichawana was to take them away, Chief Bongani would do anything for his best friend and he would leave his area to try to save them. You have to understand, he was desperate to save his own child's life.'

'At the expense of other people's?' Joss said, wiping his face with his hands. 'The longer we talk here, the further away those poor kids get. They are young boys, Francis. Just like your son. What were you thinking?' He slammed his hand down on his desk.

Francis jumped to his feet. 'I was trying to save my son! He took him to a camp and I could not find him. I tried and I tried but I failed. Zimbabwe's bush is large. Thomas was lost out there with those *madomba*. I would do anything to bring him home.'

'Are you sure he took your son to a camp?' Hillary asked.

'Yes. He told me Thomas was too soft for a boy; he would come back from the camp a man. A fighter.'

'Then we can find them; I know where most of his camps are. God help me, but I helped set them up,' Hillary admitted.

Amos tapped on the door of the office before opening it. 'Miss Peta, we have a small problem.'

She looked up at him. He motioned with his head.

'Excuse me,' she said as she followed him out.

'Look, see that *bakkie* that the visitors in our office came in? It is the one that was dismantling the spotter's camp in the game reserve. Look – same number plate,' Amos said.

'You've got to be fucking kidding me!' Peta swore. 'Have you checked it out?'

'No, I did not want those people finding us too close.'

'Dammit,' Peta said, dragging her fingers through her hair. 'Okay. I'm going back in there. If you hear shots fired it's probably them shooting the secretary dead.'

'Do not joke about something like this, Peta,' Amos said.

'I'm not,' Peta replied, as she strode back into the office.

Joss looked up from where he sat, his face lined in worry. 'Hey, Peta, everything okay?'

'No, it's not,' she said, turning to Hillary. 'Whose *bakkie* did you drive here in?'

Joss frowned and sat upright in his chair.

'I signed it out from the company fleet. In my job I can take a *bakkie* when I need one for work purposes, and the foreman at the construction company gave me this one when I asked this morning. When Mr Ndou finds out that I took it and what I have done, he will kill me. Why are you interested in that *bakkie*?'

'So who else gets to use it?' Peta asked.

'Anyone who signs it out from the company.'

'Do you happen to have photographs of the people who can take it out?'

'Yes,' Hillary said as she dug in her handbag and took out her purse, removing a flash drive.

Joss put it into his laptop and went to the file Hillary named. They ran through the pictures.

Peta recognised a face from the surveillance pictures that Amos and Julian had brought back from the spotter's camp. She pointed. 'Him. Same man. Who is this?'

'Adam and his boy Brighton; they are professional hunters. Adam is the son of the foreman, but he does not work for Ticha-wana Ndou that I know of. I put him on my file because twice he has written off company *bakkie*s while driving with his father's permission. What is this about?' Hillary asked. 'What else is going on?'

Joss unlocked a cabinet in his office. He removed a folder and put it in front of Hillary and Francis.

'That is also Adam and Brighton,' she said. 'Why do you have pictures of them setting up a hunting camp?'

'They're dismantling a spotter's camp inside the Chizarira Park.'

* * *

They had been flat out since midnight, but sleep was the last thing on Joss's mind. That was totally occupied by the boys.

They had decided to split up. The anti-poaching squads would remain at home, along with Peta and Amos. Madala White, Julian Seziba, Makesh, Timberman and Obias were all sitting at the table with them, as was Mary.

When Mary saw Francis, she knew that he had told Bongani that she had been spying on them, and reporting to the King of Thieves. The news was nothing they didn't already know, but what puzzled them all was that Ephraim had been taken – he had been her eyes and ears. Timberman had had to pry Madala White off Mary when the information came out, as he attacked her in rage that her stupidity and greed had put both their boys in trouble.

'Bongani,' Mitch said, 'as much as I dig, a lot of the Zimbabwean records are not computerised. It looks like Crew-Build was one of the companies that someone from pretty high up in the government simply gave to Tichawana – he never bought it, just took it from its previous owner, much like the farm invasions, only at a corporate level.'

Hillary said, 'He is comrades with the president. They trained together in Zambia, and he was part of the 5th Brigade.' She passed them yet another page from a file.

'You have gathered extensive information on him,' Bongani said. 'Stay close to your friends but closer to your enemy? You played a dangerous game, Miss Hillary.'

'Someone had to do it,' she said.

Mitch shook his head. 'His construction company is profitable but there's no way he can make that amount of money from construction. Not here in Zimbabwe, where there's nothing being built. The amount of foreign exchange going through this account is incredible.'

'It is more than a construction company. It is also a front,' Hillary said. 'He ships ivory and rhino horns to China. He takes blood products and makes them look legitimate. I think he is beginning to run guns, but I have no proof of that yet.'

'You are a very brave person,' Bongani said.

'Not brave. Desperate. I needed all this evidence for Reason Sazulu, an agent in the International Criminal Court. Only then could my family's killer be brought to justice, because I was never going to get him any other way. He put them in an unmarked grave deep in the bush, and for many years I have collected this evidence against him.'

'There are four camps that specialise in training apprentices for the construction industry. Is this correct, Hillary?' Mitch said.

'You found that fast.'

'If it's on a computer, Mitch will find it,' Joss said.

'There are two camps in the Gwanda area; the second is just a little north of the first. His other camps are in the Masvingo area. Then he shows as owning another construction warehouse just out-side Bulawayo, in the Turk Mine area, but it's too well funded to be a warehouse. Something else is happening there. This also says that he owns – well, part owns – half of a trucking company that is registered in Malawi,' Mitch said.

'Are you looking for the training camps, or are you looking for his warehouse where he stores his illegal goods? His other ware-house is at Beit Bridge itself,' Hillary said.

'I'm trying to find out if he had access to an aviation company,' Mitch said. 'Helicopters don't just disappear, they belong to someone.'

'Adam's brother owns an aviation business in Zambia; he has helicopters there. I know that Tichawana has hired those before, because I saw a photo of him standing next to Adam's brother, with the helicopter in the background. Mr Ndou loves to hunt. That is the old friend he has gone to, to borrow the helicopters to raid Bishu Village.'

'Why am I not surprised about that?' Mitch said. 'But don't mind us while we double-check you and everything you say as far as we can. We don't want to be led into a trap, now, do we? It could be just another psychopathic game to this man. Send the damsel in distress to us so that we focus our attention one way and forget to look the other.'

Hillary shook her head. 'He is exactly that. We are trying to bring down an extremely well-connected poaching mastermind, and a powerful serial killer as well. He helped create mass graves in the 1980s and he funnels money to the government, so he is well placed with his peers. They will do everything they can to protect themselves. If you go in to take him down, believe me, you are going to come up against many bureaucrats who will stall everything. They will "lose" things to protect their own backs.

'I have studied him for years now. I know this man, and I want him dead as much as everyone else in this room. I have been spying on him for a long-long time, trying to bring down not only him but also Philip Samkanga, who was known as Black Mamba during the *Gukurahundi*. They served together and have remained in contact. Black Mamba knows the president from the old days too. That was how I found him, in the paper standing next to our president.'

'Philip Samkanga is bad news,' Bongani said. 'As corrupt as you can get, and he is still in charge of a lot of people within the army. Does Tichawana have much contact with him in his office?'

'Never in his office. They often meet at functions, and talk on the telephone,' Hillary said. 'Once or twice, they hunted together in the Mana Pools area.'

'Sounds like the deranged loyalty that my half-brother would attract,' Bongani said.

'Now this is interesting,' Mitch said. 'I added Philip Samkanga's name to the search. Apparently, there was a shipment of rocket launchers that were supposed to come into the Harare army camp a few months ago, but they mysteriously disappeared. The brigadier in charge of the stores was suspended, because they suspected he was in on the theft. In the same month there were two hundred and ninety kilograms of stocked rhino horn that disappeared from the ZimParks Harare headquarters. The head ranger there was suspended, pending a full investigation. There is a page on conspiracy theories run by someone who doesn't even live in Zimbabwe. He claims the crimes are connected.'

'I remember that horn theft,' Peta said. 'I spent a month dehorning those rhino in the park; I thought that we were doing the right thing to keep them safe from the poachers. And they still haven't caught the bastards who stole them.'

'The man in charge of the investigation of all these crimes, by order of the president, is none other than Philip Samkanga,' Mitch said.

'Hillary, which training camp do you think he's taken the boys to?' Mitch asked as he sat next to her.

'His favourite camp is his newest one in Gwanda. He visits that one the most. He hunts in that area to feed the camp. There is something special about that place to him. It is not like the others. He spends time there, and always says he is going to check on the kids' training.'

'I think we are going to need more policemen involved other than our friend in Binga,' Peta said.

'If you reach out for help, Detective Sargent Kudzanai Mathobeni will warn all the others on Mr Ndou's payroll, and they could further endanger the children,' Hillary said.

'Then we don't,' Joss said. 'We'll wait to call in the police. We're already a strike team. Mitch and I are more than capable of taking down one facility, once we have more intel on it. Hillary, are you able to draw a rough map for us of the layout?'

'Yes, I can.'

'We hit that camp first, and we hit it fast. Go in, get our kids, and get out. Then we can call in the police. They can hit his construction company in town and his compound outside Turk Mine, and any other places we need looked at. Surely Gideon Mthemba must have at least a few other police he knows are not rotten apples? He can get them to check the warehouse in Beit Bridge. We'll leave the anti-poaching guards here, just take a few of the trackers with us. The men here will guard the safari lodge and the people in the village.'

'I'm coming too,' Bongani said.

Joss shook his head. 'That's what he wants – to get you outside of your area.'

'I know. But if we do this like you suggest, we go in fast, he will not expect us to have this type of information.'

'True,' Mitch said.

'We know his goal. He is counting on Bongani leaving here, to go and try to save the children,' Joss said. 'But he isn't expecting us to go in so soon. When he gets the intel from his spies that Hillary is here with Bongani, he'll know his operation is blown.'

Hillary smiled. 'That might work.'

'There is more,' Peta said. 'We have the location of what we believe are mass graves. There was a man who marked them; he was trusted by the people, who got him to mark each with a cross. He appears to have been working with Adam Smith, or Tichawana Ndou, or both. We are still trying to put that puzzle together too.'

'I will be very happy to have something concrete on the mass graves,' Hillary said. 'I know we cannot touch him yet, but it will help to tighten his noose when he is taken away and tried for these atrocities he has committed. Do you have the name of the man who was marking the graves?'

'Kenneth Hunt.'

Hillary frowned. 'That cannot be right. Why would that spotter be marking mass graves for the people? He worked for Mr Ndou.'

CHAPTER
30

Cold Graves

Peta sat in Joss's lounge, the baby monitor on the table turned up to its loudest so she would hear Sophia if she so much as farted. She had the men from the district's different anti-poaching units doing patrols around the perimeter of the safari camp, and she had brought all the villagers into the safari area for safety. They had people camped in the stables, and on every available surface within the lodge. The guests had been briefed on the severity of the situation, and they had surprised Peta by being accommodating and not complaining when she asked them all to remain close to the lodge and not go out.

It was already past eleven pm, but she knew she wouldn't sleep, not with Joss, Bongani, Amos and Mitch, along with one of her own anti-poaching guard units, driving to the dawn raid on the youth camp.

'I need to work out how Adam and Tichawana knew about the spotters' camps in Chizarira,' Peta said.

'I can help you with that,' Hillary said. 'It is another of my boss's projects. I just cannot believe that Adam is caught up with him. I guess it was right in front of me and I did not see it.'

'The spotter's camp?'

'There is a map that Kenneth Hunt apparently has; it shows the good places to watch the migrations of the animals in this area. I have never seen this map myself, but there was a copy on his computer. It was not in Kenneth Hunt's possessions when one of your lions ate him in the park, and the police have said they do not know where the computer went. Mr Ndou always pressed him for a copy of the map, but Kenneth Hunt always told him that it was private and he was not entitled to see it.'

Peta humphed. 'That must have gone down well.'

'I was asked to find a way around it, to find the places he stayed. Many of the pictures of the animals that Kenneth Hunt sent with his report were done on a digital camera. I used the metadata in those to pinpoint where his camps were. If you look in my files, you will see that he had two favourite camps in the Chizarira and three in the Matusadona. He also had three spotting places in the Mana Pools area.'

Peta frowned. 'Why so many?'

'Hunting concessions in the safari areas next door to the parks. Mr Ndou has more blood ivory and rhino horn coming in from up north than he can process, so his scheme was to register bogus hunting companies to pay for concessions of the animals of similar sizes, then he paid the local chiefs the small portion of money owed to them, without the work, and they could sell that tusker again, and make more money from it. He turned the commodities legal without having to actually hunt for the animals and going to the expense of outfitting a real safari hunt. Hunting trophies are allowed to be shipped out, no questions asked.'

'That is quite sickening.'

'Mr Ndou and Mr Mlilo are both looking for the computer. Mr Ndou thinks that one of the policemen in Binga stole it. One of your game guards at Chizarira is on his payroll. He was not with you when you found the body, but he reported as much detail as he could afterwards.'

'Does your boss know you listen to every conversation?' But in her head, Peta was ticking off names of the guards who were with her that day in Chizarira, and she sighed with relief that she had sent her trusted men with Joss, and not a mole for Tichawana without knowing it. The only person remaining in camp the day they found Kenneth Hunt had been the new gardener, and she would arrange that his sorry arse got fired as soon as she could.

'Hell, no! Or I would be dead. I will happily throw the Korean investors that he works with under the truck, and laugh as they all get their just rewards.'

Peta opened her eyes wider. 'He works with the Koreans? He isn't the head honcho?'

'He is his own boss, but he is not clever enough to be the big boss,' Hillary said. 'He is what you would call a contractor. He has to work with other people to make everything happen. Organised crime is more structured than people think.'

'Who does he contract to?'

'A Korean businesswoman, who pretends that she is a little old granny. I think she might live in Sandton in South Africa. I never got her name or phone number. She came to visit him just once after he had lost a shipment of ivory and horn to customs. He sweated from the moment she arrived until she left, and he does not stress for anyone, not even the president. She owns the club he loves to visit.'

'That's interesting. I assumed that he worked totally for himself,' Peta said.

'You do not know this man at all,' Hillary said.

'No, and I'm beginning to think it's just as well.'

'The graves?' Hillary asked. 'How many of those have you found?'

'We have a map with a fair number on it.'

'You should let me get in touch with Reason Sezulu at the ICC. He could help you with them.'

'At the moment we're just trying to not scare the villagers into removing the crosses.'

'Can I add my family's gravesite to your map?' Hillary asked.

Peta looked at her. 'Do you know where it is?'

'It is not something you ever forget. I am here for help. I will not have a job when this is over, and I will be lucky if I can still live in Zimbabwe. Reason Sezulu warned me it might come to this, that if I was serious about putting Mr Ndou in jail, it would get ugly. But I still did it. If you have more information on the graves, Reason will help you; he is not in anyone's pocket, and he lives in Brussels, so they cannot touch him there.'

Peta got out her copy of the map.

Hillary ran her fingers over each cross. 'So many crosses. So many people dead by his hand.'

'We've still got to prove it,' Peta said.

'Proving the graves are there will achieve nothing. I have to get Tichawana Ndou and Philip Samkanga for other crimes. In my heart I have always wished that one day I can bury my family in a proper ceremony so that their spirits can cross over. So many restless spirits in this country. One day all the people's spirits will find peace.'

Peta squeezed her arm. 'Joss and Mitch have contacted a friend in the British Army who has been enhancing satellite imagery, and we're going to look through those, and on the ground, see if any closer surveillance is necessary. Many of the sites in Rwanda have been found like this, so having the places marked will make their job easier.'

Hillary shook her head. 'No. This news can never reach the president; he will simply send in a digger and take all the bones away, blame the colonial times, claiming the graves are from then, like he did once before. No one will ever get to DNA test the bones, and no one will ever know which bones belong with who, as he puts them somewhere else. He will never allow the proper historical excavation of the graves.' Hillary paused. 'Surely now Mr Ndou has taken the children, we can bring him to justice?'

'We have to prove that he knew about the abduction of the boys and that he's responsible. Even with everything you've shown us, we'll still need legal counsel on all this, to see if we can bring him to court.'

'I know.'

'Do you know that Hunt was double-crossing your boss? We found that many of his reports were duplicated but there were differences between what he emailed and the ones he had in the field. There were many files on his computer that were locked away, but once we got past them, it was interesting reading.'

'Why would he do that?'

'According to his computer files, he was a desperate man. And he needed atonement for the crimes he had committed. He felt it was his duty to save the tuskers, save some of the last big breeding herds of the rhino in Zimbabwe. Those same herds that his own grandfather had seen, and recorded where they were.'

Hillary shook her head. 'He was sentimental? I never saw that side of that man. Never.'

'No. I wouldn't call it that; I think it was more that the historian in him couldn't destroy everything. Couldn't destroy the history of his country. From what I gather from his files and diary, when he was visiting the same places his grandfather had spoken of, he noticed that the graves of those his grandfather had cared for had fallen into disrepair. He began to restore them, putting crosses where they should be, ensuring the names and dates were correct. While he was doing this, the villagers noticed, and he told them who he was. Many of the older people remembered his grandfather, or tales of the kind man, who was one of the last Native Commissioners. They asked him to mark their graves too. There were too many names to put on the grave markers. He knew that if he put multiple crosses, it would draw unwanted attention. Instead he began marking them too, with a single cross, and recording where they were.'

'You have all that on his computer?'

'Yes.'

'And the Black Mamba? Did he have any files on him?'

Peta shook her head. 'There's no mention of him.'

'This does not make sense. Kenneth Hunt worked for my boss. Why would he be putting crosses on graves?'

'There's a sort of justification statement for his actions on his computer. He was apparently building a case against Tichawana too. But unlike you, who wants him behind bars, we are unsure if he wanted to blackmail Tichawana for more money, or if he wanted to quit, and needed dirt on him, and this information was an insurance policy to ensure that Tichawana would let him go. I think that's why he was marking the graves. He wanted out, but Tichawana wasn't letting him go, so he was finding an alternative route.'

'Dangerous game. He was lucky the lion got him and not Mr Ndou,' Hillary said.

'Apparently after he was kicked off his family farm in the Concession by the war vets, Hunt was extremely angry and got himself into trouble, and debt. To try to dig himself out, he did a job for your boss, moving ivory for him, through Zimbabwe and Mozambique to be shipped out of Maputo. He apparently hated what he was being forced to do to survive in a country that was changing from one he understood to one he no longer had a place in. Where his own family's story was about to be erased from the history books.'

A soft knock sounded on the kitchen door. She heard Madala answer it, and muffled voices.

Julian walked into the lounge. 'Miss Peta, it is all quiet outside. I thought that I might sit with you ladies for a while. Take my turn on the watch so that Madala could get some sleep.'

Peta smiled. 'You are welcome to come in and sit with us while we wait. And we both know that Madala is getting no sleep either tonight; we might as well all be awake together.'

Peta knew Joss was a marine when she had started dating him, but nothing had prepared her for the sick feeling in her stomach, knowing that he was out there in the night, sneaking around, saving the boys, risking his own life while he did it. Even with the information they had gathered from Hillary, Tichawana's youth camps were going to prove an interesting case, as they were not sure which one the boys were in. If they were lucky, they would slip into the first one, and quickly find out if they were there or not. If they were unlucky, they would have to move on to the others, and the darkness of night might disappear while they were still checking.

She thought of the fact that Joss was in perfect health and super fit, just as any able-bodied marine like Mitch was, just that he had prosthetics. And while he acted like they were an extension of himself, she worried that they might be the part that let him down out there. That part that wasn't one hundred per cent Joss.

She looked at the baby monitor. If something happened to Joss, she wasn't sure just how she would tell his beautiful daughter that her new daddy was hurt, and she prayed that it wouldn't come to that.

Peta straightened her back in the chair and lifted her chin.

Her Joss was a Royal British Marine Commando. He had told her that he had done millions of missions like this during active combat; the only difference now was that instead of having five other highly trained marines with him, he had only Mitch by his side, and Amos and Bongani with their bush skills. She prayed that that was enough to keep them all safe and to save the children.

CHAPTER
31

Combat

The mud map Hillary drew was pretty accurate. She had also marked the most likely places they might encounter trouble.

The strike team consisted of only four: Joss, Mitch, Bongani and Amos. A full unit of six anti-poaching guards from the Chizarira, who Peta had called on for help and knew she could trust, remained hidden with the vehicles, ready to extract the children when they had them, and protect their departure.

Joss's team had parked a little way away, hidden in the bush, and they walked towards the school. They had borrowed night-vision goggles from one of the private anti-poaching teams from the Victoria Falls area who were funded by an international organisation and were stationed a few kilometres up the road, ready to be called in if needed.

The training college had two parts: in the front was the school, and at the back, the boarding house. That was where they suspected they would find the boys, if they were here. Joss hated that the boys had been gone twenty-four hours.

The perimeter guards had offered little resistance and all six of them had been taken out quickly and permanently, with Joss and

Mitch doing the work. They had passed a hanging tree that had recently been used, the smell rank, flies still buzzing around despite the night breeze. Some animal had been hunted and skinned, then the meat taken to the kitchen. They crossed over the tree line, their most vulnerable position, without anyone noticing them. The smell of wood smoke was heavy and clung to the establishment.

Mitch signalled the window was only a few steps away, and Joss slid along. Mitch found the edge of the windowsill and drew himself up and over. He reached down for Joss, gripping his arm and hauling him in. He did the same for Amos and Bongani as Joss covered him inside.

They were in a kitchen and they stilled, listening. No one had stirred, not even the cooks, who Hillary had warned were always up early. Joss signalled to Mitch, and they began clearing the rooms as they went, Joss in front, then Mitch, Bongani and Amos.

There was an eerie stillness throughout the boarding house. They stopped outside a padlocked room. Joss stuck a scope under the door while Mitch looked at his small computer screen. When he brought his equipment home with him, Joss had never imagined that he would have been using it on a mission.

'Storeroom. Move on.'

They moved to the next door and repeated the procedure. That too was just a storeroom. In the third room they saw boys up against the wall, their hands bound to a pole above their heads. When their legs got tired, they would need to hang by their arms. Their bodies were slumped in exhaustion.

Mitch nodded.

Joss took the large bolt cutter from his pack and cut the lock. The clink they made was loud, but Mitch watched the boys. Not one of them stirred.

Joss slowly opened the door and veered left. Mitch crouched low behind him, providing vital cover in case of resistance. Bongani walked through and went right, while Amos waited outside the room. They checked the room for guards, then Joss and Bongani looked at the boys. Lwazi and Ephraim were not among them.

Bongani put his hand over one of the boys' mouths, and his eyes shot open.

In English, he reassured him, 'I am not here to hurt you. I need to know where they put the new recruits that came in yesterday.'

The boy swallowed, his eyes still large.

Bongani cut him down, still holding his hand over his mouth. The ropes had sliced into his wrists and his knees buckled underneath his body. He slumped in a heap on the floor and shook his head.

Bongani tried in Ndebele, but the boy shook his head, attempting to talk.

'Quietly. Understood?'

The boy nodded. Bongani removed his hand.

'I do not know where they are. I do not know.'

'Did you volunteer to come here? To be trained?' Bongani asked.

The boy shook his head.

'You are going to need to help us cut your fellow trainees down, quietly. Make sure that none of them makes a noise. We will collect you on the way out once we have found our own boys, do you understand?'

The boy nodded. 'What if the guard comes?'

Bongani looked around. 'There are lots of you. Overpower him until he cannot hurt you any more,' he said and then the team walked out of the room, knowing that the boy was too scared and too relieved to do anything but what they had ordered.

They looked into the next room, and found nothing, but the next one had children in it again. This time they were sleeping on mats on the floor.

Once more Joss cut the padlock. They went into the room, sweeping it for guards and finding none. Bongani stepped quietly through all the children. Most of them were young girls. One woke up and stared at him. Quickly he placed his hand over her mouth.

'Do not scream; we are here to help you. Do you know where they put the boys who came in yesterday?'

She nodded.

'Quietly,' he said as he removed his hand.

'The ones who were brought in the helicopters?'

Bongani nodded.

'In the school buildings. There are rooms under the floor. They put them there and tied them up. I saw them when Corporal Mazaiwana took me for his turn last night, before he locked me in here.'

'Did you volunteer to be here?' he asked.

She shook her head. 'My sister, she is also here and I cannot run away because she already has a broken leg, and she cannot run far. I will not leave without my sister.'

'Is she in this room?'

The girl nodded and pointed to the mattress next to hers. The girl lying there was younger than she was.

'Can you wake her up quietly and get her ready to come with us? If you wake the other girls you know are not happy about being here too, once we have our boys, we will come past to collect you on the way out. We also have some boys in the back room who are waiting to escape.'

She nodded.

'Can I trust you not to raise the alarm?' Bongani asked.

She nodded again and crossed her chest with her hand.

They left the boarding house and went to the school area. Within a few moments they could hear the boys. Their children were not silent, they were whispering loudly. They hadn't been broken, but they were scared. Relief flooded Joss as he listened to them.

'They will come for us, I know it,' Lwazi was saying.

'How can you be so sure?' asked a voice they didn't recognise.

'Because that is who they are. Chief Bongani, he looks after his people, and Joss, he is a marine. A commando. A British SES soldier – you know, a green beret, like they sing about in the songs. So is Mitch. They are not scared of anything.'

Joss stilled. If only that were true. Both Bongani and Mitch knew what taking up a gun against another human was costing him. He was the one who had laid down his weapons and walked away, chosen to take a chance on life in Africa instead of returning to the front lines. He was the one who had brought them all together, and the motivation for the kidnapping. His humanitarian heart had been exposed. He'd been taken advantage of, manipulated, because of it. Every man with them knew the cost of this mission and that, if it went wrong, they were on their own.

Mitch looked at his screen. 'Three guards. One on each side of the door and one sleeping a little away from the kids at four o'clock.'

'I'll take left; Mitch, right. Bongani, if you can get that third guard. Amos, hang back and defend the corridor in case we make too much noise and someone wakes. Try to get those kids to keep quiet when we go in.'

There was no lock to break on the door, and the guards on the inside never heard the team as the two marines cut their throats and placed their silent bodies on the floor.

Joss had his hand in front of his mouth, signalling for the boys to be quiet, and Bongani rushed at the third guard, his kill just as effective, if not as neat, as the trained marines'.

'I knew you would come,' Lwazi said. 'I knew it.' He threw himself at Bongani as best he could since he was handcuffed to the boy next to him, and then chained through that to the wall.

Joss took the key off the guards and opened the cuffs on Lwazi's hands, then he passed it to Bongani to free the other boys. He smiled. 'Of course we came. Now stay real quiet; there will be time for talking once we get out of here.'

Lwazi hugged Joss. 'They took Ephraim to a different room. They beat him up in front of us and they took him away. They said that his grandmother was the one who told them everything on how to get us away from you and Bongani, so now he could tell them more about Bongani, because he must know more.'

'Do you know which direction?' Joss asked.

'No.' Lwazi shook his head. 'He was bleeding, and the blood, it was bright red when he spat it out. He is hurt bad.'

Bongani unlocked the last boy's cuffs and freed the boys from the chain. They crowded around him, and he seemed to know them all.

'Bongani, you and Amos take them back to collect the other kids. Mitch and I will look for Ephraim.'

Bongani nodded. 'Come, quickly,' he instructed the boys as they made their way along the long passage and through the back door towards the boarding house.

Joss put the scope under the next door and Mitch looked at his screen. 'One body lying in the middle, not moving. On concrete. No sleeping mat. No bounds.'

'No guard?'

'No.'

Joss opened the door slowly and Mitch covered him.

Ephraim lay curled in a foetal position. Joss checked for a heartbeat. It was there, but faint. His breathing was shallow.

'Dammit, kid. Don't you die on me,' he said, and he tapped Ephraim's cheek to wake him. But even as he did it, he suspected that Ephraim wouldn't wake without help. He was in bad shape. His fingers had been broken, as had his wrists. Someone had beaten his head with a blunt object, and his jaw was dislocated, if not broken.

'It's okay, Ephraim, I'm here; I've come to take you home,' Joss said.

Ephraim's eyes opened but they were bloodshot and Joss didn't know if they focused or not.

'I'll carry him,' Mitch said. 'You make sure no one shoots us.'

Joss nodded.

Mitch shouldered Ephraim. The teenager groaned in pain.

'I know, but we have to get you out of here. Quiet now. If you can understand anything, you need to be quiet,' Joss said.

Ephraim quietened as though he had passed out again. Joss suspected that he was a dead weight across Mitch's shoulders.

'I can't tell if he is alive or dead,' Mitch said.

'It doesn't matter; we are taking him out either way.'

They exited the school building. They were almost out the back of the boarding house when the gunfire started.

Joss peered around the corner of the building and across the lawn area before the fence. Bongani and Amos had almost got all the kids into the bushes. The gunfire wasn't close to them; it was coming from the front of the school.

He saw the kids as they ran in a tightly packed group into the bushes and blended into the undergrowth, safe. A guard with a shotgun aimed in the air came around the side of the building. He was looking up.

A peacock settled back on the roof. He tousled his feathers and *craaaawwwwed* at the guard. The guard took aim and shot. The bird fell in an ungraceful heap off the roof, tumbling to the guard's feet as a second guard joined him.

'Breakfast,' the first one said and pointed and the second guard shook his head. The first guard picked up the bird and walked with an awkward gait towards the kitchen, as if the bird was heavier than he expected and the long tail feathers were getting in his way.

'Go now,' Joss said to Mitch, and he too turned his back on the building and ran, constantly checking behind him, protecting Mitch and Ephraim.

They got to where Bongani and the children still walked and looked around, slowing their pace to match.

'How many kids did they have in that place?' Joss asked.

'When we came back, they were all here, and already many had run into the bushes in front of us. There are another hundred or so. There were these four big dormitories, and the girls had woken everyone up. Those boys who were tied up, they had woken all the boys too. Once we told them the guards were definitely dead, they began to run out, just trying to get away. I gave Lwazi the map that Hillary drew of the area. He and the other Bishu Village boys are leading the pack as they run for the bus depot. I told them we would get buses for them there, as long as they all stuck together. Those too weak to run can go in our vehicles, once we follow them through the bush.'

'When those guards find no kids, they're going to come after us like bulls out of a gate. They will hit us with everything they have,' Mitch warned.

'I know,' Bongani said. 'I am hoping that these men we have with us are enough to protect the kids now that we have too many to drive out ourselves.'

Joss slowed slightly to jump a small ditch, and checked behind him again. 'This kid had better live or I might just be finding your half-brother, putting him upside down in that hanging tree and doing some skinning of my own!'

'You will have to stand behind me in that line,' Bongani said.

'You okay?' Mitch asked, looking at Joss.

'Yeah, just as well I have been pushing so hard in training. How much further do those kids have to run to the depot?'

Bongani looked ahead. 'Five kilometres.'

'I'm worried Ephraim won't make it. He needs a doctor now,' Joss said, then stopped talking as all hell broke loose behind them at the camp.

Their escape had been discovered.

*   *   *

Joss helped Mitch to get Ephraim flat in the back of the *bakkie*. He checked again for a heartbeat. It was faint. He nodded to Bongani, who sat with three other boys and four girls already in the vehicle. Each was drenched in sweat and exhausted. They hadn't even made it past the *bakkie*s, left behind by the others, who ran towards safety now with a pack mentality. The girl who had carried her sister along with her broken leg was now safely in the back too.

Bongani went to the driver's side, and Mitch jumped in the passenger seat. Joss knew that the Chizarira team were already in the second *bakkie*, getting ready to move into position to protect their departure.

The gunfire signalled that the other guards from the house were rushing through the bushes almost blind. The sun was not quite up, and every time they fired their weapons, the flash from the barrels would blind them again. They tried to scare the running kids into stopping. Only this time it wouldn't work because the *bakkie*s and the rescue party were between the fleeing children and the guards, and the children knew this.

Mitch adjusted his night-vision goggles. 'Coming in fast at ten o'clock.'

Joss took his .303 and held it ready. He looked through the telescopic lens and pulled the trigger, the sound loud and solid in the night, different to the *pop-pop* bullets of the guards.

The training camp guards stopped, unsure where the gunfire had come from. Some of them dropped to the ground, while others attempted to hide behind tree trunks.

Bongani kept the *bakkie* idling so that Joss could aim.

'Two o'clock,' Mitch said.

Joss took down another guard.

Mitch watched as the man was thrown backwards with the impact. 'Bloody hell! What bullets are you using?'

'Hollow points,' Joss said. 'They deserve the best I can offer.'

'Remind me to never piss you off,' Mitch said as Joss took out another pursuer.

Two of the guards had been smart enough not to rush into the bushes; instead they had got a vehicle and were racing towards them now. Joss and Mitch could see the *bakkie* gaining on the guards, spotlighting them so that they didn't run them over. Mitch took off his night-vision goggles and aimed at the spotlight.

It was gone in a splintering of glass.

The approaching vehicle stopped as Joss put a barrage of bullets through the radiator and into the engine block, before silencing its driver and passenger. He kissed his father's .303 on its walnut butt. 'You are a great weapon to have on our side! Any more surprises?'

'Not close,' Mitch said. 'Leave them to the Chizarira guards to clean up.'

Joss gestured to the other vehicle and the guards manoeuvred into position and immediately began to drop the other pursuers, not wasting any ammo, proving their skills were just as good as Peta had said they were.

Bongani started the vehicle rolling forward. 'I counted sixteen, including the two from the stopped vehicle, and Joss got ten,' he said.

'If they are out there, Peta's team will clean them up,' Joss said. 'It's time for us to go and protect the kids at the bus stop.' He was grateful they had the extra team hidden to protect the buses the whole way to Bulawayo. Away from the place where nightmares were manufactured.

'What do we do with all these kids, where do we bus them to?' Mitch asked.

Joss smiled. 'The Baobab Tree Orphanage, that'll be the best place. I'll call their director once we're on our way and tell him to expect us. He's an Aussie like you.'

* * *

Joss used his right hand to close Ephraim's eyes. 'I hope you know that we came for you, and you didn't die alone in that room. We were with you.'

Bongani passed him a long plaster from the first-aid kit. With shaking hands he stuck one over each eye to keep them closed, taking deep breaths to control the anger that raged inside.

Bongani put his hand on Ephraim's shoulder. 'You have passed over to the other side now. Know that I will look after your grandmother. Go in peace, and may your journey be a safe and pain-free one.'

Joss looked up at the sky. The last stubborn stars were still trying to glow brightly despite dawn's light starting to lighten the sky. 'At least he got to see the stars one last time.'

Mitch nodded. 'To die knowing you are free after being a captive is a gift of its own.'

Joss shrugged out of his combat jacket, and placed it over Ephraim so that the children couldn't see the face of death. 'I swear to you we'll find the man who took you, and make him pay. His life for yours. Even if Bongani and I have to track him till the end of our days.'

CHAPTER
32

The Fire Glows

Tichawana heard the ringing of his cell phone and ignored it. But it rang again.

And again.

He pushed the woman who was draped over him away, and she fell to the floor, dragging with her the other two women chained to her. They landed in a heap. He smiled at the tangle of limbs next to the bed as he reached for the phone.

'This had better be important—' he began, then quietened as he listened. He stood up and began dressing. 'I'm on my way to the emergency house. I will call you when I get there.' He stabbed at the end-call button, and put his phone on the nightstand. 'Clear out,' he instructed the girls.

Still a little dazed, they gathered their robes and walked silently to the door.

'Wait. Do any of you have a car?'

The oldest woman nodded. 'Is parked at back of club.'

'Good, where are the keys?'

'In locker at clubhouse.'

'I am going to unchain you. You go get them. Meet us at your car.' He reached for his keys, unlocked the small padlock and removed her leather collar.

She rubbed at her neck.

'When we are all in the car, I will remove the chains from the other girls, do you understand? If you do not come back or you call for help, I will kill them both.'

She nodded, bowed her head and silently moved to the door, then slipped away.

'Right,' he said as he put his shoes on. 'Time to go.'

The two women were so used to being chained together they moved as one. They walked quickly in front of him, sensing his change in mood. They didn't try to attract attention; they were too well trained to do that. He was breaking the rules of the club by removing them. He knew it. They knew he knew it. He just had to believe that they would not turn him in to the manager and guards who patrolled the golf club. Besides, he owned the women, even if this would be the first trip he had ever taken them on.

They reached the staff car park, discreetly hidden by a hedge. The older woman was already at the driver's side of the car. No longer in her silk dressing gown, she wore Western clothes, a T-shirt and some faded jeans with holes in the knees. And she had on studded black boots.

'Get in back,' she said, 'stay down on floor.'

She was not going to turn him in. He let out a small sigh of relief that he would not have to kill them. After their years together, he had grown fond of them.

He opened the back door and climbed inside. The older woman sat behind the wheel, and when the two younger girls got in the back, he passed them the key to unlock their chains.

They closed the door and the older woman started the car. She began driving out of the car park. She threw the girls some clothes. 'No go in street in dressing gown.'

They changed while he looked down at the carpet, willing the woman to drive faster.

'Where to?'

'Head towards the Matopos. I will give you instructions when we get there.'

For half an hour they drove silently south, until the driver pulled over to the side of the road. He raised his head and saw they were just before the Matopos turn-off.

'We served you for many years. There is bond between us when we are chained to you; now chains are gone. You a rich criminal. We – us slaves. But we are not fools. If we leave you here on the road, you will send people. Find us. But if we drive you to your place, you keep us safe? You not kill any of us?' the driver said.

'I will not harm you; you have done nothing but please me all these years. Turn left at the next junction and continue to a sign that says Giraffe Lodge. Instead of turning to the lodge, turn right, and head down the dirt road until you come to a farmhouse,' he said.

He saw the tension in the woman's shoulders ease slightly.

They were no fools. He was still their master. They were still his slaves, but for now the four of them would run together, because when the bullets started flying, he'd have three other bodies he could use as shields.

Fifteen minutes later they climbed out of the car at the old farm-house. Once it must have belonged to some settler, who'd built it from local stone, and then later made it look more colonial, but he didn't care about that as he pushed the front door open. He cared that the thick stone walls were impervious to bullets. He could hole up in this house for months, and unless someone shot a rocket down the chimney, there was no way he had to leave.

He took his phone from his pocket and dialled Denisa Mlilo's number. 'I'm clear.'

'Good.'

'Have you got a full report? What happened?'

'That brother of yours had help. He moved too fast. We did not expect him to find the boys or attack with such speed. Twenty-four hours and they came to Gwanda and took the children back. They freed all the others. I am following the buses now to see where they drop them.'

'What about the extra guards?'

'Dead. The police were called in, and they have begun to raid your other training facilities. But they only have six names so far – that is what my man in the police force has told me. They also said that one of their boys we went to Bishu to fetch is very badly injured, possibly dead.'

'Possibly dead? He is either alive or he is dead, which one?'

'I do not know.'

Tichawana closed his eyes. 'Which camp has not been named to the police?'

'Mutare.'

'Give instructions to all the staff to abandon their posts and reassemble in one month.'

'What about the youths still in training?'

'Bury them deep.'

There was silence on the other end of the line.

Tichawana asked, 'What else? What else did my brother do?'

'Not your brother directly, but I am sure they are working with him. The police also raided your warehouse in the Turk Mine area, and I have it that the police force are on the way to Beit Bridge.'

'This is too much information for them to know so fast. Which lieutenant talked?' Tichawana yelled.

'We don't know yet. But Mary, the one we had on the inside at your brother's village, she is not talking any more. Her mouth is closed tighter than a chicken's butthole.'

'Make her talk. Hurt her grandchild.'

Denisa said, 'They already hurt her grandson; that is why she will not talk.'

'Kill her. She is a liability. Find out who betrayed me.'

He hung up before the man could say anything else. The phone started ringing almost immediately, and when he looked at the number, he took a deep breath.

'Madam Lu Liang,' he said politely and with as much respect as he could inject into his voice.

'You have been compromised. You need to clean up your house.'

'Yes, madam.'

'You are to relocate to Tanzania. The Monkey Beach Safari Lodge. Be there within a week, or I will have you cleaned too. I cannot stand incompetence.'

'Yes, madam.'

She hung up on him. He threw the phone at the fireplace and it split apart, the battery and the cover scattering over the polished concrete floor.

Silently, the oldest of the women went over and picked up the pieces, and passed them to the youngest. 'Fix this. He need it.'

The youngest put the phone together while Tichawana watched, and then she brought it to him. It started to ring again.

This time he flopped down in the leather lounge before answering.

'Talk!'

Adam's voice came through clearly. 'The police just raided your construction company and your house. Your home staff have been taken in for questioning, as have the construction crews who were at the site.'

'Is Harry with them?'

'Yes.'

'Then no one will talk. They won't find anything in the crew; they know nothing.'

'My father will keep them in line, yes. They also raided the club.'

'So?'

'They found your vehicle there and they seized your hunting rifles. They are saying that you kidnapped three women employees.'

Tichawana shook his head. 'They came with me of their own free will.'

'Be careful.'

His eyes flicked to the oldest of the women. He had owned her first, and for the longest. He was certain that, out of all of them, he needed to be careful of her the most, but he was sure she knew nothing of his business dealings.

'Anything else I can do to help?'

'I need a camo Hummer. Get hold of the Black Mamba, tell him we will need to speed up that shipment he promised me last month. Fetch my tracker from Esigodini. Get my hunting rifles back. We have to move our plan up. We need a pontoon boat that will hold the Hummer.'

'The vehicle will take a few days. When do you want your tracker ready?'

'Have the boat waiting in Milbizi. Bring the Hummer and my tracker together.'

'Will do.'

Tichawana rubbed his forehead. 'Do you know how my brother found my camp so fast, and what information he gave to the police so that they had the audacity to raid my operation?'

'Still trying to put it all together. We know that Francis Kanobvurunga didn't react like we expected when his son was delivered. Instead of coming back to you, he seems to have gone mental, and the police got involved. He was taken into the Bulawayo police station. From what we've managed to find out, he was collected from there by your secretary but they've disappeared.'

'Hillary? Why would she fetch Francis Kanobvurunga?'

'Detective Sargent Kudzanai Mathobeni called your office when he couldn't get you on the cell. He told her to fetch Kanobvurunga before they took him to hospital. So she did. She booked a *bakkie* out from the fleet from my father and no one has seen her since.'

'So where did she go?'

'I don't know.'

'Any CCTV footage? Surely you know which direction she drove in?'

'That's been broken for years.'

'Typical Third World country.'

'What about the package arriving at the end of the week?'

'Get hold of your client, and tell him that there has been unrest. Delay your safari. I will stop all deliveries until after I am chief. You find Hillary.'

Tichawana ended the call and sat tapping the phone against his teeth, then he got up and went to the drinks trolley and poured himself a goblet of brandy. Gulping it down in one swig, he poured another.

Hillary had Francis, but why would she collect him and where the fuck did she go?

'Is anything we can help?' the older woman asked.

'No. Go choose a room, down the passage to the left. The maid will give us some lunch. I'm going to shower. I have work to do; do not disturb me.'

* * *

Four days later, Tichawana heard the Hummer arrive, the crunch of gravel loud in the quiet bush. He walked onto the veranda.

His tracker was sitting in the passenger seat, grinning.

Adam climbed out of the driver's seat. 'I've brought a few hand grenades that we had stashed. I figured we might need them. Also got these for you.' Adam opened the back door and removed a familiar sports bag. Tichawana's hunting rifles.

'You have done well.'

'I aim to please.'

A Land Rover drove in and parked behind the Hummer.

'My tracker, Brighton. Figured four of us was better than two,' Adam said.

CHAPTER
33

Breath of Air

Joss sat on the veranda of the lodge. In his right hand he nursed a
Zambezi beer. He watched the movement below him in the bushes
as Mandlenkosi came to catch his nightly fish. The leopard was old
and losing condition; his days were numbered.

'Kosi was born right here, raised by his mother, until he left for
a while. When she died, he increased his territory to include hers.
He's not as fast or as agile as he once was, but he remains nearby,'
Joss said as he lifted his binoculars.

'I could dart him for you, check him out,' Peta said. 'See if there's
anything I can do to make him feel a bit better, if there's something
that makes him eat such small prey now.'

Joss shook his head. 'He's old – the drugs could kill him. I can't
take the dignity of dying in the bush away from him. I can't believe
how he has deteriorated lately, though. He's still so beautiful.'

'That he is,' she said, and threaded her fingers through Joss's.

'It is just how life is. You are born, you live and you die,'
Bongani said.

'No, there is more to it than that: you live and you love—' she said.

'Bring me a bucket,' Mitch said.

They laughed.

'It's nice to relax for a while. We seem to have been on the go since forever,' Mitch said.

'I'll drink to that.' Joss took a sip from his beer. 'And I'll raise one to Ephraim too. But don't drink too much.'

'To Ephraim,' Bongani, Mitch, Hillary and Peta said together.

Joss said, 'I'm still not convinced we're not in for a hard time one of these nights. I know everyone has settled down this week, but there will be retribution. There has to be. From what Bongani has always told me about his half-brother, and from what we know from Hillary, there is no way he'd lose everything like he has and not come and try to take Bongani out.'

'That's why we are by his side, constantly,' Mitch said.

'It's good to have you here. Hope it's helped you with your decision on what you want to do with your life,' Joss said.

Mitch nodded. 'Yeah, but got a bit of research to do before I can commit.'

'Sounds interesting,' Amos said. 'You make it look so easy to have a career, and then change it. Do something else. I could not imagine doing anything else now that I work with Peta.'

'I knew I wanted a change, then I had this break and the opportunities have presented themselves. I guess I've been lucky,' Mitch said.

'Tell us about it when you can,' Peta said. 'I'm almost dying of curiosity now.'

'I will,' Mitch said.

'How was Lwazi on your run this afternoon?' Peta asked.

Joss shook his head. 'Quiet. Skittish. I'm worried for that boy. I don't know how he's going to come back from the torture they put them through, and from losing Ephraim. Bongani, Madala White and I were talking about him. We think we might look into finding him a counsellor. He hides his hurt well, but he needs to let it out. He has been through so much for a boy his age.'

'What are you going to do about Ephraim's grandmother?' Hillary asked.

'Nothing. I think what happened to Ephraim shook her up badly enough,' Bongani said.

The leopard jumped onto the edge of the rocks near the lake.

'Get your camera ready, Mitch,' Joss said.

Mitch lifted his camera to his eye and looked through its telescopic lens.

The click of the shutter was the only sound for a while as Mitch watched Mandlenkosi crouch at the edge, where the murky water of Kariba and the sand of the land mixed. The leopard stilled, lifting one paw and silently placing it in the water, then slowly lifting the next, as if stalking. His tail was still; just the tip flashed as he dived into the shallows. A moment later, the leopard's head rose for a second before he jumped into the water again, back arched, diving into the pool where the rocks, the grass and the water met. This time he came up with a very large catfish wiggling in his jaws. The leopard walked back through the grass towards a tree on the edge of the lake and jumped into it.

Joss watched as the leopard, silhouetted against the backdrop of the dead trees, ate the fish, then licked its lips and preened itself, cleaning the smell of the fish from its coat.

The sky darkened, making the leopard appear artificial in its tree, a black shadow.

'That photo will be worthy of *National Geographic*,' Mitch said. 'And you were all here when I took it. A fishing leopard.'

Joss grinned. 'Let's hope one of these days soon we can get out on the water and you can enjoy yourself, do a little tiger fishing, maybe catch a vundu.'

'I want to go check on the Bishu villagers tomorrow,' Bongani said. 'Talk to them, see how their boys are doing.'

'You did remember that tomorrow is when I planned on darting Torn-Ear again?' Peta asked. 'He still doesn't trust me enough to check him without being tranquillised.'

'I did not forget. You will have plenty of help,' Bongani said. 'I will just take Joss with me. Mitch, any objections to staying with Peta?'

Mitch shook his head.

Peta smiled. 'Amos and I will be fine with Ndhlovy and Torn-Ear. I suspect she will guard him again anyway.'

'We can go later in the day,' Joss suggested.

'No, that's okay. You guys go – the sooner you get there, the sooner you can come back,' Peta said.

There was movement at the door of the dining room, and Julian Seziba came onto the veranda. 'Chief,' he said, nodding in respect.

'Yes?' Bongani asked.

'I was following the elephants, making sure they keep out of trouble. But today I see spoor. There are men here, in the bushes. Two of them carry heavy luggage, like hunting weapons. I followed their tracks. There is a camo vehicle hiding in the bush that they brought in on a big boat.'

'Did you see who they were?'

'No. I walked back to the elephants, and came in with them tonight. But I could feel their eyes watching me.'

'Thank you,' Bongani said. 'Would you like to join us?'

Julian shook his head. 'Timberman is unarmed and waiting for me in the stables. These elephants are special, so tonight we will watch them close-close. But we wanted to borrow a .303 just in case.'

'Tell you what,' Joss said. 'How about we take turns? I'll take first watch.'

Mitch put his beer on the table. 'So it starts again. Joss, you lied; you told me this place was quiet, even boring. I'll see you there, Julian, at, say, twenty-one hundred hours?' He set his watch without looking up.

'I'll take midnight,' Bongani said.

'Gee, so you're leaving the worst for me. Fine, I'll take graveyard, from three am till sun-up,' Peta said.

'You need to be rested for tomorrow. Those elephants are depending on you ... I will take that shift,' Amos said.

'Bongani and I will be going out to track these sons of bitches at first light,' Joss said, 'then we can decide if we're still going to Bishu.'

Bongani nodded, then clapped Amos on the shoulder. 'Come on, guess our rest time is over.'

*   *   *

Joss walked towards his house, then detoured to the stables. Ndhlovy saw him and greeted him, her rumblings loud in the still of the evening.

'Hey, girl,' he said as she approached, and he rested his forehead against her trunk. She moved her trunk over him, as if reassuring him that they were alright. But she constantly moved her weight between her feet.

'I know, the timing of having to defend this place couldn't be worse. There are men out there who are making you nervous. Peta will check on Torn-Ear tomorrow and then you can probably go back into the Chizarira. Julian will be your own guard, walking all the way.' He scratched her ear, and smiled at the soft rumble coming from her.

He heard the click of Mitch's camera behind him before he realised he was there.

'I thought I'd see what you were up to,' Mitch said, still taking photos.

Ndhlovy flapped her ears at him when he took a step closer.

'She still doesn't trust me.'

'She's restless. I think she's waiting for Peta's confirmation that Torn-Ear is okay before she moves her herd. She knows there's danger out there.'

'I'm amazed by how intelligent they are,' Mitch said. 'And still in shock that people shoot them for their ivory.'

'I know. A little of me would die if that happened to her.'

Mitch took a few more close-ups of Joss and Ndhlovy before Bongani arrived with Julian. Each had a .303 on his shoulder.

'That elephant and Joss, they have a special bond,' Julian said. 'Never in my years, even when I was working in ZimParks, did I see a wild elephant trust a human like this.'

'I guess we saved each other,' Joss said. 'Look after them tonight, make sure they have extra food to keep them in camp, not browsing out there, just in case. We will touch base with you guys later.'

'You sure you want to leave me behind in the morning?' Mitch said.

'I'm trusting you to watch over Peta and Sophia.'

'With my life.'

'I'm counting on that,' Joss said as he touched Ndhlovy one last time, and kept her trunk in his hand until he had to drop it or she had to step forward. He broke the contact and walked away, Bongani and Mitch following.

As he neared the front door, he stopped. In front of him were the five *N'Goma*s.

'Chief,' Abigale said. 'The snake has returned; he is camping on your borders. You will need our help to cut off his head.'

CHAPTER

34

Witchcraft

Bongani walked in front, just a little to the left, and Joss followed closely.

They had tracked like this for many hours when he was a boy. Then, his rifle strap had been taken up as much as it would go, and his mother had added more stitching to shorten it even more. Now he carried his .303 across his back as if it was his assault weapon. He was sweating because walking in the sand was hard enough with normal legs, now it sucked at his shoes and it took a heap of energy to lift one foot and put it in front of the other. He was just happy that he was so much fitter, probably as fit as he had been as a marine. He certainly drank less beer now.

Shaking his head, he brought his mind back to Bongani, who pointed to tracks in the sand where a vehicle had parked. It was exactly where Julian had said it would be. There was a stomped-out cigarette close by. Bongani picked it up and, after looking at it closely, smelt it.

'*Dagga*-tobacco mixture.'

Joss circled around him, continually looking at the ground. 'Definitely four men. One wears expensive new boots too. Look at this print.'

'The rich one walks at the back, then my half-brother. Look, his boots are still different sizes, from where his foot was broken badly and did not set well when he was a boy. A second tracker, who walks like a man of the bush, leaving hardly any footprints, and then the hunter, who is heavy on his feet and imprints in the sand well. They have used this hiding place more than once – the tracks here are older, then newer ones again today,' Bongani said.

'What would they be looking at from here?' Joss said. He did a slow three-sixty. 'That *koppie*.' He pointed. 'I bet from the top of that you can see across into the safari lodge. We've been under surveillance.'

'The *N'Goma*s are never wrong. They said the snake is back. They said he had not yet come through their *muti* lines, but they are worried that he will, despite their power. Even if he is no longer scared of the ancient magic, he is not taking a chance. He is hovering outside my territory.'

Joss frowned. 'Okay, so they don't think that their *muti* works on him now?'

'You heard them; they are unsure. Perhaps he no longer believes or fears them. Or he tries hard to think he does not believe. But we are an ancient people, and traditions run deep roots into us. Perhaps he no longer has a soul,' Bongani said. 'But they are correct that he has not crossed over the line yet. They said that he camps on my border. We are not on my land at all, we are in the safari strip, the five-kilometre stretch that runs around the lake. Perhaps he is still scared of the *N'Goma*s after all and they have underestimated their power over him.'

Bongani walked away from Joss and came back with a branch. 'Right, we know what they are up to; let us not leave them any trace that shows we know. Let him think that he is setting his trap.' He began wiping their tracks from the area.

Joss walked back the way they had come, and then he turned towards the *koppie.* 'I think we should look up there.'

Bongani nodded.

Joss kept a steady pace on the game trail that wound its way up the *koppie,* deliberately not going on the path the others had trodden, Bongani behind him all the time, wiping out their tracks with the branch.

They crested the small hill. Looking south, Joss had a clear line of sight to Yingwe Safari Camp. They found where the men had sat, even the remnants of a small fire.

'They seem comfortable,' Joss said as he began to walk a grid search. Bongani did the same in the opposite direction.

'Over here.' Under a camo net, Joss found an ammo dump in a large metal box: a few boxes of rounds and six pineapple hand grenades.

Bongani gave a low whistle, then looked to the safari camp. 'Lucky no missiles to blow up the camp and the village.'

Joss shook his head. 'No, not in their stash.'

'If Hillary had not told us of the Philip Samkanga connection, I would not have believed this possible in my country today. I have not seen hand grenades for many years. This country is so full of corruption, I do not know if we will ever get out from underneath the tyranny that is our leadership.'

'This isn't such a bad weapons dump; I've seen much worse,' Joss admitted. 'Almost makes it not worthwhile to have here. Perhaps they are still building it up?'

'*Eish.* Scary thought.'

Joss shrugged. 'If Hillary is right, Tichawana certainly means to eradicate you. Let's just hope this is the only arsenal,' he said as he began loading the hand grenades into his backpack.

'What the hell are you doing?' Bongani asked.

'Removing their ability to use these on us.'

'But then they will know we are onto them. Can you not defuse them, take out the detonators?'

Joss shook his head. 'They're too well sealed. We should take some of that ammo too. Help me empty the boxes into my backpack, and refasten them so they think they have still have ammo and our theft isn't discovered quickly.'

Bongani smiled. 'You are crafty.' He helped Joss unpack the bullets then return the empty cartons to the box. 'Right, now to remove our presence.' He cleared the area of their prints with his branch as they made their way back to the safari lodge.

Joss was scoring in his head: Bongani 2–Tichawana 1.

The final showdown was going to unfold in a few days, and there was lots to prepare for.

*   *   *

Tichawana moved his feet again.

He could not stand still. The day of the boy's funeral had arrived, and it was going to be a glorious celebration for all. Tichawana chuckled aloud at the thought of his brother being so arrogant as to have a public funeral for the boy who had died; an open invitation for him to move his army into position and attack.

Today was the day he would kill his brother and take the chieftainship of the Binga area as his inheritance.

Tichawana watched as Adam and Brighton threw a large hunter's net over the pontoon boat parked at the edge of the lake. The sun was just rising in the sky and already the heat was pressing down on him. He wiped his brow with what had once been a white handkerchief, now streaked with brown after the hour on the open water from their camp on the other side of Binga. They had passed a few kapenta boats returning to the harbour, but no one would have given them a second glance as the pontoon boat was made to look as if it was on a safari, fishing lines in the water. At first some of the lines had dragged tight, hidden beneath the surface, the remains of his Korean slaves trawling behind. But he had cut those in deep water along the way. Their feet were weighed down with bricks, ensuring that they would sink to the bottom and never again see blue sky. They were another loose end he needed to tidy up. A commodity he could repurchase, and train anew when needed.

The Hummer had been under its own camouflage net to keep it hidden for the few days before they had arrived, waiting for them on the shore under a tree. Ready to get them to their final destination.

'I'm still not fond of this mooring,' Adam said. 'The steep drop-off into the water isn't good. If the boat moves when we need to reload the Hummer, we'll lose it. We should move to where we unloaded her earlier in the week. It's a much better position. This is fine for passengers loading, but not if we have to put that *bakkie* on board again.'

'You do not need to worry about reloading it; today I will drive my Hummer across my lands as chief, and not come back here,' Tichawana said.

Adam stayed quiet as he finished tying down the net, and double-checked the anchor rope that ran from the boat to one of the trees on the shoreline further up the bank. Once he was happy, he walked to the Hummer and climbed into the passenger seat.

'Ready?' Tichawana asked.

Adam nodded.

Brighton and the tracker sat silently as they bounced along the track they had followed several times before. Finally they parked under a tree near the base of the *koppie*.

Tichawana climbed out of the *bakkie*. 'Bring my pack,' he instructed his tracker, who quickly shouldered the bag and set off in front of his *baas*. Brighton followed Adam as they made their way up the small *koppie* to watch the happenings of the Yingwe River Lodge and Chief Bongani's village.

The tracker looked around. 'Adam, someone has been here.'

'Someone or some animal?'

'People. Look, they wiped away their prints but now they look too much like a snake with no scales. Snakes are never that fat and they weave along.'

'I'll tell Tichawana. Look sharp, you two,' Adam said as the tracker nodded and he and Brighton went to fetch everything from under the camo net.

Adam joined Tichawana where he crouched low on the *koppie* edge, watching through binoculars.

'The trackers are bringing the ammo closer,' Adam said. 'Yours said that someone was in the camp.'

Tichawana stood up and walked to where the trackers were still removing the net. He ripped it aside. 'Open every box.'

He watched as they opened them to find that all of their hand grenades were gone, and most of their ammo too.

'He did this. He knows we are here!' Tichawana shouted.

'No,' Adam said. 'He knows we have a camp here, and had stashed ammo. He doesn't know what day we are planning the attack. He can't know that, or we would have walked into an ambush on the way in. He doesn't know our full plan.'

Tichawana was silent. He looked around wildly then took a deep breath to regain his composure and control.

'He would never let me walk into his property, *N'Goma muti* or not,' Tichawana said. 'We carried in lots of extra ammo anyway, and more grenades. We stick to the plan. Once those buses arrive and the party is over, we can get my brother. Those recruits all know that they are only there to make it look like there was a riot. They know not to kill him.'

Adam nodded.

Tichawana walked back to the spot from which he could observe the village and the lodge and sat on the ground.

Adam flattened the few pieces of grass that grew there and sat beside him. 'So today is the day. You think once you kill your brother and those five *N'Gomas*, you will at last be able to walk on your land? The land of your father.'

'I am counting the minutes.'

Tichawana lifted the binoculars and saw that the elephants had already begun to move out from the stable area for their morning foraging, but unlike the previous times, they were heading north, through the opposite end of the village. The matriarch was leading them away from the lake as if she knew that there would be large crowds there today, and she needed to get her herd to safety. He could see the three men who followed the herd everywhere just behind them.

He smiled. The people under his brother's care were about to be reminded how a chief should rule – like his father had, with fear and a hard hand. And showing such devotion to this ragtag group of elephants was a weakness he would exploit to his advantage. The large bull that travelled with the herd, which the vet had helped heal, was going to be the crowning glory when he got to stick a bullet through his heart. His head mounted on his wall, with those tusks, would be Tichawana's reward.

*   *   *

On the morning of Ephraim's funeral, busloads of youngsters began arriving at the village. Bongani watched as yet another bus arrived to swell the numbers. Youths he did not know, and he was certain did not know Ephraim.

'Look at all these people,' Peta said as she bent down and replaced the pink-striped sun hat on Sophia's head for the third time.

Sophia looked at her and reached up and pulled it off. She began sucking it instead.

'Oh, honey, I know you are getting your two-year-old teeth now, but you will get sunburnt if you don't wear your hat.'

'Sunburnt? Seriously?' Joss said. 'You slathered two tons of cream on her – no UV rays are getting anywhere near her. Just pass her the cold gel ring and hook its string onto the side of the pram so she doesn't drop it, then she will leave her hat on.'

Peta did as he suggested, then carefully took the hat and put it back on Sophia's head. This time she ignored it, happy to be sucking the cool ring instead.

When Peta straightened, Joss reached for her hand and pulled her close to him.

'Sorry to disturb you,' Amos said next to her. 'Bongani is asking if you two would go stand with him.'

Joss pushed the pram towards Bongani. He noticed that there were police everywhere, and the media had also begun to arrive to take pictures of all the mourners for the boy who died during the rescue that Gideon Mthemba had been given credit for. His fast response had effectively stopped Tichawana's operation in its tracks, but King Gogo wa de Patswa had gone to ground and no one had managed to find any trace of him. Joss and Bongani had told Gideon of the cache of ammo and the tracks, and he had moved a few units of police in for the funeral, ready for unrest.

Ready for Tichawana's homecoming.

'Too many of these youths are wearing the same black tracksuit pants and boots,' Joss whispered.

'You want to bet these youths have been bussed in by my half-brother?' Bongani said.

'No, thanks. I'd lose. Gideon appears to be onto them too. He's making them leave all backpacks on the buses, and getting the buses to exit the area once they're empty. If they've got weapons stashed, they're being driven out of easy reach. Moving the buses away in case Tichawana walks in with something bigger like a rocket is also a good idea.'

Bongani still frowned. 'I can only hope he has not managed to get his hands on anything so substantial. I do not want a massacre at this funeral.'

Joss looked out over the horizon. 'Mitch is out there. They have set the two squads of anti-poaching guards that Peta called in last night, and Gideon's trusted men. I bet those buses will be checked when they are parked. Julian, Madala and Timberman are watching the elephants, so they are safe too. It's as if Ndhlovy gave Torn-Ear a few days to feel better, and now she knows to move. They're travelling away from the danger.'

'It is good that she began to move them, but it is still hard to greet people, knowing that any moment this could erupt in all-out war.'

Shifting her sunglasses up her nose, Peta said, 'Hang in there, Bongani; you concentrate on the funeral. Leave the warmongering to Joss, Mitch and Gideon today.'

Joss's cell rang. 'Mitch?'

'We were right. Every bus had AK-47s in the luggage area underneath and many of the backpacks had little homemade zip guns too. The mourners bussed in are the youths Tichawana called up. Look sharp up there. He brought the fight to us, on the day we expected.'

'Wonder when they'll find that they have no guns?' Joss asked.

'One bus driver broke when Gideon told him he was going to prison for driving in trouble. The driver said that when they drive out, they were instructed to only go about one click before they were to stop, unload all the passengers, and then wait for them to return.'

'Did you hang the *muti* bushels in the buses when you took the guns out?'

'Of course, mate,' Mitch said. 'Who am I to mess with what those *N'Goma*s instructed me to do? They would scare any other marine too!'

Joss hung up and moved closer to Peta.

* * *

Tichawana's mission had gone to shit. And he knew it.

He watched through his binoculars. Most of the youths did not have their backpacks on. Where were they hiding their zip guns? Their weapons? He'd watched as the buses were driven away, not all that concerned about it as they had discussed the possibility the buses would be moved on to avoid congestion. He had sat in the hot sun as he watched the youths attend the day of feasting to help the informant's son to cross over.

Then he'd seen the traitor.

Hillary stood next to Francis Kanobvurunga as she handed out food like she belonged at the village.

'It was her! Why did she turn on me?'

'Who are you talking about?' Adam asked.

'My secretary. At the funeral. She is the one who must have told my brother where the camps were. That is how they knew so fast. That is how the police knew so much about my operations. She is the one who talked!'

'Brought down by a girl, old friend,' Adam muttered. 'It is always the ladies that get us in the end.'

Tichawana smacked him hard across the head. 'Never say that again. Not if you want to live.'

Adam looked downwards.

'Look. They are back on the buses,' Tichawana said. He smiled then, knowing that all his plans were coming together. Despite the betrayal, at the end of the day he would walk into his old village and, as Bongani's only relative, he would be chief.

The buses were now at the point where it had been agreed they would stop. But as the youths climbed out, they began running from the buses, down the road towards Bulawayo. One or two of the bus drivers jumped out and started to run too. Other buses were hurrying away, hooting, trying to get the teenagers to move out of the road as they attempted to get as far from the funeral as they could.

'What the fuck is going on? The buses are leaving,' Adam said. 'They haven't removed a single weapon, and the army is leaving with them.'

'My youth army. It has deserted! When I catch those little pricks, I am going to cut their cocks off and make them eat them.'

Adam took a deep breath. 'There's still the four of us. We can sneak into the village and kill him.'

Tichawana looked at Adam. He nodded. 'You need to kill the N'Gomas first. Perhaps then I can enter the boundary.'

'My friend,' Adam said, 'that *muti* is not real. It's a mind game they have played with you all these years. There is no such thing as magic and N'Gomas' *muti* keeping you out. It is your mind. Stop believing in it and it will not be true.'

'How can you say that? You have lived all your life in Zimbabwe, been around my people for so long. Your father, he is white, he too believes in the power of the *N'Gomas*. How is it you are so sure that it is not real?'

'Because it's just superstition.'

Tichawana shook his head. 'I have felt the pain when I crossed over the border before. Many years ago. It was real. I was saved then by a man I have always owed my life to. He reminds me of that price to this day. I have done many things because of the debt I owe him. I was in a heap like a baby. I can never do that again. Take the trackers with you and go into the village. Tonight, when those *N'Gomas* are sleeping, you and Brighton, you will slit their throats. My tracker will bring my half-brother Bongani to me, then when I get into that village, I will teach Hillary the lesson of her life.'

Adam nodded. 'Come, Brighton, we're going hunting.'

'You go, bring me my half-brother,' Tichawana said to his tracker. The tracker nodded.

The three men left and Tichawana was alone. Waiting. Seething at how his careful planning had gone so wrong.

He took out his cell. 'Mlilo, the youths did not perform. Bury them.'

'There are eight busloads of them—'

'I do not care. They let me down. Do not let them get back to Bulawayo.'

'Yes, sir.'

He settled back into his place on the *koppie* to watch Adam and his small team's progress through his binoculars.

* * *

Bongani signalled to stop. Joss froze then crouched down.

'Lion,' Bongani said and he pointed to spoor on the ground.

'Same print as the man-eater Peta warned us about months ago,' Joss said. 'He's dragging his back foot – that's new.'

'What has he been eating if he has turned out of the reserve and come back here, because no people have been taken? No one complained about goats or cattle being taken either.' Bongani's hand went up again and he signalled to his ears. Joss strained to hear.

A branch broke nearby.

Then he heard another, and the smell of a *dagga* cigarette came to them on the wind.

Three men broke out of the bush in front of them and turned south, their backs to the men crouched low.

Joss studied them. There was a tracker at the back of the group who looked like a Matabele, but he was very short, and one shoulder was dropped slightly, as if he had suffered from polio as a child, or a bad beating, where a bone had broken and not healed right. He carried two rifles on his right shoulder. The man was strong, despite his disability. The white man in front of the tracker was in a camo uniform of sorts. He didn't walk as if military trained, but with an excited gait. On his shoulder he carried a .303 and an elephant gun, a Ruger 402. The tracker in front of him had a large hunting knife strapped to his leg, but no other weapon that Joss could see. The cigarette hung from the front tracker's mouth.

They had seen photos of the front two men: Adam and Brighton, as Hillary had identified them. Tichawana's people.

Bongani signalled to move off the path. They melted into the bush and remained stationary, keeping their breath muffled. Staying almost silent took energy, and Joss wiped the sweat from his forehead. Although the sun had begun to sink towards the horizon, the Kariba heat was still relentless.

'They are heading towards the moringa grove where the elephants were yesterday afternoon,' Bongani said.

'Good thing they went north this morning,' Joss said.

Bongani shook his head. 'I do not think it is the elephants they are after anyway. They are coming for me.'

Joss frowned. 'There are only three—'

'My brother is not with them. He is the one up on the *koppie*.'

Joss nodded. 'They obviously didn't expect the elephants to move away. Now they are between our two forces. The anti-poaching guards are somewhere out there, and some are waiting just before the safari lodge. With only three men on foot, they should be easy enough to stop,' Joss said as he took out his cell and called Mitch. 'Three coming your way. Stop them before they get to the lodge. They have a .303 and a Ruger 402.'

'Consider it done, mate,' Mitch said and hung up.

Bongani grinned. 'Hunting time.'

*   *   *

Mitch looked at the three men as they approached, totally oblivious to the fact that they were walking into an ambush.

Gideon stepped out from a large tree in front of them, but with enough distance that the front tracker couldn't reach him with his knife. 'We are the Binga Police. Surrender your weapons. You are surrounded.'

Mitch wanted to laugh, as the man sounded like an old 1950s cowboy movie. But he had not expected the tracker at the back to be so fast in raising the .303 from his shoulder.

Mitch shouted a warning to Gideon, at the same time as he shot the tracker.

The tracker fell forward, his rifle discharging.

The hunter and the unarmed tracker at the front hit the dirt. The man who was shot attempted to pull his rifle back to himself. Mitch shot his hand.

The white hunter and the front tracker put their hands in the air, but as one of Gideon's policemen stepped forward, the white man threw a grenade.

'*Basop*, grenade,' the policeman called as he hit the ground, and everyone flattened themselves as best they could as the explosion rocked the bush and echoed across the lake.

Mitch rubbed his ears, trying to stop the sound of church bells ringing in them. He looked around. The fallout from the blast was large. Trees were blown apart for metres. Some of the policemen were injured. They began to groan. So was the idiot poacher who hadn't thrown the explosive far enough from himself and hadn't even bothered to try and get low below the blast, simply turned away and continued to run. Shrapnel had peppered his body and his back was shredded where he hadn't attempted to lay flat.

The tracker, now with his knife unsheathed, was already up and running into the bush, towards the safari camp, leaving the white man behind.

Mitch took aim and brought him down with a single shot.

* * *

Tichawana watched through his binoculars as his small team was massacred. They were out of range of his weapons, so he could do nothing to help them or even warn them when he saw that they were walking into a trap.

His half-brother was still alive.

His own men were all dead.

Today had been a failure.

He shouldered his weapons, walked from the *koppie* carefully and jogged quickly to his Hummer. Starting the vehicle, he raced towards the lake's edge.

There was still a possibility that he could escape, retreat into Zambia. Using his boat was the only logical course, then he could drive up into Tanzania. He would come back to deal with his half-brother another time.

He parked the Hummer close to the boat and placed the .303 within easy reach on the trailer board that linked the boat with the shore, so that if his brother and the marines, who seemed to know what he was doing before he did, came from the bush and challenged him, he could defend himself.

He began to remove the net. His mind was focused on the clasps and getting them undone, cursing Adam for tying it down so well, when he heard the animal. The snarl was unmistakable.

A male lion crouched between him and the Hummer, ready to pounce.

'No. Not you too,' he said. He turned to the boat and grabbed his .303.

The lion didn't seem afraid of him. It challenged him, snarling, and yet it didn't come closer. As if it was waiting for Tichawana to make the next move.

'Checkmate,' Tichawana said as he loaded a bullet up the spout. He adjusted his stance so one foot was forward as he took aim at the lion. 'You think you can eat me like you did my spotter?'

The lion growled again and shook his large head as if saying no.

Tichawana watched its tail flick from side to side. He remembered an old campfire story that said when the lion's tail stopped moving and slammed downwards, you knew it was going to pounce. He had time to make this a clean kill.

The sweat ran from his head and into his eyes.

The lion sat there looking at him.

Tichawana heard a whisper of a noise behind him. Turning his head slightly, he glimpsed one of the biggest crocodiles he had ever seen as it launched itself at him. The pain just beneath his knee was agonising as the monster grabbed him. The crocodile shook its head from side to side, the teeth ripping and tearing skin, muscle, tendons, stopping only when its teeth scraped bone.

Tichawana fell to the ground, hitting his chest hard. He lost his grip on the rifle. The crocodile began to tug on his legs as it pulled its prey back into the water so it could drown it.

Screaming, Tichawana reached for his fallen weapon, twisting his body around and putting the barrel to the croc's head. He pulled the trigger.

But the croc didn't let go. Its monstrous jaw remained closed.

Despite the blood oozing from the hole in its head, the crocodile dragged him into the water. He loaded again and fired, but the animal's jaw remained firmly closed. He emptied the rest of his magazine into its head, but the crocodile hung on to his legs, refusing to give up. He kicked at its head with his free leg.

The crocodile was deadly still. He let out a breath of relief.

Then its body weight began to drag it over the small ledge into the deeper water, Tichawana's leg still locked in its jaws.

Tichawana screamed once more as he desperately tried to pry the teeth open with the tip of the rifle's barrel. The crocodile slipped backwards into the lake and pulled him in up to his chest. The water turned red around him.

He realised that there was a second crocodile in the water as it hit his side. It began its death spin, slowly tumbling over, turning his body against the resistance of the weight of the dead croc holding him. Tichawana knew he was about to be ripped to pieces, if the spinning did not drown him first.

He reached for the head of the newest croc, beating his fists against it as it flipped him in the water.

After the pain, only darkness.

*   *   *

Joss and Bongani were almost at the *koppie*. They had zig-zagged through the clumps of trees, making sure they would not be seen by Tichawana sitting at his higher vantage point. Slowly Bongani lifted his head above the crest of the rocks, to look at where they thought the man in his sniper's nest would be, to help his team in the attack.

'Shit, he is not there.'

Joss climbed up and looked around. The summit was abandoned. Tichawana had definitely gone.

They heard a shot from the direction of the lake.

'Now what?' Bongani said as they ran.

They heard another shot. Silence, then eight in quick succession, as if someone was panicked and just squeezing the trigger as fast as they could.

Bongani increased his pace. They had run almost the five kilometres of the protection zone, but still had a few hundred metres of uneven ground to cover. The shoreline came into view. Tichawana's boat was still anchored, but they couldn't see him anywhere.

They approached the boat with guns ready, sweating and breathing heavily.

Bongani looked around. 'Blood smear on the left of the boat. Look at all the spent *doppies* on the ground.'

'Over here,' Joss said. He could see the lion's footprints in the sand, then the lion had crouched down. It hadn't gone any closer to the boat, but after a while, it had padded away into the bush at a leisurely pace, dragging its back foot. Not scared away.

'A lion threatened him here, but I think it was a croc that got him there,' Bongani said as they walked to where he had seen the blood and the bullets. 'Look at the size of this slide mark – this croc was huge. He did not stand a chance.'

'You think he is definitely dead?' Joss asked.

'For his sake, I can only hope so. There are better ways to die, even for an evil man like my half-brother.'

CHAPTER
35

A Shifting View

Joss sat next to Peta, Bongani, Mitch and Amos. They had their feet up, watching Mandlenkosi as he fished in Kariba. The leopard was slower tonight, cautious. As if the recent activity in the area had rattled him too.

He's got plenty of company, Joss thought. The area had been rocked by the hand grenade, and many shots had been fired. This had been a targeted attack, bringing back terrifying memories for many of the people in the area.

The TV was on in the main room as they waited for the news.

'It's on,' Lwazi called and turned the sound up so they could hear outside.

'*The South African police today arrested Korean crime queen Sook Lu Liang on charges of trafficking in humans, blood ivory and rhino horns. A joint international operation ensured that Ms Liang and her colleagues were arrested, and there will be investigations into further allegations against her. Ms Liang is expected to be extradited to Europe for trial with no chance of bail.*'

'I'll drink to that. One less vampire to suck the good out of Africa. Tonight all the elephants and rhino can sleep a little more soundly,' Mitch said as he raised his glass.

'Hear, hear.' They clinked their glasses.

Bongani nodded. 'I heard from Gideon; he is still trying to cover our tracks from going into Gwanda Camp.'

Joss grinned. 'I would rather face the slap on the wrist they'll give us for that than know that our kids were there a minute more than they needed to be.'

'I agree,' Bongani said. 'I think that he is also doing his best to protect the kids who came back. Ensure their lives return to normal as soon as possible.'

Peta cleared her throat. 'I've spoken to Hillary in Brussels. She wanted to know if Reason could have a copy of the map with the crosses on it. I haven't emailed it yet.'

'Why not?' Joss asked.

'Damo and the British Military already have the map. We know the villagers who asked for those crosses are telling the truth. I don't want them spooked. Nothing can be done about them until the president dies, so giving the map to others at this stage is a risk. He could potentially desecrate the areas. I'd rather we just keep a seal on it for now.'

Bongani and Amos nodded in understanding.

Joss shook his head. 'You need to hand it over – it's bigger than us. These are professionals. They'll archive that map and when the time is right, they'll use it to get justice for the people buried there. If you hold on to it, it'll make you a target of the people who were responsible for the *Gukurahundi*. If they find out, they'll kill you. If nothing else, the last few months have proven that too many people in this country are still spying on each other and living in constant fear. Don't allow yourself to be one of them. Remember, they won't hurt you, but they will use those close to you to get to you. Like your dad and Tsessebe.'

'Joss is right,' Mitch said.

'I'll think about it,' Peta said.

Joss shook his head. 'There is nothing to think about. If you won't hand it over, we put Damo in touch with Reason directly. ICC will probably love his skills anyhow, and he can always do with the work.'

'That's a better idea. I think that Damo deserves to get something out of helping us all the time,' Peta said. 'And I don't feel like I'm betraying the trust of the people by handing the map over.'

'Good.' Joss smiled and squeezed her hand. 'I'd feel heaps better if you'd do that, and they can continue. We are too close on the ground. It's not safe for any of us to hold that type of information.'

'I'll happily organise for the link-up between them for you, Peta,' Mitch said.

'Thanks.'

'So now that this is over, what else is new and wonderful in the world?' Amos asked.

Everyone laughed.

'My sabbatical year is almost over, and I'm resigning,' Mitch said.

Joss looked at him with raised eyebrows. 'Never thought you'd leave the commandos.'

'I think I'm getting too old to be fighting for a government, mate,' Mitch said, then smiled. 'But the only thing I know how to do is fight. So perhaps it's time to be a soldier for myself instead; use my skills to help in a different way. From what I've seen here, Zimbabwe needs all the skilled marines it can get to help save its wildlife. Don't think I'm going to be any good at following other people's orders; I'm too used to being in charge. I need to strike out on my own.'

'Strike out on your own and do what?' Joss asked.

'Start an anti-poaching unit that trains the guards, so we can send a tender to the Matusadona and Chizarira Game Parks, and privatise that part of their operations. Fight the war against the poachers at a higher level than they are able to now.'

'You serious?' Peta asked.

'Deadly. I believe that if the government pays me the contract fee that they pay their guards now, and I get overseas investors and donations, we can protect those areas even better. If I start a military-style anti-poaching school like they have in South Africa, that'll supplement the income and help the cash flow.'

'That's a huge undertaking,' Joss said.

'That's why I'm counting on your support. I've approached a few guys from our unit, and they're keen. There are even some veterans in the States who have expressed interest in coming over, and they don't want huge pay, just enough to live on. They want to be useful again.'

'So how do we fit in?' Joss asked.

'I need a base to operate out of until we get the contract inside the game parks. I spoke to Bongani and he thinks that setting up across from Bishu is best – it's closest to Chizarira and this way, the villagers will have peace of mind that we're there to help protect them too.'

'I love the idea of being able to send the anti-poaching guards to you for better training. I know a heap of other parks who'll back your idea and support you,' Peta said.

'Awesome. Having the support of the local parks is what I'm going to be relying on,' Mitch said.

'I guess you won't be leaving us then, which is fantastic news. I'm kind of used to you being around,' Joss said.

36

Home is Where You Belong

One month later

Joss was still in bed when he heard the elephant's call. He reached for the phone and pushed redial.

'Mmm? Just five more minutes,' Peta begged.

'Ndhlovy has brought you another customer.' He knew he was smiling but he couldn't help it, hearing Peta's sleepy voice on the phone. He adored waking up to her in person when she was with him, and he missed it when she was away in one of the parks, but phone calls were better than nothing and they could cope with being apart. Many couples spent less time together than they managed to carve out of their schedules, and he couldn't imagine his life without her being a part of it.

'You sure?' she asked and yawned.

'Yup,' he said.

The baby monitor chirped with gurgling noises. Sophia was awake.

'Can you hear that? Sophia can hear her too,' he said.

'Awww, give her a special cuddle from me when you go get her. Let me know what injury Ndhlovy brought this time, so I know what supplies to bring with me, and hey, I guess this means I'm coming home early this week,' Peta said.

'I guess it does. You going to bring your dad and Tsessebe again? He seemed to be fine last time he visited.'

'No, there isn't time to prep him, and he doesn't handle sudden changes in his routine so good.'

'No problems. I still get you.' Joss grinned as Sophia gurgled a little more on her monitor.

'Guess you should go get her, and I should start moving. I might as well have the pleasure of waking Mitch at this ungodly hour so he can make the trip with Amos and I.'

'That should be interesting. Remember to stay back when you throw the water.'

'Water, oh, that is an idea. Thanks. See you soon. Love you.' He could hear the laughter in Peta's voice.

'Love you too,' he said even though he knew she was already distracted, and the phone was silent in his hand.

Joss got into his wheelchair. He could already hear Lwazi picking Sophia up and talking softly to her. There was a light knock on his door.

'Come in, Lwazi,' he said.

'Good morning. She can hear the elephants.'

'I believe she can,' Joss said as he kissed Sophia's forehead. 'Good morning, my beautiful girl.'

He was rewarded by Sophia blowing raspberries at him.

'Would you mind getting her ready while I do the same?'

'Sure,' Lwazi said as he took Sophia back to the nursery.

Joss listened to Lwazi's constant stream of chatter to Sophia. He smiled. Despite what Lwazi had gone through, he seemed to have come out the other side stronger. Determined to achieve in life, but more than that: extremely protective of everyone around him. He was talking to a counsellor via Skype once a week, and Joss was happy with that. He knew that you could not rush the healing process.

'Your favourite friend is here to visit again ... come on, let us get you out of that ...'

Sophia made more gurgling sounds and then gave a tinkle of laughter as Lwazi tickled her.

Joss showered and got ready. He could hear Ndhlovy calling outside now, not just her mumbles but trumpeting, as if announcing that she was there and waiting for him. He collected Sophia from Lwazi on his way past the nursery. 'You coming too?'

'I would not miss it,' Lwazi said.

Joss grinned and put his hand on his shoulder. 'You okay?'

'Better each day. I miss Ephraim, but I keep thinking how lucky we were that you came for us.'

'I'll always find you, Lwazi; you're part of the family.'

Lwazi hugged him and Sophia. 'Everything will change soon.'

'It will. Just remember that no matter what happens, Bongani and I will always be here to protect you.'

Ndhlovy trumpeted again, as if telling them to hurry up.

'Come on, best go greet her before she tries to come in the back door,' Joss said as he walked into the kitchen and stepped out, the smell of elephant strong on the morning breeze.

They walked into the stable area where they were beginning to construct a taller enclosure made especially for the elephants, so that Peta could have a clean space for her procedures on the patients Ndhlovy brought them. An elephant sanctuary: a safe haven for the injured, and an attraction that would help make Yingwe River Lodge even more appealing to the tourists.

Sure enough, there was Ndhlovy, protector and matriarch of her herd. With her was a tiny baby elephant. The other elephants were all outside the stable area.

Ndhlovy greeted Joss, Sophia and Lwazi. Sophia giggled and reached out her hands to the baby who was by Ndhlovy's side.

He looked closely at the baby. The little calf seemed fine. It was curious and Ndhlovy was reassuring it; however, Joss could feel that something else was happening here. The little elephant approached and, with its ears forward, extended its trunk towards Sophia.

Ndhlovy carefully reached over the impatient calf and put the end of her trunk into the child's chubby hands first, greeting her.

'You've had your baby,' Joss said.

Ndhlovy rumbled, the sound vibrating through Joss's hand as he stroked her. He looked between Ndhlovy's front legs and, sure enough, he could see milk-filled teats. As if to prove that the baby knew what he was looking for, it reached up to its mother and latched on.

'Congratulations, Ndhlovy,' Joss said as he put his forehead against her trunk. Sophia put her forehead against her too, and she giggled out loud.

'Dada. Lovvy,' she said.

Joss stilled. 'Did you hear her? Lwazi, did you hear her?'

'I heard. And who am I?' Lwazi asked, pointing to himself.

'Wazi,' Sophia said, then nodded. 'Lovvy.' She put her head back against the elephant.

Tears ran down Joss's cheeks. He tried to talk but his throat was choked up. He cleared it and tried again. 'You talked, Sophia.' He hugged her to him, and she spoke again.

'Dada. Dada. Dada.'

The baby elephant finished its snack from its mother and went back to Lwazi.

'Can we call the baby Khwezi?' he said as the baby's trunk wrapped around his hand.

'"Bright morning star", nice name,' Joss said. 'Is it a boy or a girl? Get down and check – it's easier for you than me.'

Lwazi laughed as he bent down. 'It's a boy.'

'Ndhlovy, you have a son,' Joss said as she came back to touch him, stroking his arm. Sophia blew a raspberry at Ndhlovy, and she turned her attention to Sophia for a while.

Bongani walked into the stable area.

'Hey, you're home, I thought you and Madala were still at your meeting in Bulawayo,' Joss said.

'We got in early this morning. I suspect he is still asleep, but I heard the elephants walk through the village, so I came to say hello.'

'How was the meeting?' Joss asked.

'Later,' Bongani said, then he smiled as Sophia clapped her hands at him in her signal that she wanted to be held. He took Sophia in his arms and gave her a kiss on her forehead.

'Gani, Gani,' she said.

'Did she just try to say my name?' Bongani asked.

Sophia giggled. 'Gani, Gani. Lovvy. Baba.' She pointed to the baby elephant.

Joss nodded. 'She's just started talking, and her first word was "Dada".' He couldn't contain his smile.

'Lovvy,' Sophia said.

'Meet Khwezi. Ndhlovy brought her own baby to meet the family this morning.'

'That is wonderful news,' Bongani said as he greeted Ndhlovy and was introduced to her baby with the same ceremony as Ndhlovy had shown the others.

Joss's phone rang. 'Hey, Peta—'

'What did she bring in? I'm packing supplies and—'

'Her baby,' Joss said. 'You were right when you said she looked ready. This is a social visit, as far as I can tell. Khwezi is a healthy, delightful baby boy.'

'That's not fair. Take photos and send them to me. I'm on my way. I want to meet him. Do you think she'll stay around?'

'I think she'll wait for you. I suspect she'll probably go snack on the moringas for a while before she heads back into the park. We can hear her herd already down at the water's edge close by.'

'We'll be there just after lunch. Mitch said he was making his way there as fast as he could. He's bringing some guys who need to learn to respect elephants, so you're going to be in for an interesting time. Don't let him scare her off before I get to say hello to her and the new baby.'

'I'll try my best.'

'See you soon.'

'Bye.' Joss hung up. 'Peta, Amos and Mitch are coming to meet Khwezi.'

'I am starving; do you mind if I take Sophia and we go grab breakfast in the lodge?' Lwazi asked.

'Good idea. Bongani and I will meet you there,' Joss said as Lwazi bounced down the path towards the lodge with Sophia.

Bongani stood next to Ndhlovy, scratching her ear.

'And?' Joss asked.

'The lawyers think it will work. If it is done legally, Lwazi will be the next chief in this area. I need to adopt him before he is sixteen. His grandfather signed the papers. He was happy knowing that Lwazi would be looked after should anything happen to him. He is extremely proud that his grandson will be my heir.' Tears filled Bongani's eyes. 'It is not the way I thought that I would ever get to have a child, but this was a good solution.'

Ndhlovy wiped away his tears with her trunk.

'Do not stress, girl, these are tears of joy,' he said. 'We can never prove that my brother is alive or dead. He will be classified as simply missing, as there was no body recovered. If he ever decides he is heir, the lineage is now clear. Myself, then my son. That sounds so alien, especially since his grandfather is still alive and well, and I had to ask him if he would want this position within my family. But it is such a relief to know that all my people will now know they have a leader in training and that their traditions will be looked after. They will have a new champion to look to when I am gone.'

Joss put his hand on Ndhlovy's trunk. 'What if you should find someone to marry? Have your own child? You are not that old.'

'The lawyer asked me the same question. And I will tell you what I told him: perhaps it might happen. But I will then be too old to guide that child on how to be a fair and just chief, and he would be very young to shoulder the responsibility of all these people. Lwazi will be almost fifty when I am ninety. Almost the same age I was when my father passed this torch to me. A man younger than that should not have to bear this burden. It will be a big responsibility, but it will be one that he will have trained for, and be ready. I will not change my mind on this.'

Joss smiled. 'I'm happy for you both, but don't you even think of leaving us any time soon. I am not ready to lose you from my life, not for a great many years to come.'

'I am not planning on going anywhere any time soon.'

'Glad to hear it. You realise that Sophia and I are going to miss them both terribly when they leave our house?'

'No need to rush them out. I was thinking I could move into one of the staff lodges while we build a better family home for us in my village, then we can move out all together into a brand new home, me, my son and his grandfather, but only once we find you another nurse.'

Joss laughed. 'I don't think that Lwazi would want to be called a nurse.'

Ndhlovy touched his cheek with her trunk, and then turned westward and began walking out of the stable area with her baby close behind her, ambling towards the moringa grove.

Joss thought back to when she had been the size of her baby, and how much had happened since then.

To him.

To Ndhlovy.

To his whole Yingwe River Lodge family.

He smiled.

He was home, where he belonged.

FACT VS FICTION

Fact: Baobab Tree Orphanage is loosely based on a real place: Khayelihle Children's Village, Bulawayo. The company running it is Australian Churches of Christ Global Mission Partners Limited, and they do amazing work with HIV-positive children.

Fact: Mass graves: In March 2011, a mass grave of over six hundred bodies was found in a disused mine shaft at Chibondo Gold Mine near Mount Darwin, one hundred and ten miles from Harare. The event was used as political propaganda by supporters of President Robert Mugabe.

Saviour Kasukuwere, the government minister of black empowerment, is quoted to have said: 'Forensic tests and DNA analysis of the remains won't be carried out. Instead, traditional African religious figures will perform rites to invoke spirits that will identify the dead.'

Many believe that some of the bodies were much more recent than the government claimed. An estimated twenty thousand civilians were killed by Mugabe's soldiers in the *Gukurahundi*; many of those victims still lie in unmarked graves.

Fiction: The placements and discoveries of these graves in my book are fictional, as is the involvement of the British Commando unit and the ICC in identifying these sites.

Fact: The decline of many of Africa's national parks is just one of the environmental conservation issues that the African Parks Network, an international non-governmental organisation, attempts to address in ten parks over seven different countries. It is not mentioned in this book and is just one example of the amazing organisations that are trying to help the African wildlife.

Fiction: Africa Wildlife In Crisis (AWIC) is not a real company, but there are many companies out there who are investing time and money into Africa's wildlife that is in peril.

Fact: Youth camps with formal militia training operated by the Zimbabwe Government were in existence in the early 2000s.

Fiction: My youth camps belonging to a private individual within Zimbabwe.

Fact: Recovering service men and women used to compete in the Ironman, or the American Warrior games; today, many compete in the Invictus Games, started in 2014, and the patron of which is Prince Harry.

Fact: More than 140,000 of Africa's savannah elephants were killed between 2007 and 2014, one-third of the total population. On average, one elephant is being poached every fifteen minutes. It is estimated that wild elephants will be extinct within twenty-five years.

Fact: Rhinos are listed by CITIES (the Convention on International Trade in Endangered Species of Wild Flora and Fauna) as critically endangered. At the beginning of the nineteenth century, there were approximately one million rhinos. In 1970, there were only 70,000. Today, there are around 28,000 rhinos surviving in the wild.

GLOSSARY

assegai	A traditional spear, used for fighting. (Bantu)
bakkie	A South African word for a pick-up truck, a ute in Australian English. (Afrikaans)
bama	Mother. (Tsonga)
basop	Beware, mind, take care. (Ndebele, adapted from the original Afrikaans word *pasop*)
boma	A fenced area used to keep animals enclosed. Also can refer to an area used for outdoor meals and parties. (Swahili)
cheelo	Demon. (Tsonga)
Chete Safari Area	Situated on the shores of Lake Kariba between the Senkwe and Muenda rivers. It is a controlled hunting area and one of Zimbabwe's most rugged concessions.
chipembele	Rhinoceros. (Shona)
Chizarira National Park	A large national park found in Northern Zimbabwe.
dagga	Weed, cannabis. (Southern African)
doppies	Shells from spent bullets. (Afrikaans)

domba	Monster. (Tsonga)
duggaboy	A buffalo. (Southern African slang)
Eish	*Wow! What?* Expression of surprise. (Bantu)
gillie	A person who goes fishing with you, loads the hook, guts the fish and does all the fishing things, allowing you to just catch the fish. (Zimbabwe slang)
Gukurahundi	A 5th Brigade operation carried out between 1983 and 1987. Suspected anti-government elements among the Ndebele community were identified and eliminated, and the people involved were given indemnity by the ruling government. (Shona)
ikanka yabo	Their jackal. (Ndebele)
ikhaya	Hut/house. (Zulu, Ndebele)
incelwe	A BaTonga woman's smoking pipe. (BaTonga)
inkosana	The chief's (boss's) son. As long as the chief is still alive he will continue to be called *inkosana*, no matter how old he is. Only when the chief dies will he be called *inkosi*. (Ndebele)
inkosi	The (chief) boss. (Ndebele)
intale	A BaTonga men's smoking pipe. (BaTonga)
kaffir	The word *kaffir* has now evolved into an offensive term for black people, but it was previously a neutral term for black southern African people. Also was used as a term for 'non-believer', referring to the black people not being of Christian upbringing. (Southern Africa)
kaross	Blanket made from animal skins. (Zulu/Ndebele)
knopkierie	An African club. These are typically made from wood with a large knob (wood knot) at one end with a long stick protruding from it. They can be used for fighting or throwing at animals during hunting. Ideal size to also be used as a walking stick. (Afrikaans)

koppie	Also *kopjie* or *kopje*. A small hill rising up from the African veld. (Afrikaans)
kraal	An area where animals are kept, usually found inside an African village/settlement, and usually circular, with barricades to keep the stock inside. Can also refer to an African cluster of huts. (Afrikaans but commonly used in South Africa)
Kukala Ku Chilyango	A death ritual where the surviving spouse, usually the wife, sleeps in the house with the dead person for a night, covered in maize meal. (BaTonga)
Kuyabila	The poems of God. (Tsonga)
laager	An encampment formed by a circle of wagons/vehicles. (Historical South African)
lobola	An African tradition of an arranged payment between a groom and the bride's family, in exchange for their daughter. Can be paid in cattle or cash, and the higher the *lobola*, the greater value the bride holds in the groom's eyes. This payment is the groom's way of thanking the parents for raising a good daughter. It is still applicable to many South African traditional weddings. (Zulu)
madomba	Monsters. (Tsonga)
mana	Stop. (Northern Ndebele)
middle mannetjie	The dirt bump in the middle of the two tyre tracks in the road. (Generally accepted Southern African slang)
Matusadona National Park	A large game park in Northern Zimbabwe.
metse	Mat. (Tsonga)
mielie	Maize. (Afrikaans, generally accepted Southern African slang)
mukulana	Brother. (Tsonga)

mukwa tree	Pterocarpus angolensis/bloodwood tree, a teak tree that appears to bleed when you cut it.
muti	Traditional medicine in Southern Africa. It can refer to medicine in general. Also spelt as *umuthi* (Zulu). (South African slang)
mywee	Short for my *wena* – translates roughly to 'Oh goodness'. (Zulu)
N'Goma	Traditional healers within the Nguni, Sotho, Tswana and Tsonga societies. (Tswana and Tsonga)
Ndebele	An African language belonging to the Nguni group of Bantu languages. Spoken by the Ndebele or Matabele people of Zimbabwe. Also referred to as Northern Ndebele, isiNdebele, Sindebele, or Ndebele.
Nehanda / Nyamhika Neranda	Shona god. Nehanda, originally Matope's sister-wife, possessed supernatural powers. She became a guardian spirit, and could transfer her spirit and inhabit other bodies. Nehanda Charwe Nyakasikana was considered to be the female incarnation of the oracle spirit Nyamhika Nehanda, and considered to be the grandmother of Zimbabwe. Some people, both male and female, claim they are Nehanda reincarnated because Shona people believe in spirit possession. (Shona)
ndende	Father. (Chitonga)
Ngi ya bonga. Kuhle uku bu se khaya.	'Thank you. It feels good to be home.' (Ndebele)
Nguni	Nguni cattle are known for their resistance to diseases, and characterised by their multicoloured skin, that can be many different colours and patterns, but their noses are always black tipped. Can also refer to a people of Africa,

including the Xhosa, Zulu, Swazi, Hlubi, Phithi and Ndebele.

nyama	Meat. (Ndebele)
nyami nyami	The Zambezi river god also known as the Zambezi snake spirit. (Tonga)
panga	A large bush knife, like a machete, once used generally to cut sugarcane, commonly used as weapons. (Swahili)
penga	Mad. (Generally accepted southern African slang)
pepe	No. (ChiTonga)
Puma, asi hambe masinyane	'Get out, come with me quickly.' (Ndebele)
riempie	Ropes made with animal hides. (South African)
rondavel	A Westernised version of the African-style round hut with a pitched thatch roof. (Afrikaans)
sadza	A thick maize meal porridge, the staple food in Zimbabwe of the African people. (South African)
shebeen	A tavern with a predominantly black patronage, not always legal in its activities. (General South African term)
Sibusisiwe	Blessing. (Ndebele)
sjambok	A leather whip, it used to be made from rhino or hippopotamus hide, but is now made from plastic. Used as a fighting weapon in South Africa. (Afrikaans)
skabenga	Used to describe a criminal or a shady person, rascal, scallywag. (General South African term)
spoors	Tracks, usually left by animals. (Afrikaans, used generally in southern Africa)
suka pangisa	'Move your arse.' (Ndebele)
Tarisai	'Here it is, take a look, everybody see this.' (Shona)

thula	Quiet. (Zulu)
tokoloshe	Really bad spirit. A *tokoloshe* can resemble a zombie, or a poltergeist, or a gremlin, any demon-like thing. A *tokoloshe* in this book refers to something evil. (Shona)
totsei	Thug or robber. (Sesotho slang)
Tribal Trust Land (TTL)	Now referred to as Communal Lands. Small scale and subsistence farming are the principal economic activities in Communal Lands. The farms of Communal Lands are traditionally unfenced and Communal Lands have resident traditional African chiefs who are supposed to see that the community as a whole is looked after.
travois	A rough A-frame made for carrying something on and dragged behind a donkey or person. (Sesotho slang)
tshama	Sit. (Tsonga)
twalumba	Cheers, thank you. (ChiTonga)
umfama	A young boy. (Ndebele)
umntwana	Little child. (Ndebele)
uxolo	'Sorry, excuse me.' (Northern Ndebele)
windgat	'Wind-arse.' Typically a man behaving badly, boaster, gas-bag, windbag. (Afrikaans)
woza	Come. (Ndebele)
yebo	Yes. (Zulu)
yingwe	Leopard. (Xitsonga)
zama uku xolisa	'Try saying please.' (Ndebele)
ZESA	Zimbabwe Electricity Supply Authority. (Xitsonga)

ACKNOWLEDGEMENTS

As I write more books, more and more people seem to be involved with making all the magic happen.

Forever in debt to Ray Somerville Coleman (Grampie) for the stories he wrote of his life as one of the last Native Commissioners in Rhodesia. I have used these for inspiration and authenticity. To my Wilde cousins for allowing me access to these Coleman family files – thank you!

Dave and Pat Tarr, for sharing the story of your baby elephant with me, which inspired part of this story. I hope you love the ending I gave it!

Gary Fonternel, as always, for everything flying and military based; if there are mistakes, they are mine.

Royal Marine Commando Alistair Burton, for the inspiration of the returning hero. In 2010, I visited Zimbabwe, and this story began cooking in my head. Al had just returned from Afghanistan. I'm so grateful that you returned whole and healthy to continue to live an amazing life. I know you will never read this book, but I hope one day it's an audiobook and you can listen. Thank you for answering my million questions on everything commando. Mistakes are all mine, not yours.

Skinny Wood, for your Ndebele translations, as always.

Isaac Kalio, who is a guide for Wilderness Safaris in Zambia, whom I have never met, for help with Tsonga words that I couldn't find on the net, and for answering my messages always, no matter where he was in the bush on safari, on his little mobile phone. I appreciate the dedication to Africa, her people and wildlife, and your help.

James Gifford Photography, for your amazing pictures of the fishing leopard, who I just couldn't resist writing into my book. Thank you for sharing those pictures with the world in *Travel Africa* magazine, and then continuing to share your expertise on Facebook with me and my readers.

Philip Hatzis, founder and partner of Tri Training Harder LLP, who chatted with me about all things regarding running and training for a triathlon competition, even though he was on holiday 'down under'. Much appreciated.

US Army Combat Medic, Sgt (ret.) Adam Hartswick, an amputee veteran who served in both Iraq and then Afghanistan, where he was wounded, for all his frankness about post-traumatic growth (PTG) or benefit finding (so the opposite of well-known PTSD), and all things humorous about being an amputee, including various sex positions and how your prosthetics can pinch 'your boys'. Any mistakes in this book are mine as he has tried his best to make my hero's life as close to real for an amputee as we could.

Michael Stokes, for his amazing photographs that made me want to write about a beautiful wounded warrior.

Robyn Grady and Gayle Ash, for cheering this book on, and who are always with me every step of the way.

Alli Sinclair, stable sister and friend, who's always at her computer, no matter the time, to chat, inspire and kick my butt, even after midnight!

Agent Alex Adsett, for being there when I needed help, and always helping me smile through everything, no matter what.

The team at Harlequin Mira, as always: Rachael Donovan, Annabel Blay, and the amazing cover fairy gods at Squirt Creative. Thank you.

Kylie Mason, patient editor extraordinaire, for the hard work in helping make this story the best it can be.

My sons Kyle and Barry, for just being the best young men a mum could ask for.

Barry, for doing my mud maps this time, much appreciated by me and my editor! (And the drinks you place on my desk randomly too, ensuring I'm not dehydrating.)

Last and most importantly: my darling husband, Shaun, whose constant belief in my abilities is an amazement to me. Thank you!

If you loved *Child of Africa*, please turn over for a taste of T.M. Clark's previous bestseller

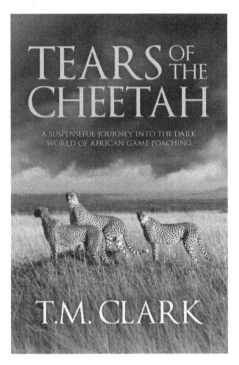

Available now!

PROLOGUE

A million years of evolution quivered, her instinct strong to kill. To survive. The cheetah mother crept forward, concealed by the tawny grass. Puffs of mist rose as she controlled her breathing in the cold morning. She dug her claws into the solid African sand, and exploded towards the unsuspecting impala. A baboon barked a warning as he spied her from a perch in a nearby thorn tree, but his alarm call was too late. The second it took for the impala to react was too long. The cheetah was already right up behind the buck, and despite its acceleration in speed to dodge the predator, the cheetah was faster, her lungs specifically designed for just this scenario. As the impala turned a sharp right, the cheetah used her tail as a rudder and adjusted her trajectory accordingly. The cheetah expertly closed the distance between the antelope and herself. One more zigzag to the left, and the cheetah extended her paw outward, tripping up the fleeing impala. In a second she had it pinned by its exposed throat. She hung onto its neck, her iron-clad bite cutting off its life's air, suffocating the buck.

Within moments, the kill was over, and the cheetah quickly pulled her trophy to a scrubby bush to recover. After the short exertion, she needed to cool down, fill her lungs with fresh air and regain her breath. Then she could feast. Once her belly was full, she would return to her cubs and call them from the bushes where they were hidden, and she would share her meal with them. At six weeks old, they were now grown enough to accompany her on her hunts, but were still very dependent on her for milk.

Slowly, the African bush returned to normal, the hype of the danger over. The doves resumed their relentless cooing, wooing each other. The baboons continued to eat the soft tips from the tree they sat in, one grooming another as the sentry on watch picked at his yellow-stained teeth. The cheetah forgotten, the death of the impala was simply another passing within the bush. Survival of the fittest. This time, his troop were safe. They would continue their day.

The cheetah chirped, calling the cubs to her from their hiding place. Three gorgeous spotted babies. Their white manes, which disguised them as ferocious honey badgers to any unsuspecting passer-by, acted as a temperature control, providing a sunscreen in the heat and warming them in the bitter cold of the early Highveld mornings.

Chirping, she called the cubs again. A loud, high-pitched sound that carried across the grassland. They should have heard her, she hadn't run so far away from them.

But they didn't come.

She retraced her steps at a trot, chirping again, looking at the bushes, knowing they should burst out at any time, their eyes bright, and their fur as beautiful now as it would be when they were adults.

But her offspring didn't come.

She ran into the bushes, her senses alert. And that's when she smelt him. Man.

The top predator of her food chain. The reek left behind saying that he had been there, and there was no sign of her cubs. Their scent had simply disappeared, and all she could now detect was the acid stench of the unwashed man.

The mother cheetah searched in circles, scanning. She climbed on a fallen tree to see if she could spot her babies, and despite having perfect view for twelve kilometres, she could not see her cubs, nor the man.

Her forlorn calls of distress disturbed the quiet hum of the Highveld, but she continued calling for her cubs.

But they didn't answer.

CHAPTER

1

Cole waited for Mackenzie to appear. Soon she'd come around the corner and begin her race along the kilometre-long stretch of tarmac that ran alongside the fence line of *nTabaGrequa* Wildlife Rescue and Cheetah Conservation Centre's exercise pens. He looked across the double cat fence on the roadside and single Bonnox square mesh fencing separating that enclosure for the next cats, giving them ample space to stretch their bodies and flex their muscles. The dust track inside was already well worn and no mountain grass was able to take root on the cats' racing track along the fence line. Three extended length, large enclosures were on the right-hand side of the visitors' centre, dotted with small shrubs. On the left were three smaller ones, being only two hundred metres long. All of them were a standard two hundred metres wide.

The cats were rotated between enclosures four times daily. This ensured they never displayed unwanted captive behaviour and it helped to keep the intelligent animals from getting bored. A few of the enrichment pens had balls in them or long ropes with knots that were used to hone the growing cheetahs' hunting skills. Boxes were a favourite toy, ripped apart in no time as the cats looked inside for the treats — meat, or feather dusters which could keep them entertained for an hour or so as they tore them to pieces feather by feather. Others simply had more trees and fallen logs, mounds and different natural features for the cheetahs to explore, and learn to use to their advantage.

In another pen a similar track cut deep into the earth, where an area was cleared of bushes and grass from many claws eating deep into it for traction as the cheetahs chased bait attached to a quick-winding winch.

Mackenzie rounded the corner and prepared to pit herself against the fastest cat in the world. Sasha, born on *nTabaGrequa* two years ago, bounded into action. Her agile body stretched to its maximum length, then bunched as her feet whispered to the ground. Her unsheathed claws created traction. Her oversized nasal passages allowed oxygen into her lungs, as her metabolism kicked into higher gear – zero to sixty-four kilometres per hour in two and a half seconds flat.

Mackenzie pushed her bicycle to overdrive. Neck on neck they sprinted, a pure adrenaline rush. Cole smiled as he watched Sasha use her long, flexible spine to spring-load each stride, out-racing the bicycle. Sasha's body was supple and majestic as it streaked ahead to its maximum speed of one hundred and nineteen kilometres. The Ferrari of the cat world.

Mackenzie wasn't bad either. But Sasha won with her three-hundred-metre sprint at the end.

The cat used her tail as a rudder to perform a fast-paced turn when she reached the end of her enclosure and pranced back a step or two as Mackenzie zipped past, then stared after her. Triumphant. Waiting for the rematch she knew was coming in about half an hour.

Watching Mackenzie on her daily exercise routine from afar was always exhilarating. Cole wondered if she noticed that he'd switched the cats again, that she didn't race just one cheetah, but half a dozen of those closest to full rehabilitation on a rotating basis.

It had been Nama's change in behaviour that had brought the cyclist to his attention at first. Usually his most foul-tempered cheetah, his unexplainable character transformation was remarkable.

His spiteful behaviour had shifted to that of a happier cat. He'd become more approachable, less moody and not as mean. Cole soon realised Mackenzie was responsible. He'd made a mental note of the time she was riding past his farm, and had watched her movements ever since. When Mackenzie showed signs of keeping pace with the old cheetah, he'd switched the cats. Sasha, who'd been watching Nama's daily race through the fence, and mimicking it in her own enclosure, was moved into the outer one. Sasha had immediately taken up the cyclist's challenge.

Soon a rotation with the cheetahs had begun, with Mackenzie helping to exercise all the cats without even being aware of it.

He watched Mackenzie as she cycled away, pushing her body to its limits. She'd done well today. He wished he could tell her how well she raced. He wished he could stop her in the street in Crystalberg, look right into her velvet-blue eyes, and tell her how beautiful she looked racing his cheetahs, streaking across the earth, so free, so full of life, but he couldn't.

Although they had a kindling friendship, she was as skittish as a newborn zebra foal. The entire town spoke of the American on the hill, an artist, they said, and a loner. How she let no one close, such a city-girl trait, and when she hadn't changed in eighteen months, the talk became more about the snobby American or the eccentric artist on the hill.

But he knew there was more to her.

A single white American woman moving to Africa. Buying the old Joubert house, which had been for sale for so long and overpriced by its deceased estate, yet the distance with which she held herself from that community didn't add up.

Almost a year ago, she'd warned him off trying to deepen their friendship into anything more. He respected that, and knew how much courage it took to admit you wanted to be alone. Hell, he himself lived by that same rule.

No attachment. No commitments. No strings.

If he was being honest, she scared him. Made him want things he didn't have the right to have. So he'd kept his distance after that, a platonic friendship, a wave here and there. A coffee at Duduzo's Kofi Shop, looking over the majestic Sani Pass, its craggy grey stone sometimes covered in snow in the winter, sometimes green with sweet tufts of veldt grasses in spring. Not that he looked at the scenery when he was constantly distracted by her long dark hair that she had a habit of pinning up with a pencil or a paintbrush in a makeshift bun, which would then slowly escape with each movement, loosening more, until it begged him to reach over and pull the pencil out completely. But he never did.

Her coffee was always a strong black with no sugar, with Duduzo constantly present as a chaperon, his big face sweating into his pristine white chef's hat, and he was always hawking his pastries and cakes. Cole often bought more and took them home in a 'doggy box' for his staff. Mackenzie always refused with a polite smile, sticking to a single buttered croissant. He died a little every time he watched her pink tongue lick the flaky pastry crumbs off her fingers.

Even then he could see that when she smiled it didn't reach her eyes, she was simply being polite. Perhaps it was that inner sadness that attracted him to her, or the fact that he was known for collecting strays. Perhaps he just wanted to fix her and remove the haunting, replace it with laughter. Help her make her life better, but she wouldn't let him closer.

Who was he kidding? For the first time in a long time, he felt a real attraction to a woman. He was pulled to her, like a butterfly to nectar. Except she reminded him of everything he still wanted and could never allow himself to have.

Cole sighed as he watched her end her first race of the day, and turned around on the tray at the back of the *bakkie*.

'She's getting better,' he said.

Siphiwe grinned, his teeth shining in his dark face. 'Aw, *Baas*. She'll never catch your cheetahs, they are too fast for her.'

'She's giving it a good try. We'll see how her rematch goes.'

The two of them jumped off the *bakkie* to the ground and began unloading the heavy bags of lime onto the dam wall.

Cole wiped his forehead with his khaki sleeve. 'Dammit, it's hot. Tell me again why I'm doing this instead of one of the workers?'

'You love your trout, *Baas*,' Siphiwe said, 'and your water test said lime was needed.'

'Smart mouth!'

Siphiwe laughed.

Together they worked for another half hour before all the bags were unloaded. Cole called a stop and threw down his soft leather gloves, then checked his watch.

He walked to the back of the *bakkie* and hopped up. 'Show time.' He looked for the cyclist, but the road was empty. He could see Sasha sitting patiently, waiting, and Cole knew she chirped expectantly, poised for flight once more. 'Strange, she's normally like clockwork on the return journey.'

'Look,' Siphiwe pointed to the section of the road further away.

Cole's body chilled.

*   *   *